Continental Drift

by James D. Houston

UNIVERSITY OF CALIFORNIA PRESS
Berkeley · Los Angeles · London

University of California Press
Berkeley and Los Angeles, California

University of California Press, Ltd.
London, England

Copyright © 1976, 1977, 1978 by James D. Houston
First California Paperback Printing 1996

Portions of this book appeared previously in
Big Moon, Foothill Quarterly, Y'Bird #1, and Quarry West

Library of Congress Cataloging-in-Publication Data
Houston, James D.
Continental drift / by James D. Houston
p.   cm.   (California fiction)
ISBN 0-520-20713-0 (alk. paper)
1. Journalists—California—Family relationships—Fiction.
2. Apple growers—California—Fiction.   3. Farm life—California—
Fiction.   4. Family—California—Fiction.   I. Title.
[PS3558.087C6   1996]
813'.54—dc20   96-8461
CIP

Grateful acknowledgment is made to the following
for permission to reprint previously published material:

AMS Press, Inc.: Excerpt from the diary of *Fray Juan Crespi: Missionary Explorer on the Pacific Coast, 1769–1774*, edited and translated by Herbert Eugene Bolton. University of California Press, 1927; reprinted by AMS Press, Inc.

Fred Rose Music, Inc.: Lyrics from *Hey Good Lookin'* by Hank Williams. Copyright 1951 by Fred Rose Music, Inc. *Why Don't You Love Me* by Hank Williams. Copyright 1950. Renewed 1977 by Fred Rose Music, Inc. Used by permission of the publisher. All rights reserved.

Peer International Corporation: Lines from *Wabash Cannonball* by A. P. Carter. Copyright 1933 and 1939 by Peer International Corporation. Copyright renewed. Used by permission.

Random House, Inc.: Excerpt from "Roan Stallion" from *The Selected Poetry of Robinson Jeffers*. Copyright 1925 and renewed 1953 by Robinson Jeffers. Reprinted from *The Selected Poetry of Robinson Jeffers*, by permission of Random House, Inc.

UniChappell Music, Inc.: Lines from *Detour* by Paul Westmoreland. Copyright 1945 by Hill and Range Songs, Inc. Copyright renewed by Unichappell Music (Belinda Music, publisher). International Copyright secured. All rights reserved. Used by permission.

Viking Press, Inc., and McIntosh and Otis, Inc.: Excerpt from *The Grapes of Wrath* by John Steinbeck. Copyright 1939, © 1967 by John Steinbeck. Reprinted by permission of the Viking Press, Inc., and McIntosh and Otis, Inc.

Manufactured in the United States of America.

1 2 3 4 5 6 7 8 9

The paper used in this publication is both acid and totally chlorine free (TCF).
It meets the minimum requirements of American Standard for
Information Sciences—Permanence of Paper for Printed
Library Materials, ANSI Z39.48-1984. ♾

ACKNOWLEDGMENTS

With special thanks to Gary Griggs, for showing me where the beast slumbers; to William Everson, for discovering the coast range; to the Montalvo Association of Saratoga, California, for the elegant peace of a Villa Montalvo residency; and to the National Endowment for the Arts, for an Individual Grant which made it possible to complete the work

Part One

Farther along we'll know all about it.
Farther along we'll understand why.
Cheer up, my brother, live in the sunshine.
We'll understand it all, by and by.

                    —TRADITIONAL HYMN

THE PROLOGUE

From high above, say gazing down from one of our tracking satellites, he can see it plain as an incision, a six-hundred-mile incision some careless surgeon stitched up across the surface of the earth. It marks the line where two great slabs of the earth's crust meet and grind together. Most of North America occupies one of these slabs. Most of the Pacific Ocean floats on the other. A small lip of the Pacific slab extends above the surface, along America's western coastline, a lush and mountainous belt of land not as much a part of the rest of the continent as it is the most visible piece of that slab of crust which lies submerged. The line where these two slabs, or plates, meet is called the San Andreas Fault. It cuts south from San Francisco, past San Jose, underneath the old San Juan Bautista Mission, on down behind Los Angeles, and back under water again at the Gulf of California.

The Pacific plate, he will tell you, is creeping north and west at about two inches per year, an example of the movement geologists call continental drift. Our globe, which appears to be divided into continents and bodies of water, is actually a patchwork of these vast plates, all floating around on a kind of subterranean pudding. What it resembles most is a badly fractured skull. From time to time the towns and cities along the fault line have been jiggled or jolted by temblors large and small, when sections of it buckle or lock, and then unbend, release, or settle. There are people who predict that one day the ultimate quake is going to send a huge chunk of California sliding into the ocean like Atlantis. They foresee this as one of the worst disasters in the history of the civilized world. They sometimes add that in a land as bizarre and corrupt as California is reputed to be, such a fate has been well earned.

Montrose Doyle will tell you all that is poppycock, both the physics and the prophecy. He will tell you that the earth's crust is three hundred miles thick, whereas the fault line only cuts down for thirty of those miles. He will tell you that if anything is going to undo this piece of coast it will be the accumulated body weight of all the people who have been moving into his part of the world at a steady rate since 1849. But it won't be the San Andreas. He has made it his business to find out what he can about this creature, because he owns fifty-five acres of orchard and grazing land that border it. He grew up on this ranch, will probably die here, and during his forty-six years he has seldom felt more than a tic across the earth's skin, an infrequent shiver in the high cupola which serves as his personal antenna and seismograph.

Montrose has studied with fascination the photographs of rotundas upended in the streets of San Francisco during the famous quake of 1906. He has corresponded with experts. And he has escorted visitors over to Hollister, twenty-five miles east of where his own house stands. An otherwise neat and orderly farm town, Hollister happens to be gradually splitting in two, because it sits in the fracture zone, like an Eskimo village caught on a cracking ice floe. By following cracks you can trace the subtle power of the fault as it angles under the town, offsetting sidewalks and curbstones and gutters, an effect most alarming in the house of a chiropractor which you pass soon after entering Hollister from the west. One half of a low concrete retaining wall holding back the chiropractor's lawn has been carried north and west about eight inches. The concrete walkway is buckling. Both porch pillars lean precariously toward the coast. In back, the wall of his garage is bent into a curve like a stack of whale's ribs. The fact that half his doomed house rides on the American plate and the other half rides the Pacific has not discouraged this chiropractor from maintaining a little order in his life. He hangs his sign out front, he keeps his lawn well mowed and the old house brightly, spotlessly painted.

One afternoon Montrose leaned down to talk with a fellow in Hollister who was working on the transmission of a Chevy pickup. The curb his truck stood next to had been shattered by the ageless tension of those two slabs of earth crust pulling at each other. Five inches had opened in the curb, like a little wound, and someone had tried to fill it with homemade concrete, and that had started to split.

Monty said, "Hey!"

The grease-smeared face emerged, irritably. It was hot. The man said, "Yeah?"

"Hey, doesn't the fault line run through this part of town?"

"The what?"

"The San Andreas . . ."

"Oh, that damn thing." The man waved his wrench aimlessly. "Yeah, she's around somewhere," and he slid back out of sight underneath his pickup.

Montrose regards that man with fondness now. He voiced Monty's own attitude pretty well, which is to say, none of this really troubles him much. Is he a fatalist? Yes. And no. He anticipates. Yet he does not anticipate. What he loves to dwell on—what he savors so much during those trips to Hollister—is that steady creep which, a few million years hence, will put his ranch on a latitude with Juneau, Alaska. He admires the foresight of the Spanish cartographers who, in their earliest maps, pictured California as an island. Sometimes late at night, after he has been drinking heavily, he will hike out to his fence line and imagine that he can feel beneath his feet the dragging of the continental plates, and imagine that he is standing on his own private raft, a New World Noah, heading north, at two inches per year.

Most of the time he doesn't think about it at all. It is simply there, a presence beneath his land. If it ever comes to mind during his waking hours, he thinks of it as just that, a presence, a force, you might even say a certainty, the one thing he knows he can count on—this relentless grinding of two great slabs which have been butting head-on now for millennia and are not about to relax.

1

Montrose was born in California, which still puts him in a minority out west. But he has at least one thing in common with almost all his friends and enemies. His folks came from somewhere else, caught up in one of those large movements that give this region its character, or as some say, lack of character—that subterranean drifting of the plates, and the ongoing drift of multitudes from their various origins toward all the murky promises of the western shore. They drift and they drive and they dribble in from every part of the globe, but mostly up from Spanish America and out from the south or southwest, and we find both these strains mixing in the Doyle ancestry. The southern by blood, the Spanish by osmosis.

Monty's granddad first, the one who tippled, the one who had to haul his ragtaggle family down out of the high hard mountain country mainly because he just plain got tired of working. This happened in the fall of 1899, which was about the time that year's depression crept up the side of Cumberland Mountain, Tennessee, and into the cabins and the cupboards and finally right out onto the hand-hewn tables of the back-country farmers and skunk hunters there. He had heard of an orchard he could pick for the picking, and his plan was to put all his kids to work gathering and drying apples to earn enough cash before winter, to get them down to Nashville, where he could put them to work again.

We see him hunched to gather golden apples in the late sun, yellow light rising from the apples themselves, while his wife and seven kids spread down the slope of the untended orchard, up into the trees, scrabbling through leaves to fill their gunnysacks. We see him rise and lean against a tree, as if for support, as if his back ails him. He is thirty-one years old. He lets one hand slide up the trunk, over the lip of a dead gash in the tree, and what does he find there, praise the Lord? A small flat brown flask of that hard cider he bottled two months back.

Falling out of sight behind the trunk, he leans into a long, world-centering pull, then sits a moment gazing up through rusty autumn leaves at the gorgeous sunlight scattered across the top of this tree. He corks the bottle, slips it back into its dark notch, and springs up, yelling, "Hey, you younguns, how you spect to fill that wagon up with apples, gittin near on five o'clock and you actin like this is Christmas and nothing to do but lay around starin out the winda. C'mown now, git to gittin," turning then to see his wife, Monty's grandma, thirty yards away beneath another tree, looking with the one look she has for him now and for the rest of their days together. It is not hatred, not disgust, not malice, not long suffering or self-pity. It is the steeled, unwavering look of a gospel minister saying to his flock with his face only, "I know your sins, and I know God's path, and you and I are going to walk that path together if I have to drag you by the throat every inch of the way."

That look is just a flicker in the gold-spattered orchard in high-country Tennessee. She drops to her knees and begins to shovel windfall fruit into an enormous basket. Doyle does the same, relieved that she didn't open her mouth, that all he has to carry is the knowledge of what she has to carry, and he long ago found this burden to be light enough. He is now floating slightly, across a bed of mulched leaves, and drinking in the apple smell, the brown rot from tiny spreading bruises, the open spots where birds have drunk. His nose squeezes all these smells to fresh, new cider before it hits the bloodstream, and three or four breathings leave him high as the orchard's highest trees, up there with the bright golden apples no one will ever reach.

Grover Doyle, Monty's dad, was four years old that day. Those apples stayed with him for the rest of his life, along with his mother's eye and his father's thirst. If you had asked him, twenty years later, why he was setting out long rows of Delicious saplings here on the coast of California, he would never have mentioned it, but those trees still glimmered way in the back of his memory, and the whole family scrabbling up and down the side of Cumberland Mountain. In fact, if you had asked him where he came from, he would confess to Tennessee with reluctance. He liked to call himself a full-blooded Texan. He bragged on Texas, sang loud songs like "The Eyes of Texas Are Upon You," and mournful tear-jerkers like "The Streets of Laredo." And like many a boastful Texan, Grover had left that land behind at the first oppor-tunity, the way his dad had soon left Nashville behind. "Born in Texas," old Grover used to say. "Born again in Jesus. Born the third time in Californ-ay-yea!"

Acreage was cheap in those days. Land that sells now for five or eight thousand dollars an acre, back then sold for two thousand dollars a hundred. Grover bought a lot more than he needed or could use, figuring that if the price of land had been going up since 1849, the trend was likely to continue. His main interests were animals, apples, and the arable por-tions of his terrain, which later on became his annuity, the chunks he sliced from the perimeter and sold off. Montrose, when his time came, inherited what remained of the or-chards. He inherited the house, the barns, his mother's love, his father's voice, his grandma's eye, and his granddad's thirst.

By spending most of his life around here, he also inherited

something his blood kin did not bequeath him. Perhaps inheritance isn't the word. This could be something absorbed, or ingested, or inhaled with the lifelong blending of apple scent and crumbling adobe and exhaust fumes and molecules of rubber dust that hang forever in the air above the freeways. He inherited a state of mind that goes right back to the Spaniards, where everything out west begins.

His land, this land, actually began in the minds of men like Hernando Cortez. In the time before Cortez named California, the land was inhabited by cougar, deer, grizzlies, eagles, eventually by the Indians. The land had not changed much, because those inhabitants had nothing to compare it to, no sense of other lands, small sense for other times. It is said that the tribe who once lived in the region where Monty's house stands now deliberately erased the past. When a man died, all his belongings were buried with him and his name was never mentioned again. Imagine what that must have been like. The only generation our generation. The only villages those we can walk to. The only time our time. If anything preceded us, it was water, until the animals came.

The Spaniards brought their pasts and their futures, like all the rest who came along after the Indians, like Monty's father, who came west dreaming, sixty years ago, a sharecropper's son dreaming of conquest, dreaming of ranches. In such a land Montrose has learned to take for granted unending waves of explorers, wizards, gypsies, visionaries, conquistadors, people who want to take what is here and turn it into something else. He has found life in his region like trying to grow a garden in the middle of a three-ring circus, with a family of trapeze artists swinging wildly above and prepared at any moment to commit suicide by plunging headfirst into his tomato vines. The odd thing is, Montrose still believes it is possible to do this and not go insane. It is a matter of conditioning. And it is a matter of continual vigilance.

Not long ago he was standing in his front yard when a

truck came rumbling up the driveway. It is fifty yards down to the county road. From the road you can barely see the cupola atop his two-story house. Whoever turns into his driveway knows who lives here or has a good reason for turning. Montrose had been listening to this truck pull the grade, waiting. When it finally lurched into view he had to grin. He had recently seen a television rerun of *The Grapes of Wrath*. He recognized the truck immediately and the style of travel first made popular by the Joad family on their laden journey west from Oklahoma during the thirties after their soil failed and the tractors drove them out. This truck was a rusty GMC flatbed, the blunt-nosed, indestructible kind of GMC, a rhinoceros of a truck, with a healthy, relentless grunting from underneath its scarred and venerable hood.

A small house had been erected on the flatbed, in the manner of a log cabin. Through a tiny window Montrose saw a kerosene lamp and, as the truck pulled to a stop, the snout of a large dog, perhaps an Afghan. One of Monty's retrievers came bounding off the porch with a short, territorial bark. Monty held him, and studied the pots and pans hanging from hooks outside the window, framing the Afghan's snout. Faded, recently washed clothes were drying over the tailgate. The couple sitting up front wore old coveralls and mail-order plaid shirts. The man wore a dark beard. His hair, like the woman's, was disheveled, and he stared out at Montrose with dark, gloomy eyes. The only difference between this man and Tom Joad of *The Grapes of Wrath* was that Joad was financially destitute. This man had left a small fortune behind. His father once held the controlling interest in a root beer chain that encircles Trenton, New Jersey. Everything else was the same. He had come west hoping for some dramatic change in his life.

He smiled cautiously before he spoke. "Anybody living in that house?"

At moments like this Montrose adopts a country manner; he assumes his granddad's Tennessee voice. He was glad to be wearing the old straw cowboy hat, the faded jeans. He pulled loose the stalk of a long yellow weed near at hand, bit it, and said, "Yep. I'm living in it."

The man controlled his disappointment. "Oh. How about that barn out in back? Anybody living there?"

Monty took his time, savoring this.

"It ain't fixed up for living in. But it's occupied. That is, I use it. Keep my vee-hickle back there, and my tools, and my workbench."

"Hmmmmm," mused the man in the truck. "How about renting? You got any space you could rent us? Like that barn? Or part of the house? How many people live in that house anyhow?"

"That house?" Monty said, turning to study the only house in sight. "That house is full, yes it is. Just me and the wife at present. But between us we manage to keep it filled right up to the roof."

The man seemed genuinely stumped by this. Alarmed. He spoke as if Montrose had been running daily advertisements and had now changed his mind without fair notice. "I thought maybe we could find something to rent around here. You don't have *anything*? What about that cottage down by the road? That belong to you?"

Before Monty could respond, the man leaned out the window, eager to share intimacies. "The name's Fowler, friend. We need a place real bad. We been here a week and haven't found a thing. I mean, we can live in the truck well enough and all that. But you know . . . we need a base of operations. We want to set up a kind of art gallery and crafts center, and get a little newsletter going."

"Newsletter?" Monty said, with true interest, since this was close to his own line of work. "What kind of newsletter?"

"Just a sort of community deal," Fowler said, "something to keep the community informed."

"Which community is that?"

Fowler turned to the woman for the first time. Monty looked

at her closely for the first time, saw she was suckling an infant. A thin woman, with opaque eyes.

"How would you describe it, honey?"

She smiled warmly, wanly, madonna-like, her voice so soft Monty moved closer to the truck to hear it. "Anybody who wants to find out what's going on," she said.

Smiling benevolently, Fowler turned back, hopeful again that something could be worked out. Monty heard the Afghan snarl, saw the snout again, this time through a porthole connecting the cab to the rear compartment. His retriever growled a menacing reply. Monty stepped back from the window.

Fowler said, "Shut up, Lorenzo." Then to Monty, "Hey man, what's the story on that number down by that gate?"

Monty waited for him to explain, chewing on his stalk.

"Looks like some kind of sculpture going up." Fowler grinned knowingly, as if they shared common insights. "Logs, tin cans and bottles, chunks of sidewalk . . ."

"You'll have to ask Wellington. That belongs to him. It's his . . . statement to the world."

"Who's Wellington?"

"He rents the cottage."

"He moving out anytime soon?"

"Not from the look of things."

There was a finality to this, accompanied by a firmness of Monty's jaw, an effect he learned from his father, a silent squeezing of the teeth that suggests the willful restraint of great power.

Fowler still could not believe the house was not for sale or for lease. He squinted past Monty, toward the shaded porch, the barn, the acreage beyond, a bit disdainful now, arrogant, as if he knew more about Montrose than Monty knew himself. The man was anxious to move on. As the flesh rose above an automatic smile, his eyes disappeared. His final words were a dismissal.

"Thanks anyhow, friend."

He backed up and swung the truck around. Lorenzo stuck his long, undernourished head out the back door of the cabin and began to bark. He lunged once, stopped short, inches from the tiny porch rail, by a length of oily rope circling his neck, tied somewhere inside.

Monty followed the truck down, to close but not to lock his gate. He let his retriever chase them to the road. As he listened to the pointless barking, as the engine faded and the truck disappeared around the first curve, he had a flashback, and then he had a premonition. He realized he had known all along this man was heading toward him. And he knew he'd be seeing him again. There was a persistence about him, the persistence of a man who has burned bridges somewhere and is determined to make some kind of stand. Times like this, Monty envies his granddad, who just got up to go when the world started crowding him, crying out triumphantly, "Goodbye, all you dried-out, suck-egg mule sonsabitches!"

2

Monty's house is redwood, cut from timbers hauled out of the coastal fog eighty years ago. He still isn't certain who built it. They say she was a widow, a Christian Scientist who wanted a high cupola so she could sit up there and contemplate the ocean on a clear day. They say she was a meditator. Monterey Bay is seven miles west. In the summer it makes a distant wedge of burnished metal, like a hypnotist's medallion. This is the only explanation he has been able to find that accounts for the steep angle of his roof, an alpine roof designed to help heavy snows slide over the side. Montrose has lived here since he was eleven, has seen snow seven times, and only twice has it lasted overnight. He calls it white rain. An alpine roof on a Victorian house, its sole function to lift a cupola above the nearest trees.

His wife, Leona, sits up there from time to time with the field glasses, gazing not west, as the Christian Scientist would have done, but east, toward the "river." She calls this a river. The river with no water. And no bottom. She envisions a deep fissure that drops, like a polar crevasse, right to the seething bowels of the earth. She knows better. When he calls it "the Grand Canyon of our dreams," Leona giggles. They used to make love out there. Nowadays she would rather not go near it, not since The Big Scare of 1969. She prefers her vision. It inspires her, she says. Her tapestries are conceived up in the cupola. Alone, with the trap door shut, she sketches baroque and involuted patterns, then brings the sketches downstairs to her workroom, her rainbow of threads and yarns and her armory of needles. Sometimes she does not sketch. Sometimes from the cupola, when the light is soft and indirect and right, she will study shadows and imagine the ground's anger, the muscular rippling that will bend this ungainly house and send her flying as if released from a catapult.

Montrose prefers the shadowy interior, the first-floor living room, cool and quiet, with, at this hour, clean new light silhouetting indoor plants—begonias, asparagus ferns—while he moves through his yoga regimen. His dance. His morning solo. "It's for the lower back," he tells the fellows in town, who know he has had that kind of trouble. "Spinal massage," he will say. "Glandular toning." Since they greet even this much with suspicion, he keeps to himself the larger reason, the appeal of things eternal.

In a headstand, breathing deeply, gazing upside down at his plants, he feels at once afloat and firmly rooted. He is alive. The air is alive. The plants are alive. The house is alive. The grain of the boards in the window casing reminds him once again that these trees lived a thousand years, in the fog and sunlight, shading giant primeval ferns. Maybe longer. They are among the oldest living things on earth. In state parks he has seen the cross-cut sections of patriarch redwoods with rings tagged back through history to the birth of Jesus Christ, and beyond. To the assassination of Julius Caesar in 44 B.C. He stares at the grain in his window casing, each dark stripe a year of aging, a year of growth. Breathing, he finds himself inside a tree. The hairs on his head are fibers feeding. His arms are rings embracing the heart-core of juice sucked up through roots that tap the deepest troughs of mountain reservoirs. Ancient Montrose hears the rush of subterranean waters.

Above him, old limbs creak. Leona is heading for the stairs. One more glance at the window casing, one last whisper of the taproot sipping, and he lets his feet jackknife to the floor. His temples drain.

From the landing she calls down, "Monty! Monty?" And from midflight, "What do you want for breakfast?"

She knows what he wants for breakfast, but never tires of

discussing these things. Nor does Montrose, when the appetites are rising. Something about the yoga gives every appetite an edge. He is ready to be aroused by Leona's question, which has for years served as a double invitation. He is astonished at how often he still wants her. For some reason he never believed such things would last—his own vitality, this house, her bosom and buoyancy, their orchards, the richness of the sunlight. Long ago he began to expect everything he valued to give way and collapse. He has been prepared at any moment for holocaust. For ashes. When Travis left, Montrose fully expected never to see him alive again. It took him two years to admit he had killed his son ahead of time, in his mind, quickly and desperately, before the bus even pulled away, in order to get it over with. Nowadays each sunrise surprises him. He feels the primitive's awe for these inexplicable returns, of a son, a moon, a season, the rich craving in his loins when Leona, suddenly behind him, reaches between his legs, teasing.

"You haven't answered my question," she says.

"What's on the menu?"

"You're such a dirty old man."

"Did I say something dirty? Only a mind depraved with lust could find anything dirty in what I just said."

His hands rush around beneath her robe.

"Not *now*."

"Why not?"

"You might miss the . . . Oh, your fingernails!"

"Sorry."

"What if Trav's plane . . ."

"If that plane lands on time I'll eat the propeller."

"It doesn't have a propeller, hon."

She bends to frown out the front window, as if a plane might at this moment be taxiing through the field between their porch and the first hills. He takes this opportunity to nudge her onto the brocade couch. She turns toward him and her robe falls open. As he straddles her, tendrils of asparagus fern flick his shoulders. Early window light tints her neck and face with the blue-white gloss of porcelain, and Montrose, nude yogi, regards this too with wonder.

The ferns, the light, the gloss of her skin, all bring to mind a wondrous day many years ago when they went romping through that orchard toward their favorite spot. Her eyes this morning are like her eyes were then. Liquid. Intimate. Yet inward. Keeping something. The phone rings. Monty's vision dissolves. He goes limp.

Leona disentangles herself and hurries down the hall to the booth, robe flapping. Monty leans back against his brocade sofa, longing to tear the phone out and stomp it to pieces.

With veiled sarcasm, Lee shouts, "For you-ou!"

He decides to take this final call, then destroy the phone. He vows to do this, while walking naked to the square glass booth where the phone resides. Travis and Grover ripped this booth from its moorings several years ago and brought it home in the pickup. It has remained in the hallway, the words PACIFIC TELEPHONE the first thing you see upon entering the front door. Leona complained at the time, saying it would be a nuisance to clean around, but Monty thought it would be good for the boys to feel they too had contributed to the household, to its design, its overall *effect*.

Against his flank and his dangling penis the varnished seat is like cold steel.

"Doyle here."

"Monty, listen. It's Nan."

"Good morning, Nan."

"Listen."

"I am listening."

"There's a fellow here who says he has to talk to you."

"I'll be in on Wednesday."

"I've already told him that. He says he has to talk to you today. This morning."

"What's it about?"

"He won't tell me. He just says it's too hot to wait."

"If it's that hot he should talk to one of the reporters. I'm not a reporter."

"That's why he wants to talk to you."

Montrose, glumly flattered, says, "Okay. Put him on."

"He won't talk on the phone. He wants to see you face to face. Says he'll come looking for your house if he has to."

Leona struts past the phone booth on her way to the kitchen, and flips up the back side of her robe. She has never approved of Nan as Monty's officemate, never quite believed he didn't set that up himself, never quite been appeased by the fact that he is only down there two afternoons a week. Her flash of bare buttocks is a taunt, a mockery. His arm lunges out the door, but misses.

He mutters, "Goddam it!"

"What did you say?" says Nan from downtown.

"Talking to me?" Leona calls coyly as she prances into the kitchen.

"How does this guy strike you, Nan? Is he new in town?"

"Aren't they all?"

"What does he look like?"

"Sort of lean. Dark hair. Dark eyes. Beard. Intense."

Montrose sees him clearly now, sitting in their cubicle, among the typewriters and swirl of pages, across the desk from Nan's poodle cut. A flashback. Another premonition. He winces. And he fills with a delicious hostility toward the invader who would ambush his life at this hour, for these reasons. Two weeks ago, when he watched the GMC grunt and stutter down his driveway, a little knot drew tight inside him. It relaxes now—the until this moment unvoiced anticipation of Fowler's inevitable return.

"He has an eastern accent," Monty says.

"You could call it that."

"Does he act like he knows me?"

"No. He's been reading your column, says you are the only writer around who sees the world with unpurchased eyes."

"Are those his words?"

"Would I say anything like that?"

Monty is certain this man, if given the chance, will sniff him out today, this morning, appear again in his yard, climb his stairs and claim his porch, occupy his couch, help himself to cigars, a Ramos fizz, eggs Benedict. Deep in his mind he hears Granddad saying, "You tell that Yankee fence-jumper I got a whole box a shotgun pellets and not much time, and if I see him closer'n fifty yards from my mailbox he better be ready to duck!"

There was a lot to be said for a world that simple. Monty yearns for it vaguely as he sits naked in his phone booth, plotting a route into neutral territory.

"I'm going to the airport this morning, Nan. Tell him to meet me at the last stoplight before the freeway on-ramp at the end of Del Mar Boulevard. I'll be moving through there in a northerly direction about an hour from now."

"You mean meet you in the coffee shop there at the intersection?"

"No. Out on the corner. Tell him . . . to appear to be hitchhiking, but . . . to stand apart from any other hitchers who might be waiting there . . . as if preoccupied, or disdainful, or . . . perhaps a little annoyed."

From her silence Monty knows Nan is weighing this. At last she says, "Have you been drinking?"

"At this hour, Nancy? No. It's a simple case of transferral."

"Transferral?"

"Of . . . unrequited lust."

Cryptically she says, "Good luck." Then, "See you Wednesday."

Click.

Moments later he is wandering into the kitchen, a goat, a satyr on the prowl. He eyes Leona. But she is at the stove now, busy with eggs.

3

Beaches border one edge of the county seat, where it hugs a
bay, facing south for warmth and for a Mediterranean light
that makes it ideal for painters. Many painters gaze into this
light through latticed windows, from the groves and from the
cliffs. Many canvases are stretched. Many houses like Monty's,
of that vintage, show on knolls and in the nearest hills—domes,
turrets, gables, dormer windows, spires, widow's walks, filigree
in fashion eighty years ago when wealthy San Franciscans va-
cationed here. Teddy Roosevelt spent one week in such a house
in 1903 and left behind an elephant hide which still decorates
the dining room. Nowadays there is a community group de-
voted to preserving such buildings, and to preserving the
groves, as well as the quality of the air that the light passes
through on its way to the windows. The group is called
SCALE, the Standing Committee for an Aesthetic and Livable
Environment. Leona is a past vice-president. There are other,
larger groups with other priorities. Houses such as the one
Teddy spent a week in mingle with high-rise condominiums,
and medico-dental centers in the shape of coolie hats, and
hundreds of rows of metal boxes parked in cleared land on
temporary footings. On any day three or four such boxes can
be seen arriving along the coast road pulled behind great
Kenworth engines, usually in two pieces. Waiting at an intersection, Montrose watches half of one such mobile home move
past at thirty miles per hour, followed by the second half, with
its interior exposed. He sees a mirror, a framed print swinging
loosely, an anchored sofa, a tiny window curtain on a door
that evidently leads out the other side toward the open road.

He thinks of *Huckleberry Finn*, which he read to his boys how many years ago—eight? Ten? Travis was the one who howled at Huck. He would be up there now, clambering in to cop a free ride, light a cigar and blow smoke out at pedestrians.

As the half a home washes past, Monty sees the old house Huck's raft collided with, back before the Civil War, washed by floodwaters into the Mississippi, floating south.

Then the mobile home is gone, and he sees the flatbed truck with its miniature log cabin, parked a block away, beyond the next light, and the bearded man in his mail-order shirt waiting there.

Approaching slowly, Montrose studies his pose, the hands on hips, one booted foot on the sidewalk, one in the street, his slender face scowling at the cars. Monty eases up to the curb and shoves his door open.

"Hop in."

"No, thanks," he says, coloring with embarrassment.

"What's the matter?" Monty says. "Aren't you looking for a ride?"

"No. I'm—"

"C'mon, I'll give you a lift. Where do you want to go?"

He blinks, scowls, trying to place Monty, finally throws his hands wide, exasperated. "I told you I don't want a ride."

"Why not? Don't you trust me anymore?"

The voice rises. "Anymore? What is this? What are you, some kind of fag?"

Monty shouts, "If you don't want a ride, what are you hitch-hiking for?"

He shouts back, "I'm not hitchhiking! I'm waiting for somebody!"

Suddenly grinning, changing his tone, Monty says, "You're waiting for me."

"The hell I am." He slams the door.

Monty reaches across and rolls his window down. "I'm Doyle."

The man steps back, tilts his head, peering into the car, squinting as if into a cave. "What's going on?"

"You wanted to talk to me."

He is blinking compulsively, as if his eyelids have been assigned the job of clearing the air right in front of his face. The blinking stops, and he is staring fiercely. "Hey, you should not fuck with people this way."

"I'll pull across the street," Monty says, and doing so, he lines up behind the mountain cabin.

The door opens. "My name is Fowler. Larry Fowler." He slides in.

"I know," Monty says, looking up at the little rough-hewn porch. "Did you find a place to stay?"

Slowly the saturnine face opens in a broad smile of recognition. It becomes a conspiratorial smile, as if recognizing Montrose not only explains the curious behavior but also grants Fowler instant, intimate familiarity. Smiling, he touches Monty's arm.

"Listen, man, we did, a few days after we checked out your place. That is the reason I had to see you. Although I didn't know it was *you*. Right? I mean, I started reading your column in the paper, man, because you are the only guy around here who understands what's happening. So I thought maybe you could use this material, or could give me some ideas about how to handle it. Actually, see, we found a place to park the truck. Some people are lending us a shed and a clearing."

He speaks as if this carries deep significance. Monty nods, grunting, "Ummmmmmmh."

"Okay. It turns out that these people are onto something that is so hot it could blow this town wide open."

He pauses again, waiting for Montrose to react. Monty has been living in these parts for thirty-five of his forty-six years and figures he has a pretty good idea where the seams and cracks and weak spots are. He knows from experience that things do not explode. They just leak, and dribble, and let out steam from time to time.

But Fowler's eyes are fixed on his like a prophet's, as if he knows things no other man dares to know. Monty motions him to continue.

"It's about this girl named Linda Kramer, the one who disappeared a couple of weeks ago."

Monty reaches for the ignition, annoyed, a little disappointed. "There's already a guy in the news room who is following that one."

Gently Fowler takes Monty's wrist, moves his hand away from the dashboard.

"I know it. That is why I want to talk to you. He'll just screw it up." (Conspiring smile.) "Reporters always screw it up. They're in such a big rush. You know what I mean? But you, you are not a journalist. You just do your column, you get in, and get out. Your life doesn't depend on maintaining the status quo in this community. By life, I mean the way you make your living. These other creeps, there are fifty people who they are afraid to cross. So there are a whole lot of stories they just don't tell, or don't tell right."

"Maybe you should go talk to the police."

"I think the police are in on it."

Again, the probing gaze, the body forward now.

"In on what?"

"Okay," says Fowler, plunging eagerly into his tale. "This field we're parking in is next to a big house. Right? And there is a bunch of people living in the house together, and one of the guys was going with Linda Kramer off and on before she disappeared. She was hitchhiking, right? On the eighteenth of March. Well, it turns out that on the twentieth she was due to testify on behalf of these friends of hers who have been indicted for dealing."

Monty's vague distaste for Fowler increases. This detail could be real news, and now he has to keep listening in spite of himself.

"The indictments were handed down after a guy named Escobido set up some purchases and informed on these friends of Linda's. The reason she knew about it is because she used to go with Escobido, who had previously been arrested for passing bad checks. The cops offered him a chance to beat the rap by informing on some people around town, after which he would be safely escorted across the county line, with instructions never to return. So Escobido, having little choice, informed, and then split, and Linda was offered the job as his replacement. Okay?

"She turned the job down," Fowler goes on, "but meanwhile all these friends of hers are indicted. They hire an attorney, who takes a deposition from Linda about Escobido and the way these busts were set up, and the offer the cops made to her. On March twentieth she is scheduled to testify before the grand jury here in town, and two days ahead of time she disappears."

"So what's your conclusion?"

"Her boyfriend says she was killed. She knew something that somebody did not want to have her talking about."

"And who might that somebody be?"

"Bigger dealers. Or the cops. Or both. Who knows?"

"Maybe she took a vacation somewhere. Maybe she got tired of her boyfriend and didn't tell him where she was going."

"I get the feeling you are not deeply moved by all this."

"Girls disappear for all kinds of reasons. Most of them come back."

A sneer flickers around Fowler's mouth. "You know, Mr. Doyle, sometimes you can be around a place so long, you think you know it so well, you don't even see what's going on right under your nose."

"How long have you been living in this part of the country, Fowler?"

"About three weeks."

"And you already think you have it wired?"

"I think this is something the public should know about, that's all. If you don't want to touch it, then help me figure out what else to do with it. I mean, I know a couple of papers in San Francisco and L.A. that would print this kind of story right now, if I could get it to the right guy in the right kind of format. If I can get my newsletter set up in time, I could even run it myself."

Montrose leans back and breathes deeply, to recover, to center his self-control. It isn't that he does not want to touch this story. There is something about Fowler he implicitly distrusts. Trying to define it, he gazes out the front window of his car, studying the portable log cabin with its tiny leaded windows, its tiny door. He thinks he sees Lorenzo in there, waiting for some signal to attack.

"Before you do anything like that," he says, "let me check into this."

"When will that be?"

"When I get around to it."

"This girl could be murdered somewhere and you are going to get around to it?"

"Look, Fowler. I happen to be on my way to the airport to pick up my son, who I haven't seen in two years. He's coming home from overseas."

By the end of this announcement Monty finds himself strangely choked with deep feeling, a mixture of remorse, self-pity, and the urge to injure Fowler in some disabling way. For a long moment Fowler gazes at him. Then the eyes slowly disappear, as he offers Monty the automatic smile, the dismissal smile.

"I understand, man."

He opens the car door, steps out, then leans down into the window for one last word. "Thanks for listening."

Driving alone always clears Monty's mind. Heading north on the freeway, he sees plainly that what so annoys him about Fowler is more than the pushiness and the persistence. It is the insinuation that nothing Monty might be concerned with at any moment could be quite as important as what Fowler is concerned with, the insinuation that Monty's sense of the world is somehow narrow and naïve, that a more generous man would have gladly leased the top floor of his house to the Fowler family, that a more worldly man would seize upon the truth of this conspiracy he has just unfolded.

Yet even this does not entirely explain it. Near the summit of these mountains he has crossed a thousand times, looking over forested valleys toward farther summits, and catching in the distance a silver flash of ocean, Montrose finds the larger view. It allows him to dismiss Fowler, much as Fowler dismisses him. He is an all too familiar character, one Montrose locates now among the blessings and the curses of the west, among all those explorers and discoverers and Cortezes and conquistadors. After traveling this far, their very sense of tradition obliges them to make some kind of profound discovery. Otherwise it simply wouldn't be worth the trip. You can't hold that against a man. He has to unearth *some*thing, once he gets here, to dramatize his life, to put his own name somewhere on this tantalizing map.

4

Montrose has two sons, Grover, aged twenty-three (named after Monty's dad), and Travis, two years younger. He can remember the first noises each one made in the maternity ward.

Grover bawled till his face turned purple.

Travis wailed.

When Grover's tiny hand first gripped Monty's forefinger, it touched lightly, then squeezed down steady till the fingers held with tiny strength, still squeezing.

Trav's hand squeezed quick, and let go, squeezed quick, and let go, and made a game of that.

The day Grover's eyes first showed signs of seeing, two weeks after he was born, they looked at Monty with a chilling steadiness such as he had seen in the eyes of alert animals, watching out of timeless pasts. He had the sense that Grover, even then, knew his main task would be the patience to wait until his arms and legs and bones and vocal cords caught up with what was looking out of those ancient, baby's eyes.

When Travis first looked, he tried to keep his eyes closed as long as he could. He opened them awhile, then closed them again, as if he didn't much care what he saw.

That was twenty-one years ago. Today Travis comes home from the army. Montrose let him join. That is, he didn't try to stop him. ("It's your decision, son.") He regrets that now. He regrets that he has never been firm enough with Travis. His problem is, he has never entirely understood him. Travis eludes Monty, in the same way Lee eludes him. He will think he has reached some understanding of Trav's character, then have to admit once again he is only guessing. With Grover it has always been easy to draw the line. He knows Grover inside out. Drawing it, of course, has never meant Grover observes the line. But at least they both agree a line is there.

"Stubborn" and "single-minded" are the words Monty uses to describe his older son. "Impulsive" and "unpredictable" describe Travis. Add "wild-ass," "profligate," "irresponsible," and "vain." For months it mystified him why Travis was the one who enlisted, while Grover refused to serve. Montrose could easily imagine Grover managing a platoon of men with no trouble at all. He even has the look of a lantern-jawed west Texas top sergeant. Red hair; a freckled and triangular face; always seeming on the verge of leaning, or lunging, toward you. Two years ago it was Grover who introduced Monty to the benefits of yoga, drawn less by the appeal of things eternal than by the emphasis on discipline. "You're getting sloppy. Dad," is the way Grover put it. "Regulate the breath, regulate the body, and eventually you can regulate the mind."

He wears rodeo shirts and lives up in the mountains, and Montrose has finally admitted (though not openly) that Grover was right, that the precedent in this matter of military service was established by his great-great-grandfather who, during the Civil War, being near the age of thirty and a resident of Van Buren County, Tennessee, fought neither for the South nor for the North, but spent those wretched years "hiding out" up there in the high country, chasing after possum and raccoon and wild rabbit, and waiting for the smoke to clear.

5

Watching a 707 taxi in, Monty scans forty opaque portholes for some sign of life. A portable tunnel is plugged into the fuselage, moments later spilling passengers out its near end, into the terminal. Monty keeps thinking the next one will be Travis. The flow is thinning, he is reaching to check the wrinkled airletter with the time and flight number, when he hears a voice, not from the plane, but seemingly from behind him, shouting, "Dad!"

He doesn't turn. So prepared is he to see Trav emerging from the plane, he interprets this as some trick of sound inside the echo-filled terminal, some odd ventriloquy. He peers into the tunnel, ready to smile. He hears the voice again.

"Hey, Dad!"

This time he turns, and sees Travis striding toward him from the direction of the snack bar, his head suddenly dipping to hear a girl just behind him. He wears a Panama hat Monty figures he must have picked up in Manila or Honolulu. Always had a taste for hats. This one sits oddly, as if jostled. Yet it isn't the hat, it's the head, something about the way Travis holds his head. The motion is unfamiliar, nothing like any moves he used to make. Montrose is looking for this, the signs of change. But he wants them to be recognizable—signs of growth, signs of manhood. A spasm of giddiness runs through him. Then Trav's eyes turn from the girl to fix on Monty. He has the look of a man returning from the grave and seeing for the first time his executioner. Monty tastes ashes, can scarcely meet his gaze. He fears his own eyes will falter. Travis blinks, and the gaze is gone, replaced by whimsy, by his cocky grin, as if that last look was just a gag, a phony hate message, to keep Dad on his toes. Monty knows Trav is capable of this. Reaching for the hand, he can't help thinking it may just have been some veteran's sympathy routine. He wavers, fiercely shaking hands, waiting for a sign.

"Travis, did I get the gate wrong? We thought—"

"I took another plane, Dad. Didn't have time to let you know."

Travis has a charming smile, perfected long before he understood how it worked. He uses it now.

Seduced, relieved, exasperated, suddenly drained, Montrose blurts, "You what? For Christ sake, Travis!"

"It was Crystal's idea," he says, urging forward the girl at his elbow. "Dad, I'd like you to meet Crystal. I met her in the Islands. She's interested in land, gardening, fruits and vegetables. I told her she could stay at our place for a few days. Sort of look around. If that's all right."

Like a man caught in crossfire, Monty half hunches, turning to glare at her. She clutches Trav's arm. Monty relaxes, forces himself to smile. She could be younger than Travis. Twenty, he estimates. And very dark, as if from sunning for months in Hawaii. White flared beachcomber's trousers. But not beachy, he is glad to see. Montrose shut the door on beach girls, with their self-serving monologues, when Travis was in high school. Crystal is a different kind of wanderer. A Rolleiflex hangs at her waist. Bright, crafty eyes size him up now while he sizes her up. Eyes like Trav's. On the verge of laughter. An adventuress. With a taste for veterans. That could liven up the place. Monty is a veteran too. Of numerous campaigns. Not that he imagines it would ever come to that. But he can tell he and Crystal will be able to get along. In any case, she's Trav's choice, and you don't start drawing lines the day your son comes home.

He throws an arm around Trav's shoulder. "Well, of course it's all right. Hell. I mean, anything's all right on a day like this. You thirsty? Let's go get a drink before we start back," winking then at Crystal in what he considers hearty welcome. Her glance is so alarmingly seductive he avoids it.

He concentrates on Travis, finding an interval, before the talk begins, to study the profile, the way he moves and conducts himself, suddenly exulting in the sheer fact of his own fatherhood. To have a son returning from . . . from anywhere, full-grown, full-bodied, not at all the son who went away, yet unmistakably that same boy. He is still compact, with Leona's straight back, and a flash of Lee's prancing in his stride. Monty sees the built-up layers of him, the original shape and nature, in ever-widening proportions, the way a tree builds. Seeing all the stages, the inner rings exposed to him as if for the first time, Monty grabs his son by both arms exuberantly, drunkenly, shouting, "Shit fire! You're gettin to be a husky rascal, Travis!"

He shoves with his shoulder, and Travis shoves back. There among the passengers rushing toward their luggage, they begin to trade light blows, feinting, fist-tapping. It is an ancient game, which always ends when Monty gives him a wide opening, and Travis drives a fist into the tensed abdominals. It always hurt, even when Trav was eight years old, and Monty has always let him do it.

6

Three abreast in the front seat, they are speeding down the Bayshore Freeway, heading home. Travis is talking, and Montrose at the wheel in his cowboy hat glances sideways from time to time, still looking for the signs, the changes. He wants to know what happened over there, though he knows it's far too soon to ask, remembering as if it were only last month how long it took before he himself could share with anyone what he'd seen in the South Pacific. It took three or four years, and even today some of his stories have not yet been told, some of his dreams have never been discussed.

Too soon to tell. Too soon to ask. Too soon for much of anything. Travis talks, but he is not with us yet. His mind is elsewhere. He has not entirely landed.

"In Honolulu," he says, "right at the end of the main boulevard that runs through Waikiki, I saw fifty Americans in aloha shirts. It was about eleven o'clock at night. They were on one of these package tours?" His voice inflects upward, his eyebrows raise as each phrase becomes a question. "They hit three clubs a night? With a two-drink guarantee at each club? Well, while they are waiting for their Gray Line bus to pick them up to take them to the next hotel, the surf is crashing in the background and they all start singing 'Swing low, sweet chariot...'"

Chuckling, Montrose picks up the song. Crystal joins in too:

Swing low, sweet chariot.
Comin for to carry me home ...

Then it's silent in the car, just Travis humming under his breath the next eight bars, which might almost be the humming within him, that waning buzz of motion, slowly draining away. This is what Montrose hears as he observes faint flickers of bewilderment, Travis waiting for something to replace that buzz. Monty recognizes the symptoms of jet lag, traveler's hangover. It never ceases to amaze him how he can live down a country road the way they do, and nearly every day run into someone just in from Rio or Manila or Jerusalem, with the smell of foreign cities still on the clothes. The traveler's soul is always far out over the water somewhere, booked onto a much slower flight, usually about four days behind the body, which can be sitting right here next to you, and talking, yet be incomplete. Sometimes you can almost see through the body. It is a double wonder—the exotic arrival of the traveler, and the body-shaped space that waits for the arrival of the soul. Monty does not yet know how much Travis has in common with those ultimate survivors of jet lag, the astronauts, who splash down glossy-eyed, their eyes and their lives out of synch at reentry and somehow forever altered on the high-speed journey home.

"Hey, Dad," says Travis, urgently, "I have to drive! Do you mind if I drive the rest of the way?"

Still looking for signs, Monty sees this as a good one. A sign of recovery. A sign of health. He pulls off onto the emergency lane. He is tired of driving anyway. Thirty-one years since he got his first permit. He could use some relief.

With the engine running, he opens the left-hand door and climbs out. Travis, sliding behind the wheel, looks up at him for just an instant with his head cocked in that eerie way, as if some glare prevents him from seeing Montrose clearly, and with the look that so disturbed him at the terminal, that returning-from-the-deepest-pit-of-hell look, that you're-the-one-who-put-me-there look. This time Monty is petrified with fear. He is sure Travis plans to drive away and leave him standing on the freeway. It is one of those science-fiction moments you cannot quite believe, a brief scene, with half-caught details that don't add up until much later. They are underneath the smooth concrete belly of an overpass, almost noon, yet the belly is slung so low and spread so wide it is like dusk. The engine roars. Monty imagines himself marooned under here for days, his clothes blown to tatters. Papers and candy wrappers have flown up into the angle where the sloping foundation pillar meets the arc. Every car that speeds past rattles papers in its wake of artificial wind. He stands studying a cloudlike blue-gray construction stain, thinking distantly of an architect in town who prizes *accidents* like this, who waves his hands describing the "aesthetic of materials in process." He is trying to detach himself. He breathes. The moment passes.

Leaning forward, Travis is testing the controls, giving Monty just enough time to rush around to the far side and scoot in next to Crystal. The car's lunge slams the door. Travis leaves angry horns back there, raising one defiant finger out the open window, hitting eighty before they've gone a hundred yards.

It was a mistake to let him drive. Yet something in Montrose accepts this situation, perhaps a boyish yearning to give up all responsibility, perhaps his own wish that Trav's return be appropriately celebrated . . . with wildness, with appropriate risks. It is among his small regrets that Travis has missed the taste of actually coming home a winner. Montrose would bequeath this to him if he could. But America is too far gone for that. How often has he seen himself, that August night in 1945, when they celebrated the ending of *his* war. He was fresh off a troop ship, Sergeant Doyle home from the Pacific, at large in San Francisco, with Purple Heart and scarlet face. He remembers tipping over a streetcar on Market, then dancing across the upturned side with a young girl whose breasts, through the years, have expanded to the size of streetlamps. In his memory they glow, leaving all her other parts in shadow. She wanted his Purple Heart for a souvenir, and he said he'd give it to her if she took her sweater off. Which she did.

Monty's pals joined him on the streetcar then, half his platoon, followed by a dozen sailors, all dancing among the windows, then nudging and shoving, finally sparring and rabbit-punching and side-stepping into panes of brittle glass. With one arm around the doomed female, one around a yeoman's neck, Monty watched a flame bloom behind his eyes—the whiskey's uppercut, not the yeoman's—and go black. The rest of that night exists for him only as other men have recounted it, legendary boozing, legendary brawls, legendary cocksmanship. Triumphant devastation, he would call it now. And yet it was so much more of a tribute than has been offered up for Travis's war, the Southeast Asian one. No dancing in the street. No plaques. No holidays added to the calendar. Perhaps a manic drive down Bayshore Freeway will help turn a few of these omissions into trophies.

A pint bottle flashes in the sunlight, on its way to Crystal from inside Trav's denim jacket. She unscrews the top, sips some and passes it to Monty, who figures this is something else he picked up in Honolulu, along with Crystal and the hat.

"Fiji Island rum, Dad," he says, glancing over to see how Monty takes this, a sly glance, like that smile of his, calculated. He looks now exactly like Leona. Travis and Leona share a whole armory of smiles and glances. For this instant he is Lee talking Montrose into something.

Monty raises the flask and says, "Welcome home, Sarge," and takes a long pull and gasps like a kid. Firewater.

Travis laughs. "It goes a long way."

Crystal laughs. Monty laughs too, just as they barrel past a highway patrolman on the far side of the freeway, whose head snaps in their direction. He would be on their tail immediately were it not for the divider strip and were he not surrounded by six matronly women, all wearing jewelry and Easter bonnets, evidently on their way to the city for a luncheon date, perhaps at the Clift Hotel, and very angry about this delay, so that the patrolman is pinned on all sides and cannot even get to his radio to warn a colleague farther down the road.

They are still laughing, and Monty is trying to advise Travis to slow down, when Crystal flips open the cover of the Rolleiflex slung around her neck and begins snapping pictures of Montrose sitting next to her. Close-ups. Profiles. "Don't pay any attention to this," she says. He turns away, annoyed, thinking: What right does this girl have? He yearns for the strength of mind said to be possessed by certain holy men in Asia who, when photographed, can will their image not to appear on the developed print. He would protest aloud, but the shutter's only clicking for fifteen seconds, then the leather lid flips shut.

Winking thanks, Crystal reaches for the radio. The car fills up with Roy Acuff's version of "The Wabash Cannonball."

> *Listen to the jingle, the rumble, and the roar,*
> *As she rolls along the woodland,*
> *Through the hills and by the shore . . .*

The dial is set for KEEN, San Jose's country music station. This is not her idea of highway listening. She jiggles the dial till she hits a talk show, turns the volume up, and offers Monty a short grin.

"You can hear country music anywhere in the world these days," she says, "but you can only hear talk shows in the States."

"Why is that?"

"We have more telephones."

The subject is earthquakes. An elderly woman is complaining that if geologists are going to keep predicting earthquakes, she wishes they would get their stories straight. "That is to say," she quavers, "either put up or shut up! Every week one a them fellas tells the newspapers there is going to be a massive shaker all up and down the state, and I want you to know I am a nervous wreck trying to get ready for all these predictions. Packing my bags. Unpacking my bags. Taking Darvon, and calling up people long-distance. I can't pay my phone bill half the time. I tell you, I simply cannot take it one more *minute!*"

She raises her voice, weeping now, shouting into the radio line: "YOU HEAR ME? I CANNOT STAND THIS WISHY-WASHY, BACK-AND-FORTH, NOW-YOU-SEE-IT, NOW-YOU-DON'T . . ."

The emcee cuts her off, saying he knows exactly how she feels and in the same modulated tones becomes the owner of a pet store describing the powers of a new brand of cat food, at which point the flask appears again in front of Montrose. He sips, and gasps again, and admits to himself that it does feel very, very good to be sitting next to Crystal drinking Fiji Island rum with his veteran son and listening to the talk show. He knows, of course, that they are near death. Travis is risking their lives with every flick of the wheel. Given the accumulating effects of jet lag, combat fatigue, one-hundred-proof rum, and perhaps as yet unspecified foreign drugs, Monty wonders how qualified Trav is for this kind of driving. But he wants to allow it, wants the boy to let off steam.

Much later, months from now, he will remember that at the very moment the emcee cut off that caller and the flask appeared, defining Monty's mood, his car was crossing the San Andreas. Perhaps coincidence. Perhaps not. The fault line cuts through these mountains, just above a large dam outside San Jose. Prophets say that when the great quake comes, this dam, like several throughout the state, will burst and the water from the reservoir will flow down to inundate the town. This road, they say, will buckle, perhaps split theatrically, creating two steep cliffs edged with asphalt and facing each other across an open maw. Of the thousands who use this highway daily, from the Santa Clara Valley to the coast, few realize that during the westward climb they cross from the American to the Pacific plate. Few care. Certainly the thought is far from Monty's conscious mind right now, far from Trav's, from Crystal's. They zip along the asphalt, sipping rum, half listening to callers, afloat on the forward motion of their journey. Would anything be revealed if we could read uncharted shadings of the mind as each rider crosses this invisible and seldom noticed boundary line? Take Monty. Who is to say what pressures or magnetisms open certain portals of the memory? Just now the glimmer of a scene began to flash for him. It flickered first this morning as he coupled with Leona. Perhaps that incomplete embrace explains the scene's return. Perhaps it is simply the nearness of Crystal, pressed against him in the front seat as they swing another outside curve. Or perhaps all three—the wife, the adventuress, and that brief acceleration through the zone of power, where two slabs of continental crust join and mate and send forth their vibrations.

As he floats in the front seat, his thigh adjoining hers, the libertine in Montrose is aroused. He begins to think of women, various women, Leona in particular, that look she wore this morning as she lay back on the brocade to receive him. Sweet, sweet Leona. He wonders how she might regard this trip. With reserve, he imagines. More likely, with a tinge of disapproval. She is not a prude. Not a party pooper. Not opposed to every form of abandon. But she practices abandon on her own terms, and does not enjoy anything that smacks of physical danger or material risk. He knows that's one reason he married her. He believes it is true that at least two kinds of women exist in the world. He would never, for example, set up housekeeping with Crystal. Yet during those periods, which vary greatly from man to man, when one wants to be free of limits, Crystal is just the sort of woman one hopes to meet. Loose. In every sense of that word. Having her along makes this wild and soldierly trip that much wilder and more soldierly. He would like to touch her. But knows he can't. Or knows he won't. She is, at this point, for him, a kind of pornography, calling forth his lusts. Savoring Crystal, he dwells the more upon Leona, her inward look this morning, among asparagus ferns, her neck and face the blue-white gloss of porcelain. The memory the phone's ring interrupted starts again, and the ferns become spring apple trees, Lee looking back as she hurtles along between the rows, two arms' lengths ahead of him. How old was she then? Twenty-two, or -three? He sees his basket crunch smooth bark as he lets it swing, grabbing for her with his free hand. She is trying to be modest about all this, to appear for some nonexistent audience as if they are merely strolling among the trees toward a late-in-the-day picnic spot.

"Monty, don't do that," she cautions, fiercely squeezing her brows. "Not to*day*." He trips on a stone-size clod and lunges, knees and elbows into the dirt, letting his basket spill like a cornucopia, as he reaches again for Leona. She leaps back squealing, pulls free from his loose grip around her ankle and begins to lope down between the rows, white trousers, pink blouse, her head turning once to repeat, "Not today, Monty!"

He leaves the wine, the basket, the olives and smoked oysters and cheese. He gathers up the quilt, rises to his knees, then waits, watching a moment longer—something in the flicker of her clothing among the trees. She is a white-and-pink bloom under dark-green limbs edged with pinkish-white where ten thousand blossoms wait for one more day, perhaps one more hour of new heat.

With the quilt flapping like a serape he follows, silent, bounding over plowed clods toward the low place where he never plows, a trough of grass, mallow, miner's lettuce, mustard greens, a weed collector's paradise, where Lee hides cuddled like a child, feigning childishness until he finds her and spreads the quilt, and there is no resistance now. She knows what he is going to do, and wants him to, wants what he wants, and lets him take it. The taking is important. His woman. His land. Her blooming is another of the promises brimming among all these trees. Her pink blouse shimmers beneath him, out here where everything is spring-green and pink-rimmed blossoms craving heat, everything, yes, until her eyes turn inward, just at the instant of his possession, of his bursting, as if the season of this blossom he has so many times possessed is now suddenly over. He sees that look and feels the deep regret for taking what he cannot let go. Regret and burning need and conquest, while he watches the eyes in the young face beneath him grow older, grow wistful and inexplicably wise.

7

A MORNING REPORT

excerpted from *One Day at a Time*, the thrice-weekly column
by Montrose Doyle

I took to the streets yesterday morning, picking citizens at random, asking a question I've been asking myself of late. Do you have a personal reason for following the news? Here are some of the replies, slightly edited, of course, like everything else these days.

RITA COLEMAN
Dental assistant

Yes, a very personal reason. My sister lives down in Carpinteria, and when that big fire broke out up in the mountains I kept my radio on 24 hours a day, just to relieve my mind that the firefighters were keeping it under control.

FARLEY NEWCOMBE
Unemployed car salesman

I keep my eye on those stock market reports. Market drops too low, I get low. Market zooms on up there, I am up there with it. I am high as a kite, checking out the market on a good day.

DON McNAB
Leather craftsman

Well, I'll tell ya. I am into disaster. Know what I mean? This is the way the world is going nowadays, one disaster after another. The only way to survive spiritually is to flow with the times. So you take earthquakes. I came out here from Minneapolis three years ago. I noticed that every day there was something in the news about quakes. So now I am following it pretty close and waiting for the big one. I am sticking around northern California so I can be here when it hits.

8

They have cleared the final rise, bringing into view the town, its summer cottages and stucco walls a distant splash of whiteness against the sea, which is itself a kind of white this hour of early afternoon, catching sun rays at a gold-flecked angle, so that the air above the town, taking its color from some mix of sea light and reflected buildings, has a texture all its own, a gossamer, white-blue vibrancy, beneath the larger, deep-sky blue above. From Travis it elicits a cowboy yell.

"Eeeeeee-yow!"

In tribute to this first look at his boyhood Riviera, Travis takes a final sip and passes the pint to Crystal. "I have a great idea," he says. "I would like to visit The Cheating Heart Saloon."

Crystal has sipped and passed the pint to Monty, who now drains the bottle and smacks his lips.

"One drink," he says gaily, secretively, "is all we'll have time for. Grover's coming by, ya know. Maybe some other folks. Leona's out there waiting to see her boy. She has plans for you, Travis. They all have plans."

"I just want to see the place. You know how some things stick with you, no matter where you go, or how many outrageous scenes you witness? Some things just hang there in front of you like photographs?"

A hot shine of understanding fills Crystal's eyes. The way some women at a moment of deep feeling touch necklaces, she touches her Rollei, a gesture Montrose notices, Trav does not.

"The whole time I was gone, The Cheating Heart kept flashing on my screen."

He accelerates, bringing new shudders as they enter town and its slower lines of traffic. Monty has to close his eyes and concentrate on rum warmth until he feels an end to the swerves and hectic braking. When he opens his eyes he sees that Travis has parked across the street.

"It's changed a lot since you've been gone."

"Everything has changed," says Travis flatly.

Surprised by this remark, Monty turns toward him, but Travis doesn't want to go into it. He wants to meditate upon The Heart's façade, making this an oddly reverent moment, punctuated by clicks from Crystal's Rollei and backed by stereophonic guitars in the distance. It is a Hank Williams reissue. Each time the double doors swing open, music swells into the street.

> *I got a hotrod Ford and a two-dollar bill.*
> *I know a little spot right over the hill.*

The building itself is of the type Leona's committee is trying to preserve—eighty-five years old, originally a general store with rooms upstairs to rent. Its style is late Frontier—brick facing, and rows of high sectioned windows below and above. A vaguely Grecian plaster fringe runs just under the roof line, in tune with the plaster triangles above each second-story window. The original roomers could step out onto a balcony supported by round wooden pillars. They could stand at the railing and look directly down into the wagons and into the mud. About the turn of the century, the building was converted to a restaurant and dining room for a new hotel next door. Later it became a warehouse, after the hotel caught fire and the center of town shifted two blocks west. By that time the wooden sidewalks had been replaced by concrete, the pillars had been torn down, and with the pillars went the balcony. For many years the vast interior stood boarded up, abandoned, waiting for the advent of the Aquarian Age, when two fellows from Los Angeles took a long-term lease and turned it into what they hoped would be the replica of a western saloon. The 1880s façade, the swinging doors, the scattered wooden tables, the long mirror behind the bar, all made it easy to believe you were stepping right into a high-budget cowboy movie. What they did not foresee was how quickly the décor would give rise to a certain style of action, or how quickly the replica would become what is now a genuine saloon—that is to say, a large barroom capable of exploding.

This is not Montana, not Nevada or New Mexico, where a few real cowboys exist. No miners or lumbermen inhabit these parts any longer. In the early days of The Cheating Heart, men came, like actors, in their western outfits, to gather at the bar and drink in the cowboy manner, standing up. Soon they were getting into real fights, they were kicking over tables and scaring the women and breaking off the ends of real whiskey bottles on the polished brass railing of the polished oak bar. Real weapons began to appear, hunting knives, and pistols, and thick bulges under the suede breast pockets of the buckskin coats. Nowadays the clientele is divided up about the way you see it in the westerns. The majority of them are bearded or mustachioed men, more or less well-meaning fellows in vests and boots and wide-brim hats just killing time at the bar or at the dartboard or playing cards; with a small but volatile contingent of true desperadoes, who are liable to show up at any time, whose tempers are short, and who ride Harleys more often than horses.

Inside The Cheating Heart no one ever really relaxes unless he is very drunk or very stoned or has recently arrived from out of town and stops in for a drink because the place has "character." For this reason the city police keep The Heart regularly patrolled: its exterior, including sidewalks in both directions, and all parts of the interior—the bar, the stage, and the two restrooms, where every imaginable kind of exchange has been known to occur.

So it is that just after Travis and Crystal plunge through the wide swinging doors, a man comes striding out, a man Montrose has not seen in over a year, a man so forlorn, so woebegone and down at the mouth—and this is the only visible clue we have to his desperate condition, the sagging, clownlike curve of his mouth between the chin strap and the goggles—that Montrose stops outside, lets the door swing to, slicing off a loud burst of song.

"Walter," he says.

"Hey, Doyle," comes the sad, constricted reply.

Taking a step in Walter's direction, with one hand out, Monty says, "What's the state of justice these days?"

The corners of the mouth turn briefly upward, then fall. "There is no justice, Montrose. I tell ya I don't know how long I am going to be able to keep this up."

"Keep what up?" Monty asks, instantly wishing he hadn't.

Walter raises one black boot and rests it on a planter box. His shoulders drop as if some dreaded moment has arrived, a moment of confession. Monty tries to overlook the ludicrous collection of artillery and riot gear he wears, tries to see through the wide, silvered lenses, and into the eyes of the man he has known since high school, since Walter was a sophomore and Monty was helping out coaching the football team. That was twenty years ago. He can't see the eyes. Lips and chin are the only recognizable features. The rest is Gestapo-like: blue-and-white crash helmet, dark-blue nylon jacket with the three-stripe sleeve, blue cavalry trousers wedging into high-top boots, the pistol, the thick belting, the blackjack at the hip, a big silver chest badge saying SERGEANT.

"Listen, Monty. You know me. I try to do a good job. That's just in my nature. Right? I don't screw around. I don't take liberties."

"That's you to a T, Walter."

"You remember when I took this job. We even talked about it."

"It was going to be this or teaching school," Monty recalls.

"Well, I'll tell you something. I goddam well should have gone the other way. I mean, I have had it up to here."

He draws a quick karate line across his throat, then looks around to see if anyone noticed this. The looking is compulsive, like a tic. Walter's head and evidently his eyes are scanning constantly as he talks.

"You see this outfit I got on? Eight hundred bucks I have to spend, out of my own money, for all these uniforms. They think it's some kind of big deal, letting us wear all this shit around town. But what I want to know is, what's the point, when everybody hates me?"

"C'mon, Walter, everybody doesn't hate you."

Monty is embarrassed. He remembers talking this way when Walter was fifteen.

"Are you serious? My wife is about to walk out on me. My whole social life is a bad joke. Every time somebody invites us to a party, as soon as people find out I'm a cop they start bitching. They expect me to explain anything that's gone wrong in the whole damn county for the past six months. They start telling me how the cops blew it here, or the cops blew it there. The conservatives are pissed because we're not tough enough with the dopers and the welfare cases and kids who drag-race outside of town. The liberals hit us with police brutality. The businessmen say we're not protecting the downtown area at night. The high school kids call us fascists because we won't let them run naked on the beach. Every time I show up anywhere out of uniform, somebody starts getting pissed off. Then I get pissed off. So I've quit going out. My wife says, What kind of life is this? All we ever see are other policemen. And Christ, Montrose, she's right! I don't really go for cops that much myself. I mean, day in and day out. It's enough to make me turn in my badge."

"Why don't you?"

"If I quit, who's gonna take my place? At least I try to do a decent job. I try to be fair. Some of these goons on the force, even *I'd* be afraid to have them in charge of anything. I ask myself, Who is going to protect this town if I don't do my share? Theft is up. Rape is up. Drugs are up. Look at this joint! Have you ever seen such a collection of freaks in your life?"

Walter's head has been swinging like a searchlight, scanning the street, the sidewalk across the street, the roofs and windows of surrounding buildings. Monty follows his gaze into the saloon, glad to look somewhere else besides at Walter's tortured face and the rims of saliva he has watched thickening at the corners of his mouth.

He'd like to get a rise out of Walter. "They're not all freaks," Monty says. "Just a few minutes ago you yourself were part of the crowd."

Walter is not amused.

Monty tries again.

"You wouldn't call my younger son a freak, now, would you? I'd have to take that personally."

"Hey," Walter exclaims. "Then I was right. That *was* Travis. I thought I saw him walking in. He's been away somewhere."

Warmed by a rush of fatherly pride at this seeming spark of interest, Monty tries once more to lighten Walter's mood. "Overseas. I just picked him up at the airport. Crazy as ever. Told us he'd be coming in on one plane, so I'm standing there waiting for him to walk down the ramp and he is already inside the terminal, sneaking up from behind. Guerrilla tactics. Keeps me on my goddam toes, that kid. Always did."

"Who's that girl he's with? She's new."

Monty thinks he sees a lecherous twitch underneath the chin strap. But before he can reply, Walter says grimly, "They're not carrying anything, I hope."

"What?"

"Most of these guys come back with their duffel bags loaded, or a hollowed-out Buddha statue mailed to themselves care of General Delivery. You know that guy Travis is talking to?"

Travis and Crystal have joined someone at a table. They huddle around a pitcher of beer. "I've seen him," Monty says.

"They used to be in a band together. Matter of fact, I think he was in Trav's graduating class."

With great weariness, Walter says, "If I were you, I'd tell Travis to keep his distance."

"Why do you say that?"

Walter doesn't explain, or chooses not to. "My wife says I'm paranoid, Monty. She says my view of the world is sick. But how can I see the world any other way, when I only see one part of it? The longer I spend in police work, the worse things look."

This last line seems to carry with it such a heavy burden that Walter falls silent, looking first at the sidewalk, as if searching for footprints, then up at the blue sky, as if to protest the heat, as if whoever removed the balcony sixty years ago and thus exposed this patch of sidewalk to the sun might still be lurking on the roof. For the first time since passing the summit on his way north this morning, Montrose thinks of Fowler and the scheme he unfolded. His impulse is to suppress a smile at the notion of Walter conspiring with someone from the bunch here inside The Cheating Heart. But that smile doesn't make it to the surface. Some niggling uncertainty erases it. Walter has become a man so confused, so whipped by accelerating circumstances, he is capable of many things no one would have expected of him five or even two years ago. It is just a niggle in the back of Monty's mind, and he would like to be rid of it, so he tells Walter about his conversation and Fowler's theory for explaining Linda Kramer's disappearance.

When he's finished, Walter moves his raised boot back to the concrete, in a gesture that could mean he has been offended. Monty thinks he sees him blinking. It's impossible to be sure. Walter laughs a hollow, despairing laugh, almost comical in its effect, Monty wishes he could see the eyes.

"He thinks we're teamed up with the dealers? Jesus Christ! It's not bad enough I got no social life, and I'm going into debt on my fucking uniforms, and I'm getting hemorrhoids from ten hours a day on the motorcycle. Now I'm a murder suspect on top of all the rest of it."

Montrose chuckles, relieved. "Not quite yet, Walter. Fowler's theory doesn't add up to much until they find Linda Kramer."

"Well . . . they did."

"Who did?"

"I guess we'll have to go talk to your friend Fowler."

"He isn't my friend."

"That's lucky."

"C'mon, Walter. Who found her? Where is she?"

"Some dogs, actually. Sniffed her out just this morning. Buried for a couple of weeks, looks like. But we're pretty sure it's her. Up in the mountains around Holy City. Hell of a thing. They say it looks like she was buried alive."

"Are you kidding me? My God! Alive?"

Again Walter laughs his despairing, hollow laugh, and this time removes his silvered, one-way lenses, revealing eyes Monty wishes now he didn't have to look at, eyes rounded with . . . what? Fear? Alarm? Desperation? The eyes are so enlarged, so stark, Monty can't help thinking of amphetamines. It's a look as melodramatic as the hollow laugh, yet it leaves no doubt that here is a man pushed right up to his limits, perhaps already past his limits.

"Either buried alive," says Walter, "or smothered first and then buried."

"They have any clues? Any idea who did it? Was she . . . violated?"

"Nothing. Nothing at all. Just a naked girl with no marks on her, and a mound of dirt."

9

Three Harleys are parked side by side pointing into the curb, equally bedecked with dark leather fittings, gleaming chrome, side mirrors, and wide black saddles. The main difference between the other two, whose owners drink now at the bar, and the one Walter straddles is the fringe dangling from their handlebars and the mudguards, which show smiling silver teeth. Walter kicks his engine to life, his boots agleam, his eyes hidden again behind the silvered shades.

"You going up there?" Monty asks.

Walter shakes his head. "Out of our jurisdiction. County usually handles the mountains. We'll be checking suspects here in town, working with the D.A.'s office. You tell your friend if we don't hear from him he'll be hearing from us."

He walks the big bike backward into takeoff position. "Good talking to you, Monty. I ought to talk to you more. I don't know what it is. I always feel better after I talk to you," leaving him then, in a wake of low thunder.

Standing at the curb, in the sun, watching Walter's crash helmet disappear in distant traffic, he is suddenly sober. The rum has reversed itself. He feels the sobriety that surpasses drunkenness. He feels clear-headed, clear-eyed, exhilarated, clairvoyant. All the workings of the universe are not only apparent to him, but amazingly transparent. There are no mysteries, no obscurities, no need for further conversation on the subject. He is standing inside a glass dome gazing out upon mankind, in the moment before he has to decide what to do next, carrying perfectly balanced in the forefront of his vision these four specific pictures:

1. *The Tortured Eyes of Walter,* which he does not want to have to deal with, since Walter's problem is at once too obvious and too elusive, "Good talking to you, Monty" being but a feeler. A follow-up phone call in a day or two would not surprise Montrose in the least. He sees now that Walter probably went into police work in order to prove the truth of a world view that began to form at about the age of fifteen. "Nobody likes me," he used to complain to Monty, after getting his face bashed in at the line of scrimmage. Now he is on the verge of some deeper, more terrible truth. He has reached some kind of flash point, and his life is ready to burst.

2. *The Thigh of Crystal,* and the tickle it sends through him, merely recollecting. He remembers reading somewhere that one sign of a mature mind is the ability to hold two opposing ideas at the same time. Even while the thought of that burial mound unnerves him, Crystal's trousered thigh vaguely titillates. His knowledge that these two images can coexist becomes a source of marvel in itself.

3. *The Mound of Earth,* which he does not want to have to deal with either. Not yet. The journalist in him would drive up there to look around. But not this afternoon. Solving murders isn't his line of work. Writing about them isn't his line of writing. Not that he is indifferent to murder, or numb to murder. Quite the opposite. The continuing pattern of bizarre and unaccountable killings in his time, in his region, is like a wound that will not heal, a deep, spiritual wound. Each new violation reopens it, cuts deeper, the leading edge of some lethal implement that he fears may gradually carve his soul to pieces. This afternoon he doesn't want to think about it. And yet the mound of earth has already imprinted itself in his imagination. Underneath tomorrow's headline he will see the girl's face for the first time. In the next two months he will see it twenty times. Two years from now he will probably not be able to pick her out of a selection of fifteen photos. But he will never forget the mound of earth. The way it looks in his mind's eye now is almost exactly how it will look when he can

no longer avoid driving up to seek some understanding of whatever creature gouged out her ragged trench and filled it in again.

4. *The Wild Drive* and that unfamiliar look in Travis's eye, which is still his first concern—his son, the welfare and condition of his son, and the homecoming, the reunion Leona and Grover even now are getting organized. He wants to give priority to this, and deal with all the rest of it later, if he must. How many sons, after all, does a man have in one lifetime? With population control catching on, the number of men with any sons to speak of may soon be drastically reduced. One has to savor these things while one can. Certain age-old privileges may soon be seldom seen again, or thought of. He has in mind not only the public occasions, such as football games, graduation ceremonies, and marriage, but also those less heralded yet somehow more indelible moments like today's return from overseas, from a battlefield. Years hence we may well discover some enterprise more profitable than war. What new forms will our deepest feelings take then? Fewer sons. Fewer campaigns. Fewer leavings. Fewer homecomings. As much as anything else, it is this sense of certain rapidly approaching terminals in history that fills him with the desire to give this day to Travis, a knowledge that the world will never be this way again. He has spent most of his life holding on to things that seem about to disappear forever, and he has learned that he prefers doing this to letting them go without a struggle, as many advise him to do. The alternative almost always leads to self-contempt. Not long ago an acquaintance in real estate advised him to put his ranch on the market because it was only a matter of time before the county rezoned it or the state confirmed a plan to route a freeway through his neighborhood, and thus reduce its value. Montrose told him that if it was a matter of time, then he would take whatever time he had coming. The time was more important than the money. He enjoyed being able to say that. He is hearing the conversation in the distance now, hearing himself declaim, *If it's only a*

matter of time . . . when another voice interrupts him, from closer in, from just outside his dome of glass, like the disembodied voice of conscience.

"I guess you heard the news."

He knows this voice. It's the one person he least wants to see right now. Without turning, he pictures the kind of face that will accompany the voice. A priestly face, with the smile priests and preachers wear when visiting the terminally ill. And he is wrong about the face. This is not at all what he sees when he turns. Fowler is walking toward him from the door of The Cheating Heart, looking embarrassed, apologetic, fearful.

"Yes, I heard the news," says Montrose flatly.

"Well?" Fowler says, as if he has been waiting for days for Monty to make up his mind.

"Well, what?"

"I was having a drink and saw you out here talking to the pig."

"Don't call him a pig. He's an old acquaintance of mine."

"Then you know what I'm talking about."

Monty can't help laughing. "You're not making sense, Fowler."

"I'm worried, that's all. When I talked to you this morning I was just guessing. You know?"

He shivers. His eyes plead for comradeship, for relief. Montrose is affected, not by the plea itself, but by the man's powers of seduction. His manner suggests that they are long-time accomplices, sharing some common chore.

"But Holy Jesus! I predicted the murder! Do you realize that? I'm into this thing way over my head. If that cop is a friend of yours, then you probably already know about cops. They are the same all over. I mean, there are always two kinds. Right? Cops who love their work. And cops who can't stand it. They divide up about fifty-fifty. So there are always cops around who are looking for a way out. When they get desperate enough they'll try anything. I have seen it happen dozens of times, where a cop takes a piece of the action, figuring it will give him a little breathing space. It's so easy to *do*, man. It's right *there*. Meanwhile it costs nothing to get rid of a chick like Linda Kramer. When I was living in L.A., I heard the going rate to have somebody iced was a hundred fifty, two hundred bucks. Around here they tell me it's more, which leads me to suspect the action is fairly big. But still, you are only talking about a few hundred bucks. And now I am living out there with my wife and kid, next to a whole houseful of people who are really *into* it, you know what I mean? I don't want to be there. It's too scary."

Fowler's eyes are growing moist, and Montrose, against his best judgment, begins to feel sorry for the man. Distantly he toys with the idea of offering him another place to park his truck, but knows this would be a mistake. Fowler has shoved his hands deep into the pockets of his overalls. He hunches his shoulders like a man standing back against a stone building to take shelter from a howling wind. The gesture reminds Monty of the log cabin on the bed of Fowler's truck. Something is inappropriate. He gets the feeling that Fowler likes to be afraid. He has known people like this before. To be with them is to be repeatedly plunged into frightening situations because that is where they feel most at home.

He makes a proposal he expects Fowler to refuse. "You and I should go talk to the D.A. He should hear what you told me."

On Fowler's lips a condescending smirk. "You're going to blow it, Doyle. Maybe that's what you want, maybe you really want to blow it."

"He's an honest man. I've known him for years."

"You've known everybody for years. That's the trouble with this town. Everybody has known everybody for years and years."

"Don't get sarcastic with me, Fowler. I don't even know why I'm standing here talking to you! What are you doing in my life anyway? Driving up my driveway! Stopping me on the sidewalk! I've got plenty on my mind without you—"

"Hey. Hey. Take it easy. You're right, man. I *should* go talk to the D.A. I mean, quietly. Under the circumstances, it is my best shot. If the D.A. knows I exist, it's a kind of protection, isn't it? Right now, I am nobody. Who do I know around here? Who knows me? Just this houseful of creeps. I need a little visibility. When I think about my kid . . . He's not even a year old. How did I get into this mess?"

Fowler is so moved by his own vulnerability, he begins to blink back the wetness in his eyes. Montrose is of two minds. He would like to comfort the man, buy him a drink, find him a soft chair to relax in. He has to admit he is drawn to Fowler, to something as yet undefinable about his personality, something exotic, almost Mediterranean. At the same time he fills with impatience, he wants to shout, "What mess?" He sees Fowler's so-called predicament as self-invented. He isn't sure. There could be something to it. But it doesn't really add up. The mound of earth? A young girl buried alive? This is just not . . . professional. He wishes he had a more reliable source of information. Linda's boyfriend, for instance. If he actually exists.

A flood of music comes pouring from the saloon, guitars and western fiddles. Bob Wills and His Texas Playboys.

> *Detour . . .*
> *There's a muddy road ahead.*
> *Detour . . .*
> *Paid no mind to what it said . . .*

Travis, singing along, seems buoyed out the door as if floating in a tub of sound. He lands on the sidewalk next to Monty, his Panama shoved back like a cardplayer's. On one of his arms hangs Crystal, on the other his old high school buddy Donald, whom Monty remembers as a dedicated miler, in whose eyes he sees a look common among customers of this saloon, a look Montrose is familiar with but has not yet learned to read. He has seen it in the eyes of dopers and meditators, but also in the eyes of vegetarians and people preparing to die. It is a moist intensity, an unblinking glassiness that seems to suggest this person recently experienced either true ecstasy or true madness. Donald wears his blond hair short and wears a plain blue work shirt that gives him the look of a prisoner. The shirt and eyes together could easily convince you he just emerged from several months in solitary confinement.

These three have consumed two pitchers of beer waiting for Monty to join them inside. They are singing along with the record, humming, wagging tongues. *Dah-daaaaaah. Dad-da-dah, dad-dah, da-dah.* Now there is an urge to dance, an urge for all present to link arms, join forces, liven up the sidewalk, counterweight the programmed lanes of passing traffic with a spontaneous human outburst. Crystal grabs Monty by the arm, Donald takes Fowler's. Monty takes Fowler's other arm, to complete the circle, surprised by the thinness of that arm underneath the plaid flannel which gives it the illusion of bulk. He looks at the dark, wiry beard and sees the unweathered white flesh beneath, a narrow jaw line, suggestions of a delicate chin. He watches Fowler's legs kick awkwardly, as they all kick in toward the center, singing, and he imagines that inside his thick logger's boots the feet too are thin, white as bone. Fowler clearly does not know what to make of this ring-around-the-rosy. He is trying to smile, can't quite manage it, as if to smile now would betray something or someone he holds dear. Montrose, in a rush of sympathy, leans in close, his voice nearly drowned under Trav's loud bellowing of the final chorus.

"I'll call the D.A. on my way home, tell him you'll be in to see him. You get in touch with me tomorrow morning."

"At your house?"

"By phone."

"Is your number listed?"

"I'll leave a message at my office."

Fowler takes this as a form of rejection. He pulls loose, backs away from the dancers with his dismissal smile crinkling up into dark eyes. Waving to no one in particular, he rushes to cross with the light, as the four six-foot speakers inside The Heart fall silent, making audible the undersound that is always there—the chattering, the clink of glass, the muffled grumble of engines lined up at the intersection.

In this small interval Monty sees Donald's hand moving toward him. In Donald's eyes he sees the look of a man who could be emerging from hypnosis, or returning from weeks alone in the Sonoran desert, or recovering from several hours of exquisite sex. As Monty takes the dry hand, he surmises that this could also be the look of a sunning snake. Donald says nothing by way of greeting. He simply opens his face in a slow, beaming smile. When Travis announces that Donald recently changed his name to Radar, and then announces that he has invited Donald/Radar home for dinner, Monty groans, as if someone just sapped him on the skull. But he does not protest. We are giving this day to Travis. And the groan itself is so timed, it appears aimed not for Donald but for a magnified and terrible scratching which fills the street as someone inside moves the tone arm back to replay the old Bob Wills classic, ending the silence, and the need for speech, and the brief sidewalk interlude. Guitars and fiddles tumble out through doors and windows, just as the light changes and a space in the traffic opens. With cowboy voices from the forties to urge them on, they sprint across the street toward Monty's car.

10

Shopping plazas surround this town, staging areas for the next advance. Around each low phalanx of ranch-style buildings lie fields of asphalt where cars and vans assemble in long rows, as if lining up for a mammoth caravan. It is always quiet out there on the asphalt. People waiting in their cars sit quietly. People walking from cars to the market or to the laundromat speak softly, if at all, like pilgrims walking in the desert. Montrose does not approve of this. He is behind the wheel again, he is soldiering again. They are into the next pint of rum, purchased when he stopped to make a fast call on Fowler's behalf. When they reach the last shopping center before the countryside begins, he detours through its parking lot to avoid the light. Speeding along between rows of cars, he leans on his horn: *Waaah! Waaah! Waaah!*

He shouts at the license plates, "Let's hear some noise out there! Let's hear some enthusiasm!"

Two small boys walking next to an elderly woman wave back with incoherent delight, rushing toward the car. Crystal snaps their picture, and Travis yells out the window, "Gotcha!"

The boys yell it back at him, firing imaginary pistols. "Gotcha! Gotcha!"

Picking up the cue, Travis and Crystal grab at each other, giggling in the back seat. "Gotcha. Gotcha. Gotcha."

Then she is lining up another shot, but Trav keeps groping at the curve of her waist, the uplift of bosom, muttering the code word with each little grab and pull.

"Gotcha. Hey. Gotcha. Gotcha."

"Cut it out, Travis."

"Gotcha there."

"How can I keep this thing focused?"

"I need woman," he growls, cave-man style. "Travis want woman now!"

He lunges, shoving the camera into her ribs.

"Ow!" she cries. "Goddam it!"

He puts his hands around her throat, still growling. "Photo girl no fun. Travis want *real* girl. Sweet skin. Soldier like sweet skin."

A swing in the road throws him against her, and he suddenly goes soft, quietly nuzzling her neck. In front Montrose is grinning, listening to the radio again, and in a fierce hurry now, finely tuned, single-minded, his sense of history propelling him along a road he knows so well he could drive it in reverse on a moonless night without once looking back to check his angle. This curve has popped them into open country. He speeds down the country road toward what awaits Travis up ahead, and everything suits his hopes and expectations except the unsettling presence of Donald/Radar at his side here in the front seat.

He has not spoken, or looked at anything but the windshield, staring through it in his saintly way, and Montrose, in quick, furtive glances, has perceived that something is missing in Donald's face. Not a nose or an eye, but . . . some essential feature. Monty is reminded of a priest he met a few years back, a young brown-robed and cherub-faced Franciscan whose task was to guide tourists through one of the Spanish missions in southern California.

"Hey, Radar," Monty says, "do you by any chance believe in Jesus?"

The head does not move. Nothing changes but the lips, which part with difficulty, as if speech pains him.

"Doesn't everyone?" he murmurs.

They zip past a stucco clot of new duplexes set against the land like cutouts. Then it's sloping meadow again, orchards spreading back toward distant knolls of eucalyptus, weathered fencing, and a stretch of road so shaded that ferns grow year round from outcroppings of damp rock. In this little grotto Monty skids to a stop, leaps out, saying he'll only be a second.

It's a spot where he often stops, selected not so much by Monty himself as by the habit of his bladder. Whatever drinking he does in town makes it unbearable not to stop along here somewhere and pee. He takes a deep satisfaction in the solitude, the spider webs, the cinnamon cast of manzanita branches he stands among, the cool, fractured, mossy rise of sandstone above him. Total quiet, except for the sounds of Crystal and Travis necking a few yards away, and then the sound of leaves crunching, as Radar wordlessly joins him, unzips, and sends forth a lemony stream as noiseless as its maker.

Montrose is annoyed. His "spot" is being trespassed, and his privacy. Then it occurs to him that this maneuver might have veiled sexual shadings. But the notion quickly passes. He sees now what Radar is missing. The lad seems entirely asexual, neither sexually attentive nor sexually repressed, but desexed, eunuchlike.

As the silence grows around them, and the wisps of steam lift above the dry manzanita leaves, it becomes clear that Radar is thoroughly at ease here. And this puts Monty at his ease again. He regards the earthy style, the scruffy, well-worn boots, firm on the feet, the threaded cuffs of his jeans in these surroundings, as somehow . . . right. There begins to rise within him a generosity toward this fellow who after all has done nothing more than pee in Monty's grotto, partake a little of his sylvan quiet. They are simply two men peeing together out of doors, sharing a small moment, puddles spreading side by side, and no words spoken.

In the glade, zipping up, Montrose sees in a flash what the mood of his entire day has been. Too much on guard. Each person he has encountered, including his own son, has called up in him some suspicion, some grave reservation. It's the very malady Walter was complaining of. Some people say the times breed paranoia. Others say the word itself is out of date, that paranoia is no longer a condition, but *the* condition. Monty doesn't need that large a theory for today. He can trace his frame of mind right back to the telephone ring this morning, their moment of love-making interrupted, the time of emptiness filled with small threats, dark innuendoes. Fowler got this whole day off on the wrong foot. Who am I standing next to here, for God's sake? This is Donald. He used to play gut bucket when they were in junior high. He does not resemble a snake. If anything, he resembles Travis. They could almost be brothers. Same lean build, same coloring, same boyishness in the cheeks and chin. This does not surprise Monty, who did the same thing when he was in high school, chose a friend who could have been his brother. The difference was, of course, that Monty had no brother of his own, as Travis does.

As they stand beneath the canopy of manzanita, ready to step back to the car, Donald's eyes could be saying to him: We have just shared a beautiful moment. Or they could be carved from pale-blue marble, as striking and as lifeless as that. In his new frame of mind, Montrose selects the former. Benefit of the doubt. He thinks again of the holy men in Asia who can will their images not to appear on negatives. Donald is like that. He could be a photograph of Travis taken in very bright sunlight.

As if satisfied that they have reached some understanding, Donald lowers his eyes, steps away from Monty, across the tiny clearing, dips under a limb, and pushes into the brush.

Monty stands there listening to the snaps and fading crackles, until Travis calls out, "Hey, what are you guys doing to each other in there?"

Back at the car, Monty says, "Donald just walked off into the woods."

Travis grins. "What did you do, piss on his boots?"

"What's he up to, Travis? I can't figure it out."

"Neither can I."

"Did he say anything at the saloon?"

"He says he's into purity. He wants to be like Abraham."

"Abraham who?"

"The Old Testament guy. The prophet."

"Is he Jewish?"

"No; he's trying to purify his life. Simple clothes. Simple haircut. Simple diet. Simple talk. Simple travel. Maybe he got tired of the car and decided to walk."

"You mean to the house?"

"Don't ask me, man."

"Don't ask you! He's your friend! You're the one who invited him for dinner!"

Monty feels the way he felt at the airport when Travis told him Crystal would be staying for a while. Caught in crossfire.

"He was my friend two years ago," Travis says. "I don't understand these people anymore. I'm starting to wonder what the hell has been going on around here."

"Walter implied that he is dealing."

"Walter's information is out of date. Radar *was* dealing. He's too spaced now to keep track of things."

"Spaced on what?"

"Who knows? Modern times. Daytime television. Vitamin E. The Book of Job. There's a thousand ways to go."

"Walter also tells me guys coming back from overseas are usually carrying something. Is he out of date about that too?"

With a prankster's glint, Travis says, "Everybody was saying it was too good to leave behind. So who knows? Maybe I did. Why? You need a refill? You feel like getting loaded?"

"Is that why you wanted to stop at The Cheating Heart?"

"I have a sentimental attachment to the place."

"I just don't want you ending up on some shit list your first week back. Walter saw you sitting there—"

"Hey. You want to know something? You are now sounding like my father."

Montrose starts the engine, concentrating on the ignition, trying to recover what he felt before Donald/Radar walked away: the willingness to trust, to let the guard down, to absorb the little mysteries and unexplainables and just give this one day to his son. Not too difficult a task, when the mysterious and the inexplicable are commonplace.

A hand falls on his shoulder. Travis says, "Don't worry about it, Dad. Really. I don't do dope anymore. I outgrew it. Now I'm just like you. I drink. And I count my blessings."

Monty turns to look at both their faces, shiny with rum and with back-seat lust, and, in their eyes, a double-edged gleam he decides to call playfulness.

11

At the turn the gate is open. Between the gate and a tree-shaded cottage stands a sprawling, high-piled jumble of driftwood, fallen logs, river boulders, scraps of sidewalk, street signs, brickwork, broken furniture, packing crates, stuffed animals, a Pontiac hood.

"Holy Jesus!" Travis laughs, as they swing past. "Where'd that come from?"

"Wellington's Revenge," says Montrose. "It's not important."

Climbing in second gear, he punches the horn. Halfway up, they begin to hear music. As they break past the willow's arch they see the band standing up there on the long front porch, next to the railing, playing "California, Here I Come," bluegrass style—fiddle, guitar, mandolin, string bass, and Grover's banjo, all the musicians ruddy from the Jack Daniel's they have been sipping since midafternoon, in their blue jeans and their work shirts and their boots.

Gravel popping, Monty swings around in front of the stairs just as Leona pushes the screen door open. The wagging dogs get to Travis first. Monty pulls them clear so that Leona, prettied up, girlish, womanly, can revive the old flirtation with her youngest. She wears a flowered blouse and bell-bottom trousers, her brown hair loose and shiny. She throws her arms around him, squeezing, while Travis, inscrutable, is for this moment the grinning, boyish, juiced lover-son.

"Hello, Ma."

"Travis, where'd you get that hat?"

"Stole it from a guy in the Islands."

"Makes you look like some kind of cardshark or gambler."

"Isn't that how you like em, Ma? Sharp and shifty?"

"I like em all kinds of ways, hon. Everybody knows that. Now let me look at you."

She stands back to study him, from shoes to gambler's Panama, takes hold of his hands, her eyes brimming, then creasing with a little frown of disbelief.

"Travis, honey, what happened to your eyes?"

"Nothing, Ma."

"Don't fool with me, now. There's something wrong."

He shrugs, speaks softly, underneath the music that jangles along right above them. "I took a little piece of shrapnel, Ma," glancing then at Montrose as if to apologize for keeping this from him, from them.

Leona waits, confusion on her face, demanding more.

"It wasn't bad, Ma. Don't worry."

She too glances at Monty, as if for explanation, as if these two have been hiding something. And you might say they have, since her question is the kind Monty would never ask on a soldier's first day back, even if it had occurred to him.

"Why didn't you tell us?" she asks Travis. "We didn't know about this, did we, Monty?"

"It wasn't bad. It wasn't much of anything. I should have let you know, I guess, but I kind of figured . . ."

"It's hurt your vision."

"I lost a little vision in my left eye. If I squint like this, the world gets fuzzy. But it really isn't anything at all. Don't worry about it. There are guys with arms and legs blown off who'll spend the rest of their lives in hospitals. I got off easy."

In her eyes there is a gathering of pain, of whatever her boy might have suffered or that she imagines he might have been through, and the accumulation of her two years' worrying, as if all this has just gone off behind her eyes in the form of a fragmentation bomb or the very grenade that caught Travis by surprise.

Unable to watch it, he turns to his father, toward the old

veteran who can better understand such things, who understands the irony of wounds. "It's fun," Travis says. "Each eye is a different kind of lens. I can flip back and forth."

He begins to wink, first one eye, then the other, saying, "Fuzzy. Clear. Fuzzy. Clear."

The comedy fails. It seems to make Lee sway slightly. Travis has to squeeze his mother's hands hard to check the sway.

12

Above them Grover's band is picking and grinning and tapping boots on the porch boards, while Grover finishes this welcome-home tune with a loud banjo chorus, leaning back Pete Seeger style, one lanky, Levi'd leg shoved forward, the taut white head slung low at his waist. Seen from the driveway, his face has mountainous qualities. At fifty his face will be craggier than his father's. At twenty-three it is rock smooth, sharp-boned, marked, whenever he smiles widely, by a gap halfway back on his upper left, where a tooth was broken off abalone-diving when he was sixteen. He never let Montrose have the tooth repaired. He liked the toughness of it then, in his junior year, liked to flash its dark gap from the backfield before signals, during night games. He flashed it just now, his version of a welcome-home grin, as Travis stepped out of the car.

This concert, which will continue till the moon rises, is Grover's idea, a tribute to his younger brother, a gesture, you might call it a peace offering. During the two months before Travis left, there had been many arguments, and since then only a couple of postcards. The arguments centered on military service, whether or not a man should take part in that, the larger issue being where a man should rightly invest his time and energy, the largest issue of all, over which they came closest to blows, being the meaning of life. Since Travis finished high school they have not been able to agree on the meaning of life.

They're both two years older now, of course, wiser in the

workings of the world, and the world itself has changed. Grover is prepared to be generous. For the past year he has lived with a woman who has been teaching him how to relax. He intends to be generous and to relax as soon as he finishes this tune, which he plays now, the way he does everything, completely immersed, until it's done. Standing on the porch and watching the scene between Lee and Travis, he sees it yet does not see it. He hears some of the words but does not react until all the licks he has in mind for this particular chorus are out of his system and "California, Here I Come" has galloped through its jangly, headlong climax to a stop.

With the last note, at just the moment Travis has tried to wink away his mother's distress, Grover grabs the banjo neck so it won't bounce and jumps down the stairs to clasp his brother's hand, punch his shoulder. His look, for one instant, is that of the football coach watching a kid hobble off the field who has just had the wind knocked out of him, a perplexed sympathy and flash of envy for the one who took the blow, for being out there where the blows were being exchanged. Just a flicker of that. Then Grover too begins to wink, like Travis. He takes one finger and pushes his left eyelid around until things go blurry for him. This isn't mockery. He wants to see how it feels, what the world looks like for Travis now. He holds his finger there and they stare at each other blurry-eyed, suddenly trying not to laugh. Beneath the eye Grover's mouth begins to work, to purse and pucker and rubber-lip, while Leona, her brow still creased, looks up from son to son.

Montrose cannot help himself. With the rum working, and the dogs straining, and Travis in his goddamned shoved-back Panama, and Grover's molar gap flashing darkly, and Lee between them like some diminutive referee, Monty starts to snicker. Hearing him, the boys are helpless. Years of gags and stunts and skirmishes and showdowns pass between them. They break out laughing. From the porch the boys in the band guffaw, and the women they brought along join in, smiling, laughing. Just that fast Leona is embracing Travis all over again, thanks to Grover and the healing powers of laughter, her tears now the ones she has stored up for him, irrepressible tears of joyful welcome, as all the eagerness she has so long held in check lets go.

13

An hour later Wellington arrives with his lady and begins to sing in the driveway. It is the welcome song of the Kwakiutl nation, he announces. He is so large and imposing that everyone is compelled to come back out onto the porch and watch this display. He is six foot four and wears a massive black beard. Black chest hair tufts out around the top of a bright-blue silk shirt, blue to match the fist-size turquoise buckle holding up his jeans. He wears black boots that scuff up the driveway dust as he shuffles back and forth, hunched forward, shouting unintelligible words and wagging his head to the tempo his lady keeps by beating a stick against a small cowhide drum.

Wellington is an anthropologist whose job with the county junior college terminates in three months. No one is quite sure why, whether he quit or has been let go. Monty associates the news of this with the first appearance of the edifice in Wellington's yard, which began as an abandoned refrigerator, has now risen to nearly twenty feet, and will go to forty as soon as he figures out the engineering. Monty knows he will do it. Wellington is a very handy fellow; he likes tools and tinkering. This is one of the reasons Monty rented to him in the first place—that, and the steady income his job seemed to promise. Monty takes special interest in Wellington's career because rent from that cottage pays the taxes on this whole place. When pressed about the future, he strokes his beard and says that his field is actually just beginning to open up for him. He talks about new realms of meaning, new connections. His field is the native Americans of the Pacific Northwest—Haida, Kwakiutl, Tlingit, and Aleut. Inspired, he says, by their high-rise, multi-image totems, he has set out to construct a monument of his own. He wants it to be composed of native materials, natural and social, to catch the full range of the region he now inhabits, everything from redwood trees to the styrofoam that home appliances come packed in. Monty suspects that this same motive explains the song Wellington now performs in the driveway. As he lumbers around, kicking at the gravel, his great arms spread wide, it is hard to believe this is anything but a collection of grunts and yodels he is making up as he goes along.

With his final note, he spreads his feet apart, stretches his arms upward in a wide V, and thrusts his beard at the sky. A great cheer rises from the porch, whistles, and rowdy huzzahs from the boys in the band, who reach again for their instruments. As they break into another tune, and as the listeners disperse, Wellington is still standing with arms upstretched, as if his monumental body has become some kind of totem in itself.

14

When this house was built, in 1889, the Christian Scientist fitted it for gas. Monty has kept the original fixtures. Nowadays he keeps the brass pipes polished. Mellow globes soften the light in the dining room, warm the darkest redwood corners, warm the distant ceiling. Tonight they warm full goblets standing on the sideboard, and all the other fittings for the banquet Leona has prepared. The globes and goblets and polished wood, and the band picking easy in the front room, all lead Monty to suspect, after forty-six years and several bottles of good California zinfandel, that this night might well be the high point of his life on the planet earth.

With Travis back, and Grover here, and Grover's woman, Holly Belle, who has become the daughter Monty always wished for, it makes tonight a winding in of all their life lines, a gathering of his tiny and precarious clan.

Holly Belle is singing now, a song she knows is one of Monty's favorites. Dark-haired, statuesque, six feet tall, she needs large accessories—large animals, large furniture, large men like Grover, large cars like the '49 Packard she keeps parked next to their cabin. Holly possesses a large alto voice, rich enough to command a total silence from the bawdy crowd at The Cheating Heart on the rare occasions when she has sung there with Grover's band. This happens to be one of the songs she sang in that saloon, and her rendition is still remembered and sometimes talked about late at night, near closing time, when the regular drinkers will do anything but face the news that they must now leave their tables and head home through empty streets, and so turn to red-eyed conver-

sations about the great moments witnessed in that room—
moments of prowess, moments of orgy, moments of spiritual
power—in this way explaining to one another why they've
spent so many hours there.

> *Life is like a mountain railway,*
> *With an engineer that's brave.*
> *We must make this run successful*
> *From the cradle to the grave. . . .*

At the chorus, all the others pitch in and pile on, harmoniz-
ing or failing to harmonize, jabbering through the unremem-
bered lines.

> *Blessed Saviour, there to guide us*
> *Till we reach that blissful shore,*
> *And the angels there to join us*
> *In God's grace forevermore.*

"Grace" is the key word here. This exuberant caroling serves
as a kind of grace before the meal, a blessing, a benediction.
Though Monty's family has never been religious in the Sunday sense, he has tried to teach them to revere the country
and mountain classics he grew up on. He remembers hearing his mom and dad sing this same song in this room
when he was ten and twelve. They came from generations
of Baptists and they believed the lyrics in ways different from
how Monty does, but such a song still fills his heart and his
eyes with a familiar Protestant warmth and glee of recollec-
tion, and an actual sense of continuities in the world—which
is exactly what the customers at The Cheating Heart are after
when they dwell on Holly Belle's rendition.

Travis happens to be standing next to her now, a brotherly
arm around the shoulder. Montrose is pleased to see the fervor
of his singing, his face flushed, his head wagging to the heavy
beat. It's a loaded fervor, as if for the first time Trav is hear-

ing and believing something about these words and purposely overdoing it in order to keep his distance from what he hears. And that is all right, Monty thinks, reading this as one of the signs. Of growth. Of change. It took Monty himself years to admit that what he hears in all so-called country music is the Okie Baptist harmonies he thought he'd left so far behind, the rich and resonant Holly Belle altos of his church-attending youth.

And when the singing's done he steps up, like the preachers and other patriarchs from that distant world, and begins to carve the roast Lee has set before him here on the polished buffet. He smiles broadly at Leona as she walks away, admiring the shiny fall of brown hair and the twitch in her behind, with true admiration for her style, the ways she takes care of herself, and takes care of all her men. He looks over at Holly bending to say something to Grover while he tunes the banjo, her high cheekbones caught in candlelight. Carving, Monty swarms with patriarchal affection for all the women here— for Lee, for Holly, for the women the musicians brought along.

He sees Travis next to Grover, tuning up the old Gibson twelve-string, showing him some little slack-key blues lick he picked up somewhere, perhaps in Honolulu, along with his hat and the Fiji Island rum and . . . Montrose does not see Crystal until he catches, from somewhere outside, a glint of white, and turns toward the window to see her near the orchard, this once without her Rolleiflex, her stride telling him she's heading out that way to breathe.

It is the moment of dusk just before moonrise, near dark, yet not dark because the subdued light of an approaching moon tints everything. He watches her white blouse and white trousers blur into the first row of blossoming trees, and he imagines showing her around the place, locating perimeters. When she disappears among the trees he wonders if she will just keep walking, the way Radar did. She is capable of that. In this light it is not mysterious at all, the urge to disappear. Monty wants to be a white flower too, among the old family apple trees. Lost. The boy living in him wants that, ever yearning for a simpler time. The father-husband-patriarch carves the roast, piling red, savory slabs on the platter, then pauses, transfixed, with these two creatures pulling, reined to him, and he is neither boy nor father, but someone else. Call it essential Montrose, with a minisecond's leisure to choose. You might say a minisecond's loftiness. Poised, he hovers here until another glint distracts him. A floating pearl.

He blinks. Leona is returning from the kitchen, almost upon him, the amber light reflecting on a necklace of cut abalone shells, like mirrors across her bodice. He loves her necklaces and bracelets and earrings and glitter pins. Again his affection swells. Before she speaks, a little pursing of her lips betrays a worry, something niggling. He hopes she's not still troubled about Travis, at least not now, not tonight. Monty has discovered in himself a fatherly pride for that wound, for the survivor of the wound. He feels relieved that he now has an explanation for that wild look in the boy's eye. He would share this with Leona. He doesn't have to. Something else is on her mind.

"The roast all right?" she says, noting his immobile knife. "Too rare in the center?"

"It's perfect, sweetheart. You never miss."

She knows her man quite well, knows he has paused to consider *some*thing. She looks where she just saw him looking, toward the orchard, where Crystal now emerges from the first line of trees, striding back toward the house. With wise amusement she searches his face.

She says, "It's nice having Travis home, isn't it?"

"Just like old times."

"The place sure gets lively in a hurry."

He puts an arm around her shoulder. "Now, you don't mean to say it's been unlively around here."

"No. I wasn't suggesting that," she says, the amusement still shining, a bit of mischief in her eyes.

Hugging her, Monty leans in close and whispers something

double-edged. It makes her smile, then giggle. His lips touch her hair.

Laughing, she says, "Don't talk to me that way, mister. I'm trying to run a good clean family restaurant."

Montrose starts laughing. There by the gleaming roast, with amber globes overhead, Grover and Travis picking "Wildwood Flower" in the next room, and the moon outside about to ignite above the nearest hills, they look into each other's eyes and laugh like lovers.

15

THE HEALING POWERS OF LAUGHTER

from *One Day at a Time*
by Montrose Doyle

I read recently that laughter can be a cure for many ailments.

Intense vibrations within the body will neutralize and realign the cells, so the theory goes, and thus has been known to prevent cancer, emphysema, and other grim diseases.

The fellow who advocated this was traveling around the world as a burlesque physician. The night he spoke in San Francisco, his lecture both explained the theory and started the audience laughing uncontrollably.

16

Late candles light the big room now, and a lemony moon. Inside and out, the air is luminous, luxurious. Wellington and his lady have eaten and gone. The boys in the band have taken their instruments and their women home, leaving the house to the family, leaving them gathered in an intimate ritual of after-dinner banter at a table littered with rinds of beef, and cheesecake, and half-filled goblets they use to chase down the brandy.

A small charge of electricity sparks around their little circle, generated by the exotic presence of Travis and Crystal and all the things that have not yet been said since they arrived and will not be said tonight. Everyone wants to know what it was like for Travis overseas, and there is something in his face, even when at rest, that prevents them from asking. He has chosen to wear his uniform to dinner, unexplained ribbons across his chest, in VFW parody of the ex-soldier patriot, but also as a silent message to all of them and to Grover in particular that his tour of duty was defendable, and potent enough, even at this late date in the history of warfare, to attract the swarthy one who sits next to him at the oval table.

Montrose has willfully kept his eyes and his attentions away from Crystal, in order not to alarm Lee, who has recognized an adventuress and who never misses a heartbeat at these gatherings. This has not stopped him from enjoying Crystal's effect. In candlelight, her lips still oiled from the roast, she seems endowed with nothing less than total sensuality. She neither flaunts this nor attempts to restrain it. She merely sits here and allows it to exude all over Grover on one side, all over Travis on the other, and there is no denying that Grover has been attentive, smiling often, peeking into the satin blouse. Travis has wavered in his reaction to this, can't decide if it's a threat to his manhood or a compliment to his taste. Crystal, of course, enjoys the compliment, while Holly acknowledges the threat. She watches Grover the way a mother would watch her son.

At twenty-three and unmarried, Holly already has a married look. She is a big woman with wide hips and has had mixed success with men. She has never called forth undisguisable lust, as Crystal does. She is not sure of her appeal, could never get away with just sitting here, the way Crystal can. But she is a glib, brash talker, and she has now steered the conversation to a subject she and Leona never tire of. It has made her the perfect companion for Leona. They can sit around the kitchen an entire afternoon trading lore.

The subject is a vast one, embracing all the strange, mysterious, and unchartable forces at large in the world—mental telepathy, clairvoyance, hypnotism, levitation, visitors from outer space, the Bermuda Triangle, acupuncture, suspended animation, unidentified flying objects, life after death, voodoo, sunspots, planetary alignment, and the runaway proliferation of everything from house dogs to nuclear weapons, which Lee views as a key signal that some cataclysm or turning point is almost upon us. Now, while the room is filled with luminous moonlight, while they all sip brandy and look at each other, and while the three men and Holly Belle add to this supernatural light their ground fog of cigar smoke, they consider the effects of moonlight upon animals and on the tides.

Montrose describes a horse he once watched kick its way out of a locked barn.

"A white horse," he says, leaning back to puff, "white as buttermilk under the moon. Just went kind of crazy this one night right about dusk. Nobody could get a hand on him. He kicked the barn door down and galloped out into the hills like there was a ghost riding an invisible saddle, and he was gone for two days. Finally came back a couple of afternoons later, his hide all torn up and his tail dragging. We never did find out where he went."

Grover observes that in his part of the mountains, which is about five hundred feet higher than Monty's place and eight miles farther inland, it is not uncommon to hear entire packs of loose dogs howling at the sky.

"Some of those dogs have pedigrees that predate the Civil War," he says, tilting back the way Montrose does, the lean, hard triangle of his face sharpened in this light until he seems to be wearing a freckled, grinning mask. "Papers as long as your leg. Makes no difference. Full moon comes out, and they join the pack, turn into wolves and jackals and coyotes. I guess it's something runs in every creature's blood. You see the same thing happening to *people* up our way too. There's some people we know, they hold full-moon festivals every month. Big open space in the trees. They're probably up there right now. They build a bonfire and drink a little wine and chant some chants and smoke a little hash and get a chain dance going around the fire, while the flutes and the drums start up, and the dancing gets wilder and wilder as the moon rises higher and higher . . . and this goes on till sunup . . ."

"And this is . . . the New Lunacy!" In drunken, mock-professorial summation, Montrose lifts his arms. "These are . . . the New Lunatics!"

"What I want to know," cries Holly, sitting up straight and slapping her hands on the table edge with great authority, "is what about earthquakes? If the moon can do things like this to dogs and lunatics, what is it going to do to the *planet?* Isn't it going to work like a huge magnet?"

As she well knows, this is a popular topic. It triggers an outburst of shouts, threats, theories, and opinions, a turmoil of yelling, nervous sipping, and heavy puffing of cigars.

"If you ask me . . ." Montrose begins.

"The moon is not a magnet," Travis says. "The moon is the eye of God!"

"Oh, glory, Travis!" Montrose shouts with glee. "You're juiced again."

"The moon is a factor," Grover says, "but a lot of other things figure in there too. For instance, wind."

"To the best of my knowledge," Monty begins again.

"The earth," Leona murmurs, "is just like a human body."

"Listen to Lee," says Holly Belle. "What did you just say?"

"The eye of God does not cause earthquakes," Travis says. "Floods maybe, heavy surf, maybe even blackouts in large metropolitan areas . . . or large empty places in the sky . . ."

His voice trails off. Leona's serene, patient smile has settled the atmosphere. Across the wall directly behind her, as if to support what she's about to say, hangs one of her hand-stitched tapestries, an eight-foot-long, bright-blue river curving like a snake, where dozens of naked people swim, float, wade, paddle canoes and kayaks, hold fishing poles, walk on the water, scuba-dive. In the moon- and candlelight, her own head almost seems a part of this pageant, as her words rise from underneath the family's babble to explain that when you live near the ocean, as the Doyles do, a full-moon night is the most likely time for quakes. "Because the earth's surface is just like the human body, you see. It is mostly water. When the tides start moving all that water around, pushing in against the shore and all, well, this is going to have an effect on . . ."

Taking in all her listeners, she smiles with deep satisfaction, fearful of such forces at work, yet sustained by them. Her hands spread wide, like a conductor's.

". . . on just about everything."

A respectful silence follows this truth, as they ponder it in the settling smoke, listening to the vast, cricket-punctuated silence outside, listening for some rumble of agreement from the deep earth.

Nothing comes.

Crystal's voice, hardly louder than one of the crickets, breaks the silence, asking Grover a question with a little edge to it, testing his capacity for wildness. She wants to know if he has ever been to one of those mountain orgies.

"I'll tell you what it's like," he says, squinting worldly eyes at her in the candlelight. "You end up tearing off all your clothes and chanting and bobbing around the fire and grunting like a cave man. It just takes hold of you. Wellington says the spot was sacred to the Indians, and avoided by the Spaniards."

"Does Wellington go up there?" Monty asks.

"He talks like he organized the thing. He calls it a power zone. I don't know. You can never tell with Wellington. He could be right. *Some*thing gets to you when you're up there. It's more than just getting loaded and getting loose. You want to whirl. No. It's more than that. . . . You want to change!"

Grover hasn't thought of this before. It stops him for a moment, reflecting.

"We only went once," he says. "It was worth going once. We never went back."

"Why not?" Crystal wants to know, still testing, her eyes asking him to jump up with her right here and whirl around the table. "Afraid of it?"

"It was a little too strange," Grover says. He turns toward Holly as if for confirmation. "Weird things start happening. The night we were up there, this naked guy, with hair that literally touched the ground when he hunkered down, was squatting by the fire, and he started skinning a dog, peeling off a strip of skin like a stripe around the belly and back. His face was absolutely blank, devoid of expression, just skinning the dog and paying very close attention to the straight line of his cut. Nobody seemed to be bothered by this at all, except me and Holly."

"And the dog," Holly adds with a bitter laugh. "The dog was still alive, so he was extremely bothered by it."

"Alive?" Travis blurts, wincing. "That's ugly. That's really ugly!"

"Listen," says Leona, fixing all of them with a gypsy's

melancholy eye. "Lorene Cuthbertson, lives up toward the summit, was talking to me the other day. She is on my committee, and after the last meeting she told me she found one of her Angus calves had been skinned and had the head cut off. She told me about other people up there have been having trouble with cattle disappearing in strange ways. Told me about one fellow found a heifer strung from a tree, with the hooves and the tail gone, and the hide stripped away, and down near the trunk of the tree a little burnt place with charred chicken bones."

"I've heard worse than that," says Holly, leaning into the light, onto her elbows. "I mean, you live out where we do, you pick up all kinds of things. There was a girl reported missing a while back, and weeks went by, and she didn't turn up. And then the rumor started going around that she had been sacrificed."

"Hold it," says Montrose, suddenly sober, rearing back. "You are not by any chance referring to the Kramer girl."

"No. This was before Linda Kramer. I don't remember what her name was. Linda's still missing. This girl apparently volunteered. .You know . . . offered herself? On an altar? At least that's the story."

Travis has become very agitated, staring at Holly, then taking in everyone with that look Monty saw at the airport, the head tilted, the eye bewildered, challenging, accusing.

"Hey," Travis says, "what is going on? Just what in the hell is going on?"

Monty puts a hand on his arm, as if to table this question for a moment.

"Wait a minute, Trav. I want to know more about this. Holly, have you heard anything at all about Linda Kramer? Even any rumors . . . like that one?"

"All I know is she lived pretty close in to town. Why?"

"They found her this morning, dead."

"I knew it," Lee says quietly. "I knew they'd find her dead. There's another killer on the loose."

"Another killer?" Travis says. "What do you mean, *another* killer?" He glares at his mother as if she is going insane.

With her very tone of voice she tries to persuade him that no event is so outrageous we cannot eventually absorb it, take it in our stride. "Last year a young fellow went berserk, wiped out a whole family. He said himself it was an execution. Walked into the house one day with a shotgun and killed five people, and then just as much as *let* the police catch up with him, as if he wanted to be caught, just so he could tell the world what was bothering him. He said he executed this family because they had three cars and a barbecue pit and two big fireplaces and a garbage disposal and a power launch, and they were polluting the environment."

The others are nodding, sadly wagging heads. Travis seems ready to catch fire.

"Are you kidding me?" he cries.

"I guess it was after you went overseas, hon."

Holly has been waiting for an opening. She turns to Monty. "Where was she?"

"That's the thing. It was near Holy City. According to Walter, she was buried alive. No clothes. No marks, as far as they could tell."

He waits for this to sink in, then asks hopefully, as if Holly might have a clue, "Now, does that add up to anything?"

Travis lets go his hold on the table edge and jumps up, shouting, *"Shit!"*

Lee's hand rises to her forehead, as if she's peering through a heavy glare. Monty's jaw muscles bunch.

"It all adds up to . . ."

While they watch him, Travis begins to tremble, seems to want to say more, to make a speech, but can't. Crystal's hand slides across, to cover his. He jerks away, staring wildly around, his mouth working, his bad eye starting to wink. For an instant he reminds Monty of an evangelist who came out from Texas one summer when Monty was a kid, to hold a revival. The man's face got like this, then his limbs began to twitch, and his cheeks changed colors, and he finally had a fit right there on the stage, screaming hellfire and damnation all the way down to the floor. Travis seems on the verge of delivering this kind of sermon, when the blood drains from his face. His stomach visibly convulses. His gorge begins to rise. His eyes bulge with a show of unexpected fear, and the vomit rushes out, spewing forth all over the remains of Leona's welcome-home dinner, snuffing out two candles and puddling his plate.

Crystal screams and pulls her hand back too late, catching some of the splatter. Leona screams, while Monty roars, "Good Christ almighty, Travis!"

For a moment he stares down stupidly at the mess he has made. Then, with chin dripping, with slimy stringers fouling his jacket front, his ribbons, his flat lapels, he rushes from the room.

The back door slams. The others look at plates and then at one another. In forlorn amazement Monty starts to chuckle, a burlesque physician's laugh at the antics of a comrade befuddled to the point of self-abuse. Slowly he shoves his chair back, moving to follow. Crystal stops him, murmuring, "Let me catch up." A sisterly concern across her unblemished brow suggests that things like this have happened before and she knows what to do. Their eyes lock, wrestling for the right to minister to Travis. Then Crystal is gone.

And with her the electricity is gone. The room goes flat. The four remaining sit here abandoned, as the sharp reek of vomit permeates the air above the table. Holly rises, heading for towels and rags to sop it up.

Monty says, "He's right, you know."

Leona says, "Oh, Monty, this is no time to kid around."

"I am not kidding around. It does all add up to shit."

"Monty," she implores, her eyes searching his for communion, for explanation, "something terrible has happened to Travis. I know it has."

"Well, whatever it was, maybe he's ended up healthier than

any of the rest of us. We sit around here after dinner talking about things that ought to make a person sick to his stomach. But we're numb. We're so goddam numb and desensitized from living in this country we don't respond to anything anymore!"

"He's drunk, Dad. Don't forget that," Grover says. "He never could drink much without making some kind of a mess. You saying that's a sign of health?"

"I'm saying maybe we have reached a point where we ought to all be vomiting our guts out."

17

AROUND MIDNIGHT

Around midnight, standing alone in the upstairs corridor in his underwear, Monty feels the first tremor. It rolls under him like a slow swell beneath a trawler. He rides it like that, his feet spread, giving with his knees. It passes, and he starts on toward the bedroom, then stops when the next tremor hits, stronger and longer. Boards creak all around him in the dark, floorboards, wall studs, rafters overhead. This one feels as if something is outside with a hand on two corners of the house, shaking it until it shivers. Gradually the hands let go. The house falls silent.

He waits a long time, listening.

When he steps through the bedroom door he sees Leona standing at the latticed window, gazing out onto the silvery field beyond. He knows she is still listening, still waiting, riveted there partly because dread runs in her, partly because she does not want to miss anything. She predicted this one, after all.

Moonlight drifting through her sheer gown defines the girlish body. He pads across the carpet, his hands reach around the outlined bosom. She doesn't move.

After a while she says, "For just a minute there I was five years old again. I was thinking about the first time I ever felt a quake, back in Oklahoma when we were still living on

Daddy's farm. They never have quakes in Oklahoma, you know. But one night something started shaking the house. I remember jumping out of bed and running to the window and looking out at a moon just like this, and then my daddy came over and swooped me up and carried me and my little brother outside away from the house."

"You've never talked about this before."

"I just remembered, standing here. It was such a jolt, pieces of the house started coming apart and falling down out in the yard. Course, it wasn't much of a house."

"Well, I'll tell you something about this house, sweetheart," says Montrose softly. "It was built to last. It was built like a ship. It'll ride through anything they send us, except the big one. And it might even ride through the big one. They say it made it through in 1906 with just one cracked window and a few busted dinner plates. I'll bet she would have made it through even if she'd been sitting on a hill in San Francisco."

Easy to soothe her now, easy to protect her in the aftermath of this little danger they just survived, the relief in knowing it really wasn't dangerous at all. His hands slide down to the soft belly and pull her close. Her body does not react. He thinks he knows what it is. He waits. When she finally speaks, there is an accusation in her voice, as if he is responsible for whatever she is feeling now.

"Did you know before today that Travis got wounded in the eye?

"Now, how would I know that if you didn't know it?"

"He could have written you at the office."

"I honestly don't think it was that big a deal to him. He just didn't get around to telling anybody."

"But it's done something to him. He's changed so much."

"He's two years older."

"It's more than that. It's like . . . something is missing. Something has disappeared."

"I'll tell you what it is," he says. "It's his soul."

She looks up, to see if he is joking.

"His soul isn't here yet, that's all. The jet age, Lee. The body gets here ahead of the soul."

"Monty . . . I'm trying to be serious."

"So am I. It's true. You've flown on planes. You know how you feel after a long, fast trip. That's how Travis feels. Give him a few days to relax and get himself together. In fact, you know what I am thinking might do Travis a lot of good? I'm thinking of driving to the hot springs sometime soon."

"I like that idea, Monty. The springs would do us all some good."

"We could drive over there and back in a day, if we got an early start."

"We could soak ourselves silly," Lee says.

"Nothing brings the soul home faster than a good hot soak."

She ponders this, then smiles up at him and turns back to the window. She wants to believe in the age-old powers of time and hot water. So does Monty, content now to let the subject rest. It's too late tonight to explore any further. He has given this whole day to Travis. He is not, by God, going to give his bedroom time to Travis too. He would like to complete what that insufferable phone call disrupted sixteen hours ago, to stitch up all the day's loose ends, his life's loose ends. His hands slide down below her belly.

She says, "Aren't you tired, Monty? You've had a hectic day." But he can feel her body loosening.

"Never that tired."

"We'll have to be quiet," she whispers, turning to face him, pushing her bosom and her belly in close.

"What's the matter?"

She nods toward the wall. "Grover and Holly are staying over. Remember?"

"What the hell do they care?" he whispers.

"They'll hear the bed. You know what a racket the bed makes."

"They're too busy climbing all over each other to pay any attention to what's going on in here."

In his ear she murmurs, "Maybe on the rug."

"I'll get some pillows then. You want a pillow?"

"Yes. Pillows, and that comforter."

"How about the moonlight? If we scoot over there by the window we can get the moonlight effect."

"You think it's more romantic with the moon?" she says, teasing him.

"It's always more romantic. There. How's that?"

She lies down on the comforter, stretching luxuriantly among the large diamonds the lattice makes. Monty lies next to her, savoring the glow of this light on her skin, amazed once again that such things last, that every month the moon displays its fullness, that these lattices some carpenter cut and fitted over eighty years ago still cast such pleasing patterns, that Lee can still stir up in him this keen yearning, and he still stirs it up in her.

He doesn't take her now the way he did when they were young and spending hot afternoons down in that low end of the orchard called the ditch. He meets her, here among the diamond pools of moonlight, and he makes trees in his mind, as their legs entwine. They nuzzle and murmur, and their four hands begin to stroke the silver diamonds as if to brush away the lines. Their hands and then their lips slide through the lines and into shadows, exploring the familiar mysteries.

Outside the crickets chirp accompaniment. The room is washed with silver water. For Montrose the window melts and turns to water. Above their long, lubricious coupling, trees appear, scented with new apples. The world is ripe. The floor dissolves and turns to earth. Leona whispers earnestly, "What should I do?"

"Do?"

"When I come."

"Whatever you want," he whispers.

"I hate it," she says.

"Hate what?"

"When I can't scream."

"Ssshhh," Monty cautions. "Do like me."

Her eyes spring wide, to see what he means. His eyes are sprung wide too. In a throaty whisper, as their bodies combust, he cries, "Yell silently!"

18

AROUND MIDNIGHT
In the Next Room

Until he was nine, Grover slept in this bed. He would listen to the voices muffled beyond the door, the rustling of bed-clothes, the long silences and laughter and distant groans, dimly imagining what might be going on in that other world. Sometimes, usually on a Sunday morning, he would push open the door, hoping to join them under the covers, to feel what it was like to be in bed with someone else. The times they allowed it were pure bliss, sharing that boundless warmth only his father and mother together could generate. The times they didn't, when they were joined, with no room between for him, their bodies making one beneath the blankets, he felt confused, abandoned. It was Montrose who would tell him to close the door. Lee would call out, "Hello, hon. Looking for some company?" Montrose, in grumpy possession of the bed, overriding the mother's sweetness, would mutter, "We're still sleeping, Grover." Then he would head for his brother's room and rattle around in there till Trav woke and Grover would needle him about something until a fight broke out, which would bring Monty thundering down the hall, squeezing jaw muscles, shouting about peace and quiet.

Grover hated him then, longed to be strong enough and old enough to injure his dad. Tonight the Montrose of those years is a comic figure in his memory, harassed, outnumbered, pulling his boys to their feet, pinching their biceps till they cried out with the pain—a warden in ratty underwear and tousled, thinning hair. He begins to laugh quietly. This bed brings it all back. He hasn't slept here since it became the guest room and they set up bunks in Trav's room, which Grover eventually took over when Travis moved out to the barn.

Lying here with his eyes closed, he hears Monty padding down the hallway toward the john, and Grover is that boy again, listening to all the vagrant sounds of a springtime night. But this time he has his own warm woman next to him, and he has solved the childhood mystery, the beguiling difference between one in a bed and two in a bed. It was Holly who helped him solve it, taught him the difference. Until she came along he had never lived with a woman. He had made love to several, spent the night with three, but no woman had yet been admitted into his orbit. They met at a coffeehouse in Berkeley when they were both seniors at the university. He has a weakness for vocalists. She has a weakness for musicians who play her kind of music well. She was writing her own songs, and it started there, one night on a bandstand, when a tune she had just completed and which they had not rehearsed came out perfectly the first time they tried it. She would like their whole life to work that way, on intuitive wavelengths. So she has not yet voiced many demands—which is how it has had to be for Grover. This is a taste he inherited from Montrose, and he will not be able to get away with it for very much longer.

Snuggled next to him in the clean-sheet comfort of the guest room bed, Holly says, "What's so funny?"

"My old man. The way he used to rough us up when we were kids."

"Must be good. You're making the whole bed shake."

"I'm not really laughing anymore."

"Well, the bed is shaking. Don't you feel it?"

"I'll be damned."

"It's a quake." Her voice is tight and quick.

"A tremor," he says, trying to stay cool.

"Oh, Lord."

"But it's passing. Feel it? Fading now. A quickie."

They ease back into the pillows.

"I try to get used to em, Grover. You know?"

"So do I."

"I grew up out here, and it's kind of a fact of life and all that. But I never do. How do you get used to— Oh, Lord. Is it another one?"

Clutching him, she giggles in crazy desperation, gallows chuckles. "What'll we do? It's bigger this time. It's really big."

Both arms around her, he tries to push down his own cold panic. He wants her to know that he is not afraid. They sit propped up in bed until the second wave subsides.

"Backing off now," he says. "It's over."

"You think that's it?"

"Has to be."

"Yes," she says, listening hard.

He says, "The Indians used to believe the earth was resting on the back of a giant tortoise, and whenever the tortoise moved, the earth would move."

She thinks about that. "I've got a better idea." She starts to laugh. "You know what it's like? It's like one of those beds in the motels, that vibrate when you put a quarter in. A great big massage that's supposed to make you sleep better."

"Except somebody put in ten dollars' worth of quarters all at once. Right? We ought to sleep like babies tonight."

"The earth is my vibrabed," Holly says.

"Yeah. That's good. The earth is my vibrabed."

They both laugh, to laugh away the echoes still trembling around them in the darkness. Then it's quiet, and he hears soft voices in the next room. He hears rustlings, distant movements. A rush of yearning and self-pity wells up inside him. He wants to weep. He wants to creep across the room and push open the door the way he used to and . . . ward off that same old boyhood loneliness that now begins to spread through him, hopelessly, deliciously, in spite of Holly clinging warm against him here. He would like to hear his father order him away from the door, so that he could follow the path to Trav's room, wake his brother and start something, some stirring of the blood, of the blood-tied memories.

She whispers, "What's the matter?"

He can't answer. If he speaks his voice will break, the urge to weep will show, and he doesn't want it to show. He does not want the loneliness to show or his helpless terror of forces vast, deep, and unknowable. He pooches out his lips and cocks his head, which means "Nothing."

19

AROUND MIDNIGHT
In the Barn

Between the house and the first row of trees stands a barn of wind-eaten redwood. Most days its planks and shingles are dusty gray, during rainstorms slick and black. Tonight the wood looks polished under the moon. The wide, peaked center room is flanked by two low sheds whose roofs flare obliquely so that the barn, from the front, on a night such as this, appears to be a rakish silver hat.

One side is Monty's toolshed. The other, years ago, Travis turned into a room for himself. It is long, as long as the barn, and ten feet across. He has a double bed in there, and a morning view of the sun through apple limbs. Animal skins cover the floor and the bed, cattle hides, deer, and sheep. The walls are decorated with the posters and magazine pages he tacked up before he joined the army. *Playboy* foldouts. Rock band fliers from San Francisco. Janis Joplin in her necklaces. Marlon Brando in his motorcycle leathers. A sign above the mirror SAYS: ABANDON ALL HOPE, YE WHO ENTER HERE!

His face pushed into sheepskin, Travis lies on the bed, while Crystal works the tendons along his neck. She kneels, rising above him, like a masseuse. They have not spoken since he bolted from the table. She found him here in the room of his boyhood, face down on the sheepskin of his youth. She has soothed him with her hands, much as she did the first night they spent together, one of those relationships that begin with the bodies and grope toward words. The bodies talk. Her hands have stirred him. He turns his face, takes a breath, tries to unmuddy his brain, unslur his voice.

"You shouldn't flirt with my brother."

" I wasn't flirting," she murmurs.

"With my brother, and also with my father. That embarrasses me."

A soft laugh. "I didn't know you could get embarrassed."

"Now you know."

"It's just getting acquainted. Don't be so touchy."

"It's not touchy to ask you not to flirt with my brother and my father. Especially in front of my mother."

"Your mother knows what's going on."

"What does that mean?"

"Let's talk about it tomorrow."

"What does that mean? What is going on? Goddam it, Crystal, what the hell is going on?"

He rolls over, just as the barn begins to move. He shuts his eyes and shakes his head.

"Hey, am I that drunk?"

"The barn is dancing," she says.

He looks into her eyes, which have grown wide with alarm and excitement. When the tremor subsides they are both grinning.

"You want to dance too," Travis says.

"It gives me ideas."

After the second, larger shake they are leering at each other. He sits up and slides his hands around her waist, up under the satin shirt. He begins to sway very slowly.

"Suppose it's the end of the world?" he says.

"Then what do we have to lose?"

Her hands, still massaging, reach for the back of his head, slide along his neck, across his chest, toward his buttons. She likes to serve him, or perhaps has learned that it pays to offer certain small services, unbuttoning the shirt cuffs, unbuckling his shoes. Her fingers skitter across his feet, his knees, little wings of flesh brushing at the cloth of his shirt where it falls back from his waist, tantalizing him the way a butterfly will when seen wooing a marigold just at one's periphery of vision. It makes Travis crazy to have her luscious surfaces again.

"I feel like getting on my hands and knees," she says.

"The last time we did that you said it was vulgar."

"Sometimes I like to be vulgar."

There is something crass and mechanical about her. He thinks of punishment. And yet she makes his flesh burn. He mounts her, plunging in, pumping furiously. Every night, most afternoons, they have been lunging into sex. He would like to do it differently. But he goes blind with the burning and the sudden bursting, and in a minute or half a minute it is done, it is spent.

They fall to the rug of animal skins, side by side. From Crystal comes a low groan, as if she is passing out, or coming to.

He says, "That felt good."

Her drowsy eyes regard him, limp.

"My God, Crystal, that was very good."

Her face is almost blank. Her eyelids barely move. They seem, for a moment, doll-like, the kind of levered lids that raise only when the rest of the doll is tipped.

"Was it," she says. Not a question, but what seems to him courteous response, as if he has disappointed her.

Travis lowers his head onto the sheepskin to rest it next to hers. He is certain he has made some terrible mistake, but is not sure how. He wonders why she has traveled all this way with him. Why has she bothered?

20

AROUND MIDNIGHT
An Open Field

At the edge of an open field, silver as the sea, and in the lee of a stand of high eucalyptus whose slender leaves hang motionless as silver bananas, Fowler's tiny log cabin sits on his GMC flatbed. During the day the mattress inside hangs up against the wall, slung from pulleys. At night, when he lets it down, the mattress fills most of the interior. Between it and the low door into the cab stands an old-fashioned wicker bassinet, where Fowler's baby sleeps. Above the bassinet a narrow shelf holds a two-burner Coleman stove welded to the wall, feeding upward into a chimney. Other shelves fenced like ship's shelving hold books, and lamps, and amulets, and small statues. Fowler is sleeping. His wife, her pillow propped, is smoking a cigarette and gazing out the small back window onto the moonlit field, listening to her husband's snore, and beyond the snore, the whir of crickets.

That is the only sound outside the truck. And that sound stops. The mattress quivers.

She thinks at first it is the grossest snore of Fowler's career, sending out its vibrations. But it happens that for this brief instant his snoring has stopped, as if switched off. From the cab, where he sleeps alone, Lorenzo the Afghan whimpers. His eye appears at the porthole. The whole truck quivers. It seems to her, looking outside, that the field is shimmering under the moon like jello.

"Good God!" she cries. "Larry! Larry!" grabbing his shoulder.

He leaps up, eyes bulging.

"What! What!"

She can't speak. Rigid, she is gazing out the window at the field, at the distant oaks, which have not yet moved.

The truck shakes again, a rippling from underneath which makes springs and axles shudder, while Fowler's wife digs her fingers into his arms. They sit staring wildly into each other's eyes until the long rippling ends.

They wait for two minutes.

Nothing.

The crickets resume.

It is finished.

Quietly she begins to sob. .

"Oh, Jesus," she says.

He touches the back of her head.

She moves away from his hand, speaking with low, intense accusation. "I can't stand it. I cannot *stand* it. It scares the hell out of me, Larry. You know that."

"It was just a tremor, baby."

"I do not want to be here, Larry. I do not want to be within a thousand miles of a place that can shake like that. One day this whole crazy state is going to shake itself to pieces, and I do not want to be around when it starts."

"C'mon, baby . . ." He moves to embrace her, to comfort her with holding. She won't allow it.

"We have to do something, Larry. This scene we're into here is hopeless. *Hope*less. We're way up this deserted road. We don't know anybody. I got the baby all day. I got earthquakes at night. The people who are supposed to be our neighbors suddenly disappear from one day to the next, and now you tell me it's because they are mixed up in that murder."

"Oh, for shit's sake, Diane. You sound like my mother."

"What do you think I feel like most of the time?"

"Don't start that."

"Well, what are we going to do?"

"I'll tell you what we're going to do. Tomorrow I am going to the reporters."

"I thought you had an appointment with the D.A."

"Too risky. No telling who owns the D.A. I go straight to the papers."

"You did that this morning."

"I made a mistake. I picked the wrong guy. I have to quit screwing around. I have to get this thing out into the open. For my own safety."

"Get what out into the open?"

"I mean, for our safety. Isn't that what we're talking about? Safety?"

"Maybe we're not talking about the same kind of safety. I'm talking about getting out of here, Larry. I'd rather be back home in Pennsylvania."

"And do what?"

"Sleep at night!"

"Hey! Hey, I got enough on my mind without having to fight you every inch of the way!"

"Don't shout!"

"I'll shout if I goddam well want to!"

"You're going to wake Ivan."

"Tough shit for Ivan!"

Hearing this, Ivan begins to whimper.

"Nice," Diane says with soft, weary sarcasm. "Very nice, Fowler."

Ivan starts to whine. In the cab, trapped, Lorenzo seems bent on drowning Ivan's cries with his own mad, lonesome barking. This, of course, fills Ivan with baby fright. He starts to howl, a full-lunged bellowing that expands inside the dark interior like a tear-gas bomb. But outside, the sound is muted by the whir of ten thousand insects. Heard from across the field, the baby's wail and the dog's futile outbursts rise like wisps of smoke from Fowler's thin chimney.

Part Two

Git so I hate to think.
Go diggin back to a ol time
to keep from thinkin.

—PA JOAD
  in *The Grapes of Wrath* (1939)
  by John Steinbeck

21

Eleven Spaniards keep watch above the main street of the town. Just their heads are showing. They wear short-rimmed Cortez helmets and pointed, newly barbered beards, and gaze down seven stories from the roof line of the Hotel Viceroy, gargoyles of the west. Below their gaze the downtown buildings, two and sometimes three stories high, press together along both sides of Del Mar Boulevard. Like The Cheating Heart Saloon, they go back to 1888 or 1910, some made of brick, some of stone from local quarries, some western-movie wooden, with frescoed, Greco-Roman borders, high windows across the second stories and shops below, where an ancient watchmaker who has been in business here since World War I bends over his elevated desk of tiny instruments to the accompaniment of Hindu temple music floating past his window along with the incense and the poncho-clad customers from Aquarian Imports next door.

In among the windows of the seven-floored Viceroy, other eyes join those of the eleven Spaniards, gazing down upon scenes they no longer recognize. This is a retirement hotel, where tenants older than the watchmaker watch mule skinners, gypsies, harmonica duets, and Hare Krishna singers in their salmon robes mingle with the shoppers. From time to time the tenants mingle too, head out for groceries, for underwear. But not today. Today they will venture no farther than the lobby, where they sit bunched up in rows of bulging chairs reading over and over what it says on the front page of the paper, and staring at the head shots.

This is perhaps the one thing they have in common with

Larry Fowler and with everyone else in town this afternoon, the lead story in the *Daily Courier*. If you were up there with the Spaniards you would be able to see Fowler in his tattered jeans and his plaid shirt striding among the shoppers on Del Mar Boulevard, on his way to the Midtown Smoke Shop, where he expects to find his name in print. He is going to the smoke shop rather than to a vending machine because the papers there are piled loose. If he doesn't find what he's looking for, it won't cost him anything. He already knows about the lead story, which has so confounded the roomers at the Viceroy. He not only knows the story; he knows what lies behind the story. It fits in so perfectly, he buzzes with a curious satisfaction—curious because he could be in much greater danger now than when there was just one murder to account for.

Around the entrance, and stacked on the sidewalk, and stuffed into wall racks, newspapers from major west coast cities decorate the door of the Midtown Smoke Shop, overflowing in a bouquet of print. Beyond the newspapers the periodicals begin, the national weeklies and monthlies, and beyond these the specialty magazines—TV and movie, fashion and glamour, horses, dogs, guns, dune buggies, hang gliders, needlepoint, crossword puzzle, bottle collection, horoscope. Farther down the long wall, there's a section of paperback books, and in the distance, beckoning, four racks of glossy nudes squirm and wink at the lures and trout flies encased across the aisle.

Fowler doesn't reach the nudes. He doesn't get past the doorway, framed there by a cornucopia of papers as he scans first the headline: THREE MORE BURIED, then flips inside, looking for his own name.

He finds it in a box, at the bottom of page twelve, among a constellation of items related to the day's big news. Two afternoons ago, when Linda Kramer's story first appeared, Fowler had appeared in the offices of the San Francisco *Chronicle,* following up a phone call to the reporter on the case. He frowns now, reading the outcome of that interview, or rather the remains of it. He squints and he scowls and he reads the last part through again.

The location of the first grave has led to speculation that the killings may have some deranged religious connection. Holy City, high in the coast range south of San Francisco, was once the center for a now defunct Biblical sect.

Another theory links the killings to local drug traffic. According to neighbor Larry Fowler, she was killed to prevent her appearance at a narcotics hearing.

"Linda disappeared precisely two days before she was scheduled to testify to the grand jury," Fowler said.

Asst. District Attorney Floyd Perrone replied, "This is nonsense, an irrelevant coincidence. We already know how she was going to testify. Her statement is on file."

But the discovery of yesterday's three victims, buried in an identical manner, might lend new credence to this rumor. Narcotics investigator Samson Newby, who inadvertently found the bodies of Roland, Bruno, and Natalie Fontaine, admits he has had their remote mountain cabin under surveillance for weeks.

With the pages spread wide and held before him at eyeball level, Fowler fills the smoke shop doorway.

"Hey, buddy," someone says.

He lowers the pages and sees the owner watching him from behind the counter, through a wreath of razor blades and Ronson lighters. "You wanna buy that paper?"

"Of course I do."

"C'mon inside then, so other people can get through."

As Fowler takes one insulted step forward, a man who has been waiting behind him eases past, heading for the counter. This man is a reporter, down from San Francisco. The town is full of reporters today, and photographers, most of them hanging around the police station or the city offices, where two television camera crews are set up, waiting for the D.A. to make a statement. This fellow does not run with the pack. He is after a background story. In the back of his mind he has the idea that one day he might do a novel on this subject.

He wears aviator sunglasses and a blue bush jacket with lapels and pockets defined by white stitchery. He selects a candy bar, a Peter Paul Almond Joy.

"Candy business must be booming," he observes.

The owner looks at him, ringing up the sale.

"Sidewalk outside is full of candy wrappers," the reporter says. "That wastepaper basket on the telephone pole, it's overflowing with wrappers."

"I'm not surprised to hear it. We been selling candy bars like you wouldn't believe. Cough drops too. Chewing gum. Cigarettes. People get nervous, I guess they look for things to do with their hands, put into their mouths. You know what I mean?"

"They get nervous about the killings. Is that it?"

The owner looks at him hard for ten seconds, as if trying to guess the nationality of an obvious foreigner. "You some kind of writer, or reporter?"

The reporter smiles broadly and begins to peel back the wrapper of his Almond Joy. "You guessed it. I'm working on a feature story. Not about the killings per se, but about the general community situation here."

While he continues smiling and savoring his first bite, the owner cocks his head, trying to see through the tinted lenses, sizing him up.

"You want to find out about the community situation," he says at last, "you ought to go talk to Walt Nesbit, owns the gun store two blocks up. His business has tripled overnight. I've sold a few switchblades, hunting knives, stuff like that. Walt is moving handguns and rifles like some kind of war has been declared. He sold out all his ammunition in two days. I mean, *all* of it. Not one twenty-two shell left in his whole goddam store."

"And is all this for self-defense?"

"Hard to say. Some of the fellas are talking about getting organized."

"Organized? In what way?"

"Oh, it's just talk. You know. To help out the police. The department's short-handed. Everybody knows that. Especially in times like this. Some kind of people's committee is what you hear mentioned. It's mostly talk. People get panicky. They got to do something with their hands and their mouths, so they wave guns around and they talk a lot."

"Would a committee like this start looking anywhere in particular?"

The owner hesitates, striving to sound reasonable and fair-minded, but unable to conceal the sharp edge that slips into his voice. "If you want my opinion, a few years ago we would never have had this kind of trouble. It's just since . . ." Here he casts a hard, accusing look at Fowler, who has feigned reading in order to eavesdrop on this conversation. "We have been invaded by what you might call the long-haired element. Don't ask me why, but in the last few years things have just been running from bad to worse. I'm not saying it was a long-hair did the killing. But it was long-hairs who got killed. These Fontaine people had hair hanging down to their kneecaps. They bring trouble. I'm just telling you what I see."

Fowler, in an effort to establish himself as a contributing member of society, puts fifteen cents on the counter to pay for his paper, returning the stare of the owner, who clearly resents this money.

The reporter says, "Yesterday's *Chronicle* implied some kind of drug connection. Perhaps a cover-up. I suppose you would say these things are all related?"

Color rises in the owner's face. His voice grows smaller, tighter, slower. "I went to high school in this town, my friend. I have watched that school turn from a wholesome, high-spirited place into a bad dream. My daughter's going there now. From the way she talks, they are serving the stuff in the cafeteria. I tell ya, if there was anywhere to go, I'd move away from here in a minute, just to give her a decent environment."

He falters, overpowered by emotion. His eyes, damp with

puzzled distaste, are fixed on Fowler, who glares back at him, suddenly charged with great purpose. Fowler feels something akin to happiness. The owner's hatred for him has quickened his senses. Turning to the reporter, he perceives that for once in his dismally checkered career his timing is perfect.

With an insider's smile, he says, "I'm the guy they quote in that story."

Glancing at the baggy jeans and scruffy boots, the reporter reacts first with disapproval. He says, "Which story is that?"

Fowler folds back page twelve, touching one finger to the paragraphs containing his name, holding his finger there while the reporter reads.

"You're Linda Kramer's neighbor?"

"Was. That is . . . I live next to the house her boyfriend used to live in."

"How about the Fontaines? Did you know them?"

"I know a lot about them."

"It says here they've been under surveillance."

"Surveillance does not begin to describe what their place has been under."

"What do you mean by that?"

"First tell me who you're writing for."

Through his tinted lenses the reporter studies Fowler. He recognizes something. They recognize each other. In this silent moment they form a brotherhood founded on mutual opportunity.

"It depends," he says. "I used to work for the Associated Press. Right now I free-lance, take assignments, string for a couple of papers on a steady basis. You read the *National Enquirer?* They pay extremely well. I have sold things to the *National Enquirer.*"

"We ought to go somewhere where we can talk," Fowler says.

"You name it. I don't quite have my bearings here yet."

"The Cheating Heart is right around the corner. They have Watney's ale on tap."

"I could use a Watney's," the reporter says, popping the

last bit of candy into his mouth, patting his hands free of invisible chocolate crumbs. "And haven't I heard about that place before?"

Surrounded by lighters and razor blades, candy bars, White Owls, and periodicals from the capital cities of nine western states, the owner of the Midtown Smoke Shop churns with fury as he watches these two depart. At this moment he is capable of murder himself.

Leaving his line of sight, they move out among the shoppers on Del Mar Boulevard, striding easily under the watchful gaze of the eleven helmeted Spaniards, and Fowler begins to tell the reporter what he has learned in the last twenty-four hours about the three new victims.

22

Up in Holly's part of the county, word of the new murders seemed to travel about a mile every eight hours. She and Grover live three miles from where the Fontaines were discovered, and Holly did not hear about them until the following afternoon.

She is not one to panic. Her impulse is to keep things in balance. During their year together she has learned to handle almost all the curious features of the life he has chosen to explore. Grover's house, like his father's, is made of redwood, though not heart redwood such as they used eighty years ago. It is second growth, lighter in hue, wider in grain, impervious to termites and structured by Grover into the shape of a large A. It is heated with wood, connected to the outside world by one telephone wire and a dirt road that turns to mud in winter. They have a chain toilet with a rusty overflow valve, and a gravity tank that is seldom full enough because a good part of the water goes to what Grover calls his cash crop, a quarter acre of (this season) organically grown string beans and russet potatoes. Tall evergreens shade the vegetable patch Holly tries to cultivate next to the house. Weasels raid their chicken pen, and raccoons rifle through their garbage. But Holly never flinches. One by one, they are ironing out the wrinkles. And Grover tells people that if push came to shove, she could lead a pack train across the Mojave Desert with no trouble. She has a venerable upright piano, and a sheaf of songs she is working on. The chords and octaves are often heard as she tinkles and tinkers, hurling handfuls of notes through the walls and out the windows at the one thing that gets to her here—the lonesomeness, the isolation, the shortage of callers, and the cold rush when she wakes sometimes very late at night and there are no lights, no neighbors, no sound, no way out, and for one awful moment, before she reaches to verify, no Grover.

Until two weeks ago she had one sure remedy for this. She would jump into the '49 Packard she keeps parked out front and roar into town for a beer. But the brakes are gone, and now the baby-blue paint job is nearly gray with pine needles and dust, waiting till some extra money comes in or till Grover gets around to looking at the brakes himself, which he is not inclined to do. The baby-blue gas gulper gets twelve miles to the gallon, highway, eight to ten in town, and this offends him ecologically. It offends his view of mountain living and he would just as soon see it shoved over a cliff.

The Packard is Holly Belle's personal symbol of independence. She views it that way, as a car, and as a symbol. Two weeks without it has sharpened her sense of isolation. Even so, she did not panic when a neighbor called with the horrible news. She merely turned to stone, listening. She placed the receiver in its cradle. She stared for a long time at her potted fern. She walked out into the yard, where Grover lay on his back in damp gravel under the VW van. It was late afternoon, almost dark, and cooling fast. She got down on her hands and knees so she would not have to raise her voice, and she told him what she had decided to do.

"Balls a fire," Grover said, a line picked out of an old Snuffy Smith cartoon, which he has been using since the age of ten. His voice, resonating upward through thin metal, was already edged with irritation at the bolts and nuts defying him. "We can't move in with my folks."

"I just called Leona. She says they'd be delighted."

"Of course she says they'd be delighted. It's the old Okie hospitality. If I called up and said the band needed steady work and was thinking of turning the house into a nightclub, she'd say they'd be delighted. But she already has a full house.

I get the impression Travis and his girlfriend are in there for the season."

"Maybe it'd be good for you to spend some time with Travis."

"I've been trying to, Holly. I guess it'll happen when the time is right. Travis does things his own way."

"I've noticed that. It runs in the family."

"C'mon. I don't need lectures. Hand me that little wrench."

"I'm sorry, Grover. About wanting to leave. But I have to get away from this particular place . . . for a while."

"Impossible. There's too much to do right now."

"I am not kidding. Get out from under there and look at me."

"I'm not kidding either. Soon as I get this bastard running, I have to take care of the septic tank before we get caught in the rain again. Toilet's gonna back up on us. I've got weeding to do around those beans. Let it go too long already. And then the mulching. If I can get it mulched, and then one good rain . . ."

He is not talking to Holly now. He is telling this to himself, reciting the chores that define his future.

"A few days is what I'm talking about," she says. "Until things settle down. Until the police find out something. Somebody is going around smothering people to death up here. It is only three miles over to Bruno and Natalie's place." She laughs the way she laughed at the tremors, with a doomsday helplessness. "That gives me pause. Did anything ever give you pause?"

"Holly, you cannot let some creep bring your whole life to a standstill. That is a kind of tyranny I will not put up with. Stop and think about what you're saying."

His voice is rising. Hers is getting softer. "Ordinarily," she says, "I would take the Packard and drive out of here myself."

"Is that what this is all about? You want me to fix the Packard?"

"If the brakes worked, we wouldn't even have to have this conversation."

Suddenly he is shouting from under the van. "Jesus Christ! Why does everything have to fall to pieces at the same time! Look at this sonofabitch! Neither one of us is going to be going anywhere until . . ."

He shoves hard on the wrench, and the wrench slips, and three knuckles crunch against metal.

A long, fierce, dark silence follows.

Then Holly says, "You can drive me over to the ranch, or I'll figure out some other way to get there. I'll start walking. If I get tired of walking, I'll call a cab."

Something in the deliberate steadiness of her voice pulls him squirming out from under the van. She left him once, six months ago, drove off in the Packard and did not return for two weeks. He survived without her, but he would rather not have that happen again. Leona told him then, after Holly left, that he was too much like Montrose. "You want to keep that girl," Lee had said with a flirtatious smile, "you're going to have to unlearn some of the things you learned from your father. I put up with habits that girls like Holly just don't have the patience for after a while. Do you pay attention to her? Do you think about her, treat her like an equal, take care of things before she has to ask and ask?"

He sits up in the gravel, sucking on his hand, his face spattered with the black crumbs of grease dust.

"Bruno was a dealer," he says. "Everybody knows he was. They also had a very freaky scene going. I have heard that Natalie was actually for sale about half the time. I mean, it's terrible that they got killed and all that. But they traveled in a different circuit than we do. It is not something we should change our whole lives about."

"I can also hitchhike," she says. "I am prepared to hitchhike if I have to, to get down to a lower altitude."

Holly is on her knees, Grover is sitting up, head to her head, and their eyes are fencing, clicking back and forth. They could remain like this for hours, but the outcome is decided in the first fifteen seconds.

23

The next morning Montrose, after the yoga, and while shaving, has three hunches in rapid succession. Like all journalists, like the reporter Fowler was seen talking to, Monty relies a lot on hunches. Since he works at this trade only part of each week, his percentage is going to be lower than that of the seasoned, full-time professionals. He is right about one third of the time.

Monty is a below-average journalist because facts have never interested him as much as ultimate causes. In this sense you might almost call him a religious writer. He sets himself apart from other journalists. Not above. Not below. But apart. Already the wire services and papers in the city are hinting at witchcraft, blood cults, Satanic rites, or are taking Fowler's lead. Here in Monty's own household, a low-keyed anxiety begins to fill the air, fed by numerous similar and as yet unfounded notions arriving by phone, by mail, on foot, carried down from the higher ridges by Grover and Holly Belle. Montrose decides he owes it to his readers to devote some space to the subject, believing himself to be the kind of writer Fowler described—that is, one of the few, perhaps the only writer in this region who can present a version unfettered by job security, deadline pressure, or appeals to the gaudy and sensational.

His first hunch is that Linda Kramer's former boyfriend might be the key, that a chat with this fellow could unmuddy the water and at the very least dispel a lot of gossip. He drives out to the house Fowler claims they were inhabiting.

In daylight the field that so frightened Fowler's wife spreads out benignly beyond a rotting fence, a wide quiet tablecloth of spring weeds. At the near edge stands a great oak, which he figures Fowler must have parked under. He sees tire tracks. He studies them carefully, the way he has seen movie cowboys study buried campfires and droppings on the trail. "They rode outta here less than three hours ago," the wise, close-lipped scout will say. "These turds'll still stick to your gloves."

He kicks at the tire tracks, raising a puff of dust. They seem recent. He hopes they are final, that they sum up Fowler's imprint on this countryside, that out of fear or impatience he has already loaded up his wagon and ridden on, like a true explorer of the west, to the next mine, the next promise. Among Monty's deeper and as yet unvoiced motives for personally wanting to get to the bottom of this case are his distrust of Fowler and a certain possessiveness about whatever happens in this county, good and bad alike, and why it happens. He would rather not have Fowler coming around telling him why.

He surveys the house and grounds. No other vehicles in sight. No sign of life inside or out. It all seems serenely disheveled and abandoned. It is not until he is standing perfectly still in the roadway, nearly hypnotized, listening to the deep noon quiet, that he hears the strange faraway duet—muted growling, and an infant's cranky whimper.

He crosses a patch of high weeds, looks through the front window into an otherwise empty living room and sees Fowler's wife sitting on a truck seat, nursing Ivan. One blue-veined breast hangs past the bone buttons of her madras shirt. Ivan is naked. The woman's feet are bare. Around her the floor is bare, the room in shadows. The sight arouses him. She seems so frail, so . . . slovenly. A ravaged madonna. It arouses the beast in him. For one gross moment he stares with lascivious disgust at Fowler's woman. Then the shadow his head throws into the room causes her to look up from the nursing. Nothing registers in her face or her eyes. She watches him like a forest animal waiting to see what he intends to do. He imagines how craven he must appear to her, gawking outside this musty window, perhaps even murderous, considering the latest news. Leaning closer to cut the glare, he sees Lorenzo lashed to the kitchen sink, and trying to eat through his muzzle from the inside. Monty moves away from the window, up old porch stairs, pushing the front door open, standing there, wary of the dog.

"I'm Montrose Doyle. I believe we met a while back."

"Yes. Hello."

"Thought this place would be full of people. From the way your husband talked."

"They all split."

"Oh, really? When?"

"As soon as the first story broke."

"So you and Larry have moved in."

Her eyes are darkly circled, her face expressionless, her voice struggling to stay in touch with eternal wonder, trying to remember that old houses like this, surrounded by fields and trees and humming insects, are all suburbs of the Garden of Eden.

"Nobody else wants to live here at the moment. So we are getting it for almost nothing. Just to keep an eye on the place. Caretaking. That's why Larry left me here."

"Left you here?"

"He's gone into town." She laughs a slow, cynical laugh. "I'm kind of a watchdog. Me and Lorenzo."

"He's not doing you much good in the kitchen. Anybody could come roaming up your driveway."

"We have to keep him tied because he started going for Ivan. I don't know why. Maybe it's all those weeks in the truck. Close quarters. Maybe when he gets used to the space around here . . ."

Her voice trails off. Ivan has begun to cry, as the milk runs out. She shifts him to the other breast, while Monty watches the maneuver, remembering how Leona suckled Grover, and later Travis, always out of doors, looking for the sun. She would shade the head with her shoulder, but keep the legs and belly in the sun. She was always a great believer in the way seasons can shape a disposition. Grover, born in winter, watched a lot of rain fall into his first three months. In his bassinet he felt the bite of five good frosts. Suckling, he would pull and drink relentlessly, till Lee was sore and raw around the nipples. Travis, born in spring, had sunshine almost every day. They lived out on the porch, and in the yard, the mother and the sunny spring child. Two-year-old Grover, already hating the loss of what could never be his again, would be tugging at her legs, knocking potted plants off the porch rail. "The other tit, Ma," he seemed to be saying. "Don't you have two? One for him, and one for me?" while baby Travis suckled playfully, as if he could take this gift or leave it alone.

"You ought to move outside," he says to Fowler's wife, "and sit on the grass. The boy might like that."

"The grass makes my legs itch," she says. "That field out there is crawling with red ants. This truck seat is the only soft place I have to sit down. Can you believe this fucking truck seat?"

She settles back into it, a movement he takes as a gesture of welcome. He steps inside the doorway and slides down next to the wall, squatting, eying Lorenzo, who snarls furiously, pulling at the rope.

Without commitment, she says, "Lorenzo."

"I came out here looking for Linda Kramer's boyfriend. You ever meet him, get a chance to talk to him?"

"Listen, he was the first to split. He left last week."

"Any idea where he went?"

"Mexico is what I heard. Maybe Central America. He could see the writing on the wall. Nothing to gain, and a whole lot to lose. Just the opposite from Larry, right? Larry has nothing to lose, except me and Ivan, and we don't really figure too big in his planning these days."

Monty scans the empty room, the empty kitchen, peers out into the sunlight. Not much to keep him squatting here. Not even Mrs. Fowler. He feels he should be moved by her plight, feels he should offer her something before he leaves. The trouble is, none of this seems real to him. In his view she suffers from a self-inflicted poverty. The victim here is Ivan. Ivan needs all the help he can get.

"Listen," Monty says, "let me move this truck seat out onto the porch for you. That way you can give the boy a little sun and fresh air, but be up there above the ants."

Mournfully she says, "It's one solid piece. You won't get it through the door. I think that's why they left it here. They couldn't get it through the door."

"Let me try."

"What'll I do later, when it starts to cool off? How'll I get it inside again?"

"Can't Larry move it? When'll he be back?"

"He didn't say."

Monty's second hunch is that a visit to the Fontaine place will be more fruitful than hanging around downtown waiting for the D.A.'s statement and the first police reports. He knows that's where the local reporter assigned to this case will be today, downtown swapping lore and beer and cigarettes with the out-of-town newsmen. The road the Fontaines lived on winds upward through woody gulches that seem to have been untraveled and uninhabited since the last mountain lion fell to the last bounty hunter, decades back. Rounding a horseshoe curve, he comes upon a row of battered mailboxes, and just beyond them, where an overgrown dirt road heads into deep forest, he sees Walter sitting on his motorcycle.

Monty pulls up next to him, rolls his window down, and says with mock severity, "Press."

Walter is not amused. Eyeless behind his wraparounds, weighted down with lethal equipment, he seems at first not to recognize Monty. He sits like a statue of a ferocious cop.

"What are you doing way the hell up here? I thought the county troops would be taking care of this."

"They're short-handed. We're helping out till they get things under control. One thing they do not want is sightseers."

"C'mon, Walter. I'm not a sightseer. I'm doing a story."

"Sorry, Doyle. The whole area is closed off."

"What's the big secret?"

"No big secret."

"Who's up there? What's going on?"

"Routine investigation. That's all I'm allowed to say."

His voice is brittle with guilt. His lips begin to squirm, of their own volition.

"I just want to look around, Walter. I'm not going to—"

"I got my orders, Doyle! Nobody gets in!"

He shouts this with a vehemence Montrose did not think Walter capable of.

"Hey, Walter. You don't have to shout. It's me. Montrose."

Walter is in a mood to shout. He seems to have been sitting here on his motocycle for hours, alone, filling with rage, and waiting for Montrose to come along.

"You wanna know something, Doyle? When this fucking case is over with, I am quitting the force for good! I am serious this time! I cannot believe the shit that is flying around my head! I feel like a goddam punching bag! About ten minutes ago I almost puked! I almost got off my bike and went over there in the bushes and puked!"

"Well, what's going on? Where's it all coming from?"

"I can't talk about it!"

"You already started talking about it."

"That was a mistake!"

"Will you for Christ sake quit shouting at me!"

Walter unsnaps his holster, pulls out his .38.

"Nobody gets up this hill, Doyle. Those are my orders."

Monty looks at the quivering pistol, then at Walter's face, trying to see through the lenses of his one-way shades. There is a long silence. The shouting match has frightened away all nearby forest noises. Flies, bees, mosquitoes, squirrels, blue jays, and woodpeckers wait to see what Walter is going to do, while Walter jerks his head this way and that, as if surrounded, or trying to isolate his reason for pulling the gun.

At last Monty says, "Maybe you should quit right now. Pack it in. C'mon, I'll give you a ride down the mountain. We can go have a drink somewhere."

"Don't push me, Doyle. This is one time you—do—not —fucking—push—me."

He punctuates this sentence with his pistol, waving it in front of his belt like a conductor's baton.

Monty waits a few moments, then gets out of his car. He walks around to the far side and opens the back door and withdraws a wicker picnic basket, which he carries to the front fender. He flips back its lid and rummages until he finds a quart thermos. As he unscrews the cup-sized cap, the clearing they stand in gradually fills with the smell of hot coffee. He fills the screw-on cup and says, "You want a shot of Bushmill's in this? I happen to have some Bushmill's in the basket."

"Cut it out, Doyle."

"Irish coffee, Walter. Lifts the spirits. It's what I'm having," he says, as he pours out a second cup, and adds the Bushmill's, sniffing in a great snootful of the aroma.

"At least try the coffee," Montrose says.

Walter appears to him now as he did one afternoon on the high school football field twenty years ago, when he was given the chance to try his foot at place kicking. It was a preseason scrimmage. Walter had been practicing all summer, and this was his big chance to get out of the interior line and into something with more dignity to it. The ball came back from center, the crouched fullback took it and propped it with his finger. Walter rushed forward with fierce concentration and missed the ball completely. The wind his foot made pushed the ball over. One of the second-string linemen scooped it up and ran untouched toward the distant goal line. The play was called back, but that was small consolation for Walter, who stood there, as he stands now, with teammates sprinting past him, hands on hips, his jaw set, staring at some despised enemy in the middle distance.

After thirty seconds of this, he puts his pistol away and accepts the screw-on cup.

"I'm not trying to pull anything, Walter. Don't worry about me getting past you. I don't need to go up there. I'll come back next week. You've got your job to do."

"Nothing personal, Monty."

"I'll just drink a little coffee and be on my way."

Monty leans against his fender, sniffing at the Irish between sips. After a while Walter says, "I had three days coming. We were going up to Yosemite. Just me and Flora. Leave the kids at my mother's. Reservations at the Ahwanee Hotel. The whole bit. We haven't been off by ourselves, away from the kids, for nine years."

"That's too long, Walter. You owe it to yourself—"

"Don't tell me what I owe myself. Two hours before we're ready to take off, the chief calls up, says three more bodies have been uncovered, the county sheriff is literally having a double hernia operation, two of his men are out sick and two others are off at some training school, the shit is going to hit the fan, et cetera, et cetera. This, on top of all the rest of it—"

"All the rest of what?"

"I'll take some of the Bushmill's, Monty. It's not my habit to drink on the job, you know that. But . . ."

"It's the altitude," says Monty, pouring.

Walter pulls his black gloves off, pulls his shades off, and runs a thick hand over his haggard face. He looks as if he has been up all night, maybe two nights. Eyes like shattered abalone shells. Ashen cheeks, with nodes of whiskers his razor missed. Razor nicks decorate his jaws like tribal markings or fencing scars. He gulps back half the cup.

"The bags were already packed for the big trip, right? So

Flora just grabbed hers and hopped in the car and drove off, said she was going to Yosemite anyway, and the police department could go fuck itself."

"She's not worried about leaving the kids behind with a killer on the loose?"

"The kids are already at my mother's, over in San Jose. That's how close we were to getting away. Jesus, it depresses me. Two more hours . . ."

"Maybe you should have told the chief this was one time you had to put duty second."

"I couldn't."

"Of course you could. You still can. It's not like you're taking advantage. You've earned three days off."

"He wouldn't let me."

Walter looks at him with eyes that seem to be remembering atrocities.

"Now look here, Walter. There's something you're not telling me."

"My life is an open book."

"You want to tell me what it is?"

"No."

"You might feel better if you get it off your chest."

Walter takes a big slug of the Irish, tosses the dregs into the dirt, and hands the screw-on cup back to Monty.

"I feel better already," he says.

Like a kid trying to make steam on a frosty morning, Walter leans up close and breathes.

"Can you smell anything on my breath?"

"Irish coffee," Monty says.

"Sonofabitch."

"Who are you expecting?"

"How the fuck should I know?"

He puts his black gloves on, his one-way silver lenses. Though they cover only his eyes, they make a mask of his entire face, turn him into a creature again, faceless among the slender trees.

24

Montrose first visited Holy City when he was thirteen. He drove up there one weekend with his dad, who wanted to see for himself what all the ruckus was about. Although Monty has passed within two miles of the place a thousand times since, and each time has pictured the town as it looked that afternoon—the slogans lettered boldly on the buildings, the winged figures, crudely painted, ready to ascend—he has never returned until today.

Visiting Holy City is his third hunch. He suspects that some truth about the killings may still be at large in the air. This is the kind of hunch he most enjoys and thus has saved it for last. It allows his mind to wander freely over the landscape, looking for essences, for suggestions, rather than for specific clues—a preference akin to what truly draws him this far out of the pattern of his life, this far into the mountains. It is not the local intrigue, as much as what might be revealed about the overriding trend of his times, a trend, a leaning, he would call it a lunge, led not by the Disraelis and Roosevelts of yesteryear, but by hijackers, vandals, terrorists, and homicidal stunt men. These are the pacesetters in Monty's world. It seems to him that more and more of us suck air in the wake of their wanton assaults.

As Monty winds down the Old Highway, his head is filled with colors, with lurid wooden storefronts, life-size statues of Santa Claus, and the patriarchal mountain man standing at the long porch rail as if waiting for Monty's dad to step up and question him. He half expects to find him still waiting there, as he has stood in Monty's memory all these years.

What he finds is a dusty post office, with a bar adjoining, and where the town used to stand, hugging two sides of a wide curve in what used to be the main road through these mountains, just an open space, the size of a large parking lot, as if a Caterpillar came in here with its blade at ground level and pushed everything over the edge, into the gorge that drops down to Los Gatos Creek.

Monty parks next to the bar, which is closed, and looks out over the gorge. Linda's grave, he has been told, was about fifty yards down this slope, uncovered by two boys and two dogs on a squirrel-hunting hike. Later he will follow the wide trail of boot prints down that way to have a look. First he will explore the scattered ruins of the town. It is not the grave that interests Monty now. It is the choice of graveyard. Why Holy City? he asks himself. Mere coincidence? Perhaps panic or impatience or some other random impulse. Perhaps not. The intersection where Linda was picked up hitchhiking is nearly twenty miles away, up to the summit ridge and down the other side to sea level. In this wide, gullied range, there are much remoter spots for disposing of a victim. Perhaps there is something to those quick guesses in the morning papers—some modern-day, mind-blown Jesus freak finding inspiration from the original Christian crackpot, returning to the scene of who knows what outrageous rituals. When Monty was a boy there were rumors that the old man, like Bluebeard, had buried women here, beneath the main street of the town. But that was over thirty years ago, and in those days he was being accused of everything from larceny to treason. Members of the Baptist congregation Monty's folks attended whispered that anyone who owned six Cadillacs and treated women the way he did was a reincarnation of the devil, a worse pox upon the land than Joseph Smith and Mary Baker Eddy.

A ruined gas station stands across the road. The metal roof that once shaded pumps hangs at a dangerous angle, ready to collapse. Beyond that, a couple of abandoned sheds, stables perhaps, and an old store with the windows gone. Was this the store the old man stood in front of? Not likely. All the town's main buildings caught fire in the late 1950s, went up like kindling in the summer heat. But this store will serve well enough, a remnant from those heydays. He kicks through low brush until he stands in front of its tumbling façade, peering into jagged window frames. Behind him, along the Old Highway, there is no traffic, this afternoon no breeze. After a long while standing in the quiet, he hears the old man call out.

"If Holy City's what you're looking for, gentlemen, then you've found it. You'll find everything you need right here."

He listens, and he hears his dad's voice answering from the middle of the street. "You must be The Comforter."

"That's what they call me."

"The fellow who built this town."

"Not a town, my friend. It's a city. One day it will be a whole lot more than that. The Lord is with us here, with all those who want to follow His true way."

Monty's dad was not an ardent Baptist. He went to church each Sunday mainly to avoid the argument with his wife. He had never trusted preachers, yet in any preacher's presence he still harbored a youthful awe. As he moved up the stairs and into the shade to join The Comforter on the long porch, his smile hung somewhere between mockery and a wanting to believe.

"I hear in your voice the tone of the skeptic," said The Comforter.

"Well, I'll be honest with you. The boy and me were just in there looking at your penny arcade—"

"The Temptations," he intoned.

"Looks like a penny arcade to me. All them little churches with peepholes in the front?"

"Inside each chapel you will find one of man's temptations. Temptations lead to sin. At Holy City we have left sin behind."

"You got one in there called 'The Legs of Queen Elizabeth of Egypt.' Now, they just don't tempt me a whole lot, if you want to know the truth. Monty neither. All full of knots and splinters. How can you charge money to look at things like that?"

"Like a true skeptic, you have missed the point, my friend. Every woman, no matter what the condition of her legs—they can be knock-kneed, bowlegged, one leg missing, or covered with hair like a gorilla—every woman becomes a queen and every man a king here at Holy City, where the world's perfect government has been established. You see that sign behind you?"

With his cane The Comforter pointed to a painted slogan, like a marquee, above the windows of a building across the street:

THE KING OF ALL WISE MEN GIVES TO THE WORLD A
NEW AND PERFECT GOVERNMENT. $25,000 REWARD
IF YOU CAN FIND ANY FLAWS IN IT. WE ASK YOUR
INVESTIGATION.

"Is that you?" Doyle asked. "The king of all wise men?"

"I have spoken with God. God reveals himself through me. And before you start thinking you are going to drive away from here with twenty-five thousand dollars in your pocket, I want you to think about what brings the biggest problems into your life. I want you to think about some of the things we have *done away with* here at Holy City. We have done away with wages. We have done away with taxes. We have done away with banks, with crime, with suicide, and with marriage."

"Is it true, then, what they say down in town?"

"What do they say? That I am a Communist? That I am a dope fiend? That I keep women chained?"

"I've heard tell that there's seventy-five men up here and only ten women."

"Well, you heard wrong, my friend. That is one example of the kind of unfounded rumor that can give you the wrong impression. We only have four women up here."

"Four women, and seventy-five men? You got to admit that could make a person stop and wonder."

"Wonder about what? Only a mind preoccupied with filth would want to stop and wonder. That is the trouble with the world down below. Preoccupied with filth. Here at Holy City we live the perfect life, we enjoy perfect health, we have the perfect government. It is"—he points again with his cane, toward another sign—"the New Jerusalem."

Young Monty turned toward the sign and saw above it a figure of The Comforter wearing the same suit, with this same cane raised like a scepter. He was flanked by two broad-winged angels. From there Monty let his gaze wander along the main street, while the men continued talking, that is, while The Comforter commenced preaching a noisy sermon on corruption that sounded too much like sermons Monty had already heard too many times. The main street had more to offer. It was like a carnival midway, striped and bannered with gaudy doors and wild promises.

He spied a low stone wall with this proclamation:

> HOLY CITY MINERAL WATER.
> THIS FOUNTAIN FOR HEALTH.
> DRINK IT ACCORDING TO INSTRUCTIONS
> AND GO FREE.

There were no instructions. But there were two statues of Santa Claus on top of the wall, their eyes as piercing and as humorless as The Comforter's. Santa Claus seemed to be the patron saint. Identical statues stood spaced around the outskirts of the town, bearded and booted, each with a motto written on its belt:

> IF YOU ARE CONTEMPLATING MARRIAGE, SUICIDE, OR
> CRIME, SEE US FIRST.

> MORTAL WOMAN IS IN CONSTANT TORMENT BECAUSE
> MORTAL MAN IS IN CONSTANT WEAKNESS.

The words "mortal woman" and "torment" revived a warm expectation in Monty's thirteen-year-old groin and lower belly. On the pretext of returning to the arcade of tiny chapels, he walked back along the street. He looked in at the chapels lined up like a row of mailboxes, with steeples and crosses and slots for coins. This was not what he wanted to see. He wanted to see one of the four women. On the drive up, his dad had been joking with him about this. "God damn, Monty! What do you think? Your mother jumps on the Mormons for one man having a house full a wives. What do you think goes on up there at Holy City? Think those poor women get any kind of sleep at all?" Monty laughed with his dad, and couldn't wait to see the place, and now he feels cheated. The Comforter must be sixty-five or seventy, leaning on his cane and spitting. Young Monty peers off into the trees, between the buildings, wishing a door would open somewhere and one of those fabled women would appear. It's a fruitless search. There doesn't seem to be anyone else around. Could the old man be up here all by himself? The whole concoction his own lonesome dream? Including the disciples who supposedly followed him out of the lowlands to found the New Jerusalem?

He looks back at the long porch where The Comforter still rants at his father. They are about the same size, in Monty's memory, both solidly built, about five ten, The Comforter one generation farther along, having trouble with his leg perhaps, although it's hard to tell. The cane could be a stage prop. They both wear hats, Doyle a rancher's Stetson, The Comforter a soiled Panama, a rumpled suit, a shiny tie. He looks a bit like Will Rogers, but there is none of that cracker barrel whimsy in his eye. Young Monty could not imagine The Comforter ever telling a joke. He wondered why his dad put up with that long and pointless sermon. Remembering now, Monty knows it was partly out of habit, after all those years of sitting through evangelical rantings of every type, and partly for amusement, for tales to carry home. But there was something else. He sees his father watching the old man, listening intently. He sees the clean, white, closely fitting shirt, the faded Levi's, recently washed, the cuffs brushing boots that show traces of manure, from a little job in the barn that came up just before they left. Doyle keeps horses and a few cattle. He is a hard-working apple rancher without much time for nonsense, who moved into this region and bought his land about the same time The Comforter moved in to found his utopia, right after the First World War. For twenty years Doyle has been hearing tales, finally drives up one day to study the devil face to face, and the devil turns out to be a nutty old-timer with his head full of dreams, which makes him, in that sense, something like Doyle. Another conquistador. They are two sides of the same coin—the rancher and the demented Christian. And they are both receding now, fixed on the porch, face to face, as the camera pulls back. The porch they stand on grows smaller, enclosed by the archaic buildings of the painted town, the side show of banners. Pull farther back, and the town is seen as a tiny clearing in the trees, beneath pines and pointed evergreens that rise in jagged steps toward the higher ridges. Now the trees merge to hide the town. From high above they make a forest cloth that hugs the flow and ripple of the spreading coastal range, and the town dissolves. Thirty years go by. From this altitude Monty sees something he did not see when he was thirteen, could not have known enough to see. Almost no one knew it then. Like a low-burning flame, it fires his imagination, a streak of light that seems at first of such immense importance he dares not dwell upon it. He savors it, lets his mind circle it awhile from above, like a moth. Holy City was built right in the rift zone, looking out upon one place in these mountains that happens to live up to Leona's vision of the fault—a long gouge, with no bottom visible. For a few miles here it follows the chasm worn into these ridges by Los Gatos Creek. Then, where the creek swings farther inland, the line continues north and west, passing under Holy City, under the freeway, heading upstate toward Woodside, Crystal Springs, San Francisco, and Point Reyes.

Again he wonders: Why here? Why Linda? Why now, or fifty years ago? Why, out of all the vales and hideaways in this long range of mountains, did The Comforter choose to plant his New Jerusalem where the plates meet? Was it chance? Or did he feel some power in the air or in the earth? Did he intuit, like a water witch, that large forces were at work right underfoot, forces large enough, if he had been able to tap them, to suit the largeness of his plan? Like Cortez, and Hearst, and Walt Disney, The Comforter had the visions of a true conquistador. Among his long-range plans, it is said, he dreamed of building a giant tower above his town. It was going to be in the form of a human figure, a modern colossus, straddling the summit and the summit road, with a radio station in its head that would broadcast uplifting messages all over the west. Gazing upward now, from the town's ghost toward where this colossus would have stood, Monty tries to picture it. A terrific idea, it seems to him. He would make only one change in the plan. He would add a female colossus, a belly dancer perhaps, so that during any tremor larger than 4.5 on the Richter scale, the man's balls would swing and the dancer's great breasts would bobble, her vast hips would writhe, while enormous speakers mounted in their heads or in their shoulders would blast out appropriate music down both slopes and into the low country. He hears Roy Acuff. Singing "Wreck on the Highway."

25

ETYMOLOGY

---

from *One Day at a Time*
by Montrose Doyle

I looked up "drift" in the dictionary this morning. The word has an interesting history. In Middle English, for instance, it was *dryft*, akin to the Danish *drift*, and Old High German *trift*, a word for "herd," and for "drifting."

The Anglo-Saxon *drifan* is related to the Gothic *dreiban,* the German *treiban,* and the Old Norse *drifa,* which originally meant "to drive."

And these hark back to the granddaddy of all western languages, the Indo-European base word, *dhreibh*. Don't worry if your tongue gets tangled around those un-American consonants. Just remember that it means "to push, to force on."

Thus the word "drift" is akin to the word "drive." To be adrift is also to be driven.

To grasp the odd connection between these two words, imagine yourself to be a hitchhiker with no clear destination. You have the urge to move, and you have just climbed into a stranger's car.

26

Taking back roads home, Monty has been watching the sunset burnish treetops and later make his rear-view a rosy square. Turning colors rise from the distant sea, as good as wine or Irish coffee. It is dusk when he turns up his driveway, high on the afterglow. The sky has turned to purple wine. Alongside his house he sees Grover's van up on blocks, its rear end underlit by a bright bulb in a small wire cage at the end of an extension cord snaking into the front room through an open window. Grover's head of reddish hair is visible, a head of coral in the light. He lies on his back on a spattered tarp with tools spread out from his shoulders. At the edge of the drive-way the dogs are sprawled like sleeping sentinels. Monty squats behind the van.

"What's the matter?"

"Spare-tank cable's stuck; got the fuel line blocked. Go more than twenty yards, the engine dies."

"Sounds like you have lost your taste for the work."

"It took me two hours to figure out what was wrong. I pulled the distributor apart, took the fuel pump apart . . ."

"How about waiting till morning, when you can see what you're doing?"

"I want to be out of here in the morning."

"What's the rush?"

"Things pile up. It's gonna rain by the end of the week. If I don't get my septic line flowing right, we're gonna have sewage up to our ankles and running down the road."

Grover, with this comment, sounds exactly like his grand-dad and namesake, old Grover. Salt of the earth and full speed ahead. Monty, for his reply, harks back one generation further, to *his* granddad, marveling, even as he speaks, at how the generations leapfrog, and deceased ancestors teach us without even trying.

"Grover," he says, grinning in under the axle. "Let me give you a little fatherly advice. You worry about your septic tank too much, you're going to get constipated. Then where are you? You got a perfect drainage system, but your asshole is wound up so tight you can't take a decent shit."

Grover has to laugh, squeezing his eyes shut with delight and a kind of relief. "Hey, everybody's giving me advice around here. I don't need advice. I need help. Grab these pliers."

"Where's Travis?"

"Gone. And he wouldn't be any good if he was here. Never did know doodly squat about cars. If you can work the cable from this end, I'll slide over and work it from the other end. That way maybe we can free it up."

Monty crawdads in under the van, reaching with pliers to get a bite on the cable sleeve, his head inches from Grover's.

"What do you mean, gone?" Monty says.

"Typical stuff he's been pulling."

"You two didn't get into it, I hope."

"Didn't have time. Holly and I drove up. Travis walked out. Bingo. End of story."

"Now wait a minute. What did you do . . . ?

"I didn't do a thing but turn off my engine and honk. He was standing up on the porch with Crystal, drinking a cup of coffee, with his hat on, like a big plantation owner. I give him a couple of beeps, because I am truly glad to see him. Right? He sets his cup on the rail and leads Crystal down the stairs. I have to admit, it was funny at the time. He did this John Wayne imitation of a cowboy running out of elbow room. He shoves back his Panama and he says, 'Gittin mighty crowded around here.' And while we are sitting in the front seat laughing at that, he grabs Crystal by the hand and they take off,

walking down the driveway. I yelled out, 'We just swung by
to take a look at that heifer a yours, Mr. Doyle.' He started
lurching and limping along bandy-legged, like some broken-
hipped rodeo star, and Crystal looking back at us, shrugging
her free shoulder as if to say, 'I don't know what this is all
about any more than you do.' We didn't think much more
about it till lunchtime. They didn't make it back for lunch.
Now it's past dinnertime, and they're still not here, and haven't
called. Leona is in there holding up dinner, hoping they'll
show. I figure they either hitchhiked into town or wandered
off into the bushes somewhere."

"I'll vote for the bushes," Monty says. "That's what I'd do
if it was me. Night like this, with the twilight coming in
through the leaves and the underbrush. They're probably just
now brushing off the stickers and starting home."

"Well, you better tell that to Lee. She thinks they have
been picked up by the gravedigger and are already buried
someplace by the side of the road."

"You're not serious, I hope."

"I'd say sixty percent serious. She's been on the phone all
day."

"About Travis?"

"About everything. In between calls, she and Holly have
been swapping disaster stories."

Monty releases a long, slow, wits-gathering breath. "I guess
I'd better get on in there."

Waiting a beat, Grover parodies his father. "What's the
rush?"

Monty snuffs a short, appreciative laugh. "No rush."

He realizes his neck is stiff from concentrating on the cable.
He lets his head drop back, relaxing onto the canvas.

"We got that wire free yet?" he says.

"Sure. It's working fine now. Been working fine for two or
three minutes."

"You mean," says Monty, "we're just lying around under
the car with our pliers hanging out?"

"Kind of nice under here, don't you think?"

"Mighty peaceful."

"There's a sweetness about it," Grover says.

"I just wish for one thing."

"And what's that?"

"An ice-cold bottle of beer."

"There's beer in the house."

"Too far away," Monty says. "I want somebody to reach in under here and just hand me a cool one."

"I believe I have some Jack Daniel's."

"That'd do. That'd do just fine."

"But it's in the cab."

"Well," says Monty, "I guess we'll just have to go get it, then."

They slide out, wipe off their hands, douse the light. In the darkness they lean back against the van's front end, which is facing west, toward the wine-stained remnants of the afterglow, while Grover unscrews the cap.

"We'll just sit here awhile and wait for Travis," Monty says before he takes his first, delicate sip and lets it trickle down, lets it settle.

"You think he's coming back tonight?"

"Hard to know. Always hard to predict what he's going to do. Maybe if we send out some welcome-home vibrations, he'll show up."

Grover takes his time on a long pull, then says, "He should have called. That's what bugs Leona, not knowing one way or another. She says it's like his eyes. Not letting anybody know."

"You worried about him?"

"Some."

"Think we ought to go looking for him?"

"I do. And I don't. That's what went on all through high school. Everybody bailing Travis out of this or that. He ought to be able to take care of himself by this time."

Monty gets reflective, nostalgic, almost maudlin. "The only difference is . . . it's hard coming back from a war. The world

you're coming into seems . . . unreal. It's too much. And
yet . . . it's not enough. Takes a while to . . . readjust."

"Sounds about like the way I feel every time I drive down
into town."

They both laugh. When the laughter dies, they sit quietly,
listening, till Monty speaks.

"Hey, you ever get the feeling that everybody in the whole
wide world is going nuts?"

"It's more than a feeling. I get an absolute certainty."

"I have to tell you about something that happened to me
this afternoon. Can't get it out of my mind. My old protégé
Walter pulled a gun on me."

"Walter the cop?"

"I keep seeing the barrel right there between us. Jumpy
bastard was actually ready to shoot."

"What'd he do that for? You two didn't get into it, I hope."

"Up there at the Fontaine place. I just wanted to look
around. He was guarding the road like a Doberman. Trained
to kill. I think he's heading for a nervous breakdown."

"I'm not surprised to hear it."

"Something crazy is going on, Grover. I mean, crazier than
usual."

"You know what they're saying up in the mountains tonight?"

"No. What are they saying?"

"They're saying that if the gravedigger shows up, don't call
the police because all the police will do is provide the shovel."

"Now, why are they saying that?"

Grover takes a deep pull and passes the pint back to Monty
with a hint of arrogance that makes Monty grin. He knows
Grover thinks he is slightly out of it, knows he enjoys one-
upping Dad every chance he gets. He waits, watching his son's
lips with anticipation, the way you watch the front tires of a
car about to turn in front of you, and with a certain awe,
since in this light the jut of Grover's chin, the overarching of

his brow, is the profile of Monty's father as a young man, yet he is also the son who keeps Montrose up to date on moonlight orgies, dope deals, scab musicians, mineral baths, draft refusal, local Indian lore, and yoga.

"This nark," Grover says, "Samson Newby, who supposedly discovered the three bodies, was actually discovered making the discovery. That's why they've got the place sealed off. It is probably why Walter is in such a sweat. This may well be the biggest fiasco in the history of the police department, and they are still trying to figure out how to handle it. There is a strong suspicion that Newby was doing something else besides stumbling upon these graves for the first time."

Though Monty's interest is growing, his amusement is waning. He hears an echo in Grover's voice, a depressingly Fowler-like echo.

"How do you know all this?"

"I know the people who discovered Newby. They live up our road. They were in custody for twenty-four hours while the cops tried to figure out how to handle their story."

"Didn't Lee tell me you also knew the Fontaines?"

"To say hello. I'd run into them down in town once in a while. That was it. They hid out in the mountains most of the time. Like moonshiners. Freaky moonshiners. You know what I mean?"

"No, I don't."

"A little too weird for my tastes."

"What kind of weird?" Monty asks.

"Two brothers, right? Bruno and Roland, who are almost identical—not twins, but amazing look-alikes—and this woman Natalie, who it seems went for both of them. They would take turns, and the theory is that the two brothers were actually hot for each other, but worked it out through Natalie, who was sort of their . . . intermediary. They were also into heavy jewelry and eye make-up and beads and weaving things into their hair, and of course they were buying and selling all the time. As I understand it, they were refugees from the Haight-Ashbury. The one time I really sat down and talked to Bruno, I got the impression they made a killing in the last days of the Haight, then got out of the city just in time, heading for higher ground. I know their place here was raided at least once, a couple of years ago, but Bruno got tipped off ahead of time and was ready for them. It was a comedy. Embarrassment on all sides, et cetera, with Bruno threatening to hire an attorney. But that was nothing like what is going on now. By *accident,* mind you, these two guys from our neighborhood happen to go driving up to the Fontaines' place at the very time Newby is in there screwing around. They knock on the doors, they look in the barn, then they start into the woods, knowing the Fontaines had the habit of hiking to a little grove back away from the house, a natural cathedral, with a straight shot up through redwoods at a pure circle of sky. They would lean against the trees and turn on. And these two guys were up there that day, of course, to make a purchase. So Newby had plenty of good cause to be staking out the place. But what they discover is Newby with a shovel, and three graves in a row, with one of the graves partly uncovered, and as of this moment it is not yet clear whether he was digging them up or filling them in."

Monty takes a long pull, absorbing the story. While Grover is sipping, Monty says, "You got all this from your friends?"

The sound of the question makes Grover defensive. "They're not bullshitting, Monty. Why would they?"

"To protect themselves."

"Hey . . ."

"If they were up there, and Newby was up there at the same time, and Newby is a law-enforcement agent, it could eventually boil down to his word against theirs."

"Hey! Whose side are you on?"

"I'm not on anybody's side. I'm just trying to think it through."

"If they hadn't come along when they did, this thing would never have been reported."

"Sounds like you think the police really do have things to hide."

"The police always have things to hide. Listen, there is a guy down in town who is about to blow the whistle on this whole deal."

"And who is that?" Monty asks.

"His name is Larry Fowler."

"Larry Fowler is an asshole."

"You know him?"

"Well enough."

"You know what he is saying?"

"Pretty much."

"And you think it's all coincidence?"

"I'm about like everybody else around here," Monty says. "I don't know what to think."

"You mean about like everybody else who wants to keep his head in the sand."

When he believes he is unmistakably right, Grover has a way of not raising his voice, which annoys Montrose intensely because he is the one Grover learned this from.

"Don't you pull that snot-nose crap with me!" Monty says. "I can still whip your ass if I have to!"

Grover's laugh is a one-note bark, a scoff. "Whipping ass is not what I'm talking about. The question is, what are we going to *do?*"

"When all you have to work with is hearsay and rumor and circumstance . . ."

"Sometimes you really embarrass me, Montrose."

"What's that supposed to mean?"

"You sound like a goddam Republican!"

"Is that your idea of an insult?"

"I just want you to know how you come across. You're sitting here worried about Travis, and then getting misty-eyed about the army and coming home from the war. If Travis hadn't gone into the army he wouldn't be all messed up the way he is now!"

"That's not the same thing. It's not as simple as that!"

"Of course it's the same thing! The army and the police department are exactly the same thing! Their main role in life is to fuck people over!"

"Well, you try and get along without em for a while!"

"That's exactly what I am trying to do!"

Over this last line a loud, sudden, terrifying *waaaaaaaaah* from the van's horn comes blaring right behind their heads. Grover lurches, as if shot. Monty jumps up shouting and finds Leona standing four feet away with one arm through the open window on the driver's side, still pushing at the horn.

27

She wears an apron, and dungarees so wide at the cuff the trouser legs overlap. Half in shadow, she appears to be wearing a long, full skirt. The sleeves of a khaki shirt are bunched at the elbows. Her hair is pulled back for kitchen work. Silhouetted against the house, she could be a pioneer, one month west of St. Louis, Missouri, and heading for Oregon, but a pioneer fed up with the hazards of the trail, venting reservoirs of impatience and unspeakable misgivings in the long, insistent blaring of this horn, which finally ceases just as Holly steps out to the porch to see what's going on.

"You boys are mighty jittery tonight," Leona says.

To still his pounding heart, Montrose presses both hands to his ribs. "I'm too old for that, Lee!"

Grover wishes he could laugh. "Hey, Ma. That was painful."

"Good," she says, unmoved, as if a point has been made in some game she long ago quit expecting to win. "Good."

Lightly Montrose says, "I guess we'll call that the dinner gong."

"There isn't going to be any dinner," she tells him.

He stands half crouched, feeling again like the sergeant caught in crossfire, this time physically, perhaps historically, surrounded—by the son who is despising his Republican heart, and by the wife who has never before leaned on a car horn like this but has always been capable of it, and by Holly, whom he would rather not have observing them at such a moment.

"I burned the food," Lee says, her voice edged with a double accusation: her fault, and somehow his. "I haven't ruined a dinner since . . . I can't remember."

He wants to see her face, steps toward her, trying to maneuver her into the light. If it is merely the ruined dinner, she will respond to touching. He slides an arm across her shoulder. Under the work shirt, the smoothness of her skin has become bark. Her frame is stumplike, unmovable.

Drawing away from his touch, she says, "Monty, I am just about ready to *bust!*"

"Well, don't bust all over me, sweetheart, because I am about ready myself! I have just had to sit here and listen to Grover tell me my head is in the sand, and then had the be-Jesus scared right out of me—"

"I heard what Grover said. I heard that whole conversation. I'd say you *do* have your head in the sand."

"Hey! I don't need that!"

"You don't see me! You don't see Travis! You don't see that girl he brought home! You don't see anything! You sit out here in the dirt like a hillbilly—"

"Travis is twenty-one years old, Leona. He has been around the world. You want me to call out the bloodhounds just because he's late for dinner?"

"I'm not talking about dinner!"

"About what, then?"

"Does everything have to be explained to you in words?"

"That's the only way I have to find out what has put this particular bug up your ass."

He knows it's an inflammatory line. But it stops her for a moment, buying him some time. While she glares, he sorts through the possible triggers for this mood. Like flash cards, they flick past his scanner. Any one could be the key. Or all of them at once. Dinner. Travis. Crystal. Age. Fear. Roaming killer. Strangulation. Isolation. Pickup. Age. Interruptions. Pickup. Aging. Forty-four's a very hard year when you've been that beautiful. . . .

She walks away from him, up the porch steps, past Holly, who wears a painful smile. In the hallway, beyond the phone booth, where he figures they are out of earshot, Monty catches up with her, takes her shoulder.

"C'mon, Lee. What is it?"

She looks up at him, with betrayed eyes, and says slowly, "Nan called."

His mind goes blank.

"Nan?"

"You know who I mean."

He laughs, incredulous, amazed. "Oh, for Christ sake. You mean Nan from the office?"

"How many Nans do you know?"

"What did she call about?"

"Ask Holly. She answered the phone."

"Is that supposed to mean something?"

"It's humiliating. That's what it's supposed to mean. What is Holly going to think? Just a call, from that sex-pot voice she uses on the phone, and no message. She'll see you the next time you're in town. The least you could do is have her call you somewhere else besides here."

"You want me to rent a room? I *live* here! This is crazy. You can't be serious. You're this upset because Nan happened to call from the office?"

Nan was, until this moment, literally the farthest thought from his mind. He would like to convey his innocence to Leona, to appear somewhat offended. It's difficult because he did have something going with Nan when she first came to town, about three years ago, a brief flirtation. She is thirty-three and divorced and very pretty, and they once went for a drive in his car. En route, her period started. After a few clumsy kisses and tasteless jokes, they drove back to the office, and that was it. The end result has been the removal of sex from their cubicle and thus, in Monty's view, a workable professional relationship. But that short drive remains alive somewhere behind his eyes. He knows Leona sees it, a flicker of guilt. He wishes there were some way to conceal the memory.

It's really ridiculous, to have his wife's disposition shattered by a three-year-old nonevent she could have no direct knowledge of.

Nan's call is almost certainly not *it,* however. Nor is the burned dinner *it.*

"What am I supposed to think?" she says. "You're gone all day, gallivanting around. God knows where!"

"I am not gallivanting around! Do you know what that word means? I happened to look it up not long ago. To gallivant is to—"

"I don't give a damn about that! What if something happened? I am stuck out here with no way to get around. What am I supposed to do?"

"Wasn't Grover here all day?"

"With a broken-down van that wouldn't start. He is so much like you, sometimes I want to kick him."

"And Travis was sup*posed* to be here. How could I know . . . ?"

"But Travis was not here, don't you see? He gets that wild look on his face, which you refuse to even talk about—"

" 'Refuse' is not the word!"

"Then he just takes off with . . . Crystal. Disappears. And I don't have any way to get in touch with you. I don't have anybody I can leave messages with. Like Nan does. What if I had to defend myself out here? There's no ammunition for the rifle. Did you know that? If Grover wasn't here, all I'd have would be that old pickup truck—"

"Hold it!"

"Which you know I can't drive."

"You don't *want* to drive!"

"I can't even get it started." Her eyes are brimming now, her voice rising. "It never starts!"

"Of course it starts. You just have to pump it. How many times . . ."

"My feet hardly reach the pedals, Monty. It makes me feel like an infant."

"The one day I use the car . . ."

"You don't know what it's like to be marooned!"

He doesn't want to raise his voice, but his honor is at stake.

"We have gone through this at least a thousand times, Lee. You want me to borrow some money from the bank? All right! I will borrow some money and buy you a Thunderbird so you can drive into town and get your hair puffed up in a beehive like all these gluepussies jamming the highways and the supermarkets. If that is your idea of . . ."

"You make it sound so—"

Her voice breaks. Her eyes are wet, her face stretched tight with hurt. "So cheap," she says. "Don't you hear what I am saying? You know what I feel like today? You want to know what it all brings to mind? I feel like I did when I was pregnant with Travis, and you were spending all your time with that Mexican woman."

"Time with who?"

"Inez. You think I was so blind and naïve I didn't see what was going on?"

"My God, Lee. Do we have to go back that far to find something to feed this . . ."

"Her kids would come up on the porch looking for her, and I'd tell them to go ask you because you were the foreman then, and they would come back and say you were gone too. And there I was, just stuck. You thought you were some kind of southern plantation owner who could just have his way with any woman who was picking for you!"

Mon-TEEEEEEE!

"Now wait a minute, Lee. That's not fair."

"But it's true."

"First of all, it was over twenty years ago. Second of all, if it is true, if that is really true, what the hell makes you think I would choose Inez? She wasn't even my type. She was twenty-five pounds overweight."

Mon-TEEEE!

Ssshhh. Ssshhh.

Mon-TEEEEEE! OHHHHHH. OHHHHH.

"Grover was just turning two years old, and your dad was too sick to work, and I was feeling so bad myself I could hardly walk around, and then having to face down those kids of hers. They knew what was going on. I haven't forgotten that, Monty."

"This is insane. How many times do we have to go through these things? If we haven't solved that one by this time . . ."

"Solving it is beside the point. I don't expect to solve it. I just want you to know how I *feel!*"

"And it is my fault, right? Whatever you're feeling is my fault! What about how I feel? Right now, I feel like a punching bag! Come home to this. I don't have to put up with it, Lee."

Her eyes leave his. Her voice drops.

"It starts me thinking. That's all."

"What starts you thinking?"

"We've made some terrible mistakes."

The way she looks up at him again, the way her muted anger mixes with fear, the fear of going too far, he knows she means "mistakes you've made." It is like a knife that is already lodged inside him, turning now.

She says, "It was a mistake to let Travis go overseas."

"I know that. Don't you think I know that?" *It's your decision, son.* "If I could roll back time two years, I would."

"He was never considerate. Or responsible. Or even very mature."

And there are some things a son can only learn from his father.

"But since he's come back, I swear to you, Monty, he is worse. I don't know him anymore."

Or fail to learn from his father.

"This morning I told him we'd be having dinner with Grover and Holly Belle, and what would he like me to fix, and he just looked at me like I was a total stranger, like he was trying to remember where he had seen me before. Like somebody on drugs. But it wasn't that. It was . . ."

Typical of everything a woman has to put up with out here.
In his belly the blade turns. It is an old knife, crusted with old words, old truths, old warnings he did not heed, or could not, or would not, so that what Travis was, and is, or is not, merges with Monty's regard for Leona, or the lack of it, each word and warning cutting as it turns, like a mass of tiny barnacles fixed to the blade. He cannot take much more of this. Her voice, her eyes are going to make him yell. Make him lunge.

"Listen, Lee, the boy's been through a lot. We don't know exactly what yet. It may well be he's in the middle of some real . . . crisis. You know what I mean?" Monty smiles at what he is about to suggest. It seems so preposterous for a son of his, and yet he half believes it. "Maybe he's got some kind of . . . religion."

This notion seems to penetrate the globe Lee has built around herself.

"It's been known to happen," he goes on. "Take the astronauts. Don't some of them rediscover God when they get back to earth? I'm only guessing, mind you, trying to piece this and that together."

He laughs a short, deferential laugh, which seals over whatever opening his suggestion might have made.

She says, "You're always guessing."

"I am merely a human being, Lee. Don't give me that look! You think you have some claim on understanding?"

"Something is going to happen, Monty! I know it. I just know it."

"Goddam it, then! What do you want me to do?"

"I *know* what you are going to do! You're going to handle it the way you handle everything!" Her voice is rising fast, a shrill pitch, to meet whatever he sends next. "Take your time! Drag your feet! Look the other way! Think it over!"

Now he roars. "Don't do this!"

Her eyes fill with fire and tears, her voice assaults him. "Let me do all the worrying! And then when it happens . . ."

"WHAT!" he bellows. "WHEN WHAT HAPPENS? WHAT IN THE HELL DO YOU EXPECT ME TO DO?"

He is standing over her, arms out from his sides, fingers curved as if he is about to lift his hands and take her by the neck. She seems prepared for this. Eyes fiercely locked with his, she does not move. His hands rise to his own neck, slapping against the tendons, as he throws his head back, in furious restraint, and steps away from her, into the unlit dining room.

28

BAKERSFIELD, 1959

Pale smoke, like weeds burning on a hot, still day, fills a dining room, cuts through the fried smell of chicken, while women yell fire and the startled men raise their eyes, peer up from waiting plates toward the window. Montrose sticks his head out and sees them running down the driveway, toward the yard. He has to smirk, inwardly, recalling his own boyhood. He also has to punish them, for Lee's sake, for her humiliation at this grand reunion that has brought her kinfolk west from Oklahoma City for the first time, and south from Hayward and north from San Diego. She is showing off her husband and her boys. The deep-fried chicken has just drawn dozens of salivating cousins and uncles and nephews and aunts toward the table, such a multitude that no one notices two of the cousins are missing. A brief quiet has fallen upon the room for the moment of blessing. The florid host has solemnly begun to thank Jesus for the gathering together of so many blood kin and loved ones in the presence of so many fine, fat, savory chickens, and here comes this rise of smoke from the floor, from lit rolls of old film, stink bombs tossed through the dining room window, adding an unforgivably acrid reek to the wings and thighs and drumsticks. Monty, catching up with them in the backyard, whips Grover first, and most, because he is older and, if we can judge by the guilt all over his freckled face, seemingly in charge, and whips Travis less, because he is younger and, at age seven, already seems to see the comedy of what they have done. There is a look in his eye, around the mouth, which seduces Monty's hand to land lighter on his backside, and Montrose instantly regrets it. Travis sees the comedy of this act too. In memory the hand swings light, and Travis smirks. . . .

29

Montrose prefers to write at night, after the house is quiet. Three nights a week he locks himself in his study with a glass of Jack Daniel's and puts his column together. He is sitting there tonight, tapping at the keys, trying to tap his way past what was dredged up in the hallway, and only partially succeeding. His outburst was like a transfusion, emptying her system, filling his. In retrospect this is what he most resents—the transfusion of rage. By now she is no doubt defused, contrite. But Monty could not go to her at this moment if his life depended on it. He sits here mentally shouting his rebuttals upward through the ceiling toward the second floor.

"What the hell should I do?" he cries. "Become somebody else? I am forty-six years old! I am what I am! Vain. Weak. Frail. Losing my hair. Maybe my grip. I try to keep track. I fuck up a lot. Take it or leave it!"

He had thought that all this would be over by now, that with the hoped-for dignity of the middle years some things about him would no longer require defending, would be acceptable. But once again, as usual, the niggling fears and embedded resentments find some toehold in her mind, and start to swarm, until she rediscovers the fundamental objection—which is the way the circumstances of their life have been unalterably shaped by *his character*. After twenty-five years of marriage he understands this process. Later on, a few days from now, he will no longer hold it against her. When the storm is over and the world a sunny place again he will tell himself, they will tell each other, remind each other, of what they have already noted many times—that this is one thing marriage is for. Life starts to pile up on you, everything going to hell, you cannot bear it one more second, and though it is on one hand the way of the world for this to occur, you can never get much satisfaction from blaming the way of the world for whatever has unsettled your life. You want something specific to blame, preferably a live person who will stand there in front of you and take some real abuse. This, in Monty's view, is the "for worse" clause in the marriage contract. He has learned to endure such moments, knowing he will be able to look back upon them as a service he was willing to provide, and Lee provides for him, when his turn comes around, although it is not in Monty's nature to vent much rage out loud. He will carry it around in his jaws and in his belly the way his father did, so that there are other signals she has had to learn to read and live with. In the calmer moments he can love all this about her as much . . .

Scratching gravel interrupts this reverie.

. . . as much as he loves her hair.

In a pause between the sentences he types and the sentences he utters in his mind, in an interval when the clicking keys are silent, and the night seems to have timed itself into an instant of pure and eerie stillness, he hears footsteps in the driveway that borders this side of the house.

He moves to the window. His desk lamp makes the glass opaque. He listens, squinting, thinks he hears footsteps receding toward the barn. His heart leaps. He is certain four feet have tried to sneak past his window and that tomorrow morning Travis, as he always used to do after a late night or a long weekend or a near arrest for disorderly conduct, will show up for breakfast in a heavy fog, as if he has been right here all along and full of amazement that anyone could be concerned about him.

He stands awhile at the window, then decides to catch Trav before they go to bed, to put his own mind at ease. He walks outside, heading for the barn light, searching for some line to open with, to set the appropriate tone, something like: "We thought you'd reenlisted," or "If you don't like the accommodations we can always rent to somebody else."

The light spills out through a half-open curtain, and beyond that curtain, before he can knock, he sees Crystal about to undress. She has a taste for tight T-shirts with enticing slogans written across the chest. This one says something about mountain climbing. He can't quite make it out. The reading lamp is behind her, and now the slogan is gone, as the T-shirt rises. She wears nothing underneath it. He expects to see Travis loom up in front, or behind her. Were Monty there where Travis is, and twenty years younger, that is what he'd be doing now, drawing Crystal to him, pawing at her, unable to keep his hands away. He doesn't want to watch this, does not want to be the voyeur to his own son's love-making. And yet of course he does. He lingers a moment longer, listening for the voice, the first move.

There is no voice. There is no movement. She is just standing there with the shirt dangling, as fixed in time and place as Monty is, he the watcher, she the watched. He was wrong about Travis. There is no lover here tonight. There is only Crystal backlit by the reading lamp and Monty lurking at the edge of his own orchard, peeking through branches.

Should he approach? Knock? Wait till she covers herself, then ask about Travis? No. Better not. She might get the wrong idea. Let it wait till morning. If the news were bad, she would have knocked on *his* door, stopped outside his window. It strikes him that perhaps she did stop there. Not to bring news, but just to look. As he stands now. Looking in at him? Those were her footsteps in the gravel, were they not? The thought beguiles him. Buzzing with whiskey, seduced by apple scents, he flatters himself with this possibility. The wrong idea. He begins to conjure fuzzy love scenes. She too is watching now, listening for something. Waiting. Perhaps she heard his footsteps approach. Or perhaps she's waiting to hear them. He tells himself he knows what she is waiting for. He thinks of himself as a provider. How easy it would be to knock, as if looking for Travis, to enter the room, to confide things. He suspects she would allow this. God knows it's what he needs right now. She has a taste for veterans. Perhaps this is what Travis has discovered. Too many tastes. For too many veterans. Perhaps this is why he has been able to abandon her. Under such circumstances it would be by far the wisest move.

Monty knows he too should move, head back to the house, stop titillating himself with vague, vain fantasies. Crystal is a user, a consumer. He intuits this. And how do you prepare a son for such loaded attractions? Well . . . you can't. What a pity. It's like the mini-cathedrals at Holy City, the arcade of Temptations. You have to pay the money at least one time, to see the splinters on the wooden legs of Queen Elizabeth of Egypt.

And yet . . .

What an extraordinary situation, to have this plentiful young woman standing alone in his barn an hour past midnight. It is almost as if Travis delivered her and then walked away, so that Montrose might stroll out here at his leisure to contemplate these rare endowments.

He prays she does not move until he can absorb her to his full satisfaction. There is a mystery here, something exotic. But also familiar. The truth is, she reminds him of Leona. It is not a resemblance. It is another kind of echo. A matter of proportion. Some bodies have one feature a man will pursue in and of itself, as if the eyes or the elegant neck or the belly or the bosom has some life of its own and might somehow be mated with separately. Other bodies are so designed, neither the eye nor the mind can separate any part from the rest. The entire body is lusted after. One imagines ecstatic head-to-toe caresses, and long, sinuous sine waves of coupling. So it is with Crystal. And so it was with Lee, the first time he spied her, in this same orchard, not forty yards from where he stands right now, when the ranch was still four times its present acreage, and she was a pieceworker's teen-age daughter gathering windfall fruit by the lug, late-season Delicious, red as blood.

The low sun was behind her, pouring through the trees, making a gauze scrim of the cotton shift she wore for picking, and though her hips were finely delineated, her lips full, her neck glossy with a second skin of moisture over the sunbrown, and around the neck loose wisps of brown hair glowed against the light, there was no one feature he could concentrate his eighteen-year-old's swooning lust upon. He wanted all of her the first time he saw her. He still does. And he deeply regrets the stages they must now live through—this inner rage, which for him is already waning toward simple anger, then the snow of pride, and the melting of pride, and finally the mere inertia of apartness—before their eyes can meet, ready to abandon all defense, and say, "It's over, it's okay now," and then their bodies touch, confirming it.

Crystal's white trousers fall out of sight below the window sill. White hip flesh above slim dark legs. She stretches luxuriously. A living fold-out. She flicks off the reading lamp. Darkness in the room, and in the orchard.

30

MONTY'S DREAM

He doesn't eat much breakfast. They have orders to advance. That makes it easy. No choice but to move toward what is coming. Insects are everywhere, tiny, in close to the eyes, and trees. It is silent, except for the tiny buzzing. He moves along in battle dress through bugs and trees and vines and heat. He stops to shove his helmet back, to drag the sweat from his forehead, and he sees them first, two men hunched loping with rifles, bayonets. The one in front is youthful, about his age. Montrose has an instant to study the lean build, the measured stride, the eyes which finally find his in the foliage. Monty lifts his rifle, aims, and does not think. He squeezes the trigger and fires at the eyes. He hears a gargled gasping that is louder than the shot, and watches the young man fall.

31

LEONA'S DREAM

She is driving into town when she feels the car's front wheels begin to shimmy. She hopes it will go away. It doesn't. The ground is wriggling beneath her car. A hairline crack appears in the road ahead. This has happened before. She knows exactly what to do. She closes her eyes and concentrates on a building she just passed, its flatness, the texture of the wall. It is made of brick and plaster, and bits of it catch under nails if you scratch it. She can feel it with her hands. Against her calves and elbows it's prickly, where she presses back, just as the crack in the street tears open. She watches loose cobblestones drop into the maw. A buggy driver reining back loses control of his rig. His horse lunges clear, dragging the buggy along at a dangerous angle, and two wheels drop into the crevice, screeching hubs against the cobbles, tossing sparks.

She hears a guttural scrape as if an old man is clearing his throat. The driver cries, "Look out!" Above her a wall of bricks is about to topple.

"This way!" he cries. "Quickly! Quickly!"

The driver now is clear of the ditch, but on the far side, strenuously reining his terrified horse. To join him she must leap the crevice. He sees her hesitate. "It's your only chance!"

She takes two steps and leaps, screaming. The earth shudders, and the crack grows wider, spreading between her outstretched legs. Knowing better, she glances down, sees the rats set free from sewer lines, the sewage mixing rapidly with sea water pouring in from somewhere. Rats are swimming in the putrid brine. Her foot, landing on the far edge, gives way under a loose cobble. She slips, grabbing at stones, sliding as if down a slope of hot gravel. Her toes are in the water when the buggy driver reaches, pulls her clear, lifts her to the leather seat. Again the earth heaves, a curse for all those still on foot, a blessing for the buggy and the desperate horse. This new thrust launches them, and they gallop off in a billow of plaster dust just ahead of the bricks.

Down broken streets they bolt, past twisted curbing, flying windows, tongues of flame. Gilt domes hang overhead, inverted like monstrous lamps. Then cobblestones give way to dirt. Houses float apart, become gardens, open fields, sand dunes stretching to the ocean. The buggy wheels are slowed by deep, white sand. Finally the horse stops, slavering, spent. They turn to watch the distant flames.

Leona says, "Do you still respect me?"

Montrose removes his derby hat, swabs his brow, his damp plastered forelock. He grins and shrugs uncomprehendingly.

"For jumping in so easily," she explains. "Just riding off with you?"

"You had no choice."

"That isn't what I mean. Do you still respect me?"

"Look. Look out there. Isn't that an incredible view?"

Again she looks at the burning skyline, enlarged every few seconds by faraway explosions, like cannon fire, that send new bursts of flame into the picture. It is, she thinks, like a film, like a long documentary seen late at night on television. She feels his hand on her thigh, and clutches the seat edge, but allows it. She does owe him something, after all. And this spectacle in the distance, framed by the water's curve and that fan of piers, contained so that one can sit back and regard it in a single glance, this in itself is warming, makes her feel lofty, and languorous. She lets herself be fondled. He is fooling around with her blouse, her skirt.

"We shouldn't," she says, reveling in the open dunes around them. Far away from this safe promontory, water is rising. It covers the piers now, trickles across twisted streetcar tracks. Seeing the streams of refugees pouring away from the city in every direction but theirs, compassion moves her to whisper, "Perhaps we should . . ." Unable to finish, she shuts her eyes while her petticoats go, her stockings. Her hair falls loose. Whatever she owes, whatever he is claiming, all this is forgotten in the hot touches they now exchange, the white knolls of sand, and silent cannons spurting flashes on the screen.

32

LEONA

The next morning over coffee she describes this dream to Holly Belle. The house is quiet. The men are gone.

"It sounds a bit like San Francisco," Holly says. "Sounds like 1906."

"I guess that's right. My personal version anyway."

"Didn't you tell me something like this a few months back?"

"I probably did. It comes and goes."

"You like recurring dreams."

"I do, yes," Lee says.

"They're my favorite kind. You dream one a few times, it gets sort of comfortable. You can relax and just go with it, even if it's very frightening."

"It's like a rerun of a good thriller."

"I don't see what respect has to do with it, though," Holly says. "Where does that fit in?"

"You have to understand that the first time I heard about this was right after I met Monty's mother. She was born in San Francisco, you know. She lived through the whole thing. She was quite a storyteller, and she started telling me this one before we ever got married. I was about seventeen at the time. It sounded almost Biblical to me. I just gobbled it up. She would change it around, of course. She would exaggerate things and add things. It was her favorite story. In later years she could make it sound like the absolute end of the world. She was eight when it happened. I guess it was the high point of her life."

Holly sips her coffee, waiting, watching Lee with puzzled eyes.

"So I think of it now as something I almost borrowed from her," Lee goes on. "You see, honey, when we came out here in the thirties we didn't have anything. We didn't even have any dreams left. My daddy had been so beat down by wind and dust and lost crops, and then dragging us kids all up and down this coast looking for work . . . Why, the first time I saw Montrose, I was literally down on my knees in the dirt scooping up windfall apples. And he was the ranch owner's *son.* Can you imagine it? I suppose part of me has never got over that."

"Now I see it," Holly says, nodding, sympathetic. "There is some part of you that still feels indebted, because he somehow . . . rescued you."

"That's the way it sounds, doesn't it?"

"I wouldn't sell myself short, Lee."

"Well, we're just trying to piece this dream together, hon. There are all kinds of ways to read a dream."

"I have to tell you something. I have a high regard for Montrose. But he is like a lot of men I know."

"In what way?"

Holly gazes hard at her, then hesitates, turns toward the window. "A man will go to a lot of trouble to keep you boxed in."

"It's true, hon. But I doubt that most men think of it that way."

"You take Montrose and that pickup. Or you take Grover and my brakes. Now, the Packard is my passport. It gives me liberty from time to time. He knows that, and he just lets it sit there."

"For him it's just another piece of equipment to worry about."

"Why is it always so hard to get your point across?"

"Men are hardly ever listening, hon," Lee says.

"Don't you ever get tired of that?"

"We all do."

Holly laughs her desperate, vulnerable laugh. "I am starting to think I may not have the nerves for it."

"Control is the key. Keeping yourself under control. Men aren't much good at that. A man tends to get caught up. He forgets about everything but that one thing that's on his mind. If keeping a man is important to you, you soon figure out that you're the one has to keep things under control. Look what happened to me last night. I said things I would have better left unsaid. But I couldn't help it. Now I guess I deserve whatever that brings along."

"Deserve?" Holly cries. "What does deserve have to do with it? All you did was express yourself! You have a right to tell him what's on your mind, get it out into the open. These killings would send anybody up the wall!"

"But it drives a man away, behaving like that. Monty's out in the orchard somewhere puttering around. I may not hear from him for days."

"Grover does the same thing. He goes out in his field somewhere and works up a sweat. I tell you, Lee, I get so agitated thinking about this, I have to go pee."

"It's the coffee. A natural diuretic."

"I'm going to go pee right this minute. Don't you move."

She watches Holly rush from the room, then turns to gaze out the window. They have been sitting on stools at the long table in Leona's workroom. This is her refuge. Her empire. She dreams here. She also entertains here. Two afternoons each month she hosts a meeting here, for the members of SCALE (the Standing Committee for an Aesthetic and Livable Environment). Then her room is bursting with opinions and documents. Right now it is quiet, the whole world is quiet, just Lee sipping coffee in her light-filled room. Facing south, and painted white, it always seems overflowing with light.

Crayon sketches on long sheets of butcher paper cover one wall. Below them lie rolls of burlap and linen and monk's cloth. Balls of yarn and spools of fine silk thread are racked in tiers near the high, padded stool she works from. Stretched on the table, with wooden hoops clamped around two half-sewn polar bears, lies the work in progress—a beach scene, about twelve feet long and five feet wide. It's a sandy beach bordering a blue-green ocean. Wild animals romp and leap along the beach and around the lifeguard stands, red rhinos, purple leopards, sky-blue grizzlies, orange kangaroos and armadillos. Offshore a few foreshortened people can be seen floating in the water. Across this scene, as if Lee is speculating that she might stitch it in here somewhere, today's paper has been spread. Low on the front page there is a picture of Larry Fowler, who seems to be waiting impatiently for his chance to enter the morning's conversation.

But Lee is not looking at the paper right now, or at the tapestry in progress. She is looking out the window and think-ing again of Mrs. Doyle, whom Holly brings to mind. They used to sit like this, like sisters. On days like today Holly is her solace, the sister she wished she'd had when she was grow-ing up in that truckful of hillbilly brothers, not one of whom had any thought in mind after the age of fourteen but chasing women and driving cars and cultivating a moonshine nose and a beer belly he could rub his hands across on Sunday afternoon. Though she has never said so out loud, she looks on Holly as successor to what has been passed down to her from Mrs. Doyle, a lineage not of blood but of sensibility. And although they have not yet spelled it out in so many words, she feels the same kinship of vision with Holly Belle that she felt with Mrs. Doyle, a vision that has expanded steadily in the years since the San Francisco legend first caught in her mind, enriched by lore from such works as the Book of Revelation and Edgar Cayce's predictions about worse and clearly interconnected upheavals of the land and the oceans. On candlelit evenings Lee will speak with playful seriousness of Atlantis, of Pele, the Hawaiian volcano goddess, of melting polar caps, and the fearsome "Ring of Fire" which encircles the Pacific Ocean from Mexico to Chile to New Guinea to Japan to the Aleutians and back around again to San Francisco. It is an enormous, shifting image that sometimes includes the complete disappearance of certain points on the map, such as the Indonesian isle of Krakatoa, which exploded in 1883, and the equally strange emergence of new locations, such as the island of Surtsey, which happened to bubble up from below the surface of the North Atlantic in November 1963, the same month John F. Kennedy was assassinated, thus opening the pattern to include the disastrous reputations of Lee Harvey Oswald, Sirhan Sirhan, Richard Speck, Juan Corona, and eventually, a year or so from now, after hindsight provides an easier perspective on this current reign of terror, the unaccountable assassin now at work in her own backyard. Each of these events is a signal, a portent, another step toward the apocalyptic turning point in the near or distant future, which appalls and mesmerizes and sustains her.

As a legend, as a pastime, as a never-finished edifice in the mind, this has served her well. She looks upon it now as a very private kind of inheritance, passed on to her, in a sense, when Mrs. Doyle passed away. It lives inside her the way the bright-hued, many-figured tapestries live, unfolding from her workroom to cover and decorate the walls of this house, and the booths at the street fairs down in town, and the shops in Carmel and Sausalito where her works have been shown from time to time. These mosaics of legend and stitchery, they are like patchwork quilts she can keep adding to for the rest of her life. On a day like today they are among the few things she can genuinely consider hers. The rest of this world out here—the ranch, the house, the barns, the orchard, this whole stretch of countryside they ride and walk through, as well as her oldest son, and Monty himself—on days like this, when she is feeling low and lonely, it is clear that none of these things belong to her. After twenty-five years she is still a

visitor here, a new arrival, an attachment. Is it possible to feel
boxed in, as Holly says, and at the same time left out? Yes.
On a day like this, that is how she feels.

She used to think she had a special hold on Travis, that he
belonged to her. She isn't sure anymore. Travis, she had felt,
was stamped by her from birth. Now he has slipped out of
reach, and this fills her with a sadness deeper than she can
show or find words for. She couldn't even make it clear to
Monty. All she did was drive him farther from her. She knew
what she was doing, and she couldn't stop herself. Dragging
up Inez like that. It was stupid. A mistake. Inez was not at all
what she had on her mind. And yet Inez is always there somewhere. Why is that? she asks herself. Because in all their years
of marriage, that was the one time she truly felt his soul sliding
from her. She has never quite understood why Inez would be
the one to hold that kind of power over him. She *was* twenty-
five pounds overweight, and hauling three kids around. But
the power was there, and Lee knows what held Monty to the
marriage then was not love. It was duty or, perhaps, mere
guilt. She hates the memory of that time, when all she had
left was the voice of Montrose speaking empty words and his
body gliding through the house. That is one thing she has
never done to him. She has never allowed anyone to undermine their marriage. There have been flirtations. There were
two adventures, years ago, opportunities that came along that
she could manage discreetly, that no one would find out about,
adventures she herself could control, and which Monty would
never more than dimly suspect, because she would never become what he became during the Inez period, allowing the
very last shred of his affection for her to be stolen away.

Even now, it is easy for her to become self-righteous on
this subject, if she isn't careful. Self-righteousness is one thing
she cannot stand in others. She would not be guilty of it herself. It is what most annoys her about Montrose, his most
Protestant trait. When he is angry or on the defensive he can
always find the words to affirm his own unassailable rightness.

Something of the preacher in him. He puts so much stock in words. She has never been good with words. This is why she's thankful to have Holly here this morning. They are of the same mind. Holly sees right through the words, in the way Travis used to, up until the time he started high school, sees the pictures in Leona's mind, makes connections words can never make. At this very moment, for example, as Lee herself is on the verge of visualizing how she is going to get through such a day, Holly returns to the workroom saying, "Leona, I feel like driving into town!"

"Now, you have touched a nerve there, Holly. I wouldn't mind that one bit."

"If they are just going to take off in their cars and their tractors and leave us here, who needs them?"

"We could go have lunch out on the wharf," Lee says.

"I was thinking of a crab salad."

"What about clam chowder?"

"And a Heineken's."

"Yes, that sounds good. Heineken's and a crab salad. There's nothing like it."

"After that," Holly says, "we could just fool around in town and catch the rally at The Heart tonight. Grover's band is supposed to play, if he can get hold of everybody in time."

Leona leans forward now to study the eyes of Fowler, who she realizes has been staring at her for some time from the front page of the paper. He is sallow, bearded, his black hair merges with a shaded wall behind, his eyes suspicious, as if he had been forced to pose for a mug shot. The caption says he has formed some kind of citizens group.

"If this fellow's in charge," Lee says, "I'd just as soon go to a movie. You ask me, he could very easily be the killer."

"Grover knows him, thinks he might turn out to be a hero."

"With eyes like that?"

"You can't always tell a hero by the eyes."

"How does a fellow like this get in charge of a public meeting? This man is capable of murder. He looks like Charles Manson."

"It's true. He sort of does. Of course, a flash bulb can do that. Or just staring too hard at a camera. You look at old photographs from the turn of the century, everybody looks a little bit startled."

"But don't you think a lot of people are starting to look like Charles Manson? I'll bet some of these young people actually work at it, getting that fanatical look on the face. They think it's fashionable."

"They used to live around here, you know," Holly says. "The Manson Family. Before they killed Sharon Tate. Some of them anyway. For a couple of weeks. So I've heard. They had a place up in the hills."

"Don't even say that. It makes me sweat."

"It's what I've heard. Then they moved on. But still. I have heard people say some of them stayed in the area."

Leona listens a moment as the sound of Monty's far-off tractor comes putt-putting through the trees. Up before anyone else, he hauled his spraying rig down to the far end of the orchard, his way—she knows—of not dealing with her for a while. Grover, as promised, left early, heading up to the A-frame to work on his septic tank. Hillbillies, both of them. Just like her brothers. And Travis—no telling where he and Crystal have run off to. She doesn't want to think about that. She stares again at Fowler's photograph.

"You know," she says, "it'd be a comfort—in a terrible, terrible way it'd be a comfort—if what this fellow says is true. It's an awful thing to think that the police could get mixed up in all this. But at least we'd know then what was at the bottom of it. That is what I can't stand. The not knowing."

"The police have some explaining to do," Holly says. "No doubt. That's what the rally is supposed to be all about."

"If I had to make a choice, I'd rather have it be the police and the dealers in cahoots, than people from the Manson

Family on the loose again. You know what I mean? At least dope dealers stick to killing their own kind. That is an awful choice to have to make. But that is the way the world is going."

"I was reading in the *National Enquirer* that the homicide rate in the United States is seventh highest."

"Is that all?"

"Higher than Japan and Sweden, but lower than Mexico and Colombia and places like that."

"Why is it? Why is it people everywhere just can't learn to get along?"

She glances down the row of trees, as the low breeze bears toward them the tractor's distant stuttering. *Why is it,* she hears the echo in her mind, *why is it people everywhere just can't learn* . . . and suddenly she is going to cry. For that question. And for Holly Belle, whose face is now so open, so sisterly. She is going to cry for Holly's youth and for all the years she has yet to live through, years Lee wishes she could have back, and for the sisters and daughters she never had, and for the man-surrounded life she herself has led. Her fathers, her brothers, her uncles, her sons, and her husband all crowd in upon her. Even from a quarter of a mile away Monty sends the metallic blupping to remind her of what she has spent her life doing—accommodating men. Here with Holly her mood is a blend of loneliness, and compassion for all wives and mothers, and the urge to embrace this young sister of hers. How much easier it would have been raising daughters, she thinks. They spread out the task of dealing with men, and there would have been many more times like this, just sitting around as she and Mrs. Doyle used to do.

It all comes welling up, and in order not to weep, she moves to the window, draws a curtain farther back, to let in more sun.

"We'll take my car," she says. "It ought to have plenty of gas. Monty can use the pickup if he has to go someplace. But Saturdays he usually works all day around the place. It's been ages since I went to The Cheating Heart. You going to wear what you have on?"

"I might change my top."

"I'm just going to leave the dishes."

"Yes, leave the dishes! In fact, sell the dishes!" Holly cries, springing to her feet. "I want to tell you something." She steps over next to Leona.

"This is a secret confession. You are the only one who knows. I have had it with dishes. I would switch over to paper plates in a second. But Grover is so ruthlessly ecological, he'd be counting the trees it would cost us to serve three meals a day."

"Or he'd be making you scrape off the paper plates so you could use them again."

"Oh, God," Holly shouts, as they break into wild laughter. "God, that's exactly what he'd do!"

33

GROVER

He works with his shirt off, blue bandanna rolled and tied around his forehead Apache style. The septic tank is buried forty feet beyond his A-frame, connected by a drain line he is now uncovering. He stops, leans on the shovel, wipes his brow with his wrist, and looks back along the trench behind him, the broken tiles tossed up, the root ends he has chopped loose, and the black snake of plastic pipe he'll install today. He doesn't mind this. It's dirty. But it's clean. There is a beginning and a middle and an end. Start early and if he does it right it'll be good for twenty years or more. Each day spent like this is a kind of brick neatly placed in the foundation he is trying to lay out for his life. And the beer he drinks tonight between sets will have twice the taste because it will be well earned.

He bends to the shovel, pushing wiry legs against it, tossing up another scoop of topsoil made damp with the leaking of the tiles. Ten feet to go, and it feels good, alone for a while, just himself and the field and the work, making progress, and no way he can be interrupted or disturbed. Some people yearn for interruptions. Not Grover. He measures an event by whether or not it allows him to continue to produce. If the phone rang inside, he wouldn't stop to answer it. If a car pulled into the driveway, he wouldn't turn. He regards the murders this way. So far they have been more a nuisance than anything else, something to be dealt with quickly in the mind, in order to avoid the waste of energy he heard his parents engage in last night, in order to get back to his crops, his equipment, his music.

He sees himself as a doer. If he read the Bible he would take this Scripture as his motto: "By his works a man is justified." He has given his work a lot of thought, and it is backed up now by a kind of faith that has come clear during the two years since Travis left. A faith not in God or in country or in the future of technology or the perfectability of mankind, but in his own capacities and in the turnings of the earth. He wants to talk to his brother about this. After Travis joined, Grover could only shout at him, about ending the draft, about ending the war, about taking America apart for a total overhaul. He remembers trembling with impotent fury and waving magazine clippings in his brother's face, photos of malnourished Asian children burned by American napalm, of Pentagon generals seen laughing at the embassy in Saigon.

When Travis left, Grover talked about leaving too, for Cuba, or Canada, to avoid the army. Monty prevailed upon him to try for CO status. When it was granted, that first summer, he began his alternative service, driving a truck for Goodwill Industries, and he started looking around for a piece of land. He wasn't sure why. He didn't see how it fit with what was coming from his mouth. But it felt right. By that time he and Holly were living together. She wanted out of the Bay Area, which was "getting ugly," as she put it, "ready to catch fire." They talked about forming a commune, they talked about starting a band.

He picked up these two acres for a good price because the road was steep and long neglected, and the house was gone, burned down a year earlier by the old man who'd built it, trying to smoke out a wasp's nest with an oil-rag torch. Everything else remained, in one form or another—the sewage system, the well, the outbuildings, the basic fencing. Grover put cash down, then borrowed some more, using Monty's house as collateral, to build his A-frame. He told people he'd never have to finish the payments. This whole country is going under, he would say with a grin—the banks, the post office, the whole shitteree.

He was cynical enough to look forward to this with a grim and vengeful pleasure. Now the war is over, and the country has not collapsed. It has just crumbled a little. He sees that this is what it's going to be like. America is not going to fall. It will just continue very gradually to fall apart. The evidence is all around him. Flimsy housing that buckles in the first rain. Garbage piling up in city streets. Flabby people staying soft on white bread and television. News from old Berkeley friends of suicide attempts by overdose. His own brother's mind perhaps permanently blown by who knows what.

Grover wants to find another way to do it. He wants to survive, and he figures the answer lies in mastering techniques that will work for him no matter what the ups and downs of the larger society. He would like to trust America. He knows he can't. Too late for that. He would like to trust Pacific Gas and Electric, but knows he can't. He would like to trust General Motors and Safeway and United Airlines and NBC and the Teamsters Union, which controls the life flow of manufactured goods to every corner of the nation, but he knows he can't. Everything he sees is either top-heavy or crumbling at the edges, or both.

"I used to be in love with the country," he told Montrose not long ago. "Because I loved it, I got hooked on its failures. I expected too much, was my problem. You have to get past expecting so much. You have to get past loving it, then you have to get past hating it. Then you can start from wherever you are and just live there, be a person on the earth, in this region or in that region, wherever it may be."

Now that his Goodwill stint is over, he picks up carpentry jobs here and there, but spends most of his time on his vegetables, his chickens and ducks, his bluegrass band, and putting this place back in good running order, which today has brought him around to the drain line, installed fifty years ago when the original house was built and now just too worn out and root-torn to mend.

His shovel scrapes at the last section of piping, where it joins the buried tank. He stops again, steps out of his trench and over to the garden faucet, where he leans to drink, looking then across at the rows of bright leaves popping from the potatoes they planted last month, and the long bean rows, Kentucky Wonders just starting to reach out for the poles, and beyond them a thicket of horse beans, his green manure crop, planted in the fall for fertilizer and shoulder-high now, white-budded. It will be cool in there between the rows.

He walks to the horse beans and steps in among the plants and hunkers down, letting the buds and shady leaves brush his neck and shoulders, thinking that as soon as the drain line is done and the beans cultivated, he had better get around to chopping down these stalks and digging them under, before the next rain, and for that matter, he had better turn his compost heap. Something has been burrowing in from the bottom. He is going to have to patch those bins. Better take a look at it now. He wouldn't want the heap to go bad. The heap and the horse beans are right at the center of his enterprise. This is the original way of the world, is it not? The original revolution. Decay and regeneration. The rhythms and cycles of the earth. Going around in circles. The horse beans grow tall, fall over, rot, revitalize the soil with nitrogen, to nourish next season's beets and lettuce and chard. The mounds of green garbage hibernate for three or four months and become new earth, each heap renewing his trust in this process. Believing this makes it easier to cope with America, which has flourished awhile and is now in decline, and it's nothing to get paralyzed about. Something new always arises from the trash and aftermath of each year's crop.

Throwing back the black tarpaulin, he nudges his shovel into a mosaic of eggshells and banana peels and coffee grounds and rotting leaves and earthworms and apple cores and hair clippings and manure trucked up from the goat farm. He turns it for the pleasure of the turning and to discover whatever has been tunneling under the tarp. Some kind of rodent, he suspects, which he will have to get rid of. It takes a lot of killing to make a garden grow—snails, aphids, cabbage moths, gophers, all these otherwise harmless creatures who won't take no for an answer.

Digging the layers back, he hears a tiny squeal, the teeniest kind of outcry, like the squeak of a shoe. He hears it again and gingerly pushes under a mat of old grass. He lifts it, and underneath lie eight hairless purple-pink ratlets, each about an inch long, squirming over one another in alarm, now that their protective nest has been overturned. Newborn rats, totally defenseless, with mom and dad gone off somewhere, so frail their combined squealing doesn't add up to a kettle's hiss, and if Grover leaves them here they will soon infest his heap and, in winter, his house. He doesn't hesitate. He lifts his shovel, bellowing into the pristine, breezeless morning of his field and his garden, "Goddam motherfuckers!" cursing not these poor doomed ones, but their parents or whatever source of proliferation requires him to kill.

He slams the shovel down flat against the squirming brood. In the instant before his scoop hits, they look to him like human fetuses three months along. The squealing stops. When he lifts his shovel they are squashed against its underside, pink and purple, sticking to it. He scoops out the mess and carries it beyond his fence and he thinks again of the Pentagon generals whose bombs fell for so long and from so high above, raining down upon the villages of Southeast Asia. He has heard on the radio, just this morning, that they continue to fall in Cambodia, even though truces and pacts have been signed. It strikes Grover that in the minds of the generals there must be a similar kind of justification for the slaughter from above. He imagines that a person holding bombers in his hand, instead of shovels, could regard the entire world this way.

34

With his engine off, Montrose can hear everything, from the tick of dragonfly wings to the deep-earth pulsing of the crustal plates where they meet beyond the low end of his orchard. It is a nonsound, which quivers many nondecibels beneath the leaf whisper and crush of grass, such as the ocean and land make on a day when there is no surf, and silent water slides along kissing the sandy beach.

He is listening to this after four jiggling hours on and off the seat of his small-time farmer's treaded rig. Up since six, at work since seven, he is now sitting back against an apple trunk, just as his granddad used to do in high-country Tennessee, pouring a little Bushmill's into his thermos cup, still hoping to work and sweat and sniff and listen his way to some interval of repose, when he hears a human sound, way down here where there isn't supposed to be anyone but him, the nearby whish and scuff of feet moving through weeds and sun-dried topsoil beneath his trees.

He squints down the rows and sees white dungarees coming toward him and he assumes it is Leona hiking out to make some kind of peace offering. He prepares to brace himself, not ready yet to meet her eyes and all they know about him and are willing once again to accept, and all that those eyes will see about herself, reflected in his. Not ready for the wife and the fun-house mirrors their four eyes make, receding into one another year by year, he feels regret and a little tide of resentment. She should know better than to interrupt him now. When the approaching figure ducks under a low bough, a Rolleiflex swings down. When the face comes into view,

Monty's arms and belly turn to water. The water of weak, demuscularized, lascivious dread. He is not ready for this one either.

With an odd grin, she calls out, "Hey, Monty. What're you doing way over here?"

"Having a cup of coffee," he says. He does not mention the Bushmill's. Instinctively he slides the bottle around behind the tree. "What about you?"

"Taking a walk," she says. "A few pictures. I love your orchard. I've been coming out here every morning."

"You want some coffee?"

"I've already had three or four cups. Any more, I'll get so wired I won't be able to hold my hands still."

She drops down in front of him, crossing her legs campfire style, and regards him with a look that implies she is in the mood for something. He could be jumping to conclusions. So easy to get the wrong idea about Crystal. Written across the bosom of today's T-shirt are the words JAZZ IS LIKE A BANANA. Each time her eyes leave his, he studies this slogan, trying to interpret it.

"What I just said isn't true," she says. "I haven't been down this way before. I heard your tractor. I came down to ask you for a ride into town. I had to bum a ride out here last night and almost got assaulted on the way. These two absolute creeps who claimed they were friends of Travis's—"

"Hold it. One thing at a time. Where was Travis? Did he just abandon you?"

"He was supposed to meet me at The Cheating Heart, and he didn't show. I thought maybe I'd missed him or something, so I got back by myself. Barely. But he never did make it home. So the message I get now is that the thrill, as they say, is gone. And I am going to be on my way. It's too bad. For me, I mean. I like it here. I can understand why you'd sit up next to that tree all by yourself. I'd like to be doing some of that myself. But it isn't my tree."

They gaze at each other in what seems to Monty to be a moment of silent communion.

"Ordinarily I wouldn't even bother you at this time of day," she goes on, "since I bet you are a lot like Travis. But I went looking for Leona, and I guess I just missed her."

"Missed her?"

She pulls a folded square of paper from her hip pocket. "Found this on the kitchen table."

In Leona's handwriting, the note reads:

Monty,
Going into town for the day with Holly. Don't forget about Grover's band tonight. I'll call this afternoon to see how you feel about dinner.

He reads it twice, then studies the last phrase. *To see how you feel about dinner* means she'd be willing to get back in time to fix something but she wants to have dinner in town. It could be an overture. Tinged with that sense of duty. But from a distance. Still cool. Still smarting from their last, loud words, those words a punctuation to their argument, and that argument looping back through the years like Leona's looping script here on the note, and all this delivered by the smooth, unblemished hand of Crystal, with whom he shares no past, and at most a short future. No loops to tighten into knots. Nothing in common but whatever's on her mind about Travis, and the accident of their two lives occurring in the same century on the same planet, and whatever magnetism has drawn their two bodies to this particular point on the globe, two feet apart in the otherwise quiet orchard and exchanging deep glances. One last look at the looped and careful script gives him a brief pang of self-disgust for what he begins to anticipate.

"You mean to say," he says, trying to make this sound casual, "that there's no one on this whole ranch right now but you and me?"

"I guess not. Can I trust you?"

"Not for a second."

"I was afraid of that," she says, her eyes suddenly so luminous, so misty and dazzling, he wonders if she wears contact lenses.

"Hey, you shouldn't look like that at a man my age."

"What does age have to do with anything?"

"Me with a wife and two grown sons and you going around with one of them. It's almost incestuous, you looking at me that way."

"I am not going around with one of your sons anymore. That's over with. What I'm trying to do is say good-bye."

"Good-bye? Where you going?"

She shrugs. "On down to where I was going before I ran into Travis."

"And where would that be?"

"Houston. My mother lives in Houston."

"You don't come from Texas. I don't hear much Texas in your voice."

"I haven't been living there for about ten years. But you ought to hear my mother."

"I knew we had something in common, you and me. I've got kinfolk in Texas too."

"Izzat a fact," she says, with a sly look, faking the dialect. "Izzat a cotton-pickin fact. I guess now you're gonna tell me your daddy was a cowboy."

"It's not too far from the truth. He was a natural-born shitkicker." Monty pushes up off the ground, tosses away the coffee dregs. "But let me tell you something, Crystal. I have to be forthright. We do have a couple of other things in common besides Texas. And I'd hate to see you go anywhere before . . ."

"Before what?" she says quickly, eyes raised.

"Before you help me solve a couple of local mysteries. Let's walk somewhere, stretch the legs. I've been hauling this rig all over the ranch. It's an unnatural pastime. Let's head that way. There's a good view off toward the water. And you can tell me some things about Travis nobody else seems to be able to explain. C'mon."

"Hey, that's far out."

"What is?"

"I was hoping you could explain some things to *me* about Travis."

"I'll do my best," he says, holding out his hand. She takes it, pulls herself up and in close, and does not let it go.

"But maybe," she says, "we could talk about that after."

"After?"

Mocking him, she says, "Monty, I have to be forthright." Then, with wide-eyed boldness, "I really like your build. You take care of yourself. I like the way you come on. I'd really like to make it with you once before I go."

In her luminous and misty eyes there is an open challenge, softened at the edges by some odd hint of innocence, of virginity. It makes him feel like two people at once, the novice here, and also the veteran.

"Your face has changed," she says. "What are you thinking? You look so serious."

He almost begins to lecture her on something he almost believes. *I guess I'm just an old-fashioned fellow, Crystal,* he almost begins. *Bodies by themselves . . . mere bodies . . . there has to be more to it. . . .*

Instead he says, "I like your build too, always have," and allows his eyes a possessive grazing of her contours, coming to rest briefly on the T-shirt slogan.

Mirth pushes her lips apart, impish mirth.

"I picked this up at a club in Copenhagen, where a lot of expatriate musicians hang out. You're supposed to ask me what it means."

"Okay. I'm asking."

"Behind the bandstand there was a big poster that said, 'Jazz is like a banana. You have to eat it on the spot.'"

His soft laughter is like leaves dropping through the orchard, a laugh of amazement at what is going to happen, with nothing to get in the way but his own caution about what she might be up to. He suspects that propositioning Travis's father appeals to her, that she is some kind of collector, another type of conquistador, and he is one variety of lover she has not collected yet, or has collected elsewhere and enjoyed and wants to try again. A tinge of perversity here. More than once he has wondered if Crystal herself might account for Trav's behavior this past week, the way she carries her camera everywhere, the kind who would probably enjoy setting up a video machine in the bedroom to play back love scenes, smoke a French cigarette and study her own technique.

If he goes through with this, he foresees long, distasteful memories, and shabby guilt, and perhaps self-loathing to be lived through in the months ahead. But in advance, while their eyes and their hands test and titillate, none of that matters much. Let her add him to whatever list she keeps. He will add her to his. There is a rare simplicity here, which is what he needs this morning. With his wife ready to bust, and one son missing, the other son calling him a redneck, an assassin on the loose, an earthquake impending, and policemen pulling guns on law-abiding citizens, what better relief than one time on the ground with Crystal? A reassuring smoothness already soothes him where the fingers touch, reminding him of the richness of life, the fullness, a thickness you can sometimes actually sink your teeth into. He finds himself falling in love, that wonderful, handy kind of undying love he'll surely fall out of by sundown. He begins to sweat and grin. In the orchard their eyes brim, and their lusts gleam, and what chance then does distaste have, or guilt, or self-loathing or inherited morality or some battered sense of tradition, or history? If there were one phrase to sum up Monty's state of mind at eleven forty-five on this Saturday morning, down here in the rift zone where the plates meet and quietly kiss, where his apple trees meet the wild pine and redwood forests so characteristic of the coast range at this altitude, it would be "Do it now, worry later."

He tugs her hand, and she pulls in closer, her head next to his shoulder, her round lens pressing just below his navel like the barrel of a musket.

He says, "You better find someplace else to put that camera."

35

Afterward, stretched out, gazing up through leaves at the cloud-patched sky, it is almost possible for Montrose to believe he is twenty-two again. His mind wanders back to those years a quarter century ago, to the girls he romped through fields and forests with, Leona among them, her young self amazingly separate from who she is now. Crystal has joined this little parade, a new and instant member, as it passes through distant groves and bedrooms with one wall cut away, like theatrical sets, and out along the dusky beaches, then into sailboats that bob toward the horizons of yesteryear, and on out past the clean, sharp skyline, skimming up into blue air above the sea, above the beach, above the treetops, where Montrose too is skimming now. Stretched out in this shady patch of grass, sipping Irish whiskey and idly stroking the breast he has admired from so many angles, he finds himself alone up there with one of our tracking satellites, gazing down upon the earth as it makes its slow turn below him. He sees the outlines of our cloud-spattered North American continent, and the cities peeping out from among the clouds like far-off stars and suns, and in each city, at any given moment, there are forty thousand hands like his, stroking forty thousand breasts.

Dreamily Crystal says, "Where are you?"

"Right here," Montrose replies.

"No you're not."

"Where am I, then?"

"Somewhere else besides here. I want you here." She feigns

the pout of a Texas belle. "How can your wife put up with you?"

It's different with the wife, he thinks. When we're together I *am* with her. Or if I'm not, she knows better than to ask such a question. She has learned to wait, learned that there are times when one has to wait, certain things one has to wait for. Any woman who lasts as a wife has to have a talent for the waiting. It is a kind of blessing a married man too easily takes for granted, Montrose thinks, until someone comes along who lacks that brand of patience. . . .

"You're gone again," says Crystal.

"So I am."

"You're already tired of me."

"No. No, not at all."

"How do you feel?"

"Good. I feel very good."

"Have you ever done this before?"

"What do you mean?"

"Made it with somebody . . . your son was going with."

"No. In all honesty I haven't."

"Do you hate me?"

"Why should I hate you?"

"For seducing you like that."

"You didn't seduce me," Montrose says.

"I didn't?"

"People don't seduce each other. That's a phony idea. It distorts the responsibility. Redistributes the guilt, if guilt is a factor. Inflates somebody's ego."

"Is guilt a factor now?"

"Sure."

"Are you sorry?"

"Not a bit."

"That's the trouble with Travis, you see."

"What is?"

"He is always telling me he's sorry, or thanking me, or

explaining what went on. Not in public, you understand. But after we make it. It is always like . . . he is very youthful about it. Like I am his . . . coach."

"And you don't go for that."

"I want to be *taken*. I want to be overwhelmed. I want to be ravished and ravaged and abused."

She rolls over on top of him, squirming in a parody of uncontrollable desire.

"What made you think Travis would be the one to ravage and overwhelm you?"

"I don't know. It just didn't turn out the way I expected. The whole thing has been weird."

"How long have you known each other?"

She doesn't answer this. Monty gets the impression she doesn't want to.

He says, "Did you meet in Honolulu?"

She sits up, straddling his loins, rocks back and forth as if she's on horseback. "He told me not to tell anybody around here where we met each other."

"I can keep a secret."

"It's kind of embarrassing."

"Well, how bad was it? What were you doing, selling tickets at a dirty movie?"

"That's close."

He waits. She seems to be weighing something. She lifts the slender Bushmill's bottle to her mouth and sips delicately.

"We were *making* a dirty movie," she says at last.

"Travis?"

"That's how I met him. It's the truth. He was my partner. We met on the set. Actually, in this guy's living room, with cameras ready to roll."

She could be making this up. Montrose can't be sure. During the past half hour it struck him several times that there was something "professional" about the way she went through her moves. Ritualized. Detached. Very methodically, with mechanical tenderness, she had slid toward his feet, his boots, removing them as if that were some foreordained starting point.

"The idea was to get two people who didn't know each other and film the whole thing. The uncertainty, the awkwardness, the spontaneous things that would happen. Unrehearsed. Really pretty strange, if you want to know the truth. If the movie ever comes to San Francisco, I wouldn't recommend it."

"Now hold on, Crystal. Wait a minute. Is this something you have been doing for a while? How do people get involved in a deal like that?"

"Why? You want to try it?"

"I mean, was Travis . . . ?"

"It was the first time for both of us. I think that's why we hit it off. That is, afterward. After the filming. The way it started, I was down at Waikiki one day just hanging around, going in and out of the water about every fifteen minutes, and this emaciated guy all covered with turquoise came up to me, like he wanted to talk, but really wanting to check my body up close. He just came right out and asked me if I wanted to be in a movie. It was supposed to start at a revival meeting, with a big sweaty crowd inside the tent. These two people are both there getting turned on by a wild preacher up on the platform, and the rock-and-roll gospel tunes. Their bodies accidentally start to touch. One thing leads to another. They get so excited they have to rush out to a motel room or something. That part wasn't too clear. When I look back on it, I don't think he ever intended to film the revival meeting part. He said we were going to start with the sex stuff, before anybody got acquainted, to catch the spontaneity and freshness of these two people who know absolutely nothing about each other. It's all just a come-on, you know, from guys who mainly want to look. They want to get you in there with your clothes off and watch you do it while they take pictures. Very sleazy. I didn't know that when I said yes. At least I didn't really think about it until later. I needed the money, and the half he said he'd pay me ahead of time was enough to make it worth the trip. So who do I end up on the bed with? Travis! He had met this same guy in a bar. They got to talking, and Trav thought it was a great idea for a movie—to get out in the open about the connection between sex and Jesus."

"Sex and Jesus? How long has Travis been talking about sex and Jesus?"

"As long as I've known him. It was all related, he said, and anybody who thought this kind of film was sick ought to take a closer look at their own compartmentalized thinking. The trouble was, once we started filming the actual scenes, he couldn't get it up too well. I was all set to go. You know, there *is* something about the cameras and the whole setup of a movie. I was getting an environmental high. But Travis, he started to giggle, and laugh. He would jump off the bed and rush toward the camera, yelling, 'Hey, you people out there in the audience! This is not a movie about fucking, it's a movie about love!' When the director told him he wasn't supposed to have any lines because they could get in trouble with the actors' guild, Travis just gave him the finger. Finally they had to bring in somebody else, because he wouldn't settle down."

"And then he hung around watching, while you and some other guy . . . ?"

"Oh, no. I told them, If he's out of the picture, then I'm out of the picture. And the director really got annoyed. He looked like he was ready to fight. He said he wanted his payroll back. But there wasn't much he could do. He looked very weaselly next to Travis, who was just back from overseas. With all his clothes off, anybody could tell he was in pretty good shape—in fact, amazing shape. So we left and took what we had and blew it on a big dinner at one of the hotels. Cocktails, onion soup, spinach salad, Chateaubriand, chocolate mousse, cognac to follow. You might say he swept me off my feet."

Still straddling, she smiles down at him with a naughty smile, seemingly amused by all she has told him. He looks at her for such a long time, her little smile begins to falter, her eyes glance away.

"Crystal," he says at last, "is that a true story?"

"Sure it's true. Why would I make up something like that?"

"If it's just a story, it's a damn good one. But if it's true, if that really happened, when I think about it, it isn't very funny at all."

"Maybe I exaggerated a little here and there. But that is how we met. Honest."

The naughty smile gone, for a moment her eyes are as naked as the rest of her. Monty feels an odd mixture of affection and rekindling desire and sadistic revulsion. He wants to trust her now, knows he can't. He reaches up to stroke her neck, her cheek, and thinks of bashing her head against a tree.

Softly he says, "There are some things I need to know. Maybe you are the only one who can tell me. Please don't kid me about any of this."

"I wouldn't, Monty. I want you to like me."

Impulsively she leans forward, nuzzling his face, aroused, squirming against his loins.

"When did all this happen?" he says. "How long has it been since you two met?"

Again she does not answer. Her hand slides underneath to fondle his spent and flaccid member.

"Let it rest awhile," he says.

Testing coyly, she says, "Can't-em get-em up again?"

"I can get it up when the time comes."

"Hey, smile. You don't act like you're happy. I don't think you like me anymore."

"I am smiling. This is my smile."

He takes both her cheeks this time, grabs her ears.

"You mean you are smiling all the time," she says, "but nobody knows it?"

"Something like that."

"You're getting more and more like Travis."

He tugs her ears until she squeals with pain. What a teaser, he is thinking, a true ball-cutter. No wonder Travis walked away. He himself should get up now and put his boots on and walk away from here. But he can't. It is the way he felt last night watching her from outside the barn, when he thought Travis's shape would rise into the backlit frame the window made, when he expected to observe something intimate and perhaps revealing about his son.

He says, "I never thought of myself as being much at all like Travis."

"He would never smile when we made love."

"And why was that?"

"Too serious about it. He has all these theories. Jesus is the triumph over pain. Sex is the triumph over loneliness. Jesus is love. Sex is love. It is all related. It is all one. That was his rap. And I was digging it, you know. At first. It sounded great. Especially after the last guy I was going with, who had four rules for living. Eat when you're hungry. Drink when you're thirsty. Screw when you're horny. And take what you want. Compared to him, Travis was a genius. In theory. That is where things always go wrong, isn't it? In practice it wasn't all that hot."

"Because he wouldn't smile?"

"Yes! Exactly! Here is this beautiful man who is so goofed up with his theories that he cannot smile when he is making love! The reason he cannot smile is that after a while we were only balling when he was lonely or confused. Now, in a certain way I don't hold that against him. Everybody gets lonely and confused. But things just kept getting stranger and stranger. Until yesterday. Yesterday I finally reached my limit. This is the part I don't understand."

There is a challenge in her eyes, as if she is testing him again, a challenge edged with frailty, like a caught child preparing for punishment. She seems to be asking him to tell her things she wants and does not want to hear.

"First of all, we go into town for apparently no reason. Then who do we run into? Radar. Again, for no reason. Like it wasn't planned or anything. But Travis decides that this is a sign, that he was *sent* into town, and they launch into this long religious rap. I don't mind religion, you understand. I grew up with it. My mother is still a part-time Baptist down there in Houston. She likes the singing. She says people don't sing enough these days. They just listen. They sit around watching other people sing on television and they forget how to use their own God-given voices."

"I might like to meet your mother."

"Religion has its points. I can take it or leave it alone. What I cannot take is a religious fanatic, which is what Travis started turning into. It was insane. We got into Radar's car and drove over to this cabin he rents . . ."

"He has a car? I thought he was trying to purify his life."

"He's still an American," she says, palms thrown wide. "Anyway, from that point on I might as well be a goldfish. Radar opens his Bible and starts reading very carefully from the Old Testament about voices from heaven speaking to the prophet Abraham, and cities getting conquered and walls caving in. What he's trying to prove is that the Bible is the true word of God. This is where the argument started. Radar believes that Jehovah is where it's at, and that Jesus is a fake and a phony. An afterthought, is what he calls Jesus. Travis got so excited, I expected him to start punching. He grabs the Bible and starts flipping through the New Testament and saying that without Jesus there wouldn't be a Bible. Jesus is what it's all about. No, Radar tells him, smiling his patient smile. No, it's Jehovah. The God of wrath. The God of judgment. Travis takes him by the shirt and yells something like: 'You shithead, the whole point of the Bible is Jesus! Jesus is *love,* you stupid sonofabitch!' And at that point I am thinking: Why am I sitting here listening to this? How do I get into these things? Why can't I just have a regular boyfriend like other people do? Travis is yelling, 'Jesus is light, you dumb bastard! Look at your goddam room! It's like a cave in here! It's like a dungeon!' He starts running around pulling up the shades, and throwing all the doors open. When he opened the front door I just got up and walked out, and neither one of them saw me leave. Now I ask you, is that the way Travis usually does things?"

"I don't know."

Monty cannot recall a time when the word "usually" could ever have been applied to Trav's unpredictable career. Shouting about Jesus is something he would not have foreseen. He is surprised by this, yet not surprised. The generations leap. Deceased ancestors shape and teach us.

"I don't know how Travis does things anymore," he says.

"Do you think I'm screwed up?"

"All of us are screwed up, one way or another."

"Seriously, Montrose. Every time I get involved, I end up in some grotesque situation. A few days before I met Travis, I had just broken off with a guy who had insomnia. He would make me stay awake with him all night going to these crummy bars in Honolulu. Finally he got into a knife fight about five a.m. down by the main wharf, and he damn near bled to death on the way to the hospital. As soon as it looked like he was going to recover, I split. I wasn't getting any sleep. I almost got mononucleosis. Before that it was a clarinet player on this Greek ship, who turned out to be bisexual, and liked to dress up in women's clothes in his cabin. I have nothing against bisexuals, but all he wanted from me was my underwear. Now it is Travis over there, waving the Bible in Radar's face and shouting about Jesus."

"And you want me to tell you why this happens?"

All the challenge is gone from her eyes, all the impish whimsy, all the naughtiness. He is persuaded that she is not making up any of this. Exposed, naked, she waits for what he will say next.

"Did you like Travis when you met him?"

Quickly she says, "Sure. Of course. What kind of question is that?"

"Think about it now. Did you ever like him, as a person?"

After a moment of quiet she says, "No. I guess I never did."

"Why not?"

"He just disappointed me, like I said. Right from the beginning."

"Then why did you stay with him?"

"I don't know."

"C'mon, Crystal. Of course you know."

"I guess I thought something would change."

"What would change?"

"I don't have to tell you."

"No, you don't. But you're the one who said you didn't understand . . ."

"All right. Just don't look at me that way. I guess . . . I didn't have anything better to do at the time."

"And is that why you came out here today?"

For several moments she looks down at him, as if on the verge of making a confession. Then the exposed look in her eyes is replaced by the naughtiness. Monty watches the change, like a cartoon imposition.

"You really want to know why I came out here today?" she says.

"Yes."

In a quick lift, she springs up and away from him, toward the nearest tree. On her knees there, with the Rolleiflex against her belly, she is focusing in on him.

"What the hell?"

Click.

"Don't move, Monty. You look great."

Click.

He jumps to his feet.

"Cut that out!"

Click.

He steps toward her, grabbing for the camera.

"Hey, Monty, this is just for fun. I don't have one good shot of you to take away with me."

He is yanking at the camera.

"Ow!" she cries. "That hurts my hand!"

"I don't give a damn! You can't just start taking pictures like this."

"Not even for souvenirs?"

"Christ, Crystal! If anyone else saw this, I'd be up shit creek."

"Who else is going to see it? Don't you trust me?"

"Are you kidding? Let me have the film."

"There isn't any film."

"Let me see the camera."

"I was just fooling around. There isn't any film."

"Flip it open. I want to look inside."

"Flip it open yourself," she says, and playfully turns away, stepping just out of reach.

He is looking at her backside, specifically her tan line, trying to decide how to deal with this, when she spreads her legs and bends over and points the camera at him upside down between her knees. It is an outrageous maneuver. Obscene. Ridiculous. Her legs are tanned and smoothly muscular, a swimmer's legs, perfect legs. Her full white cheeks are spread before him, her giggling, inverted smile below, making three openings neatly aligned. Four, counting the lens. Repelled, disgusted, weak with hate, Montrose feels his cock begin to rise.

Click.

"You bitch!"

He lunges for her, knocks her over, into the dirt and the clods and high weeds his plow missed. "Goddam you, this is too much!" he shouts. "Give me that machine!"

The camera spurts from her hands. He starts to scramble toward it, arms and knees gouging her. "Ow," she whimpers. "Ow. Oh." Pushing past her, he wants it to hurt, wants her skin to feel the clods and small stones. She won't let him past. She wants to wrestle and tickle and frolic in the weeds. Patches of dirt crumbs cling where their damp bodies touch bare soil. With both hands she reaches for his new stiffness, and he despises himself for lacking the will to make her quit. While his loins surge, he tells himself he does not want to make love anymore. She is hopeless. Doomed. Incomplete. Like Radar's face. What's missing is the part of a woman he could genuinely fall in love with, if he were genuinely going to fall in love. It is where the passion might come from, or loyalty, or tears. Is she capable of weeping? He doesn't think so. He doesn't care.

He wants to be rid of her and would get up and grab his clothes and hike naked back to the house, but now she is squatting over him again. Easing down, sliding it in, she murmurs Oooooooh. Ooooh, it's good, she says, it's so good. She is small and exquisitely tight, and having allowed this to begin, he should let her take her time. He elects not to. He wants it to hurt. He rolls her over onto her back and digs his knees into the ground for an assault, driving at her brutally, hoping it chafes, hoping it bleeds. Her groans and moans are groans of approval. Bitch, he thinks. Bitch. Bitch. Bitch. You have made me want to hurt you, and now you are enjoying it. You have made me become like you, but you are not going to enjoy what happens to you *now*. And *now*. And *now*. He would drive and plow her into the ground and under the ground, down through weeds and clods and dark topsoil and the grainy substratum he has seen from time to time in the scoop of his post-hole digger, and bury her under all of it. If his cock were a shovel he could. He could bury her this way. But he cannot. He cannot dig fast enough. Whatever he does pushes more life into her, makes her bite, and roll her head, gives her breath more voice and her voice more range. Down her cheeks the tears begin to pour, uncontrollable tears from half-closed lids. The sight of tears feeds his fire of hate and lust, makes his hate and his vision turn white. He does not want to see them, does not want to see that this is what it takes to bring tears.

He squeezes shut his eyes and listens to the cry she now spreads out through his orchard like a siren. He knows he can turn this into a scream, if he can concentrate the whiteness of his delicious rage. Lunging, lunging, he hears it start—a long, rising scream—and he watches enormous white flowers open and slowly burst and turn to liquid in his mind. Squeezing his eyes tighter, he makes the whiteness pour and flow and drain through him, changing colors as it flows, very slowly, kaleidoscopically, from white to lime, and then to pea-soup green, then aquamarine, and the scream fades, a distant moaning. Thinning. Drifting. Gone. It's quiet here. He thinks he's underwater. As long as he holds his eyes closed he can stay underwater, in this green world. Yes. Whatever else happens, the eyes stay closed. It isn't water. The blue tints wash away, leaving darker greens, all around him, a leafy, shadowed grove-green all his own, which is what he thought he wanted when he came out here, and as long as the eyes stay closed he can have it, the only sound now the tiny buzz the swirling colors make, and the short gasping inside his chest, and the breathing of the woman underneath him, who will be looking, he knows, if he opens his eyes, and he wants no one looking at him now. The eyes will trap him. They will know too much. Perhaps later, when he has his strength back, he will try the eyes. One thing at a time. Right now he wants only groves, leaves, forest shadows, meadows in the sky, and the distant breath he hears is just the breeze that moves the air and keeps the broad leaves turning.

36

At The Cheating Heart wood nymphs dance across the walls. They lock arms and whirl their slender naked bodies among the vines and grasses, underneath boughs spread above them from vine-tendriled tree trunks that frame each paneled scene. Everything is shades of green, the trunks, the grass, the boughs, the bodies green. The diaphanous gowns that swirl around the arms and legs and hips are green-tinted too. For seventy years nymphs have been dancing on these walls, since the days when the vast room became a restaurant for the hotel next door. During the decades when the floors and the ceilings and the high windows and the hand-tooled doorframes did nothing but gather cobwebs and dust, the wood nymphs dipped and leaped across the walls, anticipating the New Age and the new breed of dancers who one day would join them here. Tonight some of the new dancers will be whirling about this room, yearning, as Montrose sometimes yearns, for the old woods these nymphs alone inhabit. But before the music starts they must all listen to Larry Fowler's speech, and they must make some small contribution to the group he has formed, the Citizens Organization for Public Order, Unity, and Truth, or at least they must watch the collection cans pass through the crowd.

Tonight The Heart is hosting a true town forum. In among the embroidered vests and cowboy hats and motorcycle leathers and gypsy kerchiefs, there are cardigan sweaters and crested blazers, pantsuits and jump suits and polyester double knits. Hardly anyone present knows Fowler, but the name of his organization and the issues he is raising have touched nerves in all parts of the county. Once Fowler himself is better known, there are few who will invite him home for dinner. But they won't mind kicking in a dollar or two toward his investigations. There are fifth-grade teachers, architects, stenographers, fry cooks, and front-end mechanics, lifeguards and lifetime members of the American Civil Liberties Union and the League of Women Voters, who on one hand harbor shallow or deep mistrusts of the police department as it has developed in modern times, and who on the other hand share with Leona an urge to get these murders settled one way or another. There are many who wag their heads in secret relief that the culprit may well be someone like Samson Newby, teamed up somehow with unsavory transients like the Fontaines. With an assassin on the loose, this is better than no explanation at all, far better than a bullet out of nowhere, or a random strangler giggling in the void. If it is true that the drug-trade underworld is knocking one another off, then the rest of us are not likely to get involved. Not the healthiest environment, to be sure. Anyone can get caught in the line of fire. But in a time of wild rumor, Fowler has come up with a theory worth at least one trip downtown, and so tonight this saloon is mobbed, with believers and skeptics, anarchists and alcoholics and watchers and waiters and would-be dancers, jammed around the tables and along the bar and spilling out onto the sidewalk.

Merle Haggard booms through the speakers singing "Branded Man." Grover's band has finished setting up their own five-mike system. Now Fowler, ready to take over, is being urged toward the stage by those who recognize him from the photo and still have freshly in mind the front-page story he himself cashed in on with lightninglike reflexes to put this meeting together. With a dozen hands to help him, he is half lifted to the microphone, stuffing his plaid shirt back beneath the wide leather belt he wears to hold up his mangy jeans.

It takes a while for the farthest reaches of this multitude

to realize he is standing up here waiting for attention. Fowler signals someone, and the music fades. "Testing," he says loudly. "Testing. Five four three two one testing."

This makes a hole in the hubbub of loud talk and glass-clinking and floor-shuffle of several hundred boots and plat-forms and Earth Shoes and Birkenstocks. He clears his throat, gazing out like a dark-bearded prophet, gloomy-eyed, weary of the way this world is going and has always gone.

"My name is Larry Fowler," he begins. "We have organized this meeting for two reasons. To bring out into the open some things the men who run this town evidently want to keep hidden. And to mobilize support for an ongoing study of the kinds of things that are making it harder and harder for you and me and all our neighbors to sleep at night."

A low rush of assent moves toward the stage.

"You all know what I am talking about." And with that he begins to recount the facts of the case as he sees them—the mystery surrounding Linda Kramer's grand jury appearance, the unexplained presence of Samson Newby in the burial grove.

During this speech Montrose edges his way through the five-deep crowd out on the sidewalk and on past the double doors, to find a spot near the back wall, up against one of the leafy panels where the wood nymphs romp. He leans back against a lime-tinted calf and looks around.

He is detached from this scene, as if a movie is being shown. In the region of his loins he feels open space, a drained, eu-phoric airiness. He feels purged, as if some unhealthy crav-ing has at last been satisfied, and he is still intact. The pictures she took have been disposed of, burned to ashes as soon as Monty recovered sufficiently to crawl forward and unload the camera. Now Crystal has been disposed of too. He has just dropped her at the Greyhound depot. She wanted to start hitchhiking. He wouldn't let her. Then she asked him to come along. He could pay for things, she suggested, in return for which she would be his mistress. It would be good, she said,

because they know how to please each other. Parked near the
depot in his pickup, he entertained this idea for thirty seconds,
he looked into her eyes and foresaw that such a move would
be like draining all the blood from his body to test his ability
to survive. He gave her twenty dollars as a down payment on
a bus ticket to Texas, although he wouldn't be surprised if she
pocketed the money and started hitching anyway. Then, following her directions, he drove to Radar's place, on the off
chance that Travis might still be there. It was locked, and
dark. He drove back downtown and parked and walked a
slow, circuitous route toward The Cheating Heart, knowing
he had to go there, not clear at first why, gradually admitting
it was not to hear what Fowler had to say, or what Grover's
band would play, or because he suspects Travis will be here
somewhere too, but because his life is starting over and he
wants now to see Leona.

Scanning the room, he finds her seated at a table with
Holly Belle, next to the far wall, peering intently toward the
stage. They have a pitcher of dark beer. Another woman sits
with them. The fiddle player's wife. Between the table and
where Monty stands there are a hundred people, and no
possible path through the closely packed bodies. No way to
reach her now, and he does not want to reach her. He wants
to watch her, at this distance, regarding her profile anew. He
admires her profile. The eyebrows are thick. She does not
pluck or trim them. Her cheekbones are clear and high, a flash
of the old Cherokee who was her great-great-grandmother,
who met one of her great-great-grandfathers, so Lee claims,
at a trading post near Forth Smith, Arkansas, in 1859. Her
nose is straight, neither large nor small. In the light from the
stage this profile seems cut from ivory. He has seen it somewhere else. In different light it could belong to Travis. This
notion breaks the spell, scatters his detachment, fills him with
tight readiness, brings him away from the wall and right out
into the room. Glancing around the edges of the stage, he sees
a Panama. Though the hat brim shades the face, he's sure it's

Trav. Glancing at Leona again, he sees the head and arm and shoulder of a man who seems to be seated next to her. The man has just leaned forward to lift the pitcher and refill her glass, a large, darkly bearded man of perhaps thirty-five years, wearing an embroidered silk shirt that shines like foil. It is Wellington, Monty's tenant.

Now, what is she doing with that sonofabitch, Monty growls to himself.

Wellington sits very close to her, too close, and from the way she acknowledges the pouring, Monty gets the impression this has been going on for a while. For hours. Perhaps days. Or months. In a flash he sees that there is something unsavory, even sinister, about Wellington that he has too long overlooked. He recalls seeing him in here drinking alone and unapproachably at the shadowy end of the bar. Though he sings the native song, there is no true festivity in him. Though he can laugh a loud and overpowering laugh, he never seems genuinely amused. Monty wants to get over there. He pushes at the couple in front of him. They don't notice the pressure. Nothing gives. He wants to call out to Travis, *Get over there and talk to your mother!* No voice can find space in the air of this room now but Fowler's. Up above the Panama hat Fowler's hands are spread wide and he is shouting, "These things need to be explained!"

The audience calls out its loud agreement.

"When we ask the police for explanations," Fowler cries, "what do we get? Silence! They do not want to tip off their suspects—they say. When we ask the courts for justice, what do we get? Silence. They won't let the press report what it knows, because the jury might be influenced—they say. Tell me how you can have a jury when you don't have a killer! And how are you going to catch the killer when the cops' main concern is protecting their own skins and their own self-interest! The cops and the courts put a gag on all relevant testimony because they say they're trying to protect the investigation. My group says it's to protect the police! If we're wrong, then show us. The public has a right to know what the hell is going on in its own community. Is that too much to ask?"

From all parts of the saloon there swells a thunderous *"No!"*

"Well, then, are we just going to sit around hiding in our houses waiting till the cops decide to tell us what they think is sufficient information?"

From the crowd a louder outcry. *"NO!"*

"All right! All right! Here's what we're prepared to do. We've got a newsletter ready to go. We've got a communications center ready to open on Del Mar Boulevard. We want people who can do volunteer work. And we need support so we can take the first steps. Tonight is just a beginning. Grover Doyle is here with the Bear Flag Republic String Band. These boys have donated their services to this event. While they whip into the first number, people are going to start circulating these cans through the crowd." He holds up a one-gallon metal can with the initials COPOUT in red, white, and blue. "Your contributions will be put to good use. We can assure you of that!"

His last words are swallowed by the opening bars of "Foggy Mountain Breakdown." As Fowler moves to the side of the stage, Grover, a few steps away, shoves his white banjo head up close to a low-slung boom mike, picking hard on the first chorus. Behind him the string bass, the mandolin, the fiddle, the lead guitar, thump and tweedle and twiddle and twang. A drummer and a steel guitar have been brought in tonight to make sure the music lives up to the occasion. Now the pedal steel comes whining and sliding in to join them. The glassy-eyed drummer with his orange-flaked drums turns the Bear Flag bluegrass sound into irresistible country rock. Listeners like Montrose who may have other matters on their minds don't have the time or peace to explore them. Those who came to hear and now want to think push vainly toward choked doorways. Among the tables couples start dancing where there is no space. Monty strains to see Leona. For all he knows, Wellington has dragged her out of sight under the table. Cowboy hats are bobbing. Bangles and necklaces swing and flash. The metal cans pass from hand to hand, and long legal-size petitions suddenly flutter in the air like banners.

When the first song ends, another instantly begins, one followers of this band recognize and welcome with cheers and eager hoots. It's called "Splattered on the Windshield of Your Heart," the first Holly ever wrote. Grover has made it a standard feature of the first set of any gig they play. As the crowd starts to bump and grind and boogaloo, a walking bass line brings him to the microphone.

I used to be free as a high-flying eagle
Winging down the highway of life,
Drifting along with any current I could find,
Free from all confusion, free from strife.

Then you came out of nowhere, a-clippin at my wings.
You made me feel like a blowfly from the start.
You came highballing at me, like a diesel doing ninety,
And I just splattered on the windshield of your heart.

Rebel yells greet the lonesome fervor of this last line. Grover laughs and backs away to make room for the mandolin player stepping up to take the second chorus.

Monty has heard the song a dozen times. It still makes him smile. Tonight he wants to disapprove of Grover's role in this production. In Monty's eyes it is typical of the crusades his son is always hooking up with. He wants to be annoyed that Grover has publicly aligned himself with such an opportunist. Yet once the music starts, it is hard to be anything but wet-eyed and fatherly with pleasure at the sound. Grover has a good voice for this kind of singing, nasal but not corny, high but not whiny. The songs he does are always songs Montrose would sing if he were in a band. In Grover's voice he picks up echoes of his personal favorites—Jimmie Rodgers, Roy Acuff, Hank Williams, and his own granddad, Ransom Doyle, whom he spent a week with once in 1936 and heard Ransom's creaky, dirt farmer's version of "Ida Red" and "The Crawdad Song."

For a few moments Monty closes his eyes to savor the sound. When he opens them again Travis is standing next to his brother, guitar in hand, Panama tilted, his cocky grin. Grover's face in the spotlight mirrors Monty's first reactions —surprise, mistrust, uncertainty, delight, what in hell is the kid up to this time? He steps in next to Grover's ear and whispers something, and they both start laughing. Monty cannot help himself. He grins wide, watching them. From Travis this is surely some . . . sign. A gesture. He looks again for Lee, to share this moment, to see how she regards it. But there is still no way to see her in the jostling, jiggling throng, and now the band is accelerating, somehow augmented by Travis, who begins to pick and strum, adding a new juice to the rhythm section.

Grover sings another verse. The pedal steel takes a chorus. Then Travis steps up to one of the instrument mikes as if he has been rehearsing with this band for months. His guitar style is so bluesy, so funky and swingingly comical, he gets a wild round of applause when he's finished.

He smiles out into the crowd with the celebrity's smile that pleases everyone who's watching. When the next song begins, and he stands waiting at the vocal mike, a happy expectation overlays the swaying and jerking and foot shuffles and bobbing of heads all across the room, as the rhythm guitar and bass get the tune moving. It's a gospel tune, a souped-up version of "Farther Along." His smile hovers between parody and beatific faith:

> *Farther along we'll know all about it.*
> *Farther along we'll understand why.*
> *Cheer up, my brother, live in the sunshine.*
> *We'll understand it all, by and by.*

The fiddle player steps forward. Travis, who is supposed to give him the spotlight, remains at the voice mike and begins talking to the audience in what sounds at first like a talking blues. People nearest the band stop to look up at him. Laughter is heard, since something in his delivery makes this seem like a comedy routine.

"Brothers and sisters. As the Apostle Paul points out in his second letter to the Corinthians, a little wine is good for the stomach."

A rowdy cheer from the bar.

"Now, what he didn't go on to say is that a little more wine is good for the brain."

Someone calls out, "Amen!"

"And I am here to tell you that a lot of wine is good for the heart and the soul and the spirit of man!"

More cries. "Amen!" "Tell it, brother!"

"It is for this reason, brothers and sisters, I can no longer keep still. I have to share with you what is on my mind."

"Oh, mercy."

"Tell it like it is, brother."

"Spread the word."

While the boys in the band smile happily, cooking along behind this prologue, the voice turns somber.

"A gloomy picture has been painted for us tonight. A picture of deceit and corruption. I know you are all wondering, as I used to wonder, what can a person do about such things? I want to offer an answer to that question. I want to tell you what I now see. I want to tell you, in fact, about a new way of seeing, which was given to me over in Vietnam, where I have spent the past two years of my life. When something powerful sweeps over you, I have been told that it is important to testify to that power, to tell others about it. That is what I am going to do tonight, right here, among all you people who live in my town, and are dancing in what I like to think of as my saloon."

Among guffaws and low-grade heckles, many dancers are slowing down, uncertain how to handle this. The boys in the band watch Grover, who is half frowning, half trying to keep the show on the road, keep the music moving and the room alive.

"I damaged the vision of one eye over there," Travis continues, "but I gained something far greater. A kind of new vision. My eye became a symbol, you see. For the first time I came to understand *all* symbols. I began to understand the cross for the first time. The cross of Jesus, and the message of that symbol. And what is the message of the cross, brothers and sisters? The message is pain! And the triumph over pain! The message is suffering! And the triumph over suffering!"

The music has stopped. Grover is standing at his side, touching his arm, whispering in his ear. Travis ignores this. Some dancers squint with impatience. Some call out: "What the hell is going on? Who is this guy?" Others shout: "Let him talk! Let him testify!"

Near the stage one young girl with long blond hair is gazing at him with wide radiant eyes while unrestrained tears drop down her cheeks.

"You are worried about these murders," Travis says. "On the other side of violence . . . I see Jesus!"

A few people call out their support of this idea. Others yell for Travis to shut the fuck up so the music can continue.

"You are worried about dope dealers. On the other side of dope . . . I see Jesus!"

The outcries grow louder, spiced with cowboy whoops and rebel cheers from the vicinity of the bar.

"You are worried about the police department. On the other side of the law, and the misuse of the law . . . *I see Jesus!*"

At this point, after a brief commotion back by the double doors, Walter the cop pushes into the saloon, followed by four deputies in riot gear. They all look exactly alike except that Walter's star is bigger. Crash helmets, goggles, dark nylon jackets, black pistol butts showing at the hip, black riding

boots, and black gloves holding riot sticks like stubby quarter
staves. They line up just inside the doors, where the nearest
bystanders make a little space, awestruck into silence. Elsewhere there is so much surface noise, underneath the attention
everyone sends toward Travis, at first no one acknowledges the
newcomers, no one but Montrose, pressed against the wood
nymph's tinted ankle, confused, surrounded, sick at heart.

Loudly he whispers, "Walter! What are you doing here?"

Walter's face seems pinned and braced inside the black
chin strap. Only his lips move. "Bomb scare. We have to clear
the place."

"Are you kidding me? Who called it in?"

"How the hell should I know? I just work here. Chief sent
me over with orders to clear it out."

"Don't they call the owner first?"

"They tried, Monty, believe me. Nobody answered the
phone. Now I can see why."

The nearest ranks have spotted the deputies. An awareness
of them moves across the saloon in slow waves, as heads turn
away from the stage, where Travis is summing up.

"If it had been up to Jesus," he is saying, "there would
have been no war. Jehovah is the one who lets war happen.
Jehovah, the God of punishment. Jehovah, the God of judgment. The God of righteousness, and the God of wrath!"

Walter has a bull horn, which he raises to his lips, his
raspy call topping this last line. "May I have your attention!"

Monty edges up close to him. "Christ, Walter. Do you
realize how bad this looks? Cops coming in here at a time
like this?"

Turning from the bull horn, Walter blurts, "I don't give a
shit how bad it looks! That's my whole life story in a nut-
shell! What if the place blows sky high with all these people
packed in here? How's that going to look?"

On stage Travis is proclaiming: "But when the smoke of
battle clears, Jesus is right there, waiting for the survivors."

Into the bull horn Walter announces: "There has been a bomb threat called in to our department. We have instructions . . ."

A roar of indignation rises up, drowning his voice. All the uncertainty and impatience that has gathered during the sermon now turns toward Walter in the form of undisguised hostility. The deputies' dark gloves tighten nervously around their riot sticks. Fowler has leaped back onto the stage. Before Walter can get another sentence out, Fowler is shouting into the mike, in the full knowledge that this is perhaps the biggest break of his career.

"Do you believe what is happening here?"

A loud babble of Noes and Yeses and Goddam the pigs!

"A bomb scare, my ass!" Fowler cries. "This is a deliberate attempt to break up a public meeting! These are Gestapo tactics!"

Over the swelling turmoil Walter's bull-horn voice is straining to be heard. "This is no tactic! A bomb threat has been received! We have orders to get this building cleared!"

The crowd boos and bellows. Those still seated leap to their feet. Some jump up onto chairs and tables. Onstage Fowler screams, "We will not by God be pushed around by agents of the American Gestapo!"

This last word is blasting through the speakers when the front of the stage explodes out onto the nearest listeners, sending smoke and dust and splinters and shards of lumber into the room, and sending Fowler and the microphone spread-eagled toward the high, frescoed ceiling. Montrose sees them hover up there above the billow of dust, like a skydiver riding the uplift of some thermal current, and in that same mini-second he sees the Panama hat and, wearing it, Travis, who jumped off the stage moments before the bomb blew and is now shouldering toward a far exit with one backward glance and a grin at the booby trap he narrowly evaded. Then Fowler lets the microphone go and drops to where the front of the stage used to be, through smoke and shattered flooring, past the drums and the pedal steel and the boys in the band, who stand around the splintered edges, miraculously untouched, gazing into the maw like riverside singers at a baptism, while everywhere the wounded and the unwounded begin to yell and swirl in panic. Monty hears Walter shouting through the bull horn: "Clear out! Clear out!" and cannot tell whether it's directed at the crowd or at his deputies, who are encircled now and hopelessly outnumbered by the terrified, furious multitude stampeding for the doors.

Part Three

The Child Christine waked when her mother left her
And lay half dreaming, in the half-waking dream she
  saw the ocean come up out of the west
And cover the world, she looked up through clear water
  at the tops of the redwoods. . . .

—from *Roan Stallion* (1926)
by ROBINSON JEFFERS

37

TRAVIS

At the geographical center of town stands a concrete obelisk like a Geodetic Survey marker. Of all the things it might have commemorated, this obelisk commemorates America's wars, every one of them up to the date it was erected: the French and Indian, the Revolutionary, the 1812, the Mexican, the Civil, the Spanish-American, and World War I. It is fifteen feet high, with these words bronzed:

TO THE SOLDIERS OF ALL WARS
APRIL 1928

It names the thirty-seven men from this region who died in the armed forces between 1914 and 1918, including two of Monty's cousins, one a legitimate hero, the other a victim of ptomaine poisoning at Fort Dix, New Jersey. On top of the monument an oxidized mother eagle perches above a nest of hungry eaglets, gape-mouthed. The nest is made of intertwining metal branches, and the mother's head twists back as if screeching at some just perceived menace.

What the sculptor captured here is a certain intensity of belief; not simply a belief in war, but a town's prideful participation in battles and shows of strengths and large thefts and border incidents which would in the long run improve the quality of human life upon this earth. In the obelisk itself you can see how fine a belief this used to be. Some capable artisan was commissioned to find a powerful and patriotic and enduring image and erect it in the center of the town. In the way this obelisk is ignored you can see how things have changed. On Veterans Day, when thousands drive past both sides of the monument, few notice the eagles' nest. No one stops to read the plaque, or if they did, would recognize the names. It is around the perimeter they stop, at the beaches, the burger bars, the shopping plazas.

Until tonight Travis has been one of those thousands who never stopped to look at the plaque or the nest of eagles. He has put several blocks between himself and the scattering crowd that fled the saloon, and now he stands alone in front of the obelisk, reading the list of unfamiliar names, the dead veterans of all those faraway campaigns. Once again he re-lives his own death, sees himself running alone at dusk, back toward headquarters to turn himself in as a deserter.

While he runs he can hear, in advance, the lieutenant's mockery. *If you were a deserter, Doyle, you wouldn't be standing here in front of me.* Travis hears himself reply, *Deserter of the soul.* And again the voice of the lieutenant whose tent he never reached: *Doyle, the war is almost over.*

"Ah, well, then, I'm glad you understand!" cries Travis the deserter, sprinting in a Benzedrine terror as far as he can get from the last days of holding action, certain he'll be the last man to fall in this war against the endless enemy.

He is shouting at the jungle, *"I'm glad you understand!"* when, fifty yards away, an infantry corporal, equally deranged, leaps into the road with an Apache war cry and hurls a grenade. At first Travis thinks the man is waving at him, some comrade calling out. Then he sees with stop-time clarity that this is in fact the blow he has known was coming all along, the one he has run this far to intercept. He is rushing toward the blast when something clicks. He catches himself, dives, right into a spray of shrapnel slivers, like an automatic Singer needle stitching through his cheek.

Later, his head wrapped in gauze, he came to see that click as the moment of his death. In the days of darkness behind the bandages he used the time to contemplate what had died. Over and over, fast and slow, he replayed the scene, the corporal in battle dress appearing out of nowhere, defined against late sun pouring through a break in the trees. The crazy shout. The arm cocked, then heaving a grenade Travis never saw, yet ran toward, as if magnetized. It was fitting, he concluded, that the grenade should be tossed by one of his own countrymen. Because there was no longer any enemy. This is part of what died. The opponent. The adversary. The enemy had been like water. You could see it. You could step on it. You could hear it coming, feel it trickling down your back. But you could never get a grip on anything. Hear a noise, spin around, and it would be a five-year-old kid with sores on his arms and legs collecting Coke bottles in the roadside ditch. See a shadow in the trees, you crouch ready to fire, and a wrinkled old grandma in an umbrella-shaped hat would emerge carrying bundles. Bundles of what? Touch her, and the bundles would be garbage some platoon had left behind. Fail to touch and the bundles might explode. When the enemy is everywhere, the enemy dissolves. That leaves nothing much to fight about, nothing *worth* fighting about. Allegiances dissolve. Boundaries dissolve. His homeland dissolved. It just wasn't there. America slithered off around the edges of his mind as it no doubt had in the mind of the countryman who tried to blow him up.

He had known all this would happen. It is why he argued so fiercely with Grover in the months before he left the States. "You're wasting your time," Grover would say to him. "This war is a total loss. If we don't get out of it we're lost as a nation. Maybe it's already too late. How long can we go on burning women and children to pay for our life and our liberty and our pursuit of happiness?"

So deeply did Travis fear such questions that he would shout back, "I don't believe that! I don't believe the men who run this country would ask us to go fight somewhere unless there was a hell of a good reason!"

During that split second of a click he perceived what died. He saw the trajectory of his past two years like a dark comet— from those arguments, through his mad-eyed days of furious training, to the toss of the grenade—as one foreordained and headlong plunge toward the death of all enemies and all allegiances and toward his own self-sought destruction. And perceiving that, he altered his course. Under the bandages he came to see that dive for cover as the moment of his birth, the urge to die supplanted by the urge to live. When the bandages were finally stripped away he rejoiced that he could see anything at all. He felt he could see more clearly than ever before. He interpreted this partial loss of sight in his left eye as the price of a New Vision, the part of him that had to die in order that the rest of him might live again.

Reborn, he spent his first night drinking at an enlisted men's club, got into a fight which tore some old stitches and added new ones. This put him back into the hospital, anesthetized again, and tranquilized. Coming down from the tranquilizers, he dropped into severe melancholy and saw this as another version of the approaching grenade. He died again, and came back to life, and took it as an important lesson, as well as another beginning.

Celebrating, this time in Saigon, he passed half a night with a hooker, who disappeared with his money, his ID cards, his small stash, his camera. He died again, and this time he was not reborn for several days.

He began to suspect that his New Vision was not a permanent change, but simply the discovering of what had always been his pattern. And inside that pattern, in between the urges to die and the urges to live, were long moments of limbo, of sliding darkness, of total blindness, symbolized for him now by his days in bandages. All this so depressed him he began to plan suicide, and that led to deeper depression because it fit right into the pattern.

In darkness, while waiting to see the base psychiatrist, he met a private who believed in Jesus, a hospital orderly who asked Travis what he was doing there. Travis told him. They were alone. The orderly sat down and asked him if he had heard of the Resurrection. Travis had. "This could have profound meaning for you, my friend," the orderly said. "The Resurrection was a real event. It was also a psychological event. Forget the religious part for a minute. Forget Easter. Forget that he is the Son of God who died for our sins. Just think about what happened. Here is Jesus. He is thirty-three years old. He is a carpenter, brown hair, brown eyes, maybe five foot six, and weighing one thirty, one thirty-five. He has friends, and he has enemies, and one thing leads to another. He dies a painful and agonizing death. Right? He is put into a cold, dark cave. Everybody thinks he is finished. Three days later he comes out of the cave, back into the world, rejuvenated and ready for action."

The orderly let that sink in, then said, "Do you have a Bible?"

"Not with me."

" 'Blessed are your eyes, for they see: and your ears, for they hear.' Matthew Thirteen: Sixteen," said the orderly, whose eyes were persuasively serene and at peace. He passed Travis a flat, pocket-size New Testament, muttering, "Don't tell the shrink about this. He's hung up on Freud. Plus, he doesn't like it here. He's mad at the world. All he'll tell you is to go into town and get laid."

"I just tried that."

The orderly cocked his head, spread his hands, and smiled with beatitude, as if to say, "Exactly."

Canceling the appointment, Travis went back to his barracks and read the New Testament twice. In the weeks before his plane left he attended three study meetings organized by a young, red-bearded chaplain who wore blue-tinted spectacles and chain-smoked Tiparillos and told Travis that every show of positive energy—singing, dancing, eye contact, preparing food, body contact, first aid, sexual congress—was a manifestation of Christ's love, and that the reverse was also true, that Christ's love was just another way of describing all the strong, affirmative acts that knit together humankind.

His first day in Honolulu, Travis met the movie-maker, and after several rounds of a rum concoction called the Missionary's Downfall, the idea of a film about two people who meet at a gospel revival seemed brilliantly "right." For a few hours there he felt the ragged pieces of his life stitching together again. As he stepped naked out in front of the camera, he knew in a flash that the whole thing was monstrously wrong. Including Crystal. Stunned by her voluptuous grace, he still sensed, very dimly, that sooner or later she would kill him. That same night he died in her arms.

He was dead for a week. He remembers coming to on the plane, sitting next to her, looking out the window. He had been looking out the window for hours, but with his eyes glazed over. What brought him back to life was the first view of the coastline. In the field hospital, under gauze, the times he had tried to conjure up his homeland, all he ever got was a curving line, one edge of a topographical map coming slowly into focus, with bumps for mountains, blue ridge ribbons where the rivers are. In his mind's eye he would scan the curve from Cape Mendocino to Monterey to Point Conception to San Clemente and on across the border all the way to Cabo San Lucas and the tip of the Baja peninsula. It was, he had decided, the loveliest coastline in the world, a fine, lissome, delectable curve he longed to caress. It was, for him, a thread of hope. Perhaps his one allegiance. As they approached from the west, he felt life surge within him. This was indeed a change of view. With his New Vision came more clarity, and this time he truly had a chance to see the world afresh. Gazing down from fifteen thousand feet, he perceived something he'd never seen before. A double edge. Approaching from the east, overland, as one grandfather had done, as Lee had done, as Travis himself had always done, simply driving from the house into town, from the house to the harbor, from the house to the low-tide clam flats, it had always seemed to him some final line, a winding down. Arriving from the west, it had the opposite effect. This coastline was also a beginning. A new land. A launch pad. In the mind of Travis these two notions had quivered, colliding like magnetic fields.

The next thing he remembers is sitting in the front seat of Monty's car, as they swung out onto the freeway, heading home. As they plunged into the maelstrom of hurtling machinery, he suddenly felt the pieces of himself accelerated and strain to fly apart. His vision was fracturing into a thousand billboards, revolving signs, pizza palaces, overpasses, thunder trucks, and windshields villainous with harsh morning glare. He felt disaster hurtling toward him from every direction, like the shrapnel, while he rushed toward it, ready to explode. He turned to Montrose with his good eye, his new eye. He had not really looked at his father in years. What he saw above the wheel was an unrecognizable profile, a strange face, discolored, disembodied, floating, ready to tilt or topple, and it was then that Travis announced, grasping for some action or some thing he could physically hold and believe in until the panic left him, "Hey, Dad, I have to drive!"

Leaving the obelisk he heads down Del Mar Boulevard, peering into darkened storefronts, reading stenciled bulletins and concert posters tacked on poles and taped to windows. In the distance he hears the rumble of squad cars and fire trucks amid a low rush of voices outside the saloon. That is another battle scene he wants to leave behind, another death. He keeps moving. He is across the street from the Hotel Viceroy when Radar catches up with him.

The face is smooth, a porcelain religious mask. "I heard what you said about Jehovah," he murmurs.

He wants to revive their debate. Travis doesn't care to talk about it now. He would rather not spend any more time with Radar.

"You were wrong," Radar says. "There is nothing whatsoever in the Scriptures to back up what you said."

Glancing skyward toward the hotel roof line, Travis sees the heads of the eleven Spaniards who keep their watch above the town. He has never noticed them before. Radar follows his gaze. For a moment they stand like twins, staring up, a pair of mesmerized twins, as fixed, as sentinel-like, as the row of concrete and bearded heads seven floors above them, below the starless sky.

"I think I'll go up there for a closer look," Travis says.

"I can prove my point," says Radar quietly. "I can prove it to you beyond the shadow of a doubt."

Travis doesn't reply. When he starts across the street, Radar follows. They enter the glass double doors of the hotel, walking gingerly between the two rows of overstuffed armchairs and sofas, Radar in his blue work shirt and prisoner's haircut, Travis in straw hat and combat boots. Suspicious eyes watch them pass. Newspapers rustle. Bent and gnarled and inflated bodies move restlessly in the chairs. Travis sits down in an empty rocker next to an elderly man who is reading the worn pages of a gold-leafed Bible. He is reminded dimly of his grandfather, and he feels a sudden pang of loss, wishing there were an elder like this somewhere in his own life now, whom he could confide in, wishing he could plop down this easily next to Montrose.

Waiting for the old man to look up from his reading, Travis watches Radar move on through the lobby. A day and a half with him and he feels like an ex-alcoholic dabbling with whiskey, wincing at the taste but getting drunk anyhow. Maybe if he sits here awhile, Radar will go away.

To the old man Travis says, "You know what happened tonight?"

The old man keeps reading.

"Jesus appeared to me."

The old man looks up from his reading. "Did he say anything?"

"He said, 'He who hesitates is lost.' "

"That sounds like something he'd say."

"You know," Travis says, "I am seeing a lot of things these days that I never saw before."

The old man's eyes go vague. "Not me," he says, turning back to his Bible. "Don't see near what I used to."

Travis takes his time up the carpeted stairs. At the seventh floor there is still no sign of Radar. He prowls around until he finds a flight of steep metal steps leading to the roof. He peeks through the low doorway. No one out there.

Tarred gravel scratches underfoot as he crosses to the parapet where the line of Spaniards keep their vigil. He kneels and hangs out over the edge, like a Moslem at prayer, until his head is lined up between two of the Spaniards, gazing down at the street.

Travis finds that he can remain in this position without effort. His eyes can remain open in this steady downward gaze without effort. When his eyes move they seem to do so of their own volition. He realizes they are made of fluid concrete. On his cheeks and chin he feels the beard begin to sprout. On his head he feels the weight of the metal helmet, its cracked leather band against his scalp. He speaks to the soldier perched next to him.

"This town is very lovely, is it not?"

"Yes," replies the soldier. "I like it very much. Very much."

"It has grown."

"Yes. I watch it change. Sometimes I feel . . . abandoned."

"Do you know its name?"

"No. No, I do not remember."

"There was a mission here."

"Yes," the soldier says. "It was built to save the Indians."

"And many were saved."

"No. Very few. Perhaps none. They all died."

"In the fighting?"

"No. Not that way."

"But you remember the war," says Travis

"I don't like to. It was a clumsy war. Too much work, and very clumsy. The people living here, they ate clams and slept in straw huts. We came with muskets and heavy armor and . . . there was nothing to conquer."

"And yet you are still a soldier."

The soldier laughs a quiet, cynical laugh.

"Why?" says Travis.

"Why? Who knows why?"

"For Christ? For your country?"

"Christ is nothing but a dream."

"Christ is everywhere," says Travis.

"Christ comes and goes like a figure in a dream."

"You sonofabitch."

The soldier laughs cryptically and falls silent.

Travis waits awhile, then says, "You dirty sonofabitch."

When nothing more comes from the chiseled mouth, he lets his gaze follow the soldier's, bringing the lit street back into focus. He sees his mother pass under the lamplight right below him. As he watches her, something begins to press at his eyes. A few yards behind, he sees his father, striding along as if trying to catch up. The light picks out a bald patch shining through the thick hair on top of Monty's head. Then he sees Holly Belle, with Grover carrying the black banjo case. Silent tears begin to flow. Each figure passes through the very spot where he and Radar stood ten minutes ago. He knows that if they looked directly up at him now they would not be able to single him out from among this row of soldiers. Bearded, helmeted, weeping in the dark, Travis watches them parade around the corner, out of sight.

38

HOLLY BELLE

At nine-thirty the next morning Holly Belle is watering geraniums and margaritas around the front door of the A-frame, listening to the telephone and wondering what she is doing here. There is nothing to carry away the insistent ringing. The spring sun has brought everything to a standstill. Each ring hangs in the still air like the flowers on these plants, which seem to float, and like the treetops beyond the field, buoyant and defined against a pale azure sky. The phone rang like this, in the same kind of air, an hour ago, just as they pulled into the driveway, and there was no voice on the other end. Faraway static, then a click, and a blank line, an intolerable silence. Coincidence, Grover said, a pointless message from the overloaded headquarters of Technology, or perhaps the rednecks he believes bombed the saloon last night and are now starting to harass anyone who seemed to sympathize with Fowler's view of law enforcement. If it happens again, he said, we'll just stop answering the phone.

Holly can't stop answering the phone. On the seventh ring she picks up the receiver.

"Hello?"

No answer.

"Hello?" she says. "Who's calling?"

Distant computer bleeps send fading signals on their way to outer space.

"Hello?"

Click.

"Is anybody there?" she says. "Who is this anyway?"

Nothing.

She listens a moment longer, then hangs up and walks outside, into the bright sunshine. She puts both hands on her belly, feeling. Her period is late. She is usually right on schedule. Anxiety could explain it. Perhaps it is just the anxiety. She looks at her Packard. Its baby-blue surface is bleached nearly white with dust, its tires are spreading at the bottom. Why did she let Grover talk her into coming back up here with him? She feels more vulnerable, more exposed now than when the news of the Fontaines first arrived. She feels high-powered binoculars watching her every move. She will make it through the day well enough. There is plenty to keep her occupied. She does not know how she will do in the dark. If that phone keeps ringing, she will not want to spring awake into the kind of midnight silent blackness that encloses them out here. Things seem more bearable at the ranch, and having Lee to talk to. Maybe after a good day's work she can talk Grover into driving her back to the ranch. Yes. That would suit her fine. Days up here, nights at the ranch. For the time being. Is that too much to ask? From his point of view, it will be. She can hear his response. *We already spend too much valuable time strapped into vehicles.* He is right, of course. But too self-righteously right. Mobility is the key. She must stay mobile. She wonders how dangerous it would be to drive the Packard into town without brakes. Any more dangerous than having a beer at The Cheating Heart? In high school she had a boyfriend who drove an old Pontiac that way for a couple of weeks. He would careen down hillsides in third or second gear—riding on compression, he called it—and he would use the emergency brake on the hairiest turns. It cost him a transmission and three fenders, when the cable finally snapped. But what the hell. Is this car doing her any good just sitting here? Something has to happen. She is not going to plead with him, or even mention it to him again. That is demeaning. It is destructive to the relationship. She will try the engine. That would be a step. She hasn't turned it over for two weeks. If she can somehow get it running again, the next thing will be a course in auto mechanics through adult education. If it is true that the dawning of the Age of Aquarius happens to coincide with the full flowering of the Age of the Car, then it is surely insane to be mystified and imprisoned and defeated by something as inert and elementary as a common set of brakes.

The door opens with a rusty scrape. She slides in behind the steering wheel. It is musty and stale and hot inside. Instantly a thin film of perspiration coats her entire body. The sweat and the heat make her feel full, as if there *is* some new presence inside her and it has just doubled in size. As she touches the ignition key, something moves in front of her, down the road, next to the trees. Or maybe nothing moved. It's hard to see through the streaked and splattered glass. Maybe it was the sweat in her lashes, or a cloud of insects. Her face and neck and shoulders suddenly feel covered with small insects, microscopic fruit flies. She shakes her head and brushes her eyes and looks, sees it again, a shadow.

She listens. Now she can hear feet dragging on the packed dirt, heading slowly toward her. There shouldn't be anyone up here. No one arrives in the morning by foot. Her sweat turns cold. Hoping for a loud threatening noise, she turns the key. The starter grinds and grinds and grinds. If it starts, that will be a signal that the time has come to make her move. She isn't sure how large a move. Any move at all will do. If something is going to change, she is the one who has to make it change. If it starts she will coast on down to the first service station and negotiate the repairs any way she can—barter, flirt, wire for money, lie. The grinding now is a tiny whimper under the hood. The figure, nearly upon her, has stepped from deep shade into sunlight with arms upheld like a traffic cop. She knows this figure. It is Grover, with his shirt off, and his hair held down by the blue bandanna.

Her little laugh sounds like a groan, exhaled with the last exhalation of the starter's feeble charge. Dripping, she lets go the key and slumps back against the seat.

Grover, at the window, says, "You look frightened. Who are you afraid of?"

"You." She tries to say it lightly. "You're supposed to be down in the bean patch."

"Had to check the fences. Came the long way around. Something's been getting through, nipping at the plants. Deer, probably."

He waits for her to respond, his face fixed, his eyes steady, full of what a year ago looked to her like strength, promising rich depths of character, a year ago when they were both getting ready to graduate and more than ready to find some other center for their lives than the part-time politics that had underpinned their student years. Right now, this morning, what used to look like strength looks only like rigidity. She knows she is up too close to tell one from the other. And knowing that much, she also knows it's the wrong time to mention that her period is late; no use getting into that subject at *all*.

"What are you doing?" he says at last.

"I was thinking of going for a drive."

He laughs uncertainly. "Try the van."

"A long drive."

"Something the matter?"

"I have to get away, Grover. For a while. To think."

"Can't you think here? You have plenty of time to think."

"No. I can't. Somebody else just called. I mean, the phone rang again and nobody was there. I'm too jittery to think, if you want to know the truth."

"Why didn't you say so?"

"Why didn't I say so? What do you think I've been trying to say?"

"You want to go back to the ranch?"

"It's more than that."

"What, then?"

"Everything. Everything we're doing."

"We're building, Holly. That's the way you have to look at it. It takes time to build. You have to start where you can."

"You are building, Grover. I'm not sure I am, that's all. I'm just not sure. I'm too close to it. Too close to you. I'm going somewhere else. That's not a threat, you understand. I am not into heavy drama. I am not running off expecting you to chase after me and beg me to come back. I just need some space."

"And I am supposed to take a day off . . ."

"Did I say that?"

". . . to charge up the battery and fix the brakes and get this fucking ridiculous car back on the road . . ."

"I can find somebody else to do it!"

". . . so you can drive right out of my life?"

"I'm not talking about driving out of your life!"

"All I'm trying to do is find an honest way to live. I do not understand where all the static is coming from!"

"Haven't you ever felt like you need some space and time?"

He looks down at the ground between them, squeezing his jaws the way she has seen Montrose do. She watches the flat, smooth muscles push in and out. He says, "Where are you going to go?"

"I might head toward the Bay Area, see the old friends, maybe just hole up by myself and finish a couple of songs. I heard that some people we used to know have some sound equipment and they're looking for things to tape. . . ."

Inside the cabin the telephone rings. Grover lifts his eyes. They stare at each other. It rings ten times while they stand there motionless in the hard sunlight. Then she steps through the door and picks up the receiver and listens again to the empty line.

39

Montrose alone in his front room two days later is watching the morning news. He does not like the news. He endures it for professional reasons. He is waiting now to see how they are going to handle the discovery of the newest victims, an account of which should follow this national roundup.

A beleaguered veteran just off the plane in L.A. refuses to describe the various ways he was tortured during two years as a POW. Federal troops in full battle gear hold positions near the town of Wounded Knee, South Dakota, hoping to flush out a small band of Native Americans led by a Sioux medicine man named Leonard Crow Dog, who want redress for wrongs against their people. Senate investigations leave no doubt that ITT spent at least a million to support the right-wing overthrow of a socialist regime in Chile. It is starting to look like the men who broke into the Democratic headquarters at the Watergate Hotel last June all had FBI or CIA connections. And the cost of living index rose by two point four percent during February, the biggest monthly increase since the Korean War.

Clearly this is the wrong way to begin the day. It gives Monty the urge to demolish his TV set. This has often occurred to him. Attacking the screen would be a small but thorough form of revenge. It is the screen itself which brings so physically into his home, right into his lap and his life, these daily disasters from all parts of the earth, over which he has no control, which merely magnify his own sense of helplessness and fill him with impotent fury. This morning he feels ready to do it. Hands gripping the easy chair, he is ready to rise and move toward the set, when Fowler's ravaged face appears on the screen, videotaped at the hospital. The camera pulls back to show him in white pajamas, his hips encased in white plaster and one plastered leg slung from pulleys. His face is still singed from the explosion.

Introducing him, the interviewer says, "Larry Fowler leads a group protesting the way police and the courts have withheld crucial information from the public. In an unprecedented coincidence, his Saturday-night rally was broken up by a simultaneous police raid and bomb blast. Larry, as spokesperson for your segment of this beleaguered community, what do you think about the two bodies discovered yesterday?"

Into the extended hand mike Fowler says grimly, "It figures. It figures right down the line."

"But as I understand your theory . . ."

"It's not a theory," Fowler interjects.

"Then you believe these deaths are also drug-related."

"I didn't say that. The people came from out of state, right? Colorado or someplace."

"Idaho."

"Okay. A middle-aged couple from Idaho, touring out west in a Chevy Impala and pulling a trailer, who just happen to stop and camp overnight up in the hills. The guy works for a lumber company or something. It's perfect, don't you see."

"No, I don't think I do see."

"They are straight as a ruler. They have nothing at all to do with drugs or with the police. Because they are decoys."

"You mean two ordinary citizens are picked at random and murdered and buried naked just to throw us off the track?"

"We're not dealing with amateurs."

As they cut to a blurred helicopter view of the wooded area where the bodies were supposedly uncovered, Monty comes to his feet. When they cut back to the interviewer's unctuously dispassionate face, he steps toward the set, pausing as Fowler speaks again.

"You think it's an accident I am laid up here with a busted

hip?" Fowler asks the camera. "That bomb had my name on it. Why? Somebody wanted me out of the way, just like they put Linda out of the way. I am not even supposed to *be* here anymore!"

Monty rushes forward and rams one boot through Fowler's nose and mouth, shorting out the fourteen-inch picture tube with a quiet pop. Glass tinkles to the floor.

He looks down in awe at what he has done, relieved, and faintly pleased, then realizes the dogs have been barking outside in the yard, barking for quite a while. He thinks he hears a noise behind him, a shuffle. He thinks it is Leona coming downstairs to see what happened. He turns and finds Walter in the hallway, wearing his crash helmet, abulge with handcuffs and pistols and billy clubs, looking at him.

"I know how you feel," Walter says.

He has removed his goggles, revealing the haggard eyes. Walter seems on the verge of some final, desperate move. If they were standing together on the Golden Gate Bridge, Monty would not be surprised to see him climb to the railing and leap. He has come here to confess something, Monty surmises, remembering a similar look when Walter sought him out in the parking lot behind the high school gym to confess that he was masturbating daily, sometimes twice daily, and figured this must explain his poor showing in the fifty- and the hundred-yard dash.

"Well, come on in," says Monty. "This is quite a treat."

"I knocked. Nobody answered. Ordinarily I wouldn't have barged in on you like this."

"What do you mean, ordinarily? You haven't been out here in fifteen years. Take your helmet off."

"Can't stay long, Monty." He stares at the glass around Monty's feet.

Monty kicks at the pieces. "You know how it is, Walter. Sometimes . . ."

"Don't explain. I've been there. My wife won't let me watch

television anymore. I got four busted sets just like yours, sitting in the garage."

"It's this latest news. That couple from Idaho. Really a shocker. What's the rundown, Walter?"

"There isn't any rundown. That's the trouble. Nothing fits. They are just out here on a trip. Retired couple, passing through the county. A week ago somebody called in an Impala with a trailer rig sitting around empty way up near the top corner of the state park, looked like it had been broken into. Sheriff's office ran a check on the car, found out some relatives were wondering why there hadn't been a postcard or a call for a while. But you know how these things go. This was before the Fontaines were discovered."

"Where the hell's it coming from? Six people killed. Who knows how many more lying around somewhere. I've never seen anything like it."

"It's bad, all right."

"What else have they found up there?"

"Can't talk much about it yet."

"No new leads?"

"A few new possibilities. There could be more than one individual involved."

"You mean two or three people working together?"

"Maybe that. Maybe different people doing different killings."

"What makes you think that?"

The way Walter looks at him, the pain that covers his face, Monty has to glance away. There is something Walter is about to divulge, some reason for this visit he is gathering the courage to mention.

"I haven't seen you since the rally," Monty says. "What about the bombing? Any idea yet who's behind that?"

"There are about five groups trying to take the credit. But we've got a pretty good idea now who really set the thing."

"Can you tell me?"

"I'd rather not."

"It's up to you."

"It's kind of embarrassing."

"You mean Fowler was right?"

"Almost. A bunch of guys in town are calling themselves the Law and Order Auxiliary. They say they don't want to see the police force dragged through the mud. So they broke up the meeting, and now they are demanding that we arrest Fowler, that he is the one who is teamed up with the killers, that it is part of a massive conspiracy to take over the country by terrorism and anarchy and destroying public confidence in the police department. I tell ya, Montrose, I don't approve of their tactics. I mean, seven people got banged up the other night, in addition to your friend—"

"He's not my friend!"

"But the way things are going, the LOA could be right. We've got letters from them down at the station, and handbills they are starting to send around to a selected mailing list. I shudder to think what Fowler will have to say when this information hits the papers, or what will happen to him if he doesn't have the sense to shut up and not say anything for a while. I despise that little bastard for all the grief he has caused us. It is hard enough trying to solve a case like this, in the best of circumstances. Still, I would hate to see his body added to the list. For that matter, Grover better keep his eyes and ears open. Coming in there with his band like that. These vigilante types could take it for granted he's a fellow traveler, if you know what I mean. If I were you, I'd keep the whole family away from The Cheating Heart."

Walter is staring again at the broken glass. With great effort, he pulls off his helmet and shakes his head.

"Is that what you came out here to tell me, Walter? That Grover might be in trouble?"

He doesn't seem to hear. "I'll tell ya, Monty, this has got to be absolutely the worst period of my entire life. If I live through this, I think I'll sell everything I own and leave the fucking country for good. I hear there are still places down in Australia or New Zealand where a man can make a life for himself."

Monty realizes he has not seen Walter with his helmet off for several years. His hair is black and damp. Strips of it lace his white scalp like seaweed. Without the goggles and the chin strap and the helmet, he looks like a man who has been awake all night waiting for the firing squad.

"How are Flora and the kids holding up? She come back from Yosemite yet?"

Avoiding Monty's eyes, Walter says, "I didn't come out here to go into my personal problems. Maybe someday when I'm off duty."

"My time is your time, Walter."

"I don't quite know how to tell you this."

"You want a drink? A cup of coffee?"

"I have to talk to Travis."

"What about?"

"Actually, one of our detectives wants to talk to him."

"About what?"

"Just a couple of things that can probably be explained. I told them I'd come out here and talk to you first and see—"

"Goddam it, Walter! What are you trying to say?"

Still gazing at the floor, he says, "An investigator found his fingerprints on the front doorknob up at the Fontaines' place. And . . . it just . . . needs to be explained."

A knife begins to carve at the bottom of Monty's belly, releasing a slow upward trickle of dread and rage. He holds it down and stares hard at Walter's anguished, guilty, boyish eyes, wanting to be able to reject all his opinions and judgments and scraps of information. He steps across the room, takes the blue elbow and turns him toward the front door, whispering, "Whatever you're talking about, I don't want Lee to hear it. Not yet. All right?"

"Sure, Monty. This is hard on all of us."

They walk onto the porch, down the steps, across the yard to the first row of trees, where they stand in the shade of an overhanging bough.

"Now let's run through this again. You're telling me some investigator found Travis's fingerprints on a doorknob at the Fontaines' place?"

"It didn't take long to check. We had him on file from his high school days. I didn't realize he had a record."

"I wouldn't call one charge of car theft when he was fourteen—a charge which was dropped, by the way—I wouldn't call that a record."

"Well, they had his prints, and they checked out."

"But why is this just now coming to light? Your people have had over a week to take that place apart."

With a humiliated grin, Walter says, "The first time through the house they forgot to check the front door."

Monty laughs with relief and disdain. "They what?"

"They checked the windows, the drawers, the closets, the trash can. They forgot the front door. Like I told you before, this is not Scotland Yard. Some of these guys have to sleep in their shoes so they won't forget to put them on in the morning."

"And the doorknob is not the first oversight that has been made in this case. Am I right?"

"You mean Newby?"

"Among other things."

"Newby can be explained."

"I'm listening."

"An official statement is being released in one, possibly two, days that will explain everything. Thanks to Fowler, the goddam *governor's* office has been calling us, wanting to know what's going on."

"Fine. When all that is cleared up, and the bombers identified, and Linda Kramer's deposition made public, then maybe Travis can come in to answer questions."

"C'mon, Monty, don't make this job harder than it already is."

"All right, now listen to me, Walter. You and I both know the police have their backs to the wall. As much as we hate to admit it, Fowler is on to *some*thing. Somebody has screwed up somewhere. And badly. And they are grabbing at anything they can find to take the heat off for a while. Am I right?"

Walter's face seems ready to crumble into ashes. He glances off toward distant trees, trying to compose himself.

"You want to see the prints, Monty? You want photocopies?"

"You're not telling me everything you know."

"I'm telling you everything I can. You have to trust me. Don't you trust me?"

"Barely."

"The last thing I want to do is pin something on Travis. In fact, this is one time I hope to God the department has blown it so bad you can sue them for mental cruelty. I'm on your side, Monty, I swear it. I already talked the chief out of serving a warrant for his arrest, at least temporarily."

"Arrest?"

"It was mentioned."

Monty smiles, trying to be generous, to accept Walter's gesture. "If you ask me, that is way out of line."

"I have also played down his sermon at the saloon, until I have a chance to talk to him personally. . . ."

"What are you getting at?"

"All that Jesus stuff. I don't know if he really is a believer, or if he was just kidding around or what. But some reporter could get hold of that and have a field day. With the first body buried right there at Holy City . . . and now his prints on the doorknob. And him being a veteran, just back from overseas, perhaps trained to kill. You know how reporters think."

"My God, Walter, that is reaching for it! That is really stretching! Didn't you just tell me the couple from Idaho have been dead a week at least? It was a week ago somebody first reported their car?"

Impatiently Walter nods his head.

"You go back and tell your fingerprint committee that when this thing started, Travis was several thousand miles away. He didn't get home until the day they found the Kramer girl!"

Walter kicks at a dirt clod and shifts his weight. "Now, that raises a delicate point, Monty. You told me yourself he did not come in on the plane he was scheduled to come in on."

The eyes lift to look at him again, and Monty thinks he sees, underneath the frowning and the twitches, a grim flicker of pleasure, as if Walter has been waiting for this moment. Monty feels the knife carve again. This time he cannot suppress the trickle. It spreads through him like cold mountain water.

"As I recall, they caught an earlier flight."

"Are you sure?"

"Of course I'm sure."

"Did he have his bags with him?"

"He wasn't carrying bags. Just a light valise. He had all his stuff shipped straight to the house."

"Was it dated?"

"I didn't look."

"I have to pay attention to things like that, Monty. I can't help it. Part of my job. Flora says I'm paranoid. Maybe it doesn't mean anything at all."

"You're goddam right it doesn't."

"But it does raise a question."

"I'll call Pan Am. I can get the passenger list for every transoceanic flight that week."

"I think that would be a good idea."

"But I don't have to. Travis can explain this whole thing in thirty seconds."

"That's what I'm trying to tell you. Is he around? If we could just sit down somewhere . . ."

"He's not around. He hasn't been around since . . . He's out . . . somewhere. He'll be back . . . before too long."

"You're sure?"

"Am I sure? What is this? You think I'm hiding him up in the attic?"

"I don't think anything. I just do what I'm trained to do. And believe me, when this case is over, I kiss this fucking uniform good-bye."

40

He is watching another TV screen, one without a picture. A
black square. Inside the square a white spot bounds from side
to side, from corner to corner, a proton looking for a way out
of its molecule, a falling star gone berserk. If you insert a
coin, two electronic paddles appear on the screen, and by turning a knob you can move one of the paddles to deflect the
spot and send it back toward your opponent's side of the
screen at some new and surprising angle. At the moment no
one is playing the game. Between the pinball machines and the
drinking fountain the white ball moves quietly and con-
tinuously inside the square, bound after bound, hour after
hour, day after day, now here, now there, in what seems at
first to be a random and asymmetrical pattern. Standing in
line at the Greyhound depot, Monty watches the screen,
thinking he and this spot have a lot in common. Both follow
a seemingly unpredictable track that is in fact programmed,
predestined, arranged this way who knows why, or how, or
when, and too late now to alter any of it. This is how he is
starting to feel.

He has been to the sheriff's office to study blowups of the
fingerprints. He has called Pan Am long-distance about passenger lists and been given the run-around by suspicious voices
so on guard against hijackers and vandals they will reveal
nothing over the phone about flights past, present, or future,
except ticket prices, and these are subject to change. He has
called his attorney and implored him to seek out this information any way he can. He has driven back to Radar's cabin,
where he left a note asking Travis to make contact as soon

as possible. He has stopped at The Cheating Heart, where he left messages at the bar and cash register. He has come to this depot on the remote chance—which grows more remote to him the longer he stands waiting in line—that he can track down Crystal, the only person besides Travis himself who might explain away the mysteries of the recent past. He feels as if he is being covered with lead. The burden of his fatherhood weights him down like a lead suit. He cannot move. From here he does not know where he will go next. He has a hunch, a premonition, that his life is closing in on him.

Waiting to speak to the ticket clerk, gazing around at the posters advising him to drop everything and take to the road, it occurs to Montrose that he should not mention Crystal at all when he reaches the counter. There is something about this depot that encourages abandon, something unkempt, and tawdry, and anonymous and vaguely liberating. He has the urge to buy a ticket, to take the next bus out of town, transfer to another bus and then another, and in this way put himself into some distant landscape, another region, perhaps another reality. He has the money, and there is a great tradition for this. The impulse still lives in his blood. His father did it, and his grandfather, and his great-grandfather before that. With life bunching up around him like a pair of tight coveralls, Great-Granddad Doyle piled what he owned into a run-down wagon and drove it west from Virginia, through the Cumberland Gap and into high-country Tennessee five years before Abraham Lincoln was elected President. Those were the days, and Monty hankers for them now, waiting in the Greyhound depot, tiny nexus for arrivals and departures, descendant and distant cousin of all stagecoach terminals and pony express stations, covered wagon caravans and railroads nailed into the mind with golden spikes. It is a hankering that quickly subsides. Seven miles beyond where his own house stands, the west ends and the water starts and does not stop until you reach Hawaii, and before you know it the water starts again, yawning toward Japan. He has been to Hawaii twice, and twice returned to the mainland. Those were not his mountains. That water was not his natural habitat. For Montrose there is no more driving, no more drifting. He long ago chose to make his stand right here where he grew up, where he met his wife, where they raised their sons. Long before the days of the stagecoach and the iron horse, the Indians who inhabited this region had reached a similar conclusion. They had no plans for going anywhere. From their villages along the shore, which was the only shore they knew, they looked out at the ocean, which was the only ocean they knew, and they sang a song about "dancing on the brink of the world." Monty likes that idea. In happier times he has been able to see his own life this way, as a certain kind of dancing. But not today. Today his presence on this coastline, and the attractions it has had for him, wherever they may have originated, seem programmed, as programmed and inevitable as the endless ponging of the electronic spot.

The woman in front of him walks away and he steps up to the counter.

"Can I help you?" says the clerk, head down, noting something with a well-chewed pencil stub.

"I hope so," Monty says. He knows this man, but cannot recall his name. Years ago they worked together on a committee to pass a school bond proposition. The man considered himself a comedian and in Monty's memory delayed the passage of many a motion with his terrible gags.

When his eyes lift Monty says, "How you doing?"

Blinking behind horn-rims, the man smiles with crafty amusement. "Montrose Doyle. I'll be drawn and quartered. You taking a trip somewhere?"

"No. I'm looking for a girl."

The clerk adds a nasal rasp to his voice, throws his mouth out to the side, imitating W. C. Fields. "You came to the right place, amigo. Blonde, brunette, or redhead?"

"Brownish, with a little sunshine around the edges," Monty

says, trying to overlook the silliness. "She might have bought a ticket last Saturday evening."

"That would narrow it down to about sixty-eight possibilities, yes it would."

"How about Texas? She could have been traveling to Houston."

"Houston, eh?" The sallow face brightens, with a slight professional interest, and the voice shifts to John Wayne, slower, overdoing the drawl. "I'd remember a ticket like that. We don't get many going to Houston anymore. That would take em by way of Los Angel-ees, Phoenix Arizona, and El Pay-so."

"She's about twenty, and very attractive. She might have been wearing a T-shirt that said, 'Jazz . . .' "

" 'Jazz,' " the clerk says happily, " 'is like a banana.' Oh, yeah." His voice picks up the edge of a streetwise hipster and hustler. "Ooooh. Who could forget *that* one? I'd be tracking her down myself, but"—he shrugs his shoulders, eyes atwinkle with lechery—"business before . . ."

"Then she did buy a ticket."

He doesn't answer. He shifts again, into what seems his normal voice, high and clipped, and says, "I want you to know that I've been reading your columns, Montrose. Every week. The day they come out."

"That's good to hear."

"Right on target, if you want my opinion. I really appreciated what you wrote the other day about all these killings, and about the need to keep a level head. Too bad you didn't throw in that old Kipling line."

"Which Kipling line?"

"The one from his poem 'If.' 'If you can keep your head, when all about you are losing theirs' . . . then you'll be taller than they are."

The clerk folds forward, crippled with laughter.

"I've never heard that one before," Monty says.

"Isn't that a kick in the ass?"

Monty hears grumbling from people in line behind him. "Listen, I don't want to hold up all these other folks."

The clerk does not share Monty's concern. Wiping his eyes, turning suddenly somber, he leans across the counter and lowers his voice. "People get into a panic, they will do things they wouldn't even think about during ordinary times. Let me give you one example of what it's like over in my neighborhood. I would not label my next-door neighbor an alarmist, you understand. But she has what you might call an active imagination. Now she is saying that every time somebody has disappeared, this same vehicle has been seen cruising around somewhere in town or up in the hills. A green van with two bearded guys inside wearing old army fatigues. She says the license-plate frame is from some car lot up in Oakland, and she is certain they are the killers. Either these two alone, or maybe a whole group of them coming down here from Oakland or Berkeley to terrorize the community. She says hardly anyone noticed the connection, but on the same day those people from Idaho were found, a PG and E power station in Hayward was bombed. She wants to know if I have noticed anything unusual around the bus station."

"Unusual?"

"The kinds of people getting on and off the Oakland buses. She thinks they ought to all be searched."

The man says this as if he has a great deal more to share, as if he would like to be interviewed for the *Courier* and be quoted in one of Monty's columns. Part of Monty wishes he could do it that way, if only he could find the enthusiasm to swap rumors with this man or find some enthusiasm for any of the speculations which proliferate like metastasizing cancer cells.

With a little smile and a sad wag of the head, he says, "Sounds off the wall to me."

"Of course it's off the wall. But it's having an effect." The crafty smile returns, the barroom twinkle. "It's cutting into ticket sales. Can I sell you a ticket to Oakland, Montrose? That is what I'm getting at. We·have been instructed to push tickets to Oakland this week."

"No, thanks."

Behind Monty someone growls, "Hey, what's the holdup? My bus is pulling out."

"How about Denver?" the clerk says, amused with himself. "Or Miami? Portland? Minneapolis? Business is terrible, Monty. Getting worse. Nobody's traveling. It's killing us. They're afraid to move."

"Just tell me what you can about this girl, and I'll be on my way. You say she did buy a ticket to Houston?"

"As a matter of fact, she did not. She is just like all the rest. She was ready to go, then changed her mind. I remember the scene very clearly now. She stood here a long time in her T-shirt looking at the schedules, then said what she really wanted was a cheap place to stay for a few days. I told her about a little motel a couple of blocks down the street, and away she went. It's that place called the Mountain View. Of course, there's no view, and you can't see the mountains anymore, with the neighborhood built up the way it is. Isn't that a riot?"

"You're serious now. No kidding around."

"In times like this? Of course I'm serious. Now, buy something before I get fired. How about Seattle? New Orleans. Baltimore. Sioux City. Missoula. Cleveland. On a thirty-day excursion I can give you a fantastic deal."

"No, thanks," Monty says. "I'm not traveling either."

With an oddly sadistic smirk, the man says, "Afraid to move?"

Monty starts to answer, then lets the question hang, pushes past the angry customers crowding up behind him, and hurries out to the parking lot.

41

In the office of the Mountain View Motel, Monty smells fried potatoes. He smells onions. A door opens and he hears gunfire. Blue-white light from a television set coats part of the door. A heavy woman in a loose print dress passes through the ghostly light and up to the desk. She too smells of fried potatoes. She is about forty-five, weary of life and low-budget living.

She says, "Good afternoon."

"Sorry to trouble you," Monty begins. "I'm looking for a girl. Dark hair, about twenty, who may have checked in a few days ago. Named Crystal?"

The woman fixes him with a look of gloomy resignation. "Welcome to the club."

His eyebrows lift, uncertain.

"You a cop?" she asks.

"I just live around here. She's a friend of the family."

She tilts her head toward a shaded corner behind her. "Recognize any of that stuff?"

He leans forward and looks. "Those are her things, all right. What's going on?"

"She did check in. Paid for three nights. I know she slept here the first night. But after the second night, when I went in to clean up the room I noticed the bed wasn't used. Her stuff was there, but she wasn't. I didn't think much about it. I leave my customers alone. It's the only way to survive in this business. Some people sleep on the floor. Some people stand up all night in the shower stall. I could care less. This morning, though, I went in and nothing had been touched. We hadn't seen her around, and that was all the time she paid for. So I waited till noon, which is check-out time, and I brought her things in here and called the cops. You sure you're not a cop or a reporter?"

"I write for the *Courier* from time to time."

"Hey, don't quote me on any of this, okay? I can do without the publicity."

"What's there to quote? You think something happened? People must leave things behind all the time."

"Mister, I been in this business for many, many years. I have seen everything happen that you and I put together could imagine, or dream of. You never know what it's going to be next. You never know. I try to look out for my customers the best way I can. The way things are going around this town, it is just common sense to keep the cops informed. They know me. They know I am not the excitable type."

"Did she have any visitors?"

"Not that I noticed."

"She didn't make any calls or talk about going anywhere?"

"Five minutes, while she was checking in, that's all I saw of her. If she shows up again, her stuff will be here in the office."

42

Driving away from the motel, he curses Crystal for not getting out of town when she had the chance. He curses himself. He should have gone into the depot and bought the ticket and escorted her right up the bus steps. He is already seeing her dead. He sees the grave, and he sees the headlines, and he remembers that he has done this before, killed someone in his mind. He did this to Travis, before the boy went away, to get it over with, to ward off the specter of . . . what? Of the actual death? No. Of his own responsibility for it. Prepared at any moment for holocaust, for ashes, he feels the moment may be near, Crystal's disappearance another turn in the spiral slowly closing around him.

Then he thinks: My God, this is crazy thinking. She left some gear behind. So what. It could mean anything, knowing her. Maybe this. Maybe that. Death, of course, cannot be ruled out. Death is one of the things it could mean. Knowing her as he does now, knowing what she stirred in him, he imagines she must always live very close to violence. Didn't Monty himself want to hurt her? For a moment there he wanted to hurt her badly. Other men who have made love to Crystal must have felt some of that.

But this is too gruesome, he thinks. I'm killing her again. Turn on the radio. Something to divert the mind. The worst features of times like these, of crimes like these, is the loss of boundaries. Trust dissolves. Loyalty dissolves. Belief dissolves. Everyone a potential victim, everyone a potential killer, everyone defenseless, threatened, on guard. At this very moment the culprit could be lurking in the back end of his pickup.

The thought makes his head turn. He stares back through the glass.

That pile of canvas. Did he leave it there last night? Did he stack it that way? It doesn't look right. Too large. He pulls over, leaves the engine idling, gets out and walks back. He pushes at the canvas. A package of air, puffed out by passing wind. As he straightens it Monty tries to appear purposeful. He looks around. Some old fellow wearing wide suspenders is clipping a hedge. The sun is shining. The air is comfortable.

Inside the cab again, he fools with the dial. Sometimes he can pick up KRAK out of Sacramento, one of the great country music stations of the west. In recent years he has listened to it as far south as Bakersfield and as far north as Moses Lake, Washington. As he brings in the station his spirits lift; he rides along on half-held hopes that when he gets home there will be some news of Travis—a call, a note, a lead—and that right around the next curve he may find Crystal hitchhiking, and she will then be able to answer all his questions, or that at the very worst she has run into another con man like the movie-maker, who has enticed her down yet another side street of modern life, and that the gear she left behind is like the insomniac boyfriend and the bisexual clarinet player and like Travis and Monty himself—things she is through with and has merely walked away from. He feels he should be resenting this habit. Right now it is a way of preserving her. With three days gone since she joined him in the orchard, a warm haze has gathered around those antics. It seems like weeks or months ago, and he was years younger than he is today. He doesn't want to hurt her now. If anything, he would like that day back, the way he saw things then. He would settle for a small part of that day, for the instant he saw her walking toward him through the trees, the youthful rush he felt. It may have been the last moment of his boyhood.

Why don't you love me like you used to do?
How come you treat me like a worn-out shoe?

> *My hair's still curly and my eyes're still blue.*
> *Why don't you love me like you used to do?*

Hank Williams sings it, as Monty waits at the last intersection, deeply moved by some elusive truth lodged among
the lyrics or in the haunting, steel-guitar voice of the dead
singer. When the light changes he stomps on his pedal, lurches
past the low, sprawled shopping center, out into open country,
his pickup rattling through wooded and familiar foothills
lusciously green after spring rains.

Listening to Hank and heading home, he is reminded again
of Wellington and the tin-foil rodeo shirt pressed against
Leona at The Cheating Heart. In his mind's eye he has seen
it many times these past three days, the intimate reach of that
silky arm behind her chair. He has imagined caresses, imagined
liaisons in her workroom, Leona decorating the private parts
of Wellington with yarns and fabrics. Jealously he posed lame
questions, to which Lee replied, "You have Nan. I have
Wellington."

"Have?" said Montrose hotly. "Have? I don't have Nan. I
work with Nan. She's a friend. A colleague."

"Well?" said Lee, with a coolness to match his heat.

"Well, what?"

"It's the same thing."

"It isn't the same thing at all."

"Of course it is. He's a tenant here. He's interested in
tapestries. He say's he's interested in the committee—"

"I'd say *that* interest is the farthest thing from his mind."

"All he did was buy me a couple of beers. Is that a sin?"

"He can't be trusted."

"You're the one who decided to rent to him."

"That was a mistake. There is something slack about Wellington. Something depraved."

She laughed at that, a haughty laugh.

Trying to press the issue, he could only flounder, his suspicion mixed with possessiveness and undermined by shameful

images of his own recent conduct. Lee saw the guilt that rounded his eyes and centered his pupils as he spoke. She could only guess at its origins. She added this to the cloud surrounding her. That is how all their conversations have been going. Clouds have filled the house. She has let her eyes do the talking, and her neck, and her back, never mentioning Travis, for example, until today. The longer Trav's absence from the house, the less she has said about it in words. She and Monty have been walking past each other through clouds and fog, on opposite shores of a wide canal, until today, when Walter's report and the latest news made it impossible to remain so far apart.

For her sake he is glad she has had something to prepare for—today's meeting of the Standing Committee for an Aesthetic and Livable Environment. It is a working lunch, which could not be postponed. They have a policy paper to prepare and present. A revision of the county's general plan is in the works, an important vote comes before the planning commission this week, and SCALE is lobbying hard for park space, bike trails, high-rise controls, a five-year moratorium on freeway expansion. Expecting this meeting to be over by midafternoon, she had asked Monty to get back before dark. He assured her he would. It was the first thing they had agreed on since the day before the rally.

The sun still hangs above the trees when he passes the mailbox. He finds cars parked halfway down the drive, and more cars filling the gravel crescent in front of the porch. He pulls around behind the house and parks between the barn and the first row of trees.

In the quiet moment after he shuts off the engine he regards the light across the barn's graying planks, a leathery, wistful glow, the color of times past, of things lost. When they were ten and twelve the boys bounced tennis balls off this wall. When Monty was that age he used to stand against the barn on winter days, out of the wind, to catch the warmth that always seemed to gather there. Today it is framed by boughs of white-pink blossoms at their fullest. His eyes grow moist. If he sits here much longer he will weep. He reaches for his pocket knife.

He climbs out of the pickup and slices a small branch from the nearest tree, to present to Leona. It is one of their small, seasonal traditions, one of nature's bouquets, from him to her.

Approaching the back steps, he hears voices, the formal tones of a meeting still in progress. He is a dues-paying member of this group, often writes up their achievements in his column, but he never goes to meetings. He decides to slip into the kitchen, find a jar and some water for the branch, grab a snack, and make a few calls on the kitchen extension. He is through the back door and standing next to the refrigerator, when Lee appears across the room, in the hallway entrance. He cannot tell whether she is here to greet him, or merely by coincidence, on some other errand. She lets the door swing to behind her. She cocks her head, as if deciding something, or as if trying to identify him.

As her glance takes in the apple bough she seems to smile. He isn't sure what sort of smile. He sets the bough on the table. She is stepping toward him, now standing in front of him, gazing up at his face, into his eyes, asking to hold and be held, to receive and be received by him. His arms go around her shoulders. Her arms slowly encircle his back. He draws her close, and their bodies meet for the first time in days, lightly, then with pressure, his cheek pressing the soft, clean fragrance of her hair. Through the clothing he feels that they are beginning to merge, her energy with his, her need with his, her life with his. Her face against his shoulder does not want to be caressed or kissed nor does he want to kiss it now. Closing his eyes, he sees that in this entire world she is the one person he can unquestionably rely on, his one true source of stability. All his doubts, all his guilts, all his frailties, can be coped with if he has Lee to hold to, his wife, his sweetheart, his mother, his first girl and best companion, his old flame, his lover and his mistress, and pillow, and pillar, his anchor, and anchorage, his rock. Were she not here to meet him this afternoon, he feels that his own haphazard ping-ponging would pitch him into a bottomless void. From the way she holds to him he believes she feels something similar. She is not crying, nor is she holding back sobs. She is just holding, as he does, holding on for dear life. For this moment the voices from the other side of the house grow faint, recede, until the house is empty, the earth deserted, depeopled, except for these two who stand alone in their kitchen in their tree-surrounded clearing fifty yards up from the county road, seven miles inland among the foothills of the coast range. They are bonding now, regenerating. No words uttered, no sound heard.

Inside Monty some of the sorrow subsides, the turning of the knife subsides.

They back away from the long embrace.

The voices return. Two women are talking at once. Chairs are scraping. Papers are being shuffled. Monty murmurs, "I love you, sweetheart. I guess I haven't mentioned that in quite a while."

Still holding lightly, she says, "I know it, Monty. I love you too. Very much."

She waits, then says, "I'm glad you got back early."

"Sounds like you still have lots of company."

"This turned into a bigger thing than I expected. A woman is here from Sacramento. She just finished a trip studying communities all across the country."

"Maybe you should get back in there."

The way she shakes her head, he knows she wants to talk. He leans back against the refrigerator.

"Grover called about noon," she says. "He'd heard the news on the radio. He wanted to know if we were okay."

"Well, now. That was a thoughtful thing for him to do."

"He said he might be gone for a day or so. He's going to try to find Holly. She took off yesterday on some kind of trip."

"By herself?"

"I guess so."

"Damn! She picked a hell of a time to travel."

"Grover sounds pretty anxious."

"They having trouble again?"

"He wouldn't say. So I guess they are."

"What did he say about Travis?"

"He said for us not to worry, said he wouldn't trust a policeman's opinion any farther than he could throw the police station. Travis is in bad shape, he says, but not that bad. Then he said as soon as he has a chance he'll try to find him or find out what he can."

"I wish he was right about the police, sweetheart. But I saw those prints, and they check out; there's no doubt about it."

She searches his eyes, wanting to talk this through and not wanting to, fearing the answers. "What do you honestly think Travis was doing there?"

"It's hard to know. He might have brought some dope back with him, like Walter says a lot of fellows do. He might have gone up there to move it. Or could be, he thought somebody else was living in that house. He used to have pals all through these hills."

"It might have been any number of things, then."

"I've been racking my brain all day. I can't figure it out."

"Do the police know when those prints were put there?"

"Anytime within the space of about a week."

"So it could have been before the Fontaines were killed, or it could have been after."

"That part is still fuzzy."

"But if it was before, that means Travis would have been home maybe a week before you met him at the airport. And that just isn't possible, is it? Right here in the county?"

"I just don't know, sweetheart. I've been thinking about that one too. Walter's right about the baggage, you know. There was no baggage at the airport. And that crazy look on Trav's face the minute I saw him. That eye of his. It has started me thinking."

"You're not thinking he's involved, Monty. You don't think that."

"No, I don't. Not for a second. Something else is going on, something he could clear up for us very fast. But that is how the police will be thinking. They need a suspect they can believe in, and I am trying to stay a step ahead of the police. I told you what Walter said about his sermon."

"You want to know what I heard in that sermon? We haven't talked about this yet, Monty. I have to tell you, it wrenched my heart. It was fear I heard, just plain old fear. I couldn't bear to watch it."

"Fear of what?"

"Fear of . . . I don't know. . . . Fear of emptiness."

She turns away, shutting her eyes against sudden tears. From behind he slides his arms around her, searching for words to soothe, to reassure. But it is the wrong time for that. He has his own misgivings to express, and Lee is the only one he can tell them to.

"A while back," he says, "I told you his soul would be coming in on a later flight. But . . . I'm not sure anymore. The war took something from him. Maybe that is what you saw, when he was on the stage. Something gone. Some empty place. I don't mean hunger. There is a kind of emptiness like hunger, that a person will keep trying to fill. This is different. This is like something has been carved right out of him. I think he is smart enough to know that much about himself too."

"Did you feel that when you came back from the war? Maybe it's something a person has to go through."

"It changed me. I felt bad about some things. I grew up some, I guess."

When she speaks again her voice sounds hollowed, as if she is trying to make casual a question that has been on her tongue for hours, perhaps for years. "Did you ever . . . have to kill anybody, Montrose? You've never talked much about that. An enemy, I mean?"

He waits awhile, chewing on his lips, thinking how to phrase it. "Yes," he says quietly. "Yes, I did."

"I always felt that you did."

"But it was a different kind of war. I came back . . ." *through the trees, loping toward him through the trees and wet heat and fog of insects, and he did not want it to be him, aiming, and did not think, he saw the eyes and fired at the eyes, and watched* ". . . I came back feeling proud of myself, more pride than guilt anyway. I am not saying I am still proud of what I did. But back then I was, at that age, in those times. Nineteen forty-five. A hundred and fifty years ago, it seems like now. But Travis, whatever it was that happened over there, the boy takes no pride or satisfaction in it."

"Has he talked to you at all about what went on?"

"Not a word."

"We have to find him. That's all there is to it. Do you realize we have only seen him once in the past five days? He has hardly been here. And we haven't talked to him at all. Where do you think he's staying?"

"If I knew, I'd go get him."

"Maybe he'll show up again, like he used to, all of a sudden."

"That's what I'm hoping."

"I wonder if it's anything we've done."

"Don't start thinking that."

"I'm not going to be able to stand it much longer, Monty. This on top of everything else. I thought if I kept busy I could keep my mind off things. . . ."

Her voice is speeding up now. He says, "We can't panic, sweetheart."

"Then come to find the paper full of that couple from Idaho . . . They weren't much older than we are, did you know that? Just out here on a trip. There is an interview in today's *Courier* with the fellow who found them, a contractor who was driving up that way yesterday and stopped for lunch where there was a view, and he happened to notice two mounds back by a culvert. It gave him an odd feeling, so he called it in on his two-way radio, and there they were, about a quarter of a mile from where their trailer was parked. Naked. And bludgeoned. And animals had been digging into the dirt.

Animals, Monty! Fifty-two years old, and bludgeoned to death not ten miles from here. They weren't drug dealers. They weren't out hitchhiking or looking for trouble. Just two ordinary people who happened to be passing through. It's getting too close. I feel something getting too close to us, Monty, and I'd like to get away from here for a while. I'd like to move into town. For a while. What would you think about that?"

"Moving into town? I don't know what I think about that."

"Just rent a couple of rooms. An apartment or something."

"That is easier said than done, Lee. There are the dogs. There are the chickens. It may sound trivial, but we can't just abandon the chickens. And the watering. Sometimes this place gets to be more like a prison than a ranch. You can't get away even when you have to."

"Let me show you something. You tell me if I'm seeing things, or what. C'mon in here."

"We don't want to disturb the meeting."

"Don't worry about them. We'll go into the dining room. That's where the paper is."

"Something new in the paper?"

He follows her down the hallway to the dining room table, where the spread-out *Courier* lies, already open to page three.

"They have a map of the county here," she says, "with a bunch of *X*'s and circles to show where all these victims have lived or have been found, where the Kramer girl was hitching or last seen and where those people had their trailer parked. Now look at this and tell me what you see."

"Some wild man's version of tick-tack-toe. God, that's a depressing sight."

As he continues to study this map he sees something that makes his eyes go wide, something he realizes he has known all along, in the way he knew ahead of time that Fowler would be appearing in his driveway, knew it before he knew it.

He stares at the newsprint until the *X*'s and the circles start to merge. His vision blurs. The page turns white and seems to grow smaller. The page is down below him, a square that is dropping through the table, a small bright square in a dark region that becomes a forest, a bright spot, now a speck, disappearing inside that shadowed crease in the landscape. The crease opens, then fades.

He is looking again at the spread-out *Courier*, at the inky and hastily assembled map.

Lee says, "Now tell me. Am I going crazy or are these three *X*'s all in a row?"

"Looks to me like they are."

"Those are the gravesites, Monty. One two three."

"Yes. Yes, I see that."

"They look to be four to five miles apart, in a line aiming south and west, and . . . each one . . . is getting closer to our place. Doesn't it look that way to you?"

"I'll tell you something else about these *X*'s. It occurred to me that day I went driving around up in the hills, but it seemed so farfetched I just filed it away with some of my other hallucinations. It's still farfetched, but it's hard to deny when it's right there in front of us now, isn't it?"

"What's right in front of us?"

"The fault, Lee. According to this map, all three of these gravesites lie right along the fault line."

"No, Monty. That can't be. That's too awful to think about."

"This is where it runs," he says, tracing with his finger, "coming down from San Francisco, under what used to be Holy City, right along the summit road, then heading on south toward San Juan and Hollister. I didn't catch it when I stopped at the Fontaines' because Walter wouldn't let me in. Their cabin must be half a mile beyond the road, and then the bodies were buried quite a way down past the cabin, which would—yes—put them right in the rift zone. This is exactly what's going on. What kind of maniac would dream up a scheme like that? I'd better put in a call right now, make sure the police are aware of this."

Her eyes are still fixed intently on the map. "It's coming our way," she says. "That is what I have been feeling. This is almost like . . . a warning. See the way it starts over here and points toward the ranch? We are right in the path of something!"

"Whoa now! Let's not leap to wild conclusions, Lee. There are lots of folks out in this stretch of country. There are hundreds of houses and ranches. Not to mention hikers and travelers and tourists. People coming and going all the time."

"But they don't all have property located the way ours is. I'm serious, Monty. I want to get away from here. Before we do anything else, I want to move into town for a while. You can call it panic or nerves, whatever you want. But something is coming toward us. I feel it. You have to believe me this time. I was right about Travis, wasn't I? Something has happened to him, something neither one of us yet understands."

The phone rings, and her body jumps as if shot. They look at each other. She starts toward it. Monty holds her, hurries back into the kitchen, and grabs the receiver halfway through the third ring.

"Doyle here."

Silence.

"Hello?"

Nothing.

"Hello!"

He listens hard, for a breath, some background noise. He hears distant static, the faint echo of an operator's voice, half a sentence from some other line a hundred miles away, then silence.

Again he says, "Hello?"

Click.

They stand side by side in the kitchen looking at the black receiver.

"Who was it, Monty?"

"Beats the hell out of me."

"Didn't anybody answer?"

"Maybe it was Grover trying to call back. He's got some kind of funny connection up there. What do you think?"

"He wouldn't be home," she says. "He's gone off looking for Holly."

"Then who the hell called?"

"It's the second time today that's happened."

"You didn't tell me that."

"I didn't think anything about it until now. Middle of the meeting, the phone rang and I listened, and then it made that sound, you can't tell if it's somebody hanging up or just something automatic."

"I wonder if it was Walter. Maybe Walter has come up with something and is trying to get hold of us. I need to call him anyhow."

He dials and the duty officer answers, a fellow named Frank, whom Monty knows, and who tells him that Walter left the station five minutes ago.

"Did he try to call here, by any chance?"

"I wouldn't know, Monty."

"Maybe I can catch him at home."

"Not likely. He's working overtime again."

"Oh, really? What's up?"

"Can't talk about it on the phone."

"Give me a hint."

"All I can say is that the shit has once again hit the fan."

"It's not another grave, Frank, another body."

"I can't go into it."

"How about a trade?"

"A trade? What kind of a trade? What are you, Monty," Frank says with a little faraway laugh, "some kind of secret agent? You working for the CIA?"

"I'm looking at this map in the *Courier,* Frank, and I notice that all the graves so far happen to be following the trace line of the San Andreas. Isn't that curious? It could be coincidence, of course. But I thought some of your people should be aware of it."

"We're already looking into that. A couple of other callers noticed it right after the paper came out. In fact, it's getting to be like a talk show down here, with all the goddam activity on this case."

"Then something else *has* turned up."

"I didn't say that."

"Whereabouts, Frank? Is it in the mountains again, down at this end of the county? I have to know."

"Monty, the detectives don't want any reporters out there yet. There'll be a press briefing as soon . . ."

"I'm not a reporter. I'm a common citizen who happens to live out here. I need to know what's going on. My family could be in danger. C'mon, Frank."

"In that case, just follow the parade. Look for the goddam searchlights. I wouldn't be surprised if you find somebody up there selling peanuts and hot dogs and bumper stickers for souvenirs."

43

He changes into his boots. He puts his rifle into the pickup.

"What's that for?" she cries.

"I don't know."

"What do you expect to find?"

"Don't know, Lee."

"Are you all right?"

"I have to check this out, Lee. It's something I have to do."

He has a hunch, an unthinkable and grotesquely fascinating hunch. He now feels he knows the killer, knows more than he would like to know about the mind at work. The gravesites seem so carefully chosen, he *knows* that the next victim or victims will be found somewhere on a lonesome stretch of mountain road between the third site and the far perimeter of his ranch. This road happens to follow the fault zone for about five miles before looping down toward the lowlands. Between that loop and the edge of his acreage it is rough, roadless back country. "Unless this maniac has four-wheel drive and a chain saw for cutting through scrub oak and timber and a taste for true self-punishment," says Monty, as he consults his file of detailed topo maps, "it has to be right along here. That is the only place it could be."

He does not call anywhere to check this out. He does not want it to be true. He wants this to be the lamest hunch of his career.

With her house full of people, Lee can't go with him, and she wouldn't if she could, would never go out looking for whatever's on the loose. Knowing it's coming is bad enough. She wants to head the other way. In the driveway she holds him a moment longer with her eyes through the pickup window, wishing she could hold him from this expedition.

He says, "If this meeting breaks up before I get back . . ."

Her face is fixed in a tight, troubled smile. "The way things are going, they'll be here till dinnertime, maybe even past dinnertime. We're already talking about adjourning to a restaurant or some such thing. Where are you going to eat?"

He doesn't hear the question. He says, "I'm going to call Tom Warfield. He has a beach cottage I know he'd let us use for a while, for a few days anyhow. It's in a built-up area. Houses all around. You'd feel comfortable there. We can take the dogs with us and figure out a way to get the chickens fed."

He is easing away from the barn. She stands back, with a little wave. "I'll be home as soon as I can," he says, "and I'll arrange all that tonight, in the morning."

As he heads down the driveway, past the scattered cars, it occurs to him that he should explain things to Wellington. As he nears the county road he sees that Wellington's VW is gone. He cannot recall when he last noticed it parked in front of the cabin. Beyond the screen of low trees it looks as if the cabin door is open. He swings in past the ramshackle highrise totem, and stops. On the tiny porch he knocks and shouts, "Wellington!" and waits, hears nothing. He pushes the door fully open and peers inside.

The front room is such a jumble of open books and papers and maps and strewn shirts and artifacts and congealed TV dinners and empty bottles, it is hard to tell whether hours or weeks have passed since someone last set foot in the place. Monty looks into the equally cluttered and seemingly abandoned kitchen and bedroom, then heads back to his pickup, shutting the door.

Billowing dust back onto the porch as he roars away, he spills a little stored-up feeling on his black-bearded and jobless and philandering tenant. An open door at a time like this. It is typical—in fact, more than typical. It is unnerving and ominous, thinks Montrose, who rented to him figuring the fellow could be counted on at certain times. Yet as things have turned out, Wellington's monumental collection of odds and ends is the perfect symbol for his character and the life he leads—sprawling, unkempt, erratic, perhaps unstable.

In a rush now, Monty dips his visor against the low sun coming straight at him through the glass, and thinks that he would like to get rid of Wellington. This idea and the motion of the driving seems to free his mind. Fearing what he will find up ahead, yet knowing it will be there, knowing that even though a spiral is closing in around him something will soon be clarified, one way or another, he is for these few moments beyond resisting it or brooding over it. He hurries toward what looms in the distance, thinking that it is time to clear the air. Give Wellington notice, take a few days in town, for a fresh perspective. Better yet, take that trip to the hot springs. Yes, when this is over we will all of us find some new starting place, somewhere to begin again. With no looking back. It is—yes—the looking back that does you in.

By the time he reaches the high road the sky has turned to flame. Just over the earth's curve some distant metropolis has caught fire. The glow of its burning ignites the trees and slopes. Half a mile ahead of him he sees other lights flickering against this glow, dark red, dark blue.

Coming around a long turn, he finds fresh flares burning pink on rutted asphalt, and a young deputy guiding traffic past the vehicles clotted around the next pull-out. They can't block traffic here. It's the only route through this stretch of country. Monty has driven it before. This is right where he imagined they would be, where the road and the fault line follow a high ridge above a deep, creek-cut gorge. Passing slowly, he sees patrol cars, an ambulance, a ranger's truck, half the clearing cordoned off with ropes, and beyond that the string of hurriedly parked cars belonging to reporters, photographers, TV cameramen, and a few stray travelers, who all gang around among the eerie lights of blue and red revolving lamps and road flares.

He pulls up beyond the last parked car and walks back, reaching the cleared place just as someone shouts, "All right! Make a little room! Make some room, please!"

The ambulance is backing toward the ropes. Beyond an embankment the hats and heads of half a dozen men can be seen. Four of them are carrying a blanket-covered stretcher. As they struggle up over the edge of the bank, one man stumbles. His partner, adjusting to the extra weight, steps on a corner of the blanket, pulling it clear. There is an astonished outcry, a burst of commands. In the instant before a white-clad ambulance attendant rushes forward, Monty sees the dark hair, the once-brown face now ghastly white, the body still striped by tan lines, two days buried yet strangely fresh in this lingering light, and sprinkled with crumbs, with smudges of dirt and smears of dust that take him back to their rolling under the boughs, when their sweat-coated bodies caught patches of dirt. It makes him sick. His throat goes dry. His stomach turns. He shuts his eyes and sees her in the noontime orchard, crumbs clinging to her legs and belly. His eyes spring open, day becomes evening, and he finds her being unearthed.

The blanket drops over her. The stretcher bearers hurry to the open rear door and slide her in. The attendants leap on board, the door thuds shut. The ambulance purrs toward the road with its roof light twirling.

One of the sheriff's cars swings out in front, as escort, and they siren into the dusk, while the reporters and cameramen bunch toward the sheriff, eager for a statement, muttering reverently, babbling and wisecracking among themselves, even their wisecracks tinged, in the dusky light of sundown, with awe and wonder.

"How did she die?" someone asks.

"Just like the first one," someone replies.

"Smothered?" asks another.

"Or buried alive."

"Incredible."

"They say the hands and feet were tied."

"Was she molested?"

"Not from the look of things."

"But who *was* she?"

"Nobody knows yet."

"Can anybody figure this goddam case?"

"Does anybody have any coffee?"

"I'm through trying to figure it. I have had it with these wild rides into no man's land."

"It's too bizarre. It has to be one of these cults."

"I keep coming back to the Manson Family."

"What about the Mafia?"

"It's too sloppy."

"Whoever it is, they want to be caught. They're tipping their hand. This grave was right where anybody could spot it, just driving down the road."

"How do you know that?"

"That's how they spotted it. Some thrill-seekers."

"Gimme a sip of that stuff."

"Whatever happened to good old-fashioned homicide?"

"What do you mean by that?"

"I mean for money, or for revenge, or crimes of passion. In the old days your average killer at least had a motive a person could relate to."

"What about terrorists? Some kind of underground outfit."

"Not likely."

"Hey!"

"Yeah?"

"Did you hear what I just said?"

"I think I heard it."

"Underground! Sonofabitch! This whole thing could be some kind of diabolically symbolic act of—"

"Too easy."

"Think about it. You know where we are standing at this

very moment? I checked it out on the map. This whole area through here."

"You mean if she started now we could be swallowed up."

"Like noodles."

"It hasn't gone off since 1906."

"She sure as hell isn't going to start shaking tonight."

"I wouldn't get overconfident."

"What the hell's the connection? What kind of freak would bury somebody in a place like this? No notes. No explanation. Terrorists always leave notes."

After a thoughtful silence someone says, "Maybe it is another way to shake people up."

They all chuckle nervously, against a cold breeze that seems triggered by the winking out of the last spot of brightness in the western sky.

Montrose, at the edge of this group, and out of the shine of headlights, finds himself trembling. He cannot control it. He moves away, toward the cover of some scrub oak at the edge of the clearing, and the trembling becomes silent, convulsive sobs, his whole body heaving wretchedly for Crystal, and for Travis, and for Leona, who has yet to hear this news, and for himself, and for all the sad ways men fend off their specters. Poor Crystal. The folly. The pointless waste. Driving home from the airport, sipping rum in the front seat and listening to the talk show, who was she, between those two tipsy soldiers careening down the road from the summit, her eyes shining at the ocean in front of them? Just a woman on the loose, one of Travis's girls, with a mother in Texas, and Trav at the wheel, and all of them for that brief hour on the loose, so oddly innocent. The memory undoes him, the innocence of it next to what's been learned this week, this past hour. These days you cannot look back without grief and helplessness and that gouge of loss for even last week's brand of innocence.

Again he sees her in his orchard, that face set against bright leaves. Astraddle him, she grins down bewitchingly, and he sees now that everything about her, every gesture, every turn of phrase, was calculated, edited, and there had been nothing spontaneous about the free-floating adventuress who came gliding toward him through his April blossoms. There were certain things she wanted, certain things she wanted hid. He has no way to know with certainty what they were. He can only guess, with guesses that lead where he does not want to go. He hears her evading the question of when she met Travis and how long they might have been together and why in fact she stayed and traveled with him. Perhaps she knew that Travis *had* returned early to the mainland. If so, were there other secrets she could have been threatening to reveal? She liked abuse. Perhaps this was a way of forcing Travis to assault her, the same way she goaded Monty to attack. That is what she came looking for; he sees it clearly now. She sensed he had some anger in him that could be put to good use. Perhaps she misjudged Trav's limits. The boy has never been known for his restraint. What if Crystal told Travis about coupling with his father? That perverse streak in her. Some kind of test. She liked to talk about her lovers. Maybe she talked too much. Maybe Travis went too far.

A hand falls on his shoulder. He turns, as if stung, and sees Walter, helmet and field jacket backlit against the garish clearing.

"Didn't expect to see you up here," Walter says.

Monty shakes his head, blinking fiercely, to bat the tears away.

"Neither did I."

"You all right?"

"No."

"I just realized something," Walter says.

"What's that?"

"Where I've seen that girl we just dug up. She was with Travis that first day I ran into you downtown."

"You don't forget much."

"It's my job."

"She was with him a lot, until a few days ago."

Walter inhales deeply, looks up at the sky as if praying, then lets the breath go, in a great weary sigh of resignation.

"What happened?" he says.

"They broke up. Got tired of each other, something like that."

"What else?"

"What do you mean, what else?"

"When was the last time you saw them together?"

"I guess it was . . . before the rally."

"What kind of relationship did they have?"

"What are you getting at, Walter?"

"You know what I'm getting at."

"There isn't necessarily any connection."

"But there's a possibility. Anybody could figure there is a strong possibility. Especially if he still hasn't turned up."

"Can you put me in touch with Samson Newby?"

"I wish I could."

"Under the circumstances I think I deserve a chance to hear his version of what happened at the Fontaines' place."

"I couldn't agree with you more. I wish he was still in town."

"Where is he?"

"Transferred."

"You've got to be kidding."

"This won't make you feel any better. It'll probably make you feel worse. But it will be in all the papers tomorrow, so you might as well hear it now."

Cautiously Walter looks around, then he steps in so close Monty can hear the smallest leather clicks his belts and holster make.

"Newby was in narcotics, right? He supposedly had the Fontaines staked out for months. When those kids showed up last week while he was out there, they couldn't tell if he was digging up bodies or putting them away. Well, it turns out that he had just discovered them. He had been gone for a few days and just got back and noticed something was funny and started poking around. That part is very simple. All you have to do is check the coroner's report. The messy part is the reason he had never closed in on the Fontaines. He too was dealing, you see. This is why he had been gone, and also why he was so anxious to find them. They had an arrangement. Very small-time, of course. Very clumsy, in my opinion. That is the problem. There was nothing going on with Newby. All very small-time and clumsy and very embarrassing for the department, and so they have hustled him out of town, just like he was some third-rate informer they can't use anymore. That is the story on Samson. He was never anything but a big pain in the ass, as far as the department was concerned. If it wasn't for Fowler, we might have been able to cover it up. But Newby is not a killer. I know the guy. His wife cut out on him a while back. He has two kids, one of whom is now in juvenile hall for compulsive vandalism. He has psoriasis. His life is a shambles. Just like mine. He never was a suspect."

Monty looks at him and weighs this story. He believes it. This is about the way he expects the world to work.

"Who are the others, then?" he asks.

"Others?"

"Who are the other suspects?"

"If that was Travis's ex-girlfriend, I would say that at the moment he is near the top of the list. I don't guess you have seen him yet."

"No. We expect to . . . hear from him, though. Anytime."

"Can I ask you a favor?"

"Sure."

"Would you come into town and identify the victim?"

"What?"

"I'm sorry, Monty."

"That is really rubbing salt into the wound."

"You're probably the only person around here who knows her."

"Goddam it, Walter!"

Again he sees the body, tagged this time and stretched out on a table, and his hopelessness turns suddenly to anger, at her death, and at whoever murdered her, and at Travis, for the anguish he puts people through, never letting anyone know what in hell he is up to, this lifetime of thoughtlessness.

At Walter he shouts, "You like this whole idea, don't you!"

"No, Monty, I don't. . . ."

"Bullshit, you don't! You'd like everybody's life to be as fucked up and miserable as your own!"

He watches the stricken eyes expand.

"Isn't that true?" Monty shouts.

He leans toward Walter, hoping he will reach again for the .38. He would like one small excuse to lunge.

But some journalists have turned toward this outburst. Two of them recognize him, calling out, "Hey, Monty! Is that you, Doyle? Didn't see you over there. Didn't know you were covering this one."

These two step toward him and then two others, drawing Monty and Walter inside the loose edges of their throng, where steaming thermoses and many flasks of liquor have appeared. Dark has fallen quickly, and with the dark a sharp, damp chill no one is prepared for, smelling faintly of the sea and the moist scent of pine rising from the slopes below. Where the headlamps converge there has been a brief huddling, as they listened to the sheriff, and then a round of quick laughs as they held their fraternity together a few moments longer. Now Walter and Monty are surrounded and pushed apart and find themselves moving, mumbling, shambling toward the cars, inside a crowd any one of whom in this light, at this altitude, could be a rapist or a gravedigger or another target— detectives, police officers, rangers, camera crews, reporters, feature writers, acid-eyed and bearded mountain men. Reluctantly, in silence, Monty accepts what Walter asks him to do. His engine soon is one of dozens warming up, his lights sending two more bright bayonets to pierce the night.

They all swing around, raising dust in the cleared space,

around the deputies assigned to guard this site until the investigation can continue in the morning. They line up to make a long cortege of squad cars, rented Pintos, taxicabs and pickup trucks snaking slowly along the turns and through the trees, gathering speed. Inside, heaters whir against the early chill. Outside, a haze of dust gives body to the headlight beams. Seen from a distance, say from across the gorge, silhouetted against this shine their own lights make, beneath the edge black ridges cut in the darkening sky, they could be some modern-day wagon train or party of explorers caravaning down from the high country, bearing headlines, threading west.

44

If Montrose, before returning to the ranch, had lingered in town and stopped one more time at The Cheating Heart, he would have found Travis sitting alone at a dimly lit table drinking what he figures could be his final bottle of beer. In his pocket he has the note his father left at the bar this afternoon. He has just learned from the bartender that the police want him for questioning. Now the bartender, with face averted, as if to hide this conversation from a lip reader, is talking on the phone. Travis doesn't care. Fuck it, he is thinking, let them come. He is waiting for whoever it will be. It is past midnight. He is too tired to care, too tired to move.

For two days he has been walking the beaches, talking from time to time with the Spanish soldier he first met on the hotel roof, discussing war with him, and adventuring, and Jesus. "For a while there," Travis would say, "I thought Jesus was with me." And the Spaniard would stroke his beard and shake his head and say, "No one is with you. It is a very long and lonely journey."

For two nights he napped on the porch of an unoccupied cottage he discovered, hoping each night he would not wake up in the morning. He has died again, and this time he is not sure why. He didn't love Crystal. He didn't even like Crystal. But he wanted her to stay with him, be with him, sleep next to him. When she walked away he figured she would be back sooner or later. When she did not return, when it dawned on him she might be gone for good, he sank into darkness. He is convinced he will never be able to keep a woman. Something inside him repels women. Like an insecticide. Drinking, he has returned to the battle zone, where he died the first time, and he is punishing himself with memories of Asian prostitutes, the ones he let humiliate him, when someone sits down next to him, scooting in so close he can feel the body heat.

He expects to see the plainclothes detective who keeps tabs on this saloon. But it is Radar, saying in his soft, religious voice, "Do you believe in messages?"

"Yes."

"There was a message on my cabin door."

"Not from me."

"It's from your father. It says get in touch immediately."

Travis looks into Radar's eyes and sees a woman there. He suspects that if he mentioned making love, Radar would consent without hesitation.

"I knew you'd be here," Radar says.

"What do you want?"

"I want to take you somewhere. I want to show you something."

Travis doesn't answer, but he feels a warmth begin to percolate through the coolness of his death. He is in the mood for something. Anything. He doesn't care.

"There are signs," Radar says. "Signs everywhere. Prophecies and warnings. But no one wants to hear them."

He does not like Radar anymore, but he likes this warm buzz of old times, the sense of intuiting what Radar means. In the days when they played basketball together, two on two, the instant before Radar's hand or eye would cue a pass Travis would be moving toward the spot. Sometimes he would be reaching for the telephone, to call him, and the phone would ring and Radar would be speaking. Tonight it is clear that Radar is the one he came in here to wait for. Not the cops. In his mind this is more than coincidence. It is the fourth time he has run into him. Travis believes that things come toward you because you attract them. He is repelling women, but he is attracting Radar. It is time to find out why. There is something to be handled. Some kind of test. Perhaps it is going to be a test of his faith. He had thought his faith was long blown out to sea, that he would never again be able to believe in anything. He has begun to think of his New Vision as nothing more than recurring blindness. Now it strikes him that if a thing can be tested, maybe it still exists, and so he soon finds himself leaving the saloon by the rear entrance.

Driving out of town, Radar says, "I took Abraham as my middle name not because I am Abraham but because I am like Abraham. I am here to bear witness, to body forth. You did not understand what I meant about Jehovah, you see. Jehovah is a very ancient God. I want you to understand this because you are my only friend. All my other friends have deserted me. I don't want you to think I have anything against Jesus. It is just that Jehovah is more ancient. That is why he is more powerful. The Bible is a book about power."

Travis replies with something he does not believe any longer. He knows it is the kind of thing he would have to say if he were facing a true test. He says, "There is no power greater than Christ's love."

"Except the powers of Jehovah," says Radar quietly, "the deep, primordial ones."

"Christ heals all wounds."

"But Jehovah's powers are deeper than blood, deeper than soil, deep in the earth. When I saw that message from your father on my front door, I heard your father's voice, and I knew then that you and I should go into his forest, and that there was a way to show you what I mean."

"My father's place? Is that where we're going?"

"Eventually."

"We shouldn't go out there, man."

"Everybody gets used to it."

"What the hell do you mean by that?"

Radar doesn't speak again for a long time, and Travis is blinking hard, trying to clear his head.

"I don't like this," Travis keeps saying. "Hey, man, I really do not like this at all."

Then they are cruising down the county road. He sees his father's mailbox go by. Half a mile past the mailbox Radar stops, shuts the engine off, climbs out and slams his door. Travis feels for the door handle. It isn't there. It has been sheared off or dismantled, and the paneling is smooth. He has heard girls talk about hitchhiking, and this is one of the things you are supposed to check before you get into a car. He has to wait for Radar to come around and open the passenger side. He shuts his eyes hard, to push down the nausea, and he is thinking that he and Radar are about the same size and if it came to hand-to-hand he could take Radar, he always could, and Radar should know that. He expects to see a gun or a knife drawn from the sheath Radar is wearing at his belt. But when the door flips open it just swings wide. No one is standing there. Radar is already around back, by the trunk.

Travis hears the trunk lid lift, hears him rummaging through tools. He does not want to know what is going on. He will walk, and when the dark has covered him he will run toward the house. He starts down the road, sobered by the adrenaline rush, thinking: Oh shit, oh shit, how did I get way the hell out here in the black of night . . . when Radar calls, "Hey, Travis, did I tell you that Crystal left a note on my door too?"

The question stops him. Travis did not know this. The thought of it makes him groan, that she would have any reason to go looking for a warped sonofabitch like Radar, and because it is just the kind of thing she *would* do.

"When did that happen?" Travis says.

Radar doesn't answer. He climbs over the low rail fence carrying what looks like a shovel, wading into the forest as if his eyes can see in the dark. He calls back, "I thought you knew about it."

"No. I haven't seen her."

"I thought she might be with you tonight. I expected to see her."

"I don't want to talk about Crystal," Travis says. "Okay? As far as I'm concerned, she's dead."

Radar's voice comes to him as if from farther away. "How did you know that?"

"What did you say?" Travis shouts.

He hears the sounds of movement, footsteps heading into the trees. His head swims with sudden terror and rage, already knowing what he dares not admit he knows. "Hold it, Radar! Hold it right there! Tell me what you just said!"

But the crackle and whish of footsteps move still farther into the dark and into the trees.

45

BEFORE DAWN

She doesn't know what time it is. The sky outside seems less dark now. She can't be sure. Next to her Monty turns and breathes in a way that tells her he isn't sleeping either. She almost reaches out, almost speaks, but does not, dares not share with anyone what's on her mind. It is too strange, something she herself would read about in the *National Enquirer* with skeptical fascination, something she has kept to herself for so many years it is embedded in her imagination the way a tumor gets embedded in the flesh, and she regards it that way, as a part of her, yet something separate she can study and explore.

It begins in Berkeley, when they were ten months married and renting a three-room shack on Durant Avenue while Monty finished his third year at the university. He was drawing money on the GI Bill and working part-time as a janitor. She took junior college classes and waited on tables four nights a week. Weary of being too weary to enjoy the few hours they had together, come spring vacation they dropped everything and drove a hundred fifty miles north and east to the rim of Lake Tahoe and rented a beach cabin with a view of the water and snow-capped peaks beyond. Every morning they made love on a long double bed with fitted sheets, in the afternoons they hiked and sunbathed, at night they ate in restaurants or cooked outdoors in the mountain air, and made love again. He was twenty-two at the time, and she was twenty. Handsome they were, and beautiful and slim and full of vigorous, stored-up embraces. It was their second honeymoon, and also the week Grover was conceived.

His seed was planted there, in the Sierra—that is to say, on high, firm ground—and in her view the time and the place of the planting of the seed is just as meaningful for people as it is for beans or beets or carrots, which, if planted during a waxing moon and watered well, will respond to the magnetic pull of the moon's expansion and extraordinary light and open faster. Magnetic light will draw the water and bring the sprout quicker through the soil's skin and make a stronger plant. If seeded during a waning moon, the plants will come up, but at a different rate, waiting through their first nights in a different brand of light, thus finding another rhythm for their few weeks or months in the world.

She thinks of herself in these terms, and Monty too, and hopes one day to meet Holly's mother and find out about the woman she already sees as Grover's wife. Talking to her own mother many years ago, Leona learned that she herself was conceived in the Oklahoma farmhouse her family lived in until they abandoned it in 1934. "That's the only place your dad and me ever had for lovin'," her mother had said, "the back room in that old frame house, and nothing outside the winda but dirt and whatever crop was comin in, or not comin in."

Whenever Lee is feeling small and ordinary, or less than ordinary, or whenever she is feeling isolated, with wide dry spaces between her and everyone else, this is how she accounts for it.

In Monty's case, she learned from Mrs. Doyle, on one of those days when they spent long hours trading lore, that he had been conceived in Tennessee. This was a revelation. Born in California but conceived in 1925 when Mr. and Mrs. Doyle had traveled back to the old family homestead outside Nash-ville for a big reunion. Since then it has been no mystery to her that at least half of him wants to be a dirt farmer and listen all the time to country music and fake his down-home accent when strangers stop him on the road.

She doubts that he knows this fact about himself, since Mrs. Doyle did not think it proper for women to discuss such things with men. And Lee would never mention it to him, for fear it might start a conversation that would lead around to Travis. That is the part she doesn't want to have to share.

The sun cut bright through the apple trees that afternoon. Ridges and slopes of soil beneath the blanket pushed up against her loins. She remembers that she was wearing white dungarees and a purple blouse she knew he liked. It was going to be a picnic, but Monty dropped the basket, chasing her, and then they laughed, fighting at the buttons in their haste, both eager. They were always eager. They had been waiting till she was safe. He was not supposed to come into her. She didn't want him to. Grover was then just a year and a half and plenty to handle. She wanted some breathing space. Monty came into her anyway. She let him, and afterward they looked into each other's eyes with unspoken questions and talked about how good it had felt.

That was the summer they had moved back to the ranch. With Grover always underfoot, they had fallen into the habit of leaving him with Grandma while they hiked to the far edge of the orchard. They had a spot down there, a cool grove they used to call the ditch. It made them feel lascivious to murmur to each other about taking a little stroll down to the ditch. They didn't know back then what had put it there. It was just an oddly pleasant feature of the land. Nowadays it can make her hands sweat—ever since 1969, when the ministers and the psychics started predicting publicly that a big chunk of coastline was going to break off and fall into the sea. Until then she had never given it much thought, this legendary crack in the earth that was supposed to be the breaking edge; and come to find out that Monty's ranch was sitting right on the ocean side of that crack.

There were people who actually fled the state in the spring of 1969, moved inland to Idaho or Missouri. There was more to this than earthquakes, they said. They were leaving to be safe from tidal waves and the massive floods Edgar Cayce, the medium from Kentucky, had predicted would inundate California sometime before the year 2000. They were leaving to prepare for the Second Coming of Christ. She heard a preacher from Oakland reading from the Book of Revelation on the radio, and this had chilled her blood, because he had an Oklahoma voice like one of her uncles back home, which made it impossible to ignore.

" 'And I beheld,' " the voice proclaimed, " 'I beheld when he had opened the sixth seal, and, lo, there was a great earthquake; and the sun became black as sackcloth of hair, and the moon became as blood; and the stars of heaven fell unto the earth, even as a fig tree casteth her untimely figs, when she is shaken of a mighty wind. And the heaven departed as a scroll when it is rolled together; and every mountain and island were moved out of their places.' "

Hearing this, Lee too began to talk of moving, or taking a trip somewhere until the deadline passed.

But she also dreamed of watching it happen, dreamed of observing this catastrophe from some secure and elevated vantage point, as if from a helicopter, gazing down with awe and grief at the wreckage wrought by these fearful convulsions of the earth and the inpouring of the seas, filling valleys and burying cities forever.

Montrose told her the whole thing was nonsense, although she knew he wasn't sure, not at the beginning when the predictions began. He was worried enough to start studying the subject in earnest, for his own peace of mind, bringing home magazines with seismic wave charts and geological maps and cutaway views of the earth's crust that proved the fault line was not nearly deep enough to break this state in half.

When the fateful day came and went and the ranch had not moved, the sun did not turn black, no tidal waves rolled toward them from the lowlands, and the whole coast somehow survived, intact, without so much as a quiver, she gradually relaxed, eased it all out of her conscious mind.

For two years she relaxed, until February of 1971, when that big quake rumbled up out of nowhere and ripped through San Fernando, down in the southern part of the state. The pictures in the papers made it look to be the very thing the prophets and the mystics had predicted. Sidewalks split open, hospitals caved in, freeway overpasses landed on the cars. Aftershocks followed, and more damage, and more prophets arose who said this was just the prologue, the end was near, and the worst was yet to come.

Then the earth fell silent once again. The prophets fell silent. Again her fears subsided, gathered back into the cocoon of her mind, where islands emerge in silence from the deeps, where blazing volcanoes explode around a distant Ring of Fire. Since she never goes near that part of the ranch now, weeks can pass when she scarcely thinks about the ditch. When she does, it never worries her much. She hasn't let it, until today, yesterday, last night, when her fear started up again, in a way she had not anticipated, never dared let herself anticipate. That map in the *Courier,* put together with Walter's news, and now Crystal—it makes certain things she has always carried in her bones too fearful to allow her mind to dwell on.

Travis was conceived where the tremors lurk. Monty calls it the zone of stress, where rocks and boulders stretch and strain. Lee sees it as a bottomless river, a fissure plunging to the heart of the earth, and she thinks of it as a realm of violence. Tonight she cannot shake this notion from her mind. There is no way to talk it out, no one she dares mention it to. Bad enough to have such thoughts. Speaking such thoughts can give them power, make them truer than they already are. She longs for the light of day to come and burn these hovering nighttime visions from her mind.

46

MONTROSE

They are always there, but Monty doesn't always hear them.
Like far-off tracers, they move in silence, tracking in the
mind, acquiring sound only when summoned. Tonight, this
morning, the bullets come quietly to life. There are dozens.
No way to tell how many found a target. Two of them make all
the noise, buzzing like the insects buzzed, insistently, so tiny,
sometimes so close in next to the eyes, they can't be seen at
all, a tiny buzzing blur. Insects were everywhere, and trees.
It was morning, not long after breakfast. He didn't eat much
breakfast. They had orders to advance. He followed orders
then. In those days it was easy. He believed in orders. No
choice but to move toward what was coming. It was silent, for
the first time in weeks, it seemed. He was moving alone
through trees and vines and morning heat. He stopped to shove
his helmet back, to drag the sweat from his forehead, and he
saw them first. Two men loping, with rifles, bayonets. He had
enough lead time, a long instant, to study the lean build of
the man in front, the cautious stride, and then the look, when
their heads turned at some sound Monty did not know he
had made. He could tell by the eyes and the mouth that the
one in front was around his age. Monty stared, as if seeing
himself in a mirror coming toward himself in the jungle, from
the far side of the world, traveling just as many miles as
Monty had traveled to reach that spot at that selfsame mo-

ment. This little reverie gave the other one some time, but not enough. Before the man could change position Monty lifted his rifle. Someone was going to be killed. He did not want it to be himself. He squeezed his trigger, heard a gargled gasping, and watched him fall. The gasping is always louder than the shot. That is mainly what he hears, twenty-eight years later. Tonight, this morning, he is forty-six. The man coming toward him is still that age, a young-eyed soldier, loping through trees with a lifted bayonet, and gasping, and Monty can regard him with a kind of familiar loftiness until the face suddenly moves in closer than it has ever come. A spotlight is switched on. This time it is the face of Travis heading toward him, with the bayonet aimed. The eyes are staring wildly, the mouth working like an evangelist's, getting ready to call upon the Lord. The face turns pale, all blood gone, the eyes abulge with some unexpected fear, and then he vomits, the soldier's gasping becomes a long agonizing retch, as gobbets spew across the dining room table, into the candles, all over the plates and Leona's linen, the slimy stringers fouling his uniform, his ribbons, his flat lapels, an eruption that is triggered by their table talk, their murder talk, their talk of some girl found buried alive, intolerable to Travis on his first day home because he . . . because he . . .

Monty's eyes spring open. He is paralyzed, made of ice, then cold fire, as the blood throbs in his temples. When he can finally lift his head, he strains to hear the world beyond his window, to see some sign of daylight, the window purple-gray and the sky waking. Unsure whether he is awake or still sleeping, he reaches past the mattress edge where his rifle stands propped and loaded. He touches metal, lets his head fall back, stares at the ceiling, trying again to kill the seed Walter first planted yesterday morning, and failing to kill it. Against his will it has been slowly blooming, a misshapen night flower, ornate and gory.

He is lying like that, arm out, fingering the underbarrel,

when he hears again the noise that roused him, or some sound within the nightmare his old dream has become. The retching gasp is like a board pulling on the stair or in the hallway. An old beam nailed up to last in 1889 and settling now into some infinitesimal wearing of its square-ended nail. Perhaps that. Or perhaps a dawn wind pushing at the house. Is there a wind? Beyond the lattice there hangs a long, slender pine limb he uses to gauge the power of the wind. The limb is motionless. Each needle tuft is still. He sits up and listens hard and hears it again. The creaking a footstep would make. It covers him with a film of icy sweat, his heart now pounding wildly. He wants this all to be part of the dream. This must be part of it. If Travis should appear at the doorway it would be proof to Monty that he has not yet emerged from that lurid realm.

The dreamer's wife appears in his nightmare, sitting up next to him, to add the intensity of her listening to this intolerable silence.

"Monty? Monty, what was that?"

Into the night he shouts, "Who's out there?" grabbing for his rifle, its cold metal touching white sheets the way you see guns in old trompe l'oeil paintings from the 1890s, the folds of the background cloth almost believable beneath the oiled and shiny barrel in repose. He clicks off the safety, points the rifle toward the door.

A scratch of shoe, a knuckle raps lightly. Someone is out there, someone got past the dogs.

He hears a voice that is not a voice but a rasp in some faraway throat that sounds like "Dad."

Monty shouts, "Who? Who's there?"

"It's him," Lee says.

"What happened to the goddam dogs?"

Lee says, "It's Travis."

"Has he come?"

"Don't hurt him."

Monty lunges for the bed lamp. Seeing this in the near-dark,

Leona dives at him across the mattress in a tangle of sheets and blankets, crying, "No! No, you won't do it, Montrose! I won't let you do it!"

He has hit the switch too hard, sending the lamp off the table. The bright arc of its falling bulb and the shock of her weight, the blind grope of desperate hands, jars the gun against his trigger finger. The shot roars just as Travis appears in the opened doorway, his face lit for an instant in the ghostly upward shine of the bed lamp still rolling on its shade. The face drops as if hurled into shadows.

Monty hears the knees and elbows thudding, but no groan, no outcry. For one instant the only sound or movement in the room is the lamp's last little rolling before the circular shade comes to rest, shining its funneled beam across the floor like a flashlight. Then a wail starts in Leona's throat, one long, low, rising syllable.

He lurches toward the wall switch, flooding the room with ceiling light. Blinded momentarily, dazed with giddy nausea from the sudden effort, Monty looks down and sees the outline of his son, spread across the floor, arms flung, hands grabbing at the carpet.

He drops to his knees and sees that Travis is breathing. He sees the clamped jaws and squeezed eyes of a man who could be fighting pain. The whole body quivers. Monty touches his shoulder and the quivering subsides.

"Son," he says, his voice thick. "Son, did I . . . are you . . . are you hurt?"

No blood visible. Under his hand he feels quick, even breath. Watching the eyes open narrowly, the mouth twitch slowly loose from its grimace, he recognizes the tensed face of a man in combat waiting for the next shell to land. Monty's chest bunches so tightly he cannot breathe.

Travis's jaws relax. The voice is dry, almost a whisper. "He was going to . . . do me in."

"I didn't mean to fire, son. It went off. It . . . went off."

"I had to cut him."

"What?"

"Had to cut . . ."

"Cut who?"

The fingers unbend, release the carpet. Slowly Travis pushes up to his hands and knees, staring down at nothing. His face is stubbled, worn, as if he hasn't slept in days. His clothes and face and arms are smudged with dirt.

Monty repeats, "Who?"

When Travis still does not answer, he leans and puts a hand under each shoulder, to urge and ease him upward.

"Are you all right? Can you stand up? What's happened to you, son?"

Sobs are rising from Monty's chest now, sobs of relief, sobs of forgiveness, sobs of dread for what may be yet to come.

Travis says, "It was going to be a test. And I blew it. I became like him. I might as well be dead. I should be."

"Travis, I can't follow this. Became like who?"

"I think I killed him. I had to. He started talking. Can you help me carry him? I don't want to leave him there. We aren't supposed to leave anybody behind."

Travis is on his feet now, hunched, moving toward the doorway, toward the shadowed hall.

"Wait a second," Monty says, reaching for the arm. "Take it easy, son."

"Can you?" Travis barks, suddenly fierce, making it an order. He jerks away from Monty's hand.

"Travis, wait. Tell me how . . ."

"He could be dying. Don't you follow that? Goddam it! God*dam* it, I don't want him to die!"

Travis is in the hallway, calling back over his shoulder. Monty thinks a blow to the jaw could stop him. It would give them some time. But he isn't going to stop him. He hears boots crashing down the stairway. He calls out, "We'll take the pickup, then!"

"No," Travis yells. "It's faster this way! Through the trees! Right now! C'mon!"

Monty turns to grab his rifle, sees Leona standing by the bed watching this. Her hand clutches the window frame like someone ready to jump out. She looks sixty. Hair loose and witchlike, eyes pouched, skin gray, as if powdered. Monty sees himself in her face, sees how he must look to her.

47

TRAVIS RETURNS

From high above she could be a butterfly, or a white-winged cabbage moth floating under the trees, her wings obscured by branches, then flashing clear, or glowing among leaves still shaded, still waiting for the sun to show along the eastern ridge. This is how she looks to Travis as he glances back toward his mother through the rows. Her wings are the wide white sleeves and flaring skirts of nightgown and robe. He does not recognize the wings or the robe. In this light the sheer cloth has a ghostly shimmer. She too is an alien creature in these surroundings. Running low and hunched, searching each path of ground in front of him, Travis sees some stranger's boots and cuffs. He is in a foreign country. Foreign yet familiar. He has run through an orchard much like this one long ago, and then forgotten it until this moment. He hears someone in dire need banging on a tree trunk, signaling for help. He listens. No. It is the shivering of teeth. He listens hard. It is a jay. A jaybird's chatter. What's a jay doing here? There are no jays out here. Unless . . . Aaahh, yes. If there are jays, then what he's looking for will come to him first in the shape of a branch broken, a path trampled, some change in this landscape he is piecing back together as he runs. The part behind him has now been reconstructed. The part ahead is still unknown, unfolding. He concentrates on limbs and leaves and clods and each worn footpath leading into the brush.

Past the last row of trees, where the orchard gives way to pine and redwood, he finds what he is looking for, and now remembers everything. He sees the wild berry thicket, a swath trampled through it. He plunges past the thicket into a dark clearing. Trees with high foliage shade this bower from the light that still hovers behind the hills, back up the slope he has descended. Around the trunks, in the damp morning air, ferns proliferate. When the sound of feet and breaking brush ceases, there is an absolute stillness which on other occasions has seemed to Travis ideally sylvan, the kind of little Eden he remembered in the late-night sleepless heat of barracks, but which now chokes him as if this quiet nave has been sprayed with deadly gas.

It does not strike him that the end of sound means others have joined him here. It does not register that Monty and Leona stand behind him staring down, as he does, at the thick blanket of composted herbage, and at the dug-in shovel blade waiting, at the ready. Near the shovel Radar lies crumpled. His close-cropped head lolls forward, as if he might be sleeping off a drunk. His hands, gathered at the sternum, are covered with blood. Travis, looking at the blood, watches it dissolve. He sees Radar on his feet again, and sees the hands without the blood, in the moment before he swung the piece of fencing. Then he sees the head silhouetted in front of him as they hiked in from the road, when the urge to obliterate took hold of him, when the words streaming back from Radar's mouth became unbearable, when he knew why he had been sitting there waiting for someone to arrive, and knew why they had come out here, and knew who Radar was. He feels that same blind fury rising, hears the invisible whish of sheath knife leaving its holster just as Radar turned in the dark with his hands spread wide as if saying, Take me. Now the fence piece is in Trav's hand again, and he is lifting it over the body, ready to swing again, when someone grabs him from behind.

"Let go!" cries Travis. "Goddam it, let me go!"

But Monty has him in a bear-hug vise and squeezes until the muscles go limp and the piece of fencing drops.

Then it seems to Travis that they stand this way for a very long time, in the cool humid silence under the trees, as if waiting for something, waiting for the light. The breath of his running slows down. And the blood slows. But not the throbbing of the blood. It throbs in his skin, filling his ears. He does not hear Leona move. His side vision catches a flash of white, and he turns and sees her lifting the shovel. He sees her slipper push down on the blade. She lifts out a shovelful of the soft, black earth and tosses it aside, making a small hole.

Monty says, "What the hell are you doing?"

She says, "We'll have to bury the body."

Travis feels the bear-hug grip release, slowly, as if the arms know they will be needed elsewhere, but do not yet know how. Monty moves toward her, saying, "Give me the shovel, Lee."

She turns on him. "Don't you patronize me!"

"Lee . . ."

"It's our land, isn't it?" she cries. "Our son? Who is going to know?"

"We don't have any choice."

"Of course we have a choice! Do you just want to turn him in?"

"No. I don't want to do that. But . . . this is . . . the police are already . . ."

"How are the police going to know?"

"My God, Lee!"

"Who are the witnesses? Isn't it our land? Our family? How is anybody going to know?"

Travis, watching this, feels his chest enlarge until he fears that it will burst. It is filling up with water, and the water rises to his eyes and coats them with a clear, searing liquid. He blurts, "I have to be turned in, Ma. I have to."

Her body jerks. "Don't say that, Travis. It isn't true."

Through this hot clear liquid he looks at his mother and seems to see her for the first time, who she is, what she is capable of feeling, what she has done for him and would be willing to do. All the sins and transgressions of his twenty-one years come pouring through his mind in an instant, and he begins to weep. He wants to turn this pouring into words. All he can say is, "Ma. Ma." He wants to sink into her arms. But she is the one who sinks. She falls to her knees, as if fainting. She is moaning.

Montrose, looking from wife to son, says, "Travis, can you tell me what happened? I have to know what happened before I can know what to do."

"He killed Crystal."

"How do you know?"

"He killed everybody."

"How do you *know?* Why would he do it?"

And now Travis sees his father for the first time, sees in those eyes that he is merely a human being, capable of breaking into little pieces, of being broken. Seeing these two so vividly, it seems to Travis the liquid pouring through him has washed away a lifetime of scales and crusts that have been coating his eyes, and he understands with extraordinary clarity everything he has ever done. Though he will not be able to speak out loud about this for weeks, the scene he would like to describe for them begins to run through his mind almost exactly as it will be heard at the trial, and the questions now forming in his mind are the ones he will ask with his voice, although here, this morning, as the blue light of dawn gives way to the sun's aura above the eastern hills, he can only ask them silently and search for answers in these new-found searching and bewildered eyes.

48

RADAR'S DREAM

When the story breaks, that afternoon, the papers in the city bill Travis and Radar as a team, playing up the fact that he is a recently returned veteran, digging out statistics about the homicidal tendencies men bring back from overseas. DEATH DUEL FOR KILLER DUO, one headline reads. VET HELD, COHORT SLAIN, reads another.

Though he curses his colleagues for such sloppy and slanderous reporting, Montrose can tell himself this theory will soon abort. He called his attorney again, from the sheriff's office, and the man told him Pan Am has already agreed to verify that Travis flew into San Francisco from Honolulu on an earlier flight the same day Monty met him at the airport. It is something, a ray of hope.

By the time those papers are hitting the sidewalk, Monty and Walter and two police detectives are standing outside Radar's cabin. They try the door, and watch it swing open into the darkness and dankness of a cave, a lair. The windows have been boarded crudely from the inside. The smells of mold and long-imprisoned sweat flow toward them and over them in an invisible cloud.

"Jesus, what a stink," says Walter, groping for a light switch. "Let's get the back door open, circulate the fucking air."

The floor is bare. A metal folding chair leans against one wall, next to a steel-frame cot with a thin tick mattress and a grimy sleeping bag that seems to be producing most of the fetid odors. Above the cot, filling the wall, there is an enormous grainy blow-up of Radar's face, and opposite that, across the room, a wall-size topographical map of northern California, ringed with newspaper accounts of tremors and quakes. Penciled arrows connect each clipping to some point on the map.

"Sonofabitch," Walter exclaims. "Look at that! It's like a goddam battle plan!"

Next to the map, seeming strangely out of place in this otherwise stripped and spartan room, stands an old-time, ornately carved roll-top desk, scarred and nicked and layered with grimy dust. It is the kind of desk Monty ordinarily would covet, might imagine standing in his own studio. Seeing it here, he is filled with revulsion, perhaps because its contents are so similar to what he himself might stuff its drawers and pigeonholes with—more maps, and pamphlets, tide charts, pages of scribbled notes, various versions of the Bible, Prescott's *History of the Conquest of Mexico, The World Almanac*. In among the notes they find astrological readings, letters to federal agencies, and finally, tied shut with a piece of twine, a copious journal which Monty knows, as soon as he sees it, is going to contain more of what they are looking for. On the cover is written:

THE LAST DAYS OF RADAR ABRAHAM CORTEZ

He lets the detective untie it and examine it for prints. Then he opens the volume and flips through. In all entries but the first, the writing is scrawled and various, as if written in a rush, with letters sometimes large, sometimes small, slanting now to the right and now to the left, as if two or three people took turns at the writing. The first entry, however, is very neatly printed, in the form of an amateur's legal document:

I Donald Yates do hereby change my name permanently and throughout all time taking the names conferred upon me time and time again through the voices and in dreams, which are these three names.

RADAR—which is a device for receiving super sensitive messages, and which stands for all things in technology.

ABRAHAM—who was willing to sacrifice the one he loved the most in order to show his respect for power in the universe and who was rewarded for doing this, and who stands for all things patriarchal.

CORTEZ—who said he was a Christian but who conquered with the sword of Jehovah and named the state of California and who stands for all things heroic and necessary.

DONALD YATES—is hereby declared dead.

The next entry, dated six months before Linda Kramer disappeared, begins:

What is God? God is the power in the universe. God is the force that keeps everything in motion and in its proper place. What is an earthquake? It is a manifestation of that power. Throughout the ages men have killed each other in order to show their respect for the power in the universe.

The next entry is undecipherable. The fourth, dated a week later, has the heading ANCIENT LAW:

In the case of Abraham and Isaac you have a man who is not only willing to murder to show his respect for the power. He is willing to murder his own son, lay him on the altar and slit his throat if God gives him the go-ahead. This is one example of the age-old custom. Genesis Chapter 23, And they came to the place which God had told him of, and Abraham built an altar there and laid the wood in order and bound Isaac his son and laid him on the altar upon the wood. And

Abraham stretched forth his hand and took the knife to slay his son. Thus willing to slay his own son, he won God's approval and he prospered all the rest of his days and became a legendary person.

This is followed by a dream, undated:

I had a dream in which I saw caves full of water. Long deep caves with men and women swimming toward the surface toward some kind of light. I heard voices in the distance calling my name. They called me by many names and all the names were my real name. They called me Radar and they called me Abraham and they called me Hernando Cortez and Donald and other things. And the water behind them turned dark. It was rushing water, like in an irrigation canal and pushing toward the mouth of the cave in the distance where the people started crawling out one by one. They formed a column behind me for some kind of a march. We were out in the open. No trees. No clothes. The men and women were naked. The light was very bright but I couldn't tell if it was sunlight or moonlight or both at once or maybe an eclipse. There was no heat and no cold and no glare and no shadow, just these men and women carrying weapons and marching and all of them knew my name.

After several pages of illegible commentary on various articles and clippings Scotch-taped to the pages, Monty finds this entry, again entitled ANCIENT LAW:

The Aztecs had one of the most advanced cultures in North America and they sacrificed their own people by the thousands. They even got volunteers for this. Why? To show their respect for the power in the world. They did not want the power to get out of balance. These are small disasters. The death of any one Aztec was a small disaster. Enough small disasters can prevent a large disaster like the disappearance of the sun, which is one thing the Aztecs feared, or like a major quake along the San Andreas Fault which the scientists now say could produce one of the most terrible calamities known to man. I say it could be worse than that. It could bring life as we know it to an end. They say that enough small earthquakes going off here and there can let off the pressure and that way maybe the big one won't strike. But it is going to take more than that. It is going to take much more than that. In 1906 when people knew nothing at all about these things San Francisco Bay became a lake of fire.

Montrose shows this entry to Walter, who has been rummaging through the drawers of the desk. He reads it slowly, blinking, and swallows and looks at Montrose. "Lord preserve us," he murmurs. He shakes his head and calls to the detectives. "Hey, you guys come over here and take a look at this." And then the four of them are standing under the bare-bulb ceiling light gazing down at the scribbled pages, written here in this room some solitary night with these books open and maps and scraps of scattered research spread around, and the metal folding chair pulled up to this once-elegant roll-top desk.

"It gives you the chills, doesn't it," Walter says, "to think that a nut like this can be running around loose for months or even years, getting ready to make his move."

Driving back in the squad car, Walter and Monty are silent, weary, mulling over what they have seen. Walter parks outside the station and slumps into the seat.

"Things like this make me want to leave the country," he says.

"Where would you go?"

"Switzerland. Easter Island. I don't give a shit." Walter shoves his helmet back.

Monty says, "What else do you know about him?"

"Not much. A loner. On the streets a lot. We used to watch him pretty close. He was handling small amounts of dope. Although that had tapered off. I tell you, when I saw him in the saloon with Travis that first day I smelled trouble, I just smelled it. Once a guy gets into drugs it is all downhill. If you want my opinion, drugs is going to be the downfall of the whole United States."

"There has to be more to it than drugs."

"Not in my opinion."

"What I mean is, it's too easy to blame things like this on drugs alone."

"I'm not an intellectual, Monty. I just know what I see on the streets."

"It's like the war. Drugs are one of the symptoms of what's going on. But not the cause. Drugs release things that are already looking for a way to get released."

Walter turns quickly, his eyes widened with a boyish fear. "What's the cause, then?"

"I don't know."

Monty drags his hands across his face, pushing fingertips against his eyes. "I mean, I *do* know. That is, I have theories. I have thought about this. But right now I am too damn tired to remember what they are."

"You've been through a lot," Walter says.

"And it isn't over. It's just beginning."

"At least it's looking better for Travis."

"Are you kidding? He's just been booked on suspicion of murder."

"I've been in this business long enough to foresee things, Monty. I foresee self-defense."

"You don't know how much I want that to be true."

"I really do. Not only that. I want you to know that I will do anything in my goddam power . . ."

Here Walter stops. His voice breaks. Monty turns and sees him swallowing hard, concentrating on the windshield. "Listen, Monty. For what it's worth . . . I want to thank you."

"For what?"

"For what you said last night."

His mind goes blank. "Last night?"

"That I was glad somebody else's life looked as fucked up as my own."

"Oh, that. Hey. I'm sorry about that one, Walter. Please."

"Don't apologize. You did me the biggest favor of my life."

"I wasn't thinking."

"You were right on target, you hit the nail on the head. Deep down inside, see, I *was* glad. That's how sick a person can get. While I was looking at that journal and all the other shit we found over there, and thinking about the word coming back from Pan Am, all of which from the department's point of view is going to turn this case around, I said to myself I should be ashamed, because I was glad that Travis looked so bad. I guess I have always kind of envied you, Montrose. That's just how sick a person can get. It made up my mind for me. I am going into the chief's office right now and give notice. Fuck it. I have had it with this line of work."

"What do you think you'll do?"

"I got a few ideas. We have a little money saved up. I might buy into a sporting goods store or maybe open up some kind of sandwich joint. I don't know. Right now I feel like a huge safe has been lifted off my shoulders. Thanks to you, Monty, I am a changed man. And believe me, I am going to spend my last days on the force working to make things keep going Travis's way. You know, if we can produce an explanation for those fingerprints on the doorknob, your boy could end up being a goddam celebrity in this town."

49

THINKING OUT LOUD

from *One Day at a Time*
by Montrose Doyle

Out west we thrive on legends. There is the legend that this is the land of promise. And there is the legend that this is the end of the line. And there is the legend that a great shaker is coming that will prove the truth of the second legend once and for all. And there is the legend that anything goes.

Over the years they have given us some true saints and heroes. And some truly lethal madmen.

I am just thinking out loud here, trying to make some sense out of what we now know about Radar Abraham Cortez and his grisly scheme to save his part of the world from apocalyptic destruction by sacrificing a few innocent souls to the inscrutable powers in our midst.

If I don't do this . . . well, it doesn't make very much sense at all. It is just another thread unraveling from the raggedy edge of what used to be the social order. And I don't know how much longer I can live with that.

Legends are a kind of last defense. I am thinking that I would rather have a legend than a madman out of nowhere.

50

At the preliminary hearing, the district attorney was puzzled. "Let us assume for the moment," he said, "that Mr. Doyle did not arrive in San Francisco until after the first two killings occurred. What about the Fontaines? How is it possible for a lone assassin without a firearm to physically overpower three people—two men and a woman—in the middle of the day?"

The answer, according to witnesses familiar with the Fontaines' habits, was paralysis. In the cathedral-like grove they called their power zone, they often smoked themselves into a stupor. Radar had been there several times before. They would not have been alarmed by his approach or indeed by anything else. Certainly they would never have suspected how he had redefined the meaning of the cosmogeomagnetic power they were out there trying to tap.

"But how, then," the D.A. next wanted to know, "do we account for those fingerprints? Mr. Doyle claims that on the day after he returned, Radar suggested the Fontaines as one way to move the hashish Mr. Doyle had smuggled in from overseas. I will for the moment overlook the implications of the hash itself. And I will grant that it is within the realm of plausibility, if they found no one at home, for Mr. Doyle to try the front door. But what could Radar possibly have had in mind, if these so-called dealers had already been dead at least a week, and by Radar's own hand?"

The defense called this further evidence of his deranged condition and called in a consulting psychologist, who testified that Donald/Radar Yates had a mental record going back at least three years, although until something like the present case brought to light the need for such data, no single person other than Radar himself could have known or cared to know his whole history. Four times he had been admitted to clinics in four parts of the state, twice voluntarily. Four times his tendency of mind had been described as schizophrenic. Four times he had been released after a few weeks of therapy.

Local witnesses who knew him were not surprised to hear this. He was remembered by some as vice-president of his high school junior class, an erratic drummer in the jazz ensemble, a second-rate miler who finally lettered in his senior year. No one knew much at all about his private life or his family. His mother, either widowed or separated, had moved here from Nebraska when he was ten. Summers and falls she worked in the vegetable canneries. In the off-season she drew unemployment. After he graduated from high school she moved into a trailer court, and about a year ago she had left town for good, perhaps alone, perhaps with a companion. There were no brothers or sisters or girlfriends. Adrift, Radar had enrolled for one semester at a junior college, then dropped out to live on food stamps, odd jobs, and intermittent dope dealing. He had been known to fast for several days at a time, to gaze at the sun, practice headstands, take peyote, write spontaneous verse, read tarot cards, to dabble in Subud, dianetics, Christian Science, the writings of Aleister Crowley, and the Jehovah's Witnesses, while gradually withdrawing into the crazed monastic solitude made palpable to the jury in his journal and in the photos taken inside and outside his cabin.

With this much established, the outcome was never in serious doubt. For the community the trial was mostly ritual, an occasion to voice and vent and purge. When Monty's column on the subject appeared, it drew a great flood of letters to the editor, and letters to himself. There were also open letters to the police, and to the state department of public health, and to the governor. Monty came to see each of these outcries springing from a deep need to describe those things we fear the most, to find the words or pictures that can contain them, in the hope that this might bring them under some control. Sitting through the days of testimony he came to see the trial itself—the probing by attorneys, the press coverage, the photos and maps and flashbacks to similar crimes in other states, the coroner's reports, the pileup of documents inside and outside the courtroom, the circling and recircling of key events—he came to see all this as another effort to depict, and by depicting at such length, to surround, and to siphon off some of the power certain forces have, before they capture us, or before the fear unhinges us—uncharted urges in the mind, and in the sky, and in the earth.

In his moments of detachment this is how he could view the trial. In his column he could voice the local feeling. But more often, as he sat in the courtroom, he looped back to events he would never write about. While the lawyers circled, Montrose circled inwardly and wished he could take Trav's place, endure this for his son, feeling he himself should be on trial here, the old conquistador within who had let his son be crippled fighting another country's wars.

He relived the day Travis stopped him on the porch to announce defiantly that he had decided to enlist. With a little foresight, Monty could have made things happen another way. ("It's your decision, son.")

And yet it goes back even farther. In Bakersfield fourteen years ago he let his hand fall light on Trav's young butt, his anger and his force reined in by the youthful smirk, appealing to that youth in Montrose, the reek of burnt film and chicken fat wafting down the driveway to surround them while the son made the father accomplice to his tiny crime.

Around that moment a thousand gather, a lifetime of waverings, leniencies with the boy he never understood, half hunches, microscopic sins of omission, as well as the monumental oversight that he simply did not see, two years ago, how different this war would be from his own. Everything Monty now knows, it seems to him, he has learned in these past two years. Before Travis left, part of Monty still believed in war and soldiering in the old-fashioned, 1945-and-earlier sense. He sees this now as yet another form of innocence, peeled away by television and the sheer rate of change and the opinions of his older son, but peeled away too late to save his younger son. He blames himself for not seeing sooner, for not hearing Grover sooner, for letting the war take that looseness in Trav's character and tear it full of holes. He takes the blame for not admitting soon enough how fast the world and its wars were shifting, for not grasping soon enough what it means to live backstage with the cameras, and how twenty-four-hour-a-day video coverage can undermine any tradition, put the strain on any belief. Christ on the cross could not survive that kind of exposure.

Sitting in the courtroom, he thought about what moved him to raise the rifle when he heard Trav's foot in the hallway. He had believed, and yea, had hoped, the time had come to pay for all this, to have things turn full circle. In that fevered, wakeful sleep Monty saw his frailties coming back to him in the shape of Crystal, who was dead because she had been chosen by Travis; and that kind of choice, or pattern of choices, was coming back to him in the shape of a son made vengeful by some knowledge of what his father had done to him. In that darkness before the first dim glow of dawn Monty saw topo maps, the valleys white, the uplands pale green, with looping altitude lines terraced toward the breastlike peaks, bulging in his mind, becoming a full-blown landscape, with swales and ridges. He saw four crude altars spaced along the shallow crease, and his ranch lying in the path they marked, and it seemed to him, as he hallucinated and calculated, that his house and ranch had been waiting eighty years for whatever was approaching, some dark guarantee in the deed his father purchased, in the homestead, or in the land, in the landscape's history, and the leapfrogging west. In that fantasy it was Travis who had embarked upon this scheme to terrorize his father and then bury him the way the others had been buried, crazed by what the war made visible, despising his father for sending him, for allowing him to be sent. The father would be next, and it would happen there in the rift zone that was the boundary and dividing line old Grover chose by chance or perhaps was drawn toward—who knows why?—and bequeathed to all of them. In that fitful, fevered half sleep, knowing he deserved it, Monty was awaiting this role, almost gave himself up to its ghastly justice, was almost ready to savor the rich irony that at such a murderous intersection he would at last come to know his son. Those were his dreams when the young-eyed soldier came loping toward him again with bayonet raised. Then he had no choice but to reach again for his rifle and spring awake with survival uppermost in his mind. Now it is clear that if anyone fulfilled a stark destiny that morning it was not himself, but Travis. And Monty's lot, rather than bowing out at the end of some gloomy drama of retribution, will be to take whatever he has learned and gird up his loins and continue. Just continue. And continue.

In the end Travis was charged with one count of murder. To prove his plea, the attorney reconstructed the whole gruesome scenario. By the time Travis entered the courtroom he was, as Walter had predicted, a kind of community hero who had slain the villain in his own defense.

Travis didn't see it that way. But his attorney was able to persuade the jury because the official version of what had happened was on tape. A consulting psychologist had recorded it in the county jail a month after his arrest. It was the first and only time Travis had been willing to talk at any length about what had happened, his monologue triggered by Crystal's final roll of film, which had been discovered inside her Rollei-flex, near the road, four miles from where she had been buried. Two of the last five shots were of Radar's cabin, taken from the sidewalk. The door is closed, the shades are drawn, the small front yard is high with weeds. The other three were taken inside his car, from the front seat, the first of these a profile, the next two showing anger and high agitation as

Radar turns, then seems to be lunging toward the camera. It was not the substance of the photos that moved Travis to speak, but the quality, the tilted candid-camera style so typical of Crystal and everything she did—random subjects, impulse photos, never quite in focus, the border often fuzzed with streaks of light. The sight of these prints moved Travis to tears. As the tape begins, the first words are catching in his throat:

I already knew he had killed her, you see, from the way he was talking when he started into the trees. And I had to go in after him. I didn't want to know any more, but I had to know. I was also very fucked up at the time. I don't just mean what I'd been drinking. There is a kind of shell shock I think anybody feels when they come back into this country after they've been gone for a while. I went over the fence where he went over and one of the rails came loose in my hands, one of those old rough-cut redwood rails down there where the ranch angles out to touch the county road. I kept it and hiked in after him and it was like he wanted to be sure I was close enough to hear him before he started talking again. He said, "Yeah, her note was Scotch-taped to my door and when I read her note I heard her voice and when I finally found her she didn't want to come out here either. She begged me to let her go," he said. "But I couldn't do that, you see. Not without permission." "Permission" is the word he used. "Have you ever had a woman beg you for anything, Travis? I don't like it," he said. "I tried to make her be quiet before we got as far as we were going to go. She begged me to let her out of the car, and I wanted to. If it was up to me I would have," he said. "But she had been selected and once a person gets selected that is it," calling all of this back to me over his shoulder while I am trying to catch up with him and yelling, "Where is she, Radar? What did you do with her?" But it was like he didn't hear me. He kept saying, "I couldn't stand the begging, man, I could not fucking stand it, I really couldn't." Things like that, until I was going crazy with hate and grief and stumbling after him, and when he finally stopped and turned around I almost ran into him. I was close enough to hear the blade against the leather and I knew this was it and I started swinging the fence rail, which caught him on the wrist and knocked the knife loose. It fell between us. I went for it and came up aiming for his gut, and that is how it happened. He lured me in there with this stuff about Crystal and then he pulled the knife. . . .

Here there is a long pause on the tape, and in the attorney's judgment this was as much as the jury needed to hear to be convinced that Travis, and perhaps the whole Doyle family, had been next on Radar's list. Switching off the recorder, he pointed to a large-scale local map, where one last *X* had been added to the line that began at Holy City. After that pause, however, the monologue continues for a while longer:

When I dove for it I expected to feel his hands around my neck. Then I figured maybe I had hurt him with the rail. But when I came up it was almost like . . . he was waiting for it. He could have gone for the knife, you see. But he didn't. It was like he sucked me in there so I could do him in. Like he chose me for that. People choose each other for things, you know. He chose Crystal for one thing. He chose me for another thing. That's the only way I can explain it. I don't think of myself as a killer. But maybe he figured I had the capability. I guess he was right. Because I did it. He made me want to do it. He made me become like him. There was a guy overseas, a corporal, who chose me for death. Did I tell you about him yet? He threw a grenade at me. And it worked. I died. Why does this happen? Why do I get chosen for things like this? He was supposed to be on my side, right? But he turns out to be the one who is trying to blow me up. I get back home and here comes my old basketball buddy, with a new name, coming on like a freaky stranger. This is what I don't know how to handle. There is nothing you can count on. There is just me and nothing. That is where I am right now. That is what my new vision revealed to me. I see how I got here. But what is the good of seeing when what you see is that it is just you and nothing? Can you tell me that? You're a psychologist. Where do I go from here?

Part Four

The banks were grassy and covered with fragrant herbs and watercress. The water flowed afterwards in a deep channel toward the southwest. All the land that we saw this morning seemed admirable to us. We pitched camp near the water. This afternoon we felt new earthquakes, the continuation of which astonishes us.

> ——FRAY JUAN CRESPI,
> chaplain and diarist for the
> Portolá Expedition, soon after
> the Los Angeles River is named
> and crossed, August 3, 1769

51

The first explorers to pass through this region did not see any other people. The local tribes were keeping out of sight. The explorers saw streams, which they usually named for saints. They saw deer, and trees, which they identified, an abundance of trees, including the mysterious redwood, which amazed them. "They have a very different leaf from cedars," wrote Fray Crespi, the diarist, "and although the wood resembles cedar somewhat in color, it is very different, and has not the same color." There are still more trees than people here. Leona and the members of SCALE would like to keep it that way, perhaps improve upon the ratio. Although the odds are against them, they have no intention of giving up the fight.

As you approach from the sea, before the town comes into view, all these trees conspire to make the hills and mountains beyond the town a high border of dark dark green. If you are flying in, as you near the town you begin to see tiny glints and sparkles down there among the eucalyptus clumps above the shore, among the pines and oaks and bay and acacia along the streets, and in the groves that separate the districts. These would be the dormer windows and diamonds of stained glass catching the sun, and windshields moving through intersections, the eyeglasses of pedestrians, wrist watches turned to reveal the time of day (11:38), sometimes the season (summer) and the date (July 10), and crates of empty beer bottles stacked behind The Cheating Heart, and truckloads of bright galvanized fittings for the chimneys above the tile roofs of a shopping plaza under construction just past the city limits.

The glints and the sparkles are the evidence that can be

seen from above of the life that continued to be lived in and around the town, even while new and unforeseeable tremors rose from below to shake the trees and houses, and while an invisible assassin became his own final victim. In those few weeks everything changed. And nothing changed. Terrors emerged. And then subsided. Weapons were purchased and kept loaded awhile, then stored in closets with other weapons. Another increment of apprehension and dread was lodged in the heart of each citizen, filed within easy reach, like the guns, for future reference, while daily life continued. Among the many glints along Del Mar Boulevard is the shine of fresh seagull droppings on the cement helmet of one of the soldiers still keeping his vigil from the roof of the Hotel Viceroy. Near the bridge across the river there is the flash from a lost hub cap as dark-bearded Wellington lifts it from the grass, picturing in his mind's eye exactly where it will fit on the shapeless edifice which, after a long and soul-searching pilgrimage down the Big Sur coastline, he now views as his life's work. Inside a telephone booth at the edge of a lonesome Texaco lot, the glinting dial is at rest, seldom used now that the Law and Order Auxiliary has lost interest in anonymous harassment. Out next to the last freeway off-ramp there are bright flashes from the belt buckle and boot snaps of a young girl hitchhiking somewhere alone, a girl who has already forgotten the warnings, and the details of the trial, or perhaps never heard them, or perhaps has recently arrived from some other part of the country, where papers carry only local news.

The gleams and sparkles flash skyward, into the white-blue vibrant light that rises from the sea to coat the air above the town and above the hills beyond the town. Think of it as a cushion of softening light that spreads inland for miles and that now bears us inland past the first line of hills, where the houses and glints thin out, and past the second line of hills, where houses and roads and cars are widely scattered, and finally up the slope of the third and higher line of hills. Looking down, we can almost see this land the way those original

Spaniards saw it. On a day like this, when sea breezes have cleansed the air of fumes and haze, the light that coats the air and the land must still be as it was two hundred years ago. There are no people in sight, only trees, a cloth of forest green that hugs the upward flow and ripple of the hill country, until we zoom down closer and the trees part, and we can pick out one clearing, where furrows are turning green in a small field next to a small house.

Down along the fence that runs below this house, two figures can be seen, two men, one wearing a Panama hat, the other a blue bandanna tied to hold his hair back. It is hot and bright and the man in the Panama seems ill at ease in this heat. He cannot stand still. The sport coat he carries is shifted from hand to hand. He pulls at his hat brim, picks at the barbs in the fence wire. The man with his hair pulled back is leaning on a hoe and seems content to be doing this. His shoulders are brown, his Levi's faded, recently washed, the cuffs brushing boots that show traces of the goat manure he shoveled onto his compost heap earlier this morning. He is running with sweat. His eyes squint hard and searchingly at the man in the Panama. But his body is at ease. He seems fixed, like one of the trees. With Holly back and planning to stay, this is precisely how he feels, for the first time in his life—centered, rooted, fixed.

Beyond the A-frame her Packard can be seen washed and glowing, on permanent display as a car and as a symbol. Grover has decided to compromise one of his principles and help her keep the gas gulper running. He was amazed by the sense of relief that flooded through him following this little surrender.

From that same vicinity piano music can be heard, gentle bluesy ragtime chords floating toward them from the top of the slope, where she is trying to finish the first few measures of a new composition before she breaks for lunch. The piano has just been tuned and installed in a studio he built next to the A-frame, as a welcome-home present. The day Holly first read about Travis's arrest in the San Francisco *Chronicle,* she called the ranch to talk to Lee. Grover happened to answer the phone. After five minutes of guarded conversation, as they exchanged the recent news, he told her something he had never told anyone. The idea that he actually said this can still make him stop and stare vacantly across the field. "I'm not going to make it without you, Holly," he said. "You're horny," she said. "That too," he said. She was there in two hours, and spent the first day helping Lee. The next morning, while they were driving up here, she told Grover she had been afraid she was pregnant, that was part of the reason she wanted to get away, but when her period finally started, what she felt most was disappointment. "I realized then that I wanted your child, Grover," she said, her eyes brimming with expectation. They made love that morning as if they had both spent these days of separation in the arms of new partners who had taught them things they couldn't have imagined. Grover fell in love that morning, after a year of cohabitation. He whispered words to her that had never before entered his mind, and they stayed in bed until noon heat forced them out of doors, mapping what they were going to do together, and do separately, the things they would change and the things they would keep the same. He felt ropes falling away from his body. He had spent his whole life bound and knotted inside layers of tightly drawn ropes, which began to unravel at last as he and Holly lay there falling in love.

Leaning on his hoe, Grover says, "How did you get up here?"

"Hitchhiked to the bottom of the road," Travis says, "then just followed the music."

"I didn't think I'd be seeing you before tomorrow."

"I wanted to talk to you. I figured tomorrow there might not be a chance, with everybody around. We haven't really had a chance to talk much."

"I've been thinking that myself," Grover says. "You thirsty? You want something to drink?"

"What time is it?"

"About quarter to twelve."

"I try not to drink anything before noon."

Under the hat brim Travis's eyes dart around, looking at Grover with a twinkle of sardonic amusement, then past Grover, up at the hills, down at the ground, at Grover again, then past him again.

"What are those things over there?" Travis says.

"That's escarole."

"Looks like the back of somebody's head caught in a bad wind."

"It's a real hardy kind of lettuce, is what it is. I just plant enough for me and Holly. She likes it in the salad. C'mon. You want to look around the place? You haven't been out here before. You want to walk?"

"I ought to be tired, after that goddam hill. But I guess I'm in better shape than I thought I was. Yeah, I'd like to walk around. It feels good up here."

Moving past the escarole, toward the field of head-high bean vines, Travis says, "I wish I could get into something like this."

"Give it a try."

"I mean the way you do, full bore."

"You could stay here awhile, if you want to, see how it feels."

"That's what Monty said," says Travis with a melancholy grin. "In fact, those were his very words."

"I have already mentioned this to Holly, in case the subject came up. She said she'd love it. She'd love the extra company. Truth is, we're looking for people we think we could share the place with."

"Thanks. But no thanks."

"The band is practicing here now. Part of our new policy to expand the social life. There's a spot for you in the rhythm section, Trav. I'm serious. We would use you. We're starting to work every weekend—clubs, parties. It could be just like—"

"Can't do it. I wish I could. But I can't. I have to get

away from here. For a while. I'm sick of seeing my picture in the paper, and people calling me on the phone."

"What are you going to do, then?"

"I don't know yet. Hey, what's this bushy stuff over here?"

"You ought to recognize that. Oregano. Lee's been growing it for years. Take a sniff. It's potent," says Grover, tempted to challenge him on this matter of what he is now going to do. "By his works a man is justified" has been one of Grover's unspoken credos. No works, no man. But he holds his tongue. He and Holly debated this very matter not long ago. As he watches the loose-limbed, offhand, and random way Travis bends to sniff the herb, he hears her telling him that if you try to measure everyone by such a standard you will end up in the isolation booth, self-righteous and old before your time.

"Maybe I'll write a novel," Travis says.

Grover laughs softly at what sounds like the start of one of Travis's gags. This is what he would like to do with Travis—not challenge him, but laugh with him, reach back to the times when they could laugh.

"You think it's out of the question? Listen. Three different guys have called up about doing a book based on my experiences. Free-lance writers. Two of them called long-distance. I don't want to get into ripping off myself like that. But I think I could do a novel. At my own pace. You might even be in it, Grover. Did you ever think you'd be in a novel?"

"I'd want a percentage."

"No more than half. What time is it now?"

Squinting upward, Grover says, "Close to noon. Maybe a little bit past."

From the inside pocket of the sport coat he carries, Travis pulls a pint of Southern Comfort.

"Care for a snort?"

"It's a little early," Grover says.

"Afternoon, they say, is the period of sociability."

Travis tips the bottle for a quick sip, then holds it out.

Grover looks from the label to his brother's mischievous face. Trav has been drinking a lot, too much, and Grover doesn't want to encourage this, but he has been waiting a long time to make contact again. This is the first real gesture since Trav came home, this bottle, a gesture and a backyard challenge. One sip can't hurt, thinks Grover, knowing one sip is not what Travis has in mind, knowing that if he drinks anything at this point in the day one of two things will happen. Grover will belt a few swallows and fall asleep by midafternoon, or he will continue drinking until he passes out. In Travis's eye there is a sardonic and seductive glint. Grover reaches for the bottle, takes in a mouthful of the syrup-flavored whiskey, wincing.

"This stuff'll rot your teeth out," he says.

"I've got this little pension coming in from the government," Travis says, sipping again. "I can scrounge on that one for a long, long time. If I want to. This is one of the things I need to talk to you about. I am twenty-one years old and I have this disability pension for the rest of my fucking life. It isn't fair. It undermines my incentive. Look at you, you're dripping with incentive. How does this happen? You are dripping with incentive and I don't have a goddam clue."

"Sure you do. You just need some time. . . ."

"Do you believe in anything anymore, Grover?"

"Plenty of things."

"Give me an example. Do you believe in God?"

"In a sense."

"What sense?"

Grover sips and gathers his thoughts and says, "There is a source of power in the universe that keeps the planet turning and the crops growing and our bodies working and our eyes shining. I believe in that."

"What else?"

"I guess I believe in what I'm doing. I believe in Holly Belle. I believe people can be better than they are."

"You're a lucky sonofabitch."

"Why do you say that?"

"All the things you have. I don't believe in anything. Not one goddam thing."

"That's not true."

"How do you know it's not true?"

"If it was true, you wouldn't be standing here."

As he says this, Grover regrets the harsh edge to his voice. He can feel his brother's mood shift. Two years ago this was the kind of remark that would have started a loud argument about the meaning of manhood, the meaning of war and peace. When Travis first got back, Grover was prepared to resume this old debate. He had speeches on standby, ready to deliver. Now he waits for Trav's rebuttal, the outburst, and he is relieved when it does not come. The need for that kind of conversation is long past. Piano chords float toward them above the bean rows and potato rows. Travis grins his melancholy grin.

"I'd be blowing my brains out, right?"

"Something like that."

"Maybe I am. Maybe secretly that's what I am doing. The shrink says I have a negative orientation."

Travis hunkers down under a shade tree at the edge of the garden, picking at the grass between his shoes. There is an awful lonesomeness about the way he moves that reminds Grover of himself during the days when Holly was gone. He sees himself hunkering under this very tree the day after she drove away and there was no piano music, just himself out here with his field and his tools, and it was not what he had expected.

He hunkers down next to Travis. After they have each sipped from the pint, he says, "Hey, Trav. Promise me something."

"What?"

"Postpone secretly blowing your brains out until we get to

the hot springs tomorrow. I wouldn't want you to miss the springs."

"Monty tells me there are monks over there."

"Students mostly, studying to be monks."

"Where do visitors fit in? Don't visitors crowd up the place?"

"They let people in during the summer," Grover says. "It helps pay the bills. Everybody has to pay the bills. Even monks."

"Why does somebody become a monk? What do they believe in?"

"Ask somebody when we get there."

"If I go, I probably will."

"What do you mean, *if* you go?"

"I may not be going. I may be changing my plans."

"What the hell for?"

"I don't know if I can spend that much more time with Monty and Lee."

"Hey. C'mon. They're counting big on this. It's your own family, for Christ sake. They've been through a lot on your account. What's the matter with you?"

"That's the other thing I want to talk to you about. I want you to do me a favor."

Grover waits, uncertain.

"If I take off, you tell them what I'm telling you. Tell Monty that I'm . . . going out to try a few things."

"Why don't you tell him?"

"I can't. I mean, I can't handle it . . . yet. I'm just coming out of a very bad place."

"I know that, Trav."

"I don't know if you do or not. It's a place you've never been, except for maybe half a day."

"Give me an example."

Travis grins suddenly, his wide, charming grin.

"You know what it's like the next day after a really terrible drunk where you have mixed all the wrong things and totally lost track and the next day when you can finally get up off the floor, each individual step is like a large and painful project?"

"Okay," Grover says, "I've been that far. We've been that far together more than once."

"It's like you are walking on broken glass, and if you step down too hard or move too fast your whole body will shatter into little pieces and you will be sprinkled all over the floor like the glass, and that is the way I have been feeling for months. Like a skin filled with broken glass. Always on the verge. I just couldn't handle much. One thing at a time, one person at a time, and for a while I couldn't even handle that. You remember the day I walked away from the house just when you and Holly drove up? I couldn't handle it. I'm really sorry about that, Grover. It's been on my mind."

"Forget it. Water under the bridge."

"You follow what I'm saying?"

"Sure. I follow you."

"You won't hold it against me?"

"Hell, no."

"Then listen. Also tell them that whatever I get into, I'll be back. Okay? For them not to worry? I want them to know this, because . . . I care about them."

"It would be a lot better if they could hear this coming from you. Monty's carrying a lot of blame, you know."

"For what?"

"He blames himself for what you've been through."

"Hey, that's crazy. He doesn't have to do that."

"Well, he does."

"Tell him to stop thinking that way. I don't blame him for anything. That's kid stuff. That's the whole goddam problem, isn't it? If I had somebody to blame, I'd know which way to move."

"Get on the phone right now and call them up and tell them what you're telling me."

"I can't."

"Can't is also kid stuff, Trav."

"I can't do it yet. I want you to. Can I have your word? You're my brother. You're the only one I can ask."

Staring at the ground, Grover thinks about this, finally says, "Yeah. You have my word."

Travis shoves his Panama back, as if some bargain has been struck. He cocks his head, listening. For a while the only sounds are the gurgle of whiskey through the bottle's neck and the faraway piano tinkle as Holly works out some phrasing in the melody line.

Travis says, "Sounds good."

"She's been practicing a lot."

"You know, I realize while I'm sitting here that I have never had a woman in my life. I have had sweet young things and hookers and pretty bodies here and there. But never a woman."

"Someone will come along."

"I think that's what I'm afraid of."

For a moment Grover wishes he were an Eskimo, so that he might be able to give his woman to his brother for a day or a night, to warm away this lost lonesomeness and maudlin self-pity the Southern Comfort nourishes. Then he is glad he is not an Eskimo, and he is glad they are drinking. If they drink enough, Travis will forget that he does not plan to make tomorrow's outing.

52

A ROMAN TEMPLE,
A SPANISH SAINT

from *One Day at a Time*
by Montrose Doyle

Thirty miles from San Francisco a temple has been erected. It stands out there by itself, among trees, and in the lee of a long dark ridge that rises between the fault line and the sea.

It is a circular temple, some twenty feet high, and Romanesque in style, with concrete pillars supporting a ring that is open to the sky and decorated with lions' heads.

In front of this temple lies an oblong blue reflecting pool. As you approach you begin to hear the water, first from the gush of it constantly filling the pool, then from the roar underneath the temple.

You climb circular stairs and the noise grows louder. You step inside the ring of pillars, lean over a low parapet, and the roar surrounds you. Nothing can be heard but the thunder of water pouring over turquoise tiles and into a spillway that carries it out to a natural trough of a reservoir that is the western end of the Hetch-Hetchy system.

The temple was built over the head of the spillway in 1938, and it happens to be standing in the rift zone because the fault itself etched out this chain of long troughs which engineers, a hundred years ago, decided would be the very place for storing San Francisco's water.

The roar, and the wind-riffled lakes, and the shaded slopes, and the absence of other buildings make this a place of astonishing loveliness, Sierra-like.

It smells something like a mountain stream right here, two hundred miles west of the

Sierras, a high mountain stream that has run awhile through concrete. The roar is of a mountain river, the color so beguiling you could almost leap in and ride the rush on out to the lake.

Someone foresaw that urge. Below the parapet a circular steel grate has been installed, to prevent the smell and sound and look of mountain water from seducing you too much. You stand and watch it pour into the troughs the fault dug millions of years ago, one of which gave this whole long crack its name.

In 1895 a geologist named Lawson studied the pattern in the western landscape which a few people were just then start-ing to talk about. He concluded that its path could be seen more clearly in the crease this chain of narrow lakes had tried to fill than anywhere else he had observed between here and the border.

He gave it the name of the northernmost stand of water in this chain, a name that had been chosen much earlier by a party of explorers up from Mexico. After another long day's march through uncharted country, thankful for the cool valley and a lake to camp beside, they had been pleased to honor San Andreas, Saint Andrew, whose name day it happened to be.

53

Bundled like loose baggage, Grover and Travis are sleeping off hangovers in the bed of the pickup. Up front Montrose in his cowboy hat and Leona and Holly Belle listen to the talk show, waiting for the fog to thin beneath the penetrating midsummer sun they know is up there somewhere. Heading south, they move past a steady two-lane stream of vehicles rolling along the coast highway toward town—the U-Haul trailers, the station wagons with glossy surfboards stacked on the roof like cargo. There are cars hauling torpedo-shaped trailers, and cars towing yachts four times the size of the car, and jumbo campers towing tiny foreign cars like lifeboats, and great Winnebagos with side ladders leading to the sun roof, where the trail bikes and scuba tanks are strapped. They pass mobile homes, and moving vans, and high-wheeled live-in vans with waves and flames along the side panels and bubble-out portholes that offer quick views of floor-to-ceiling shag rug interiors.

On the radio a prominent psychic is being interviewed. She has just predicted that California will not fall into the sea. "A new continent can be expected to appear soon," she is saying. "Within the next twenty-five years, or perhaps sooner than that. Doric columns have already been sighted just off Catalina Island. No one is talking about this, but they are slowly rising toward the surface. There will be flooding, but no apocalypse. We can look forward to a steady series of small upheavals. As this new continent continues to emerge, coastal cities like San Diego and Los Angeles and San Francisco will gradually be surrounded with water, becoming offshore islands by the year two thousand. . . ."

This could be the flood, Leona thinks.

"Anybody listening to that stuff?" Monty asks.

"Not me," says Holly with a lazy smile. "Too early in the morning for predictions."

"Yes," Lee says. "We ought to be able to get through one day at least without predictions."

Monty brings in KTOM, the country music station from Salinas. "K–TOM Country, one thirty-eight," sing the happy voices on the signature loop.

This could very well be the flood Edgar Cayce was talking about, thinks Lee. *Not rising oceans and tidal waves. But this river. This one we're in the middle of right here, pouring toward us and around us, pouring all across the land.*

A one-time school bus painted maroon rolls by, with home-made drapes covering most of its windows, and a stovepipe rising from the rear end, then another Winnebago, then a dune buggy with a Model A grille, then a late forties GMC truck with a log cabin on the flatbed, a shingled roof, a dog inside, and faded Levi's drying on a tiny clothesline.

Maybe this is the river and we are already drowning and we are just now finding out about it.

Holly says, "Wasn't that Larry Fowler who drove by?"

"Looked like him," Monty says.

"I thought he'd be long gone."

"Not Fowler," Monty says. "He won't be going anywhere for a while. He has some adversaries now. He has a few followers. He finally got that newsletter going. I've seen it downtown. He calls it *The Searchlight.*"

Lee says, "I still think there was something to what he was saying."

Monty looks at her. A fine sermon begins unfolding in his mind. He hears the words, but holds them. They have discussed these things too many times already. Before the trial, he and

Grover had a long debate on the subject of Fowler. After much shouting and many threats and accusations, they discovered that they agreed completely. They agreed that Fowler was wrong and that he was also right. Wrong to imply the cops had much to gain, but right to say they were hiding things. You hang around a place too long, you can start overlooking details a newcomer won't hesitate to make noise about. You can take them too much for granted, these sad meanderings of human error at the neighborhood level. He has to admit he learned a lot from Fowler and that he misjudged him at the outset. Monty felt superior to him mainly because he himself had been here first. Glancing sideways at Lee's sharp profile next to him in the cab, he also has to admit he has too often regarded his own wife in this same way. Why? Because he has been here longer? Because he is some kind of proprietor? What arrogance to scorn the small-time conquistador in Fowler, when Monty himself has still not outgrown the habit of taking from his wife, or simply taking this and that for granted.

One person by himself, she is thinking, *doesn't do what Radar did. Or even what Travis did. It does take some kind of a conspiracy. A gathering together. A multitude. You get all these cars and trucks and gasoline pumps on every corner and people pouring in like this, crowding up the place, heaping up and breeding and spreading asphalt on every livable spot the poor earth has to offer, it starts driving every one of us crazy one way or another. And is this not the flood, is this not the pouring in that Cayce talked about, and oohhhh, is it not just now beginning? ...*

On the radio Mother Maybelle Carter is singing "Will the Circle Be Unbroken," backed by the hill-country sound of an unamplified twelve-string. Monty switches it off.

Lee says, "I thought that was one of your favorite numbers."

"It is. But it's the wrong time for music, don't you think? On a day like this? Distracts the mind?"

"Yes," Lee says, suddenly smiling at him with a smile he

has not seen in weeks, months. Playful, suggestively edged, a smile of recovery.

"A person wants to arrive there clear and empty," he says, "like an empty vessel. Know what I mean? Ready to be filled."

Yes. We can leave the country music behind us awhile. Along with the prophets and the predictions and the headlines and the trial and the chickens and that new German shepherd he bought and the second rifle and all those padlocks and dead-bolts you have to have for country living. Let's leave all that behind and make this a day of peeling back whatever we can ... whatever we can. ...

The traffic and the low-hanging silver-gray overcast seem to go together, a package deal, concealing the landscape, as they roll past artichoke fields, and Fort Ord's target ranges, and the Mediterranean port town called Monterey, its fishhook curve of bay like pewter in this light. They drive under clouds, through shreds of fog, until they turn inland where a huge shopping plaza marks the last intersection before the coast road heads on south for Big Sur.

A mile up the river valley the traffic has thinned, and the sky turns clean, as if someone just now scrubbed it.

Thank goodness. We have left that overcast behind at last, along with most of the vans and the Winnebagos and the smell of their wheels and the smell of the burger pits and taco bars and pizza palaces they drive in to. We all drive in to them, if they are there, and we will sit at the steering wheel drowning in the smell. ...

Ten miles up the valley there are no more stores, no gas pumps, and few houses, just a narrowing wedge of groves and pasture, as the surrounding hills converge. Turning due south, they pass the last house and cluttered yard and bounce off the asphalt onto a dirt road cut into the first ridge of the Santa Lucia Range.

Climbing out of the flood now, leaving all of it back there below us for a while ... for a while. ...

At a high outside curve Monty looks back and down the

way they have come. Through madrones and oaks he catches
a glimpse of startling beauty, a rise of velvety mounds, softly
creased hills above the Carmel Valley. Each crease looks
seamed with quartz or silver. As his eyes flick away toward the
nearing curve, this view almost reminds him of something
else; he can't think what, and doesn't want to stop yet. It will
come to him.

Trailing their plume of pale dust, they climb through heavy
timber, steep slopes of scrub oak and more madrone and
manzanita, soon high enough to see a plunging dark valley
to the west where no humans live, and above this valley raw-
boned ridges pushing at the sky, first one visible, then another,
farther west, until the road tops out along the mountain's
spine, and he pulls over.

Grover and Travis sit up groaning, squinting, tangled in
their sleeping bags. Monty tells them this is a good spot to
stretch and breathe and come to your senses, pee if you have
to and give a moment to the sky and the timber and the view.
And he is right. The boys climb out and find that from this
promontory the view itself can clear the head and revive eyes
that seemed permanently ruined by drink.

Here the ridges are lined up like wave crests from west to
east, as if some ancient storm of tidal waves had rolled across
the land and had solidified, one crest at a time. To their right,
between the road and the high cloud bank above the coast,
three green ridges thrust, sharp and still in this bright air, and
layered with glossy shades of deepening green. To their left
another ridge humps up, like the spine they're standing on, but
lower, so that they look down at its steepness, then past it,
toward the last ridge in this range, a long bulge called the
Sierra de Salinas, brown and buff and angular, its humps
dissected into triangles and sloping planes. Below that bulge,
out of sight from here, lies the Salinas River Valley, spread
between this range and the Gabilans, which are pale blue at
this distance, in some spots hazy brown, their details disappear-

ing in the sunlight, nearly merging with one more range, of darker blue, and farther east, called Diablo.

They drink from the canteen, and drink in the air, and walk back and forth from one side of the road to the other while they exclaim about the view. Though it is very much on Monty's mind, he does not mention that the northwest-southeast trend of the rift zone lies just beyond the Gabilans, thirty miles from here—like the Salinas River, an invisible but prominent feature of the landscape. He doesn't mention this out loud for fear certain words spoken might take the edge off the fullness of this moment. But as he takes the wheel again, with one last glimpse to the west and east, he is thinking that each of these craggy waves, each ridge, is a wrinkle in the earth's crust, forced upward into such grand shapes by the ancient pushing of the crustal plates, which happen to meet over there, six or seven wrinkles inland from the sea. This image brings home to him with ecstatic clarity that it is all one, another package deal—the dreaded leaps and jerkings of the fault line, and these marvelous vistas that can restore a person's soul.

His head filled with this, Monty feels like preaching, or singing. He sings "She'll be comin round the mountain when she comes." Feeling twice enlarged, inspired and gigantic, he begins to take the downhill curves recklessly, coasting unbanked turns like a stock-car driver, making the women cry out with alarm, Lee clutching his sleeve, while his sons bang their fists on the metal backside of the cab, cursing and laughing and grabbing for handholds as the pickup careens down deeper into the wilderness.

At the rocky bottom of this world of ridges, they come upon a high Japanese gate. Thick, straight, skinned logs support a wooden pagoda-curved arch that has the effect, in this setting, of a three-pronged buck leaping into the road. It is unexpected, surprising and awesome, yet clearly belonging, and in this case a good deal more appropriate than Monty's truck, which brings into the small clearing outside the gate its puttering exhaust and battered muffler and steaming radiator and chattering valves.

When he turns the engine off, a deep quiet falls around the clearing and the gate and the dozen other dust-covered cars parked there, a quiet sharpened by the faint tumble of a creek nearby. There is no wind yet, no one else around. They climb out and stretch and unload their towels and the picnic basket and walk to the gatehouse, where a young man in brown robe and close-cropped hair appears at the window and gently asks how long they'll be staying.

"Just the day," Monty says.

The wooden gate swings and they all walk through into a narrow granite canyon which seems to catch and magnify the gurgling rush, so that the sound of water fills the air above and around the built-up vegetable plots and the small, sun-drenched plaza ahead of them, and the wooden gong hanging outside the zendo, and the low stone and wooden buildings along the borders of the creek.

Travis has stopped, looking back at the young man. He walks to the door of the gatehouse.

"Are you a monk?"

"I'm a student."

"Can you tell me what that means?"

The young man regards Travis with unblinking eyes for such a long interval, and Travis, his gaze steadied perhaps by true intensity, perhaps by a morning-after stupor, seems so willing to wait him out, that Montrose says, "We'll meet you at the bathhouse."

They move on.

With that short hair and skinny neck and eyes that never blink, he makes me think of Radar, who saw things that I too have seen, and still see. But Radar did not know about the islands. He only saw the flood. This fellow in the brown robe,

*there is a genuine peacefulness about him. He knows what
lies outside his gate. If I listen, I can almost hear what he
must hear. It piles up like a wall of water that pours this far
and comes to a sudden halt. Here, we are with him now. And
the gatekeeper, he sits in there listening and watching it. That
is what he is smiling about. It will stay there until we drive
back into it. The pickup will take us back. But not this morning. This morning we move in the other direction. We have the
rhythm now, the hang of leaving things.*

They leave their shoes and sandals on a rack by the railing
of a footbridge that crosses to the bathhouse.

They leave all their clothes, stepping out of them directly
into sulfury steam, down underwater concrete steps into tubs
the size of small rooms, filled with water so hot each few
inches of the body has to stop and learn for itself that what
seems to be excruciating pain is in fact ecstatic pleasure.
Groaning and exclaiming, they begin to inch into the slippery
water.

"Beware of the pelvis!" Monty cries. "Watch out for the
pelvic trauma!"

"My pelvis needs this," Leona says.

"Is it hotter than last time?" Grover says, still standing
near the top step.

"It isn't hot at all," Holly says. "It's fantastic."

"In that case," Grover says, and he dives a shallow headfirst dive into a hundred and fifteen degrees and comes up with
hair slick and his missing molar making that dark gap in the
back of his grin.

"That hurt," says Monty. "You made a wave my balls
weren't ready for."

"That was nothing," Grover says, pushing water Monty's
way.

"Aieee! No waves! No pushing!" Monty cries, just as Travis
appears at the iron railing, white-skinned and slender, testing
the water with one toe, then pulling the foot back. With
extreme caution he takes one step down and stands ankle-

deep as if waiting stoically for his feet to burst into flames.

He smiles his cocky, seductive smile, saying nothing, ignoring their jokes and jibes, taking his own time. Five minutes later he is in there like the rest of them, up to his neck, and the talk quiets down while the aches and the pains and the nameless ailments in the neck and in the balls of the feet and in the small of the back join the clothes and the shoes and the pickup truck, as healing water bathes the skin with liquefied minerals, opens the pores and unties the knotted tendons and lets the muscles rest.

A year ago Grover brought Lee and Monty here, calling it a birthday present, not because either one of them was born that day but on the theory that a trip to the springs can bring you back to life. That is how Monty has been thinking of today's return journey, as a birthday gift to Travis. He looks at the body of his son in the water, made white and slender from the stress and exhaustion of the past three months. The sight of it fills his throat. He wants his son to know, to remember, that places such as this still exist in the world, who knows for how long, but still do exist, today, right now. He wants his son to discover the healing powers of the mineral springs that have been flowing here for centuries, or for millennia, warmed by the hot pudding our piece of the earth's crust floats on, or perhaps by some deeper heat, from below the magma and below the mantle, some heat caught four billion years ago when the spinning gases and swirling dusts first coalesced and that continues to radiate in all directions from the hard metal core.

Can this kind of heat be presented as a gift to Travis? Or received? He doesn't know. He isn't sure. As he feels himself begin to be dispersed among those gases and those dusts, he gets the impression that something else is on Trav's mind.

Down in the creek bed, where mountain water pours over the rocks, they are cooling off, between soaks, lying among the glossy boulders and gazing at the sky, when Travis says there is going to be a meditation session for visitors and he wants to attend. He has to be at the zendo in fifteen minutes, so he thinks he will start drying off.

Having soaked enough for this round, Lee and Monty decide to dry off with him and head downstream for some undisturbed sunshine. They take towels and bathing suits and leave their clothes in the bathhouse and their shoes in the rack and Grover and Holly Belle neck-deep again in the tubs. These two will soak awhile longer, then try the steam grotto, and then the creek again. Their eyes are languid, their voices soft. They will be married before the year is out, with a big wedding at the ranch, under the apple trees, champagne to follow, and country music. By this time next year they will have a young son named Grover, who during his first few months will know diaper rash and an insatiable craving for his mother's milk and will be awakened late at night by the aimless barking of stray dogs and will fall asleep again in the crib his father carved from second-growth redwood.

Crossing the footbridge, Travis tells his parents what he learned in his brief dialogue with the gatekeeper, how this wooden gong in the plaza marks the tempo of their days, how the students rise before dawn, to meditate and study until breakfast, how they eat in silence, then work in the gardens or in the kitchen or maintaining the buildings and the grounds of the Zen center. At night there is more meditation, and study, and more gonging and early sleep.

Monty is surprised by Trav's animation and soft eagerness. Kidding him, he says, "I thought you got enough of that stuff in the army."

"Does it sound like the army to you?"

"That gong before sunrise. The all-day schedule."

"Don't knock it," Trav says. "Takes a big burden off the shoulders, believe me."

"I wouldn't knock it, Trav. There are dozens of ways to get to heaven."

Several other visitors are gathered near the plaza, on the flagstones outside a low-roofed wooden building. The student who opened the gate is now opening the doors of the zendo, beginning to explain the meditation ritual. They are all taking off their shoes and sandals. Travis joins this group, looking back at his parents with a smile that is oddly shy, as if apologizing for what he is about to do, as if this is not at all what he had led them to expect. It could be the smile of a man about to tell an off-color story; and this little interlude could be a kind of jest, a lark. Or it could be a gesture, a portent of the way Travis will be going, toward the stillness of the mind. Montrose would like to think the head-clearing steam and the deep heat of mineral baths perhaps opened some new portal in his son. But there is no way now for him to know with certainty.

Leona takes his hand, and they cross the plaza, heading toward the creek trail.

And is he safe now? Is Travis safe? Did he finish something back there in the realm of violence, drawn into it, to the very place of his conception, like a salmon? He had no choice. Maybe he will never have a choice. We all live in the midst of violence. Making love is a kind of violence. The seas and the roads and the television channels all hum with violence. And the wars. Could it be that he returned in violence, the way a salmon will travel upstream to its place of origin, to spawn, to release? Could it be that he finished something there? When I first saw him standing next to Radar's body in the grove, I thought this was the final bursting, and all the pent-up dams of the world would come roaring down to swallow us. Yet now, today, we have all reached another island, and here is Travis drawn again, to this brown-robed fellow who makes me think of Radar, with his hair cropped short and his unblinking eyes, though he must be the opposite of Radar, Travis drawn the way a magnet will fix itself to any shape of iron, and he is . . . at least for these few hours . . . is he safe?

In the still, hot air, their bodies loose, they follow a path that winds back and forth across the creek bed, among the trees beneath the walls of stone. The path is sandy. The tumble and gush of creek water fills the narrow canyon and *Now we have to leave the children behind. Let them go. For these few hours we can peel back the children too, and even our thoughts of the children. Leave them there with that old-fashioned telephone I saw in the office. Monty says there is only one wire running into this canyon, and it is hooked up to the phone. No radios here, no country music, no television, no flashing signs, no stereophonic speakers, no microphones. The flood runs on electricity and gasoline. We are leaving all that behind, with the pickup and the telephone. We are walking away from the phone.*

They reach a clearing where few trees grow, where wide granite slabs bevel down toward the water to make a low falls, and make mounds and couches of polished stone for the naked bodies scattered soaking in the sun, men and women whose entire bodies are brown, their flanks and breasts and penises and cuticles and the close folds behind their ears. Like the Zen students, the sunbathers also seek inner peace. While the students meditate and labor in the gardens and the kitchens, these devotees come for a day or a week at the springs to worship mineral warmth and fern and laurel and creek moss and the riches of the sun. Everyone drives a long way to get here, everyone leaves traffic behind with the closing of the gate. Soakers. Meditators. In this isolated canyon the two faiths mingle, overlap.

Lee and Monty have arrived at a beach made of stone, where the unclothed ogle the clothed, where anyone dressed seems freakish. On a flaky trail worn into the slabs they pause to step out of their bathing suits. They find footholds and hip niches and lie back like the others and look around. Between these steep bright walls the sun is gathered, fiercely concentrated. Monty doesn't plan to stay here long.

Lee says, "It's different from the baths, isn't it?"

"How do you mean?"

"Makes me feel self-conscious."

"Relax."

"All these younger women. Their bodies are so much firmer than mine."

"You look terrific. In my opinion you never looked better."

"That girl over there. What splendid breasts she has."

"Don't compete," Monty says. "You've got maturity. You've got experience. I wouldn't give a fig for that girl."

"Whenever you lie, your nostrils flare. Did you know that, Monty?"

"You're the only woman in the world I have eyes for. C'mon. I don't even want to look at these people anymore. Let's move downstream."

"I wish we'd found this place twenty-five years ago."

"It would have been easier to take this sun. C'mon."

They leave their belongings in a heap and move on past the shiny bodies. Below the falls they step across a grassy bank into a shallow pool and begin to wade, from pool to pool, stepping slowly to avoid small rocks half buried in the sand, guiding around the boulders, crawling over fallen tree trunks, waist-deep or ankle-deep through the shaded, fern-banked pools.

The towels, the clothes, the wheels, the wires, the children, the vans, the flood . . . We are up here now, or down here, below it, or above it. We have reached another island, and all that matters is the island we have reached. Not the flood. Not today. I remember . . . down here in this creek bed . . . I wish we had found it twenty-five years ago. It is like the days before we were married, all the boulders, and the ferns. This place is like the places he would take me to before we were married, which was before the flood. I don't remember Winnebagos then. I don't remember television. I remember doing anything we could think of to do because we were both so full of heat then and he was so good-looking and he would look at me and take all parts of my body in his hands. It was always summertime and we were always out of doors and there were always ferns and trees and shade. . . .

The creek takes a couple of turns and they are alone, just Lee and Monty hand in hand wading down the creek half a mile below the sunbathers, when they come upon a setting of slick boulders that catch the water and make a spillway three feet down onto a wide stony bench. Here they can both sit and take the bubbling rush into the lap, across the thighs. The boulders are skinned with pale-green moss, and the sound of water is the only other presence, rising toward the rim of the gorge where the sun rests, its heat broken by pine and laurel branches and by the rising coolness of the stream. They lean against the moss, set their arms against the bright clean flow, as if their arms are stones, fixed to block and turn the water.

We are now among the stones, Monty thinks, and in the stream, and maybe we have been here all the time, immersed in stone and water. Maybe this is where we really live, he thinks.

He would throw a blanket into the ferns and we would lie there. After we were married we would keep going down there. It was the first island we found, away from the house and the in-laws and the kids. And then it was not like we were married anymore. Married people don't do this, I would think to myself. Married people don't go out into the forest and get naked and throw blankets on the ferns. Mom and Dad to my knowledge never did such things. This is what kids do. Kids and pagans.

His arms and Lee's overlap to make a little reservoir, their legs entangle where the water spills, their limbs and eyes and bellies shiny as the stones. Gazing at the shine, as if at sculpture, Monty lets his mind wheel back to the hills he saw from the first high curve above Carmel Valley, recognizing it now. Those velvety folds and creases seamed with ore were the overlapping thighs and shoulders and hips and arms of enormous lovers who met there eons past, then fell asleep in a mounded tangle.

This is for pagans, I would think. It would make me feel pagan, being down in a place like this with him, and he would dream up different kinds of things to do and I would always do them and I wanted to do anything that came to mind as long as we were on that island, and still do. . . .

His mind wheels up to the highest ridge, with that view of the several ridges, then into the air above the ridge so that he is high over the coast range surveying the wrinkled border of his continent, as well as folded in the arms of his wife of twenty-five years, and half submerged in this creek at the bottom of a gorge which from overhead is just a thread line. From here he can see quite clearly that for every flick and quiver from the dark tail of the creature imprisoned below the surface, there has been some luscious rump of polished grass or majestic view or steep meadow or stand of redwood lifted toward the needed blend of fog and sun, or some rock throne squeezed into its present shape by the same slow turbulence that pushes the continents around, or some remote canyon cut into the upthrust granite by a creek such as the one they have traced today to make this reunion with their ancestral stones.

That time we went back to Lake Tahoe and left the boys at home. Monty called it our twenty-second honeymoon. I would lie on the sand with the pines behind us and I would float my eyelids together till all I could see was the blueness of the lake, nothing else, and then we were not beside a lake, we were islanders, somewhere above the water, with a cabin in the trees. I was an island princess. That is how I felt, how I always felt whenever there were no children getting in between, or relatives or automobiles or telephones. The jangle of the phone, just that alone can fall between us like a soundproof curtain. On our islands there were never any phones.

If we begin in stone we must return to stone; not dead matter, but the ageless moving stuff of earth, which Grover calls a moving circle.

The floodwaters rise, each island is smaller, yet we find them. We search together and we find them and for these few moments we have

Perhaps we two have come full circle, he thinks. Although it never ends, we have reached the place where it begins again. Within this ring of earth we two are what we have . . .

above the flood or below it the juices in our veins run young again, our eyes are pagan

Within this ring . . .

We find such simple things

I do thee wed . . .

shed old bodies we have known so long, find new flesh up there

. . . take thee as my woman once again

down here

among the wet ancestral stones

our eyes

full of light

our new bodies

meeting

in this clean water we close *once again* the moving ring.

Barbara Hall

James D. Houston was born in San Francisco and has spent most of his life on the Pacific Coast. Educated at San Jose State University and Stanford, he is the author of six novels and several non-fiction works, including *Californians: Searching for the Golden State*. With his wife, Jeanne Wakatsuki Houston, he co-authored *Farewell to Manzanar*, the story of her family's experience during the World War II internment of Japanese Americans. For the NBC teleplay based on this book they received an Emmy Award nomination and the Humanitas Prize. Among his other honors are an NEA Writing Grant for *Continental Drift*, a Wallace Stegner Fellowship, an American Book Award from the Before Columbus Foundation, a PEN/Library of Congress Story Award, and a 1995 Rockefeller Foundation residency at Bellagio, Italy. He lives in Santa Cruz.

1740

California Fiction titles are selected for their literary merit and for their illumination of California history and culture.

Disobedience by Michael Drinkard	0-520-20683-5
Fat City by Leonard Gardner	0-520-20657-6
Continental Drift by James D. Houston	0-520-20713-0
Golden Days by Carolyn See	0-520-20673-8
Who Is Angelina? by Al Young	0-520-20712-2

Forthcoming titles:

The Ford by Mary Austin
Thieves' Market by A. I. Bezzerides
Skin Deep by Guy Garcia
In the Heart of the Valley of Love by Cynthia Kadohata
Oil! by Upton Sinclair

A NOTE ON THE TYPE

The text of this book was set in a face called Times Roman, designed by Stanley Morison for *The Times* (London), and first introduced by that newspaper in 1932.

Among typographers and designers of the twentieth century, Stanley Morison has been a strong forming influence, as typographical adviser to the English Monotype Corporation, as a director of two distinguished English publishing houses, and as a writer of sensibility, erudition, and keen practical sense.